SUSAN RO

WARRIOR POSE

YOGA MAT MYSTERIES

Published by G-EMS PTY LTD
and PS LLC

An imprint of Yoga Mat Mysteries

ISBN: 978-0-6454136-6-3 (eBook)
ISBN: 978-0-6454136-7-0 (Audiobook)
ISBN: 978-0-6454136-8-7 (Paperback)

Cover Work: Tess McCabe, Susan Rogers, John Roosen, Nicholas Roosen, Pooja Khatri

~~~

Cultural Advice

First Nations people / Aboriginal and Torres Strait Islander peoples should be aware that this book may contain the names and voices of people who have passed away.

We acknowledge the traditional custodians of the lands we have written about and pay our respects to the wisdom keepers of the past, the current tradition bearers and the future knowledge seekers of the world.
~~~

To the unknown person we found and the story we never knew.

To the countries under the Southern Cross – Australia and New Zealand.

Thank you for serving as the main locations
and language base for this book.

INDONESIA – SKETCH MAP

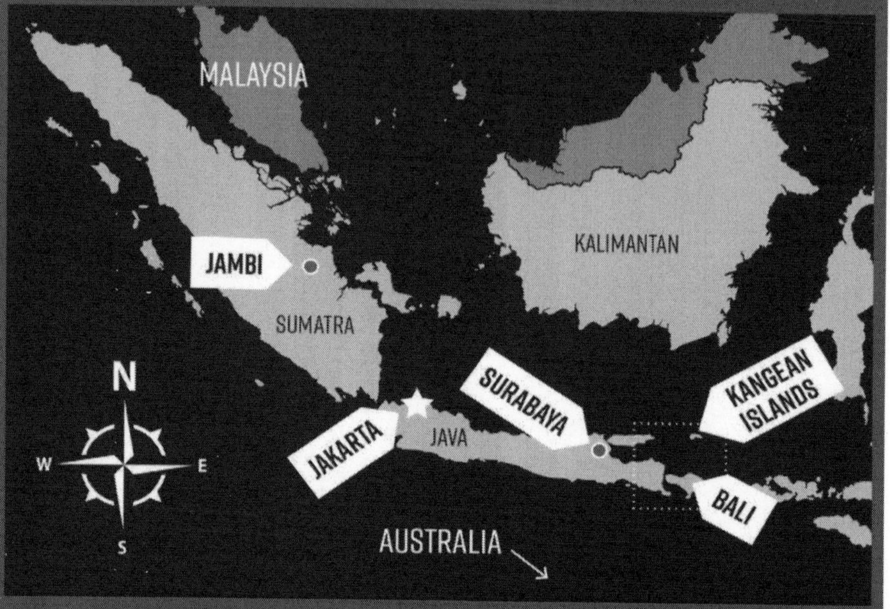

INDONESIA – DETAIL

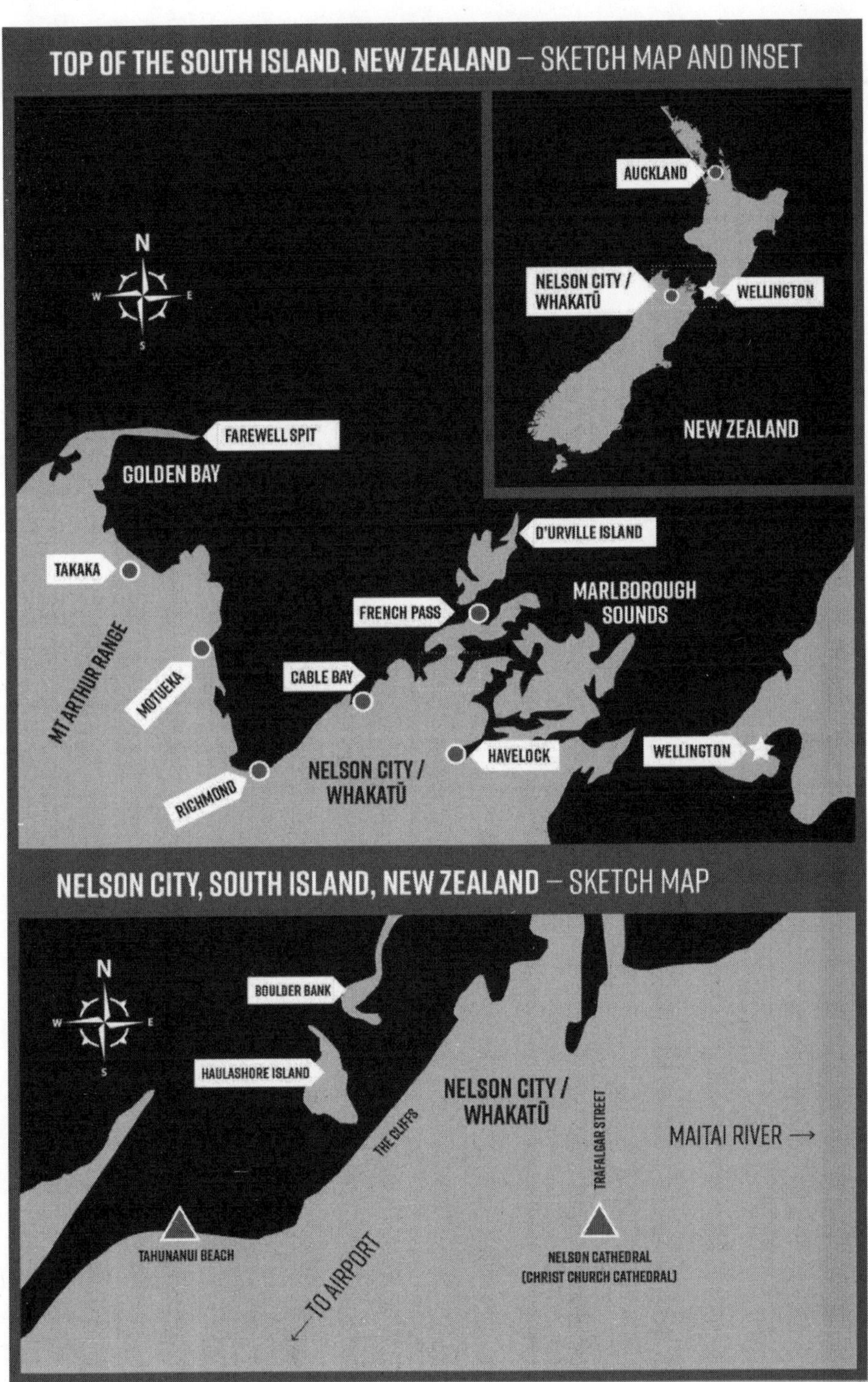
TOP OF THE SOUTH ISLAND, NEW ZEALAND – SKETCH MAP AND INSET
N
W
E
S
AUCKLAND
NELSON CITY / WHAKATŪ
WELLINGTON
NEW ZEALAND
FAREWELL SPIT
GOLDEN BAY
D'URVILLE ISLAND
TAKAKA
MARLBOROUGH SOUNDS
FRENCH PASS
MT ARTHUR RANGE
MOTUEKA
CABLE BAY
HAVELOCK
WELLINGTON
RICHMOND
NELSON CITY / WHAKATŪ
NELSON CITY, SOUTH ISLAND, NEW ZEALAND – SKETCH MAP
N
W
E
S
BOULDER BANK
HAULASHORE ISLAND
NELSON CITY / WHAKATŪ
TRAFALGAR STREET
THE CLIFFS
MAITAI RIVER →
TAHUNANUI BEACH
← TO AIRPORT
NELSON CATHEDRAL
(CHRIST CHURCH CATHEDRAL)

WARRIOR POSE

CHAPTER 1

A MAN IN THE SOUP

Inside the Betel Nut Palms Restaurant, Jakarta, Indonesia

As Ric Peters pushed his chair back from the table where Laurence Patterson sat, Patterson smirked and took another mouthful of soto soup.

Ric stood up, then strode away towards a cluster of tables, including one booth that was shrouded in vegetation. He passed a waiter coming out of the kitchen and moved through the kitchen to the rear exit, not looking back.

Behind him, Patterson suddenly bolted upright in his seat, hovering almost at attention, his eyes frozen, gazing forward, as if focused on something extraordinarily interesting.

A moment slipped by, then Patterson's ramrod-straight back began to slump.

A 22-calibre round had penetrated Patterson's forehead and entered the cranial cavity. The velocity of the round was slowed down by the skull. The bullet bounced around inside, scrambling the brains for a few microseconds before stopping. Death was swift.

Patterson's body folded forwards. His head dropped into the large bowl in front of him.

A total faceplant into the soto soup.

Later the waiter would describe that the only thing visible on Patterson was a small, round black hole on his forehead, just before his face plunged into the soup.

~~~
~~~

Earlier, outside the Betel Nut Palms Restaurant, Jakarta, Indonesia

At first, Ric couldn't find the restaurant. He glanced at his mobile phone to reread the directions to the meeting. Laurence Patterson's guidance was terse and clipped – the language of a military man used to short, sharp instructions.

'Come alone. No helpers. No tails. No other equipment. Unarmed.'

Ric expected the meeting would be brief. His gut said: *Prepare for deadly.*

The bistro was located on a side street away from the main traffic, where it perched in a jungle area that protruded into Jakarta like a hernia. The rest of the ultra-modern Asian metropolis grumbled past at full speed, ignoring this quiet corner.

Ric noted the streets, alleys and traffic. He checked his surroundings as he advanced; it was ingrained behaviour—part training and part previous mistakes. His muscles were taut with tension. He felt edgy about Patterson. The man couldn't be trusted for a minute.

Jakarta was chock-a-block with people, cars, bikes and dark doorways and Ric couldn't be a hundred per cent sure someone wasn't watching and waiting. But for what?

Elaina Williams often said she'd never be able to surprise him … about anything. In his mind, that should always be the case.

~~~

Earlier, inside the Betel Nut Palms Restaurant, Jakarta, Indonesia

At booth seven, Francis Holms had ordered the nasi goreng decorated with prawns, plus a tall bottle of sparkling water to counter the spices.

Holms was short and thin with a receding hairline, and wispy hair that refused to flatten down. His beady eyes assessed the massive planters surrounding him, which were filled with festive tropical plants.

'It's like being in a jungle without being in the jungle,' he said to no one in particular, though a real jungle would have been too complicated and chaotic for Francis. His Cockney accent made him sound like his father—an East Ender from London.

He pulled down the earlobe of his left ear, a habit when he was concentrating. 'Yes, this will do quite nicely,' he commented.

Booth seven was near the back of the dining room and close to the door that led directly to the kitchen. The owners had put an array of
~~~

planters around the restaurant to reduce noise. From Francis's booth, despite the dense shrubbery, most of the other tables could be seen. He only had to lift or lower a particular branchlet of leaves.

Earlier, moving from outside to inside the Betel Nut Palms Restaurant, Jakarta, Indonesia

Outside, Ric evaluated the risks. He had no choice in the locale and no backup. He knew the background of the man he was meeting.

That man valued money more than anything else. Ric's boss, Maximillian Oliver Williams, had bought the information as a package deal. 'On sale', as Oliver coined it.

Ric approached the bistro via an alleyway. In his experience, a back entrance was preferable, and typically allowed a walk-through of the kitchen with time to observe the staff. Two of the workers looked up, then briskly went back to their prep work.

Ric continued into the dining area. Not many customers, he noted.

Laurence Patterson, ever the military man, was sitting rigidly in a central booth that faced the main garden. He had a clear view of the entry, the side garden and the kitchen area. When Ric walked up to the table, Laurence placed his spoon squarely on his napkin as if he were still in boot camp. In front of him, the bowl of soto soup was steaming from its earlier delivery.

'Mr Peters, you're on time. I value punctuality. I trust you value my rules.'

The two men watched as several other people filed into the restaurant. Two of the customers had balloons, and an elderly lady wore red frangipani blossoms in her hair.

'I followed the rules as much as you did, Patterson,' Ric responded. He looked at this man who worked for Clarence Jenkins, the Australian Ambassador to Indonesia. Well, 'worked' was probably going too far. Patterson was now 'on the hook' to Ric's boss, and Ric was about to reel him in. He pulled a chair out, opting not to slide into the booth.

Patterson shrugged and picked up his spoon. 'I expect we'll remain professional. It's nothing personal. We're very similar, you and I.'

'I wouldn't go that far. I'm here to pick up something. That's it.'

'All right, Peters. Or do you prefer Captain Peters?'

Ric took a breath and shifted his weight in the chair. It would be easy to take a swipe at this man who thought he was so cunning.

Patterson seemed amused. 'You're very good, Peters. No reaction. I'll bet your girlfriend doesn't know what you really do. She's your weakness. You were better off alone. For companionship … rent some.' He laughed.

Ric wanted to reach over the table and … *Knock it off*, he coached himself.

He said softly, 'Patterson, if you know about me, you know what I'm capable of. Let's leave it at that.'

Patterson took another spoonful.

Ric could see he was enjoying this. Patterson liked to dangle someone on a thin line and try to make them wiggle.

But Patterson's soup was getting cold. After a short while he pulled out a flash drive from his shirt pocket and slid it across the heavy teak table.

'Is this encrypted?' Ric asked.

'Of course. The key is your commissioning date. Not many people know that.'

Ric took the drive and placed it in his trouser pocket, burying it deep. He stood up, pushing the chair back. 'We had this short armistice. Consider it over. If I ever see you, or you ever come close to her, you'll regret it. And I won't think twice about it.' Ric pointed his finger at Patterson. 'Stick to the deal you made.'

Ric walked away, passing through the kitchen and out into the sweltering heat of Jakarta.

Behind the greenery, Francis withdrew his barrel from the dense foliage, which had turned out to be helpful in the end.

'*True to death—breath*,' Francis sang softly while unscrewing the tube, collapsing it into half the size and removing the firing mechanism. It was packed into his canvas over-the-shoulder bag while he airily sang the lyrics he had created.

One down and three to go.
One fast, the other three slow.
Jenkins is two, since Patterson's passed.
Ric Peters is next, O'Neill is last.

For Peters and O'Neill, Francis was finishing a contract he'd started months before. Jenkins was the purchaser of the services, but he hadn't paid up. Patterson had been the arranger. Francis felt compelled to carry through with his end of the bargain, and then some. It was a matter of pride and reputation.

He realised there was a benefit in having Peters at the table of the man he'd shot. A built-in scapegoat! The man's lunch partner and the perfect person to blame. He'd catch up with *him* later. How tickety-boo was that?

'At least I finished the nasi goreng,' Francis whispered. Out loud he announced, 'Not one of my favourites. Not like bangers and mash …' rating the rice dish as two-star.

'I wonder if they used MSG in the sauce?' he said while counting out the Indonesian rupiahs. He left carrying his bag and walked unobtrusively out the front door.

As he strolled along the bustling main street, he contemplated the use of MSG. It tended to alter his moods. But he could never trust anyone to do things right, in a restaurant or anywhere else. It was why he was in Indonesia.

His unpaid accounts needed straightening out. It was up to him to see to it.

~~~

Not far from Soekarno-Hatta International Airport, Jakarta, Indonesia

Ric texted Elaina.

Dear Sweetheart,

After ten weeks trying to help Flynn, I've had one meeting today and there's another shortly. Then I'll catch a plane to Bali. I've sent you the details of my Bali hotel. After Bali, I'll come back to Surry Hills, pick you up and we're on our way to New Zealand.

Elaina, I can't wait to show you the New Zealand that I know. And I want you to meet my parents. They're still in shock that I'm getting married. Knowing me, they never believed it would happen. Many days, I wonder myself if it's true. Are you still wearing my impromptu glow-in-the-dark engagement ring?

I love you, Elaina … Ric

PS Flynn wants to meet up with us in New Zealand. He said he wanted to see you one more time. I hesitate to interpret what that means …
~~~

While Ric wanted to show Elaina New Zealand, he had also carved out this time to try and cross the ten-year chasm that developed between him and his father. But he didn't trust his father, and he wasn't sure the rift between them could be navigated.

He was looking for a bridge over that chasm. He was making a king-sized change in his life with a leap he had never before considered … embarking on a committed relationship.

~ ~ ~

Yoga Boronia studio, Surry Hills, Sydney, Australia

Elaina paused to talk to Priya Joshi, one of the yoga instructors at Yoga Boronia. After obtaining a law degree from the University of Sydney, Elaina decided teaching yoga was a more direct way to help people. Priya had followed Elaina's pathway several years afterwards.

'Ric's going to Bali? Really, Elaina?' Priya asked, her dark eyes searching Elaina's face.

They both were in short sleeves ready to jointly instruct an early morning class. It was almost February—summer Down Under.

'He's getting on a plane in a few hours,' Elaina said. 'It takes about two hours to get there from Jakarta.' Elaina nodded to Mia as she and Priya passed by the front desk at the studio.

Priya put her hand on Elaina's arm. 'You have to go and meet him, Elaina.'

'I've already bought a ticket.' Ric is always trying to protect me, she thought. First my father. Then my Uncle Max. And now Ric. We've been through a lot together. But I want to be able to take care of myself. How am I going to learn if I'm always left behind? And I want to help Flynn O'Neill as much as Ric does.

She rattled off her plan to Priya. 'Ric's in Indonesia trying to help our friend, Flynn. He'll be there a day or two more. I'm going to give him a hand.'

She loved Ric and wanted a future with him—but she wanted to know *something* about his work. She knew it was dangerous. That he might be away a lot. Maybe much of it without her. Those were big considerations in making a life with someone—especially with a family.

She needed more 'evidence' of the life he lived. It preyed on her mind. Bold action was required. It would help her find out where she was going with him. Or if …

'Well, you've mentioned you can't ever surprise Ric.' Priya's eyes sparkled. 'Now's your chance! Do you know where he's staying?'

'Yes, he sent his details in a text. I'm wondering what I should say when I see him,' Elaina admitted as they entered the large yoga studio. The sunlight streamed in as if polishing the wooden floor to an even glossier shine.

'What about … surprise!' Priya said. 'It would be soo romantic.'

'Definitely could use some of that,' Elaina responded. The surprise felt like she had eaten a chocolate bar loaded with sugar. Is this what Ric felt? Some type of adrenaline rush? It was certainly a different feeling than yoga!

~~~

Café near the Soekarno-Hatta International Airport, Jakarta, Indonesia

At his second get-together, Ric was meeting the South African man who, two months ago, had been sent to kill him. Was 'kill' the right word? Maybe scare off was more accurate. Hendrik Ackerman and he had dosi-doed around Tasmania for almost two weeks. Then Ric left with Flynn to head to Indonesia.

But as often happens in Australia, what is 'opposition' in one moment becomes collaboration in another.

This time they were on the same team. Hendrik would help Flynn wrap up the last two weeks in Indonesia, seeking any last small loose threads they could find in Flynn's search for his wife and daughter.

Ric still felt personally responsible for Flynn's loss and the guilt weighed on him like a Toyota truck double-parked on his chest. He didn't want to leave the search until the 'mission' was complete, but he'd promised Elaina and his family the trip to New Zealand. He knew it would seriously damage those relationships if he cancelled.

His conflict deepened when his boss insisted that he take time off. Even if he were willing to cancel, he'd risk the ire of Maximillian Oliver Williams, the male lion watching over his pride within the Australian Secret Intelligence Service (ASIS).
~~~

Ric needed to focus on the task at hand—meeting up with Hendrik, an Afrikaner of Dutch extraction. He was an exceptional tracker and bush expert.

If a lion crossed his path, he'd always be curious what it'd had for lunch … as long as that wasn't him. Hendrik worked largely for film companies in Africa. He wasn't interested in hunting any animal to kill it. His shooting was for film sequences in colour or black and white. In Africa, he'd become a social activist for the preservation of wildlife, then had moved to Australia for his health.

A non-profit organisation in Sydney had hired Hendrik to investigate the palm oil industry in Indonesia. That's where he met Flynn O'Neill who'd lived in the same area, working as an activist.

After a year, Hendrik had seen enough 'droppings' on the ground in their local village to know which way everything was going. It was an important indicator when reading the bush. Hendrik saw the signs in the village well before unarmed people were harassed, then kidnapped, then murdered by hired thugs who were heavily armed.

He had been trained to 'Act on What You See'. In Indonesia, he had made a mistake by stalling and not acting. Hendrik always regretted not getting Flynn and his family out when he saw the reality of what was happening around them.

He continued to help Flynn in Tasmania, but now had returned to Indonesia to prevent Flynn from stepping into any more 'poo'. Hendrik had come back to a place where he was not welcome, but he was there to help an old friend.

~~~

'Mr Peters.' Hendrik Ackerman approached the table at the small café close to the international airport.

'Thanks for coming, Hendrik,' Ric said, standing up and shooting his hand out.

Hendrik returned the firm handshake. While they were on the same side now, they were both in a dangerous position. The Indonesian National Police would be wildly happy to snag one or both of them.

It would be a short trial and shorter appeal. Ultimately, they'd have an early morning appointment at an undisclosed location. Firing squads were well trained—Indonesian style.
~~~

'I've got Flynn tucked up in the Orchid Airport Hotel. He's resting. It's been another long night,' Ric said. 'I've provided a summary of what we've done since we came here about ten weeks ago. There is very little left of the village you two lived in. There is even less information on what happened with its destruction. Flynn needs to understand that these meagre facts may be all that he ever finds out about the loss of his wife and daughter.'

'I'm ready to stick my boot into it, Ric,' Ackerman said. 'We'll go back to the village for a second look to see if there's anything that was missed.'

Ric figured that considering Hendrik's tracking career, he would have stuck his boot into 'it' multiple times. 'I appreciate the risks you're taking coming back here.' The police would be very interested in Flynn and Hendrik—two former activists nosing around. They needed to stay away from the limelight, edging out of the shadows when necessary.

'Is he still drinking?' Ackerman asked.

'I got him settled down after a few rough weeks. He's sober at the moment.'

'Can I expect your continued support?' Ackerman asked in a low tone. 'At this point, it's not about the big game. You've checked that out. I can handle most things, but if we get into a tight spot I may need some outside action.'

'You have my mobile details, and I'll give you some work contacts,' Ric answered. 'I can help arrange entries and exits if you need it.'

'You're a regular Bureau of State Security,' Hendrik said, smiling. 'Perhaps we should start up our own agency if I survive this.'

Ric nodded. A tracker with a sense of humour would be useful in his field.

'Don't worry, Ric, I can sneak up to a cheetah dipping down to have a drink at a waterhole and scratch his belly before he knows it.' Hendrik slid a picture across the table. 'On a different topic, in a different place.'

The image was a colour photograph of Ric and Elaina embracing in an area called the Bay of Fires, Tasmania.

Ric remembered that day. He had planted kisses on the nape of Elaina's neck as they'd stood in the sunshine of the Bay of Fires. Elaina short-circuited his caresses, kissing him on the lips.

Ric looked across the table at Hendrik. It must have been Hendrik on the overlook when he had been with Elaina. He remembered he had seen a flash above him as they stood on the rocks. Was it Hendrik's camera?

'I've always wondered if there was only one person on that overlook. Or …' Ric didn't always trust what he felt. He had to see it. He wanted some type of evidence, and preferably more than 'some'. 'Was there someone else there?'

'There was. A short guy. Eccentric. Quirky even. I took a few pictures of him and his vehicle before I went over to talk to him.'

Ric placed the picture into his bag. 'If you still have those images, can you dig them out and send them to me?' His phone signalled he had to catch the plane to Bali. 'Take care of Flynn. We'll be in touch, Hendrik. I'm available anytime as you sniff around.'

'Doing a bit of tracking helps keep my senses sharp.'

'And hopefully will keep Flynn and yourself out of any trouble,' Ric added as he left the table.

Hendrik paid the bill and checked directions to the Orchid Airport Hotel.

The dark side of Indonesia wasn't something Hendrik talked about much. He wanted to get in … and quietly get out.

Ric hadn't entered the country as 'Ric Peters'. He hoped his flight to Denpasar, Bali, could get him closer to some answers.

He desperately loved Elaina. But this relationship had amped up the conflict and stakes in his life. Their marriage was likely to put Elaina in greater danger. It might interrupt his fieldwork. He was often gone for long stretches, sometimes undercover and in chancy situations.

Bali could mean a shallow grave in the undergrowth of the rainforest. He wondered if all this worry would make him too cautious, avoiding risks, not wanting to leave Elaina as a young widow. Conflict in his past life had been external. Now it was up close and personal. Maybe too personal.

Chapter 2

Deep Dive into Exposure

Rainforest jungle, north of the capital city, Denpasar, Bali, Indonesia

The palm fronds rustled and there was a dull crackle from debris on the Balinese jungle floor that sounded an alarm. Ric froze in position—waiting and listening as he squatted under the dense foliage.

Most of the rain had stopped, leaving drizzle to slide off the tropical plants. The drops rhythmically plunk-plunked on the lower palms, then free-fell onto the ground. The warm, sweet smell of wet humus radiated from the forest floor, as if it had been sprayed with a perfume spritzer bottle called *Rapid Decay*. A chattering monkey scampered up a nearby palm.

Ric had patrolled the clearing around the shed where they were going to meet, then stepped back into the jungle undergrowth, making sure he had a clear view of the meeting place. He was in his *suss-out mode.*

Birds cackled like they were attending a festive reunion high in the treetops, along with periodic commentary from the noisy monkeys. He listened for warning screeches … nothing yet. The jungle had become accustomed to his smell and movements.

He released the magazine from his Glock, depressed the top round and pushed the magazine back in. He pulled the slide, chambering a round. This rainforest vigil should be short-lived, as long as 'living' remained on the agenda.

Two men had contacted him while he was in Jakarta. They claimed special knowledge of the attack on Flynn's village. Ric knew it had been a battle between palm plantation expansion and villagers wanting to hold onto their land—a battle that Flynn and Hendrik had not been winning.

The surprise attack had resulted in the violent murders of villagers with most of the houses left in flames. Ric and his small team had been given conflicting information, so he'd arrived after the attack had already taken place.

It didn't erase his feeling of being partly responsible for the wounded and dead left on the ground. It was always in the back of his mind, even though it had happened twenty-one months ago.

Truth was the illusive ghost, never quite appearing to reveal what had happened to the men, women and children of the village. But it hadn't stopped him searching for that ghost. The responsibility felt like a fault line in his mind, several kilometres deep.

The two tipsters he was meeting had been vetted by a 'reliable contact' named Martin Moreau. In Indonesia 'reliable' was a sliding scale. The intel could be gossip or even a quick set-up. Selling of information could quickly become selling out.

He remembered meeting up with Martin, who was the owner of Jakarta's Blue Lotus Club—well attended by notorious fraudsters and scandal-sayers who helped create the high crime rates of the area. The club thrived on its tawdry reputation. A flock of young girls were perched outside the club in ultra-micro miniskirts. Their white stretch shirts exposed more than they covered.

The two-storey colonial-style building flashed blue and red neon lights, day and night. Drinking was done on the lower floor. Upstairs, two dozen tiny rooms fulfilled the banner business of licking, flicking, skimming and gypping.

Ric stepped onto the verandah, the ceiling fans above him slapping the air around. Prostitutes circulated between tables—a calculated distraction. Two young women sauntered up to him, putting their hands on his shoulders, sitting him down. They had sized him up quickly: foreign, definitely not local, quality clothing, hard currency. Food and drink started the procession towards the more profitable services that the club could provide.

'Maybe you like two girls for short time?' the one with extremely long eyelashes and a very skimpy dress proposed. 'Nice place upstairs. You a fancy man.'

Ric politely got up. They were right on one point. Time was short; he had two days left to check anything out.

He found Martin in an unreliable card game. Five men were betting with several large stacks of US hundred-dollar notes in front of them.

Martin had confirmed that the two tipsters denied any involvement in the village attack, but they *knew* the 'big fella' players. They seemed *sangat senang* (very happy) to sell their inside story—for the right price.

However, Martin was explicit. Ric needed to travel to Bali, where two men were located. The arrangements for a meeting with them were detailed. Ric was told to bring cash in US dollars—fifties, no hundreds. Nothing and no one else.

Ric had grabbed a flight to Bali after meeting with Laurence Patterson and then Hendrik Ackerman.

As he sat in the jungle, the afternoon edged on. Ric huddled under dripping palm fronds with the rain clouds joining hands to start clapping again. The water splashed on his face and ran onto his lips. He had that queasy feeling. He smelled the classic set-up. The forest floor had the smell of rot. He wasn't going to add his body to the mix.

His thoughts were of Elaina. That last day in Tasmania outside Launceston, that last afternoon on the grass. He still had a hard time believing he was engaged to this beautiful, intelligent woman. Things like that didn't happen to people in his occupation.

What they both had wanted suddenly seemed to be happening. And then … it wasn't. He'd got on a plane, heading to Indonesia and reverting to the unknown.

Ric snapped his attention to the objective. He had wallowed long enough. He wanted the truth, and he wanted the names of people who had been the conduits of information for the village massacre almost two years ago.

He rose, still hunched over, staying low. A noise off to his right sounded like steps, snapping branches on the forest floor. The jungle was slipping into deeper shades of green and longer shadows, ribbons of light penetrating to the leaf litter.

It reminded him for an instant of another jungle, years ago. Except that time hadn't worked out very well. He'd ended up being patched together by a veterinarian. He couldn't have gone to hospital or he'd have ended up in the hands of the police.

In the distance, he saw two men emerging from the shadows. They came to the shed, edging along the pathway. He prowled further to the right, slowly slinking around them in a broad arc and coming up behind.

Each of them was holding something … revolvers! Ric slid in closer. He recognised them from the photo Martin had flashed on his phone when Ric was in Jakarta. Wayan had a patchy moustache, Kedek a blotchy beard.

'*Berhenti*! *Berhenti*!' Ric spoke in Indonesian, then English. 'Stop. Put down your weapons. Put your hands behind your head.' His Indonesian vocabulary was limited. He may well have been ordering an espresso, but he could see they understood.

Wayan was on the right. He turned quickly, aiming his weapon towards Ric's stomach. Using his left hand, Ric swept the man's wrist up past his face and Wayan lost his grip on the handgun. Kedek panicked and dropped his weapon, which landed with a thud.

'*Mundur. Mundur.*' Then Ric translated, 'Back up, back up.' He signalled for the men to raise their hands and clasp their fingers behind their necks.

Ric bent down and snatched the two handguns; both were old and tarnished. He fast marched the men nearer to the shed. In the clearing he directed them down and onto their bellies.

Lying face down on the jungle floor, they panted, gasping for air. Dirt clung to their sweating skin in the tropical heat. This promised easy mark had baffled their expectations.

Ric frisked them, turning up a knife each, but no identification.

Even with Wayan's left eye scrunched into the ground, Ric could see him watching how he held the Glock. Ric's aim was steady. His search methodical. Professional. His orders were direct, clear.

Ric figured they thought he was either military or police. Running, therefore, was useless. They waited for the next command.

One at a time, he made them take their boots off and their belts. Back on their bellies, Ric kicked their legs apart, so they were spreadeagled.

Ric heard a crunch of footsteps from the same trail where the men had appeared.

A third person? A backup? Ric ran through expected options while his Glock continued its unflinching aim at the two men on the ground.

A woman pushed her way through the palm fronds.

'Ric! What are you doing?' shouted Elaina. She wore a black T-shirt, bush jacket and boots, her blonde hair tied back with a black velvet ribbon. She had dressed for adventure. Her fiancé was dressed for an assassination.

'Why do you have a gun pointed at those two men?' She squinted as she evaluated the scene before her. 'This is how you're helping Flynn?' Her voice reflected surprise with a heavy dollop of curiosity.

Ric blinked. His worst nightmare had shown up. Two more steps and she'd be directly in the line of fire. Jeopardising his job. He wasn't used to distractions.

'What are YOU doing here?' he bellowed. 'This is dangerous. Do you know what would happen if you were caught?'

Calm down, Ric, he told himself. He took a breath and asked, 'How did you find me?' He needed to focus on the two men on the ground and what they were capable of. What the hell was he going to do now? One slip up by him and it was a bullet through his forehead. With Elaina … he didn't even want to think about that.

'I arrived at the hotel address and saw you leaving in a Land Cruiser. My taxi driver followed, but when we arrived we saw your truck was parked and empty. Then another car came up. My driver suggested I wait. When those two men headed into the jungle, I followed their trail.'

'You're very inventive,' Ric said, keeping his weapon trained on the audience stretched out on the ground. He remembered she'd spent her childhood in the outback of Broken Hill, Australia. Ric realised the risk she'd taken, even if she didn't.

'I'm following in your footsteps, or should I say following your footsteps.' She came closer to him. Damn it, she wasn't leaving! They'd have to finish this together and then they'd have to get out together.

Elaina raised her voice. 'Last thing I knew you proposed to me. You left me on a hillside. I wanted to help Flynn too. What was I supposed to do?'

Ric processed this, along with the two men who watched carefully. The previous outcome of probable death now seemed cloudy with a chance of reprieve.

'Could we please discuss this later, Elaina? I am in the middle of something right now,' Ric said. 'I'm trying to find out some information for our friend. This is not helping.'

Elaina looked at the two men on the ground with their hands behind their necks. She'd known Ric for a year and a half—unusual situations were a habit for him.

She now understood what he was doing. Elaina had to intercede to help before he did something he'd regret. He already had too much dark baggage. He didn't need any more.

Elaina bent down to the first man on the ground. She knew enough to stay back out of reach.

'I don't know who you are, but I know you are in danger. And I do know *this man* over there really well.' She was guessing that the two men on the ground would deduce compliance was their ticket to eventual freedom.

Kedek grunted and nodded.

Elaina continued, 'This man wants information. You've got to give it to him, for your own safety. Tell him what he wants to know, or he'll force it out of you. He's really good at that.'

Ric observed where this was going. Elaina's attorney-client technique was useful. He decided to lean into her improv.

Ric grabbed a shovel that was leaning against the shack. Then he stomped on the shovel close to the faces of the two men. It made a rasping, scraping sound against the rocky soil.

He took the shovel out of the ground and moved it slightly closer to their heads, providing another sound effect deafening to their ears. Yes, he could well be digging graves for them.

Whether it was the woman speaking softly, the gun, or the shovel sounds, they opted to talk. They had been sent to ambush Ric, not to be ambushed.

Wayan began in broken English, describing their life in a village near Jambi in Sumatra. They had heard of Flynn O'Neill and Hendrik 'something' and their activities against the palm oil bosses.

'One day, men came with weapons, machetes and fire. They burnt down all the villages around. Some people got away. Many did not.'

Kedek talked about the smells and the screaming in the fires. At the outskirts of the village, he had met up with Wayan. 'We had no home, no family, and then no village. We went first to Jakarta. We met a man named Martin there. But too many homeless are in Jakarta. We came to Bali.'

While in Jakarta, Martin had found they were from the burned-out villages near Jambi. Ric always knew Martin was a bottom feeder for easy, cheap information he could sell. He could see now that he sold two ways. Martin had set these two up as bait for the ambush.

Ric had spent several weeks asking questions about the village that was destroyed near Jambi. That word had gotten around, and Martin had picked it up.

Wayan and Kedek were paid by Martin to take care of Ric. He was to be eliminated before he found out any more information or asked any more questions. Someone in Indonesia didn't want him there. They wanted him dead, but Wayan and Kedek did not know exactly who that was.

Repeatedly, Ric tried to elicit more information, but it was Elaina who got a name.

'A man called Clearance,' Kedek said.

'Clear-ance,' Wayan repeated.

And that was it.

Ric bound their arms and legs and put one of the knives ten metres away. They would be able to get free, but it would take some time. He told them, 'Count to 500 before you dare move.'

Taking Elaina by the arm, he led her down the pathway and then opened the side door to the Land Cruiser for her to get in.

She paused by the door. 'I thought you might try and push me out of this quadrant of your life.' She didn't add that this hit directly on the nerve of what drove her to come. She couldn't forever feel excluded and marginalised, not fully connecting with him. There were powerful undercurrents at play between them. She didn't want them to be at cross-purposes as they moved closer. Elaina lightened the conversation. 'What will keep those two men counting?'

'That's the beauty of it, Elaina. It's the unknown of whether I am there or not. We'll be at the Denpasar International Airport and on a plane by the time they get back to their car. Besides, they'll have a hard time driving with slashed tyres.'

Elaina immediately understood the connotation. 'This is a new side of you I haven't seen before.'

'No, it's an old side of me that's always been there,' Ric replied.

Elaina's mind raced. Was this Ric's life? Petrifying one minute and exhilarating the next? A never-ending rollercoaster with no brakes and no one strapped in? Could she do this?

After Ric had finished with the tyres, they climbed into the Land Cruiser and Elaina leaned over from the passenger seat and kissed Ric on the cheek.

'I've missed that,' Ric said as he cranked the engine over, and they took off towards the airport. All the same, he couldn't help the thoughts that tumbled through his mind. How in the hell can I protect her? She wants to be a part of this. And she can't! I have enough to worry about taking care of myself.

'More of that to come. I can see you like surprises,' Elaina said, smiling. 'Sometimes I like being a little scared. It means I'm still alive.'

While she liked to surprise him, she had a strong urge to prove herself to him. How else could she earn his full trust? Or even show him that she could handle his lifestyle—and be a part of it?

He laughed. 'Living life rationally? It's highly overrated.'

~~~

Before take-off, Ric glanced at his phone. Oliver Williams had sent him a short text. He was Uncle Max to his niece Elaina but Oliver Williams for everyone else.

Laurence Patterson was found dead at a restaurant in Jakarta. He was shot in the head. You were captured on CCTV moments before he careened into his soup. If you haven't left Indonesia, do it now. Oliver.

He switched off his phone. Minutes later he could feel the plane lifting off the runway. Ric took Elaina's hand.

In photography, there is a golden exposure triangle. Too much exposure and the image is washed out. Ric's objective was to always leave a place before overexposure occurred.

He looked out the window, waiting to see a battalion of police vehicles speeding to his departure gate.
~~~

Chapter 3

More than a New Look

3 am, 82 Cooper Street, Sydney, Australia

In the middle of the night, Elaina woke up screaming.

'Elaina, Elaina, it's me. You're okay, you're okay,' Ric said, reaching over. 'You're dreaming.'

'No, no. It was real! You were trying to find something. Someone was after you. There was a loud bang. I couldn't find you. I thought you were …' Elaina started crying.

Ric had nightmares, but his were different. Bloodier. Gory, even. Very few had good endings. He stroked Elaina's shoulders, then held her hand. He gave each finger an individual massage.

She smiled. The moon had shared enough light so the shadows receded. Ric's green eyes had turned to grey.

'I always love it when you do that,' she said.

It wasn't long before Elaina was asleep again. For Ric, it was a two-hour debate, wondering if he was crazy trying to live a normal life with a normal person. Maybe this was a weakness in him. Or was it a vulnerability? He could be hurt through her being directly associated with him. Ric's brain felt as if it was at war. How much could he tell her? And what would he have to hide from her … to protect them both?

Flashback, leaving Indonesia

The flight was like an adrenaline-packed film for Ric. He pictured the action hero barely clearing the runway before police came roaring up.

However, the police didn't show. Still, Ric spent most of the six hours' flight time expecting the plane to turn around. Did the tipsters tip off the police? Had Oliver gotten to the Indonesian Government? Maybe the Indonesians figured out who he was. Did the police think that he killed Patterson?

When he saw the coastline of Sydney he took a deep breath. Once more he had made it back to Oz (the Aussie nickname for their country). Barely.

He'd been surprised how easily Elaina had tracked him down. He'd have to be more careful about what he told her. The risk was too great.

All right, Ric, he told himself. Reel it in. What's at stake can be sorted out. He wasn't going to lose her. Risk was a calculated assessment. Wasn't it?

During the flight he tapped on his portable keyboard, working up a report to Oliver. He recounted the many weeks in Indonesia. They hadn't gained much on Flynn's objective to find information on his wife, Gemi, and child, Diah. But some of Oliver's assignments on intelligence gathering had been productive.

Ric's modus operandi was not to focus on what *could* happen at any given moment. He focused squarely on what he *wanted* to happen. But on this last trip he hadn't been in charge of his time.

While on the plane, Ric reviewed Laurence Patterson's flash drive. The extensive data Patterson provided was airtight and conclusive. An Australian Government official had delayed the rescue attempt of Flynn and the villagers for personal gain. That official was Ambassador Clarence Jenkins, who had landholdings and business dealings with a number of palm oil companies.

He glanced at the ambassador's name again. Clarence. He thought about the two tipsters in the Bali jungle. They had said, "Clear-ance". It sounded like a 'clearance' sale. Or maybe 'clearing' something. It was clearing all right. Clarence wanted to clear away the evidence. And that included him. He added an additional note to the report. This time the 'tips' had been valid.

It would be up to Oliver to find the way forward.

He detailed the meeting with Patterson, noting that he was still alive when Ric left. It must have happened afterwards, even though the police felt he was involved.

To Patterson's data on Jenkins, Ric added the name Martin Moreau. *It's clear now, Moreau has been the middleman with his hands in two (or more) pockets.*

He finished the report to Oliver. Elaina was fast asleep. He'd have to try a dose of whatever 'meditation' she was using.

~~~

5 am, 82 Cooper Street, Sydney, Australia

The birds outside started early as they always did. Ric knew what was coming—a highly competitive tournament for heralding the first crack of dawn. They didn't care how many hours of sleep Ric had. Neither did the Australian sun, which was crawling its way up a blue sky.

As the dawn cracked on, he glanced at the head of blonde curls currently occupying his shoulder. He flexed his shoulder, which had been injured almost six months ago in Brisbane.

Ric hid behind the billing of 'photojournalist', and he had done a fair amount of film work in all parts of the world. But even taking pictures underwater or documenting the habitats of snakes and crocodiles wasn't as hazardous to his health as his work with the ASIS.

He'd planned a few weeks in New Zealand without the pressure of work hovering over him. At noon, they'd be off.

He looked at Elaina. The practising solicitor who had traded her law skills for yoga poses. Her studio, Yoga Boronia, had become an icon in Surry Hills, one of the many villages that made up Sydney.

Sometimes he wanted to shelter and protect her. And most of the time he wanted to keep a part of his life separate from her. Too dangerous. Too bloody … strike that, too everything.

Since Ric had left Elaina in Tasmania ten weeks ago, a lot had changed.

Elaina used to live in a different part of Cooper Street, not too far from Ric's apartment. While he was in Indonesia, Elaina suggested having two apartments was a waste of time.

'Why spend four minutes walking from one place to the other? Our lives need simplicity.' She moved in.

He smiled, realising simplicity might not be the actual result. But he'd be the blockade keeping complexity outside the front door.

Elaina's body was tucked beneath the goose-down doona. He reached across her waist and drew her closer. He put a kiss low on her neck. She was warm, soft and tasted good. She turned, drawing him into a longer kiss.
~~~

This was even better than an espresso to start the morning, Ric thought. And he really liked espressos.

'Are you ready for the flight today?' Ric asked.

'I don't know why I'm nervous. It's not like going into court and giving a brief. Well, on second thought, maybe it is. What if the jury doesn't like me?'

'The verdict will be unanimous in your favour. Though there's no court procedure and no jury. It's my parents.'

'It sounds like the same thing,' Elaina said.

'They'll love you, especially my mum. And besides, it doesn't matter. *I* really want you.' Ric kissed her again.

Ric felt more trepidation than he let on. He often spoke with his mum, but he hadn't talked to his father about anything seriously in the past few years. They had grown distant over time.

There were things he wanted to ask about his grandfather. Ric remembered Opa fondly. Before he left for university, he found out Opa had died in Africa. His father always skirted around the edges of Opa's death. And discouraged Ric from joining *any* government services. His Opa, Wilhelm, had been in the Netherlands' diplomatic corps when he died.

Ric had brooded, thinking his father was hiding something.

He'd wondered if anything his father said was trustworthy. He'd done exactly what his father advised him against. His father wasn't aware that Ric's work was neither diplomatic nor conciliatory.

Elaina looked at the watch she kept next to the bed on a box that her friend Mario had given them. Mario had passed away under a year ago. The sealed box was a wedding present to her and Ric. Mario always knew they'd be together.

'Yikes, I'm late. Bags are packed but I need to get my hair cut at Delilah's salon before Jack picks us up outside there.'

Ric swiftly squirted out two espressos from his faithful Rocket coffee machine. Elaina took hers 'to go'. They rolled their luggage to the street level and took a taxi to the middle of Sydney.

~~~

Angel Place, Sydney, Australia

Wedged into the farthest and darkest bend of Angel Place was Delilah Samson's hair salon. It was appropriately named Dead Ends Off.
~~~

Dozens of birdcages were suspended overhead in the middle of the lane. An artist, Michael Thomas Hill, and his friends had assembled the cages. Called *Forgotten Songs,* they represented the birdsongs that were once heard in Sydney. In the morning, as people walked underneath, motion detectors triggered the various birdcages, and the appropriate birdsong was heard. The nocturnal birds were heard when darkness filled Sydney's sky.

The exterior of Delilah's salon was crafted using iron and timber resembling steam punk with a dash of industrial panache. Delilah was the tall, statuesque, owner and operator of Dead Ends Off. Form-fitting outfits barely encased a muscular, toned body. Long black hair cascaded down her back like a dark and wildly flowing river.

Delilah channelled 'all that jazz' in her make-up. Lipstick and fingernail polish fluctuated with her moods and this morning both were Sizzling Salmon—a colour as dazzling as her personality.

Richard Wagner must have visualised Delilah when composing *The Ride of the Valkyries*. Delilah could easily lift up the fallen warrior, place him onto a white horse, then whisk him off to the halls of Valhalla.

'Ohhhh, it's Elaina and Ric, two of my favourite people!' Delilah purred with her deep throaty voice. 'I was wondering when you two would shake your junk through my door again. Must be something important, girl.' Delilah spoke to Elaina sotto voce, lowering her pitch for effect.

'Well, I'm meeting Ric's parents for the first time.'

'It's the big one. Wow! We need to do something special with your hair!' Delilah had changed her volume again as if the salon were a stage set.

'How about a light trim around the edges?' Ric interjected. He could see Delilah's shorts were held up by a brass-buckled belt—a gift from him. Her feet were clad in brown boots matching his own and she was almost his towering height.

'Don't worry, Ric, I'm good, really good at what I do. It'll be fantastic.'

Elaina nudged Ric towards the door and an errand.

'Okay, I'll be back soon,' Ric said, reluctantly leaving. In his divided mind he wanted to keep the trip as a separate compartment in his life. He longed to give Elaina more of his time.

Watching the door shut, Elaina tapped into another subject. 'I was thinking, Delilah. Priya and I have been talking a lot about my lack of ability to surprise Ric. He often seems to know exactly what I'm going to do.'

She didn't go into her underlying mission to open a few other doors. She wasn't a bookworm solicitor hiding behind a stack of dusty law books, or a yoga instructor stretched out on a purple yoga mat. She wanted to show Ric she was edgy, could change, and could be fully trusted and relied on. He needed to let her in more fully.

'Ooooohhhh,' Delilah said, her voice dropping off. 'You're saying some mighty fine words now, Elaina.' She began washing Elaina's hair then wrapped it in a towel. 'If you give power to the hairdresser, she is going to give you nothing but surprises in return.' Delilah brought Elaina back from the sink and took three pairs of scissors out of the drawer, along with various tubes of hair colour.

~~~

Ric returned from picking up a few things for his parents. He put his hand on the Dead Ends Off door and pushed through. Delilah was crafting the finishing touches on Elaina's hair. She spun the swivel chair around so Elaina faced Ric. Her hair seemed somehow fluorescent. Ric's mouth opened but no words came out.

'How do you like it?' Delilah asked.

'Ah … it's incredible.' Ric was having a hard time seeing Elaina's face under the wild hairdo—a tangerine-orange mass of tiny ringlets.

'I most definitely thought you'd approve, Ric. Light trim like you wanted, with a few added touches,' Delilah said. She, too, wore a big smile as if she had won an Olympic medal for the most courageous and creative hairstyling on the planet.

After several long moments, Ric said, 'They will love you, Elaina.'

Elaina couldn't hold her laughter back and bent over in her chair, and Delilah pulled the orange wig off Elaina's head.

'Like you said, sport, a light trim,' Delilah said, revealing Elaina's strawberry-blonde hair. 'We always deliver what the man wants.'

Elaina got up and walked over to Ric. 'You should have seen your face. I thought you'd enjoy my disguise.'
~~~

Ric put his arms around Elaina and kissed her. 'Some disguise,' he said with vast relief.

'Wow, Ric, this is a family establishment, you need to get a room,' Delilah said as she hustled them out the door with their suitcases.

'If it's your new mission to surprise me,' he said, 'seeing you in the jungle was one thing. Seeing your "almost new do" was two stages beyond that.'

I do have a new mission, Elaina thought. And it's a lot more than you think.

~~~

En route to Terminal 1 – Sydney International Airport

Jack McMasters, Ric and Elaina's friend, was standing outside his vehicle at the corner of Angel Place, waiting for them. Jack was a Detective Inspector in the Homicide Squad, which was part of the State Crime Command in the New South Wales Police. Homicide often worked with the Criminal Groups Squad and Organised Crime Squad.

Recently, Jack had volunteered for extra duty within the State Intelligence Command (SIC), though Jack told Ric the acronym sounded like 'Sic 'em' when they talked about the covert operations group.

Ric had known Jack for several years before he'd met Elaina. They had worked together on a number of projects (not involving photography). They were two edges of the same sword, seeking the same objective but with different slashing and thrusting techniques.

'How's Nina?' Elaina asked Jack as they got into the car.

Jack checked the traffic behind him and headed off to Kingsford Smith International Airport. His relationship with Nina Anderson had started in Tasmania, along a particularly fast-flowing river. Nina instantly became a fishing buddy after a spontaneous meeting went swimmingly well. Within hours, she knew all about how Jack tied his special Mayfly lure. It wasn't like Jack to show his Mayfly lure to just anyone. Afterwards he'd made time to be with Nina. A lot of time.

Jack thought about Nina, a resilient and competent fishing buddy. Maybe more. Too early to tell. 'She's fine. I'm giving her a helping hand now and again,' Jack noted and then he switched topics. 'Speaking of
~~~

fishing, while you're visiting the South Island, can you check out any known, or even better, little-known fly-fishing spots? When the NSW Police believe I've done enough disruption to crime for the week, you never know when or where I'll turn up. I'll send you a list of options.'

'Got it,' Ric said. 'Fishing spots for the Crime Disrupter. You ought to get a special outfit.'

'I'm wearing it,' Jack said.

Ric and Elaina both looked at his attire, seeing grey pants, a blue shirt and sports jacket.

'It's undercover,' Jack quipped with a grin.

At midday, traffic congestion squeezed into every roadway in Sydney. If a cockatoo paused to perch on a power line, everyone had to stop and discuss it. Commuters could easily sit in gridlocked traffic listening to news podcasts or holding video meetings that cinched a business deal.

'We're almost there,' Jack said. 'I'll drop you at Departures for Air New Zealand.'

'Going to be close timing,' Ric said to Elaina.

'We could jump out and run,' she offered.

As they pulled up to the curb, a security guard tapped on the roof of Jack's vehicle.

'You gotta move; can't stop, mate,' the guard stated firmly.

'I'm dropping passengers off. This is a passenger drop-off zone. I am allowed to stop for one whole minute,' Jack stated in a brisk tone.

'I don't care, mate. I was told no stopping. Move this vehicle immediately or I'll call a copper.' The guard was insistent with his hand on his phone.

'I don't think you want to do that,' Jack snapped.

Ric short-circuited the showdown occurring at the O.K. Corral, where the battle was over a parking space to get to the Departures level.

'Sir,' Ric said to the wannabe cop. 'This is a high-level police officer in State Intelligence Command. He's on a top security mission involving covert operations and an international flight to New Zealand.'

Jack's hand reached across Ric to the window. He had flicked open his badge and ID in a leather wallet.

'My God,' the guard said, eyeing Jack's credentials. He suddenly realised his importance had shifted upwards. He took out a whistle and blew it loudly. 'Stop, stop!' He waved to adjacent cars, clearing a broad path for Jack to park. 'Let this car in. This vehicle here,' he shouted, pounding on the roof as Jack took up two entire spaces to empty Ric and Elaina out.

'See, Ric,' Jack said, putting their bags on the sidewalk. 'Crime Disrupters have special powers, mostly invisible unless provoked. *And* they work both sides of the Tasman Sea.'

He didn't give Ric a chance to reply, but kissed Elaina on the cheek and got back in the car, giving a flourishing wave to his assistant in this important Crime Disruption activity.

CHAPTER 4

THE UNPAID INVOICE

Jakarta, Indonesia

Francis Holms rather liked his new job that combined both of his major talents. His specialty skills were what supported his lifestyle. Francis could hit a target at 300 to 400 metres, whether the target was moving or a still-life sunflower seed on a Van Gogh painting.

His other talents were in the field of Information Technology (IT), which always gave him an occupation he could claim on his taxes. He had taken this current job to clear up an unpaid invoice. Balancing the books was a passion with him. He hated those who tried to cheat on paying bills, almost as much as he hated bullies.

Francis had obtained the assistant's job with Ambassador Clarence Jenkins after a sudden opening had occurred. He had applied to Jenkins a day after the previous assistant had unavoidably been killed. Francis used his IT expertise to create a fake CV that sailed through security checks. He sat in front of the massive mahogany and rosewood desk, where Jenkins droned on and on.

The new job offered Francis the opportunity to flex his software development and hacking skills. Francis's more recent feat was hacking into the human resources centre attached to the Embassy and adjusting the job description of the previous incumbent.

He added enhancements to his own background, ensuring he was a 'drop-dead' replacement for the dearly departed assistant. That included recommendations from a few satisfied employers and closely matching work experience.

Francis was well aware the job outlook for hackers was certainly on the uptick. All sectors were vulnerable—including government and consulate computers. He was delighted that his hacking skillset had a much faster overall job growth rate in almost every economy.

He tuned back in. 'Absolutely,' Francis replied, unaware of what Jenkins was yakking about.

Francis cast his eyes around the room. It was situated in a well-appointed tower in downtown Jakarta. His own office was down the hallway from Jenkins. This temporary job would do nicely.

Bullies too often seem to get their way, Francis pondered, as he later sat at the assistant's desk and rearranged the supplies. He muttered a litany of how he felt about the bullies who had entered his life.

'They're manipulative, power-hungry control freaks, and believe in their own sense of right and wrong. But in the end … in the end,' he emphasised, setting up the desktop computer, 'even when they think they are sooo deceptive, they topple. One way or the other.'

While Francis could easily accomplish the duties of this day job, it was going to be such a pleasure to consider the options for that topple. Could take a week to get it done perfectly.

'Brown bread, he'll soon be dead,' he sang to himself, reorganising the digital files and noting a few interesting items. There were some folders in the system that had been set off to the side.

They were a collection of some extraordinarily eye-opening data. He doubted the man who'd hired him knew about these files. Francis's nickname for Ambassador Clarence Jenkins was 'The Ass'. The Ass would not be happy if these files slipped out the door. *Could happen*, Francis concluded.

'Brown bread, he'll soon be dead,' he repeated, lowering his voice an octave.

He smiled at the activities ahead. Tonight he'd have to decide if he was going to have Jenkins well-done or medium-rare.

CHAPTER 5

TOUCHDOWN NEAR TASMAN BAY

In the air over Wellington, New Zealand

The flight from Sydney to Wellington took three hours to cross the Tasman Sea. The sea that separates Australia from New Zealand was named after the Dutch navigator, Abel Tasman. He navigated the vessel *Heemskerck* across these waters in 1642, well before Captain Cook explored the Australian and New Zealand coastlines in the 1770s.

Well before that, the Polynesians had made their way to New Zealand over 300 years in advance of Mr T. But in Australia, the First Nations people clocked in with their shift to Australia some 65,000 or so years ago.

New Zealand was thus a recently populated land for homo sapiens.

With each shake, rattle and roll across the country, New Zealanders adhered to the adage 'Nothing is permanent but change'. Earthquakes, rapid weather changes, raging storms and Roaring Forties winds *was* Aotearoa—the Land of the Long White Cloud.

Elaina peered through the window as the Air New Zealand flight began its approach, passing over the emerald-green land below. Flying sideways into the wind was a speciality of Air New Zealand, as pilots tried to correct for crosswinds, dodge the city and ensure they didn't land in the harbour.

Elaina looked at the tall man in the seat beside her. 'I've been to your parents' house north of Sydney. The one in Manly. I know you were born in New Zealand, so did you ever live in Manly?'

'Background gathering, are you?' Ric was amused. 'The facts are: we mostly lived in Manly until I was about 13, then shifted to New Zealand.

Though we came back to Australia often, for many holidays and school vacations.'

It dawned on Elaina why Ric's friends were people he knew from university onwards. His family had routinely shifted back and forth between countries. Difficult to make childhood friendships when you are always flying away.

The hard thump onto the runway at Wellington Airport and the loud applause of passengers in the cabin surprised Elaina.

'Why are they clapping?'

'Gratefulness that we're in Wellington,' Ric responded. 'One more flight to Nelson.'

'I'm really hungry,' Elaina said.

Ric smiled. 'Let's grab something at the terminal, though we don't have much time as we're running late.' They passed through Arrivals and Immigration and headed to their Nelson flight.

Ric bought two takeaways—a cup of tea and a coffee. A giant eagle with Gandalf from *The Lord of the Rings* watched from the ceiling, seemingly okaying the purchases. Outside, Ric then marched Elaina in quick time towards their flight to Nelson.

~~~

Tarmac, Wellington

They hurried to the twin turboprop de Havilland Q300 sitting on the tarmac, waiting for the nimble hop over Cook Strait to Nelson.

'That tea's made me hungry,' Elaina said again. 'I should have eaten this morning.'

'Are you okay?' Ric asked.

'Maybe I'm being a baby about this meet-up.'

They stood by the port wing of the aircraft, waiting in line to board. Ric turned back towards Elaina, dropped his bag on the tarmac with a thud and took her into his arms. He bent her backwards and kissed her. The kiss was long and all-encompassing.

Elaina came up for air. 'Of all the things you do well, kissing is a major talent. But why did you kiss me?'

'I kissed you because you're hungry and I was hoping the kiss would hold you over until Nelson,' Ric replied.
~~~

Inside, Carol Jean and Neville Lewinski were sitting in seats 3A and 3B. Carol Jean was in 3A because she liked peering out the window. Neville was in 3B because of his enlarged prostate. He needed quick access to the aisle.

'Why don't you kiss me like that, Nev?'

Neville had been looking out the window at the time of The Kiss. 'With my sciatica?' Neville asked. 'Guess holding hands will have to do, Carol Jean.' He interlaced his fingers with hers.

Ric and Elaina boarded the aircraft. There was hooting and cheering from all the passengers on board. They, too, had seen The Kiss.

'How long is this one?' Elaina asked as she slid into her seat. 'Are all New Zealand passengers so enthusiastic?'

'In about the time you sit down, buckle your seat belt, have some water and find my shoulder we'll be there. And Kiwis live in a small country. They find most things amusing.'

They left Wellington the way they came, sideways against the cross winds, flying over the Cook Strait with its gunmetal-blue, turbulent waters whipped up by high winds.

One of the strait ferries was battling a southerly screaming in from the Southern Ocean. The bow sank into the swell and then rode up to the surface like a breaching whale, slamming back down into the sea moments later. The aircraft cruised over the intricate coastal waterways of Marlborough Sounds, which could have been Norway in the declining light.

One of the pilots came down the aisle.

'That was quite a show out there, Ric. Got the whole thing on my smart phone. Think I'll send it over to Air New Zealand marketing,' the pilot said.

'Richard, what are you doing here?' Ric asked.

'I'm flying the plane. I'm the Captain,' Richard said.

'But, Richard, you're standing here,' Elaina said, laughing and offering her hand. She had ridden with Richard Hornwell twice before in Queensland.

'Well, okay, technically that's Sally Winfield flying the plane, and she's undergoing a test flight,' Richard added.

Captain Richard Hornwell could fly anything that had wings. In Queensland, he had flown a twin-engine King Air B200 out of Brisbane.

Later, as a helicopter pilot, he made a life flight from Stradbroke to a Brisbane hospital. He'd been on secondment to G-EMS Pty Ltd, a medical emergency services provider.

'How's the shoulder?' Richard asked.

'Healing, thanks to you. What are you doing over here?' Ric asked.

'Air New Zealand is my day job,' Richard answered. 'Here for a few months, then conducting simulator training in Melbourne about six months from now. Where are you two headed?' He cast a glance towards the cockpit.

'Home to see my parents and introduce them to Elaina,' Ric answered.

Richard laughed. 'Suspect you'll find a few surprises there. Better get back to my seat—I think we're landing soon. Should probably teach Sally how to do that.'

They began the approach to Nelson, passing over an array of vineyards, farms, orchards and beaches. Ten minutes later they were on the ground. Ric and Elaina passed in through the Arrivals and Departures gate. It was one of the early indications that life in a small town is less complex, slower and, most importantly, everyone knows everyone and what they have on the clothesline that day.

~ ~ ~

Nelson, Whakatū, airport terminal

Ric's mum was waiting for them in the cavernous terminal that served the Nelson region. Kiri was tall with a robust physique, her thick black hair swept up onto her head with a wooden comb to hold it in place. She was dressed in a tan canvas skirt and wore a fuchsia flowered shirt under a soft brown jacket. Her eyes were dark and her smile seemed endless.

'Finally, I'm meeting you in person,' Kiri said to Elaina, embracing her with a huge hug then giving her a hongi, with her nose planted squarely onto Elaina's. 'This is how we welcome you to Nelson, Whakatū, at the Top of the South Island,' Kiri said. 'Now I understand why my son is so enamoured with you.'

Elaina felt warm and tingly. She'd lost her mother early in life and this felt like coming home, even though it was a home she had never been to.

Ric hugged his mother, kissing her on the cheek. 'Where's Pappa?' Ric had been dreading the meeting with his father. It had been a while.

'Waiting with the truck out front,' Kiri replied.

'You can wait by the terminal for passengers?' Elaina asked. 'I feel like I'm back in Broken Hill, where people can leave their car running and go into the airport.'

They headed out of the terminal. 'It's another one,' Elaina exclaimed as she spotted the FJ40. 'A Land Cruiser!' Amused, she whispered to Ric, 'And like the one I was in yesterday. You must collect these cars!'

Kiri explained, 'It's a Peters clan obsession. I've spent my entire life riding around in these things: when we dated, when we were on our honeymoon. Ric was likely conceived in the back of one of them. This one is called FJ-Orion.'

Elaina made a face at Ric who was shaking his head. What had he done by planning two weeks in Nelson?

John Peters was standing next to the Land Cruiser and stepped forward to embrace Elaina; and awkwardly included Ric. His father's hug did not take away the edginess Ric was feeling.

'It's good to see you two. My real name is Johannes, but please call me John.'

While Ric was taking off his backpack, John and Kiri grabbed the two rollie bags that Elaina and Ric had brought outside.

'I'll put my carry-on in the back,' Elaina said, moving behind the truck, then twisting the chrome handle and opening both doors wide. She shoved her backpack into the nearly empty compartment, dislodging the lid of a small cardboard box, which fell off to the side.

Resting in the cardboard box was a bleached, white skull. The entire skull was visible and the empty eye sockets seemed to gape at her. There was a triangular space where the nose would be.

A complete set of fully formed teeth were closed, but strangely, in a macabre way, appeared smiling. Elaina stared at the skull. She saw nothing else. The skull seemed to gaze directly back at her.

Death sat in a box before her. She'd lost her mother, almost lost her father, nearly lost Ric. All her fears reached out and grabbed at her. The sudden jolt of seeing the head of a dead person was too much.

She could hear Kiri speaking loudly, and then John trying to tell Ric something. Then she could hear nothing at all.

CHAPTER 6

TRACKING MANDU: TREE STUMPS IN THE ABANDONED VILLAGE

Province of Jambi, Sumatra, Indonesia
Hendrik and Flynn stopped in the jungle and cleared an area of humus down to the soil. They were keeping their voices low as sound travelled a long way in the jungle. The pair hunched over the space and Hendrik gathered some small rocks, twigs and several different sticks.

'All right, Flynn, what do we know?'

Flynn took a breath, looked out at where his village had once stood as a vibrant community. All that remained was a patch of land and a few burned-out stumps. 'This is close to where we lived among our neighbours.' He gestured towards what had been his home.

Hendrik marked out the perimeter of the village in his dirt-made map on the ground. Flynn nodded. 'My house was about here.' Flynn used a stone on the cleared soil to indicate the spot.

'And I was north of you in a smaller place that faced west.' Hendrik added his flatter stone to the map.

'We had heard that someone was coming to the village to help us shift. Shift out of the village at any rate. I went up to see Bayu …'

'Bayu Bintang, head of the village council.' Hendrik filled in other stones and added sticks made into arrows.

'Yes. He said someone was coming to help get us ready to move. And then a team from Australia was going to get us out, before the attackers got here. But the timing was all wrong. The attack occurred at noon while I was away from my home … from Gemi, my wife and Diah, my daughter …'

Hendrik kept the onsite action in focus. 'The outcome of the attack split us up into five groups. Of the seventy-four people in the village, about twenty-two were killed outright.' Hendrik wrote the number '22' by the recreated village.

Flynn named the villagers as Hendrik thumbed the names onto his phone.

'Yes, my neighbour on the south, the teacher, the aid worker … Bayu was killed while I stood there trying to find out what was going on—that was around noon. There was someone else standing by him. Now I wonder if that was Mandu Olda. He was the one who was coming to help shift people out.'

In his early life, Mandu Olda had been a travelling monk who had gone his own way, due to the early suppression of Buddhism in his youth. He continued on his quest to help villagers in any way he could, often dressing in the local village clothing, and participating in what he called 'the friendly neighbour' approach.

He knew of Hendrik and Flynn when he'd been working in a village not far from them. They were helping the local people fight back through legal means to keep their land.

Mandu had been contacted by a member of Ric's team to aid in the evacuation … which turned into a rescue.

'Ric says the total group rescued including the wounded came to thirty people,' said Hendrik.

'Late in the afternoon, half of Ric's team took those thirty people along the river. We got to a small airport and were airlifted out of there. I have the lists of rescued and wounded from Ric.' Flynn took a deep breath. 'I was one of the wounded, but I was unconscious.'

'About the same time, maybe 5 pm, Ric and a few others went after the attackers. The invaders had ten or so hostages,' Hendrik reflected.

'Twelve, Hendrik. The attackers had twelve hostages. Local people.'

'I had asked two villagers to check the burnt houses for bodies,' Hendrik said. 'But they never checked *all* the houses. No time.'

'When Ric got to the attackers—' Flynn stopped, thinking about the burned bodies. He couldn't go further.

'I know, Flynn. I know.' Hendrik looked at his notes. 'We don't know if Gemi and Diah were inside your house. Or left before … We do know twenty-two were killed, thirty rescued including the wounded, plus twelve hostages that Ric and his group saved. I think you are right. That *was* Mandu. So sixty-five total. That leaves about eight or nine people missing.'

They both stared at the map they had constructed on the floor of the jungle. Despite its crudeness, the realness of the battle seemed embedded with the rocks, twigs and the sticks. It was almost as if they could still see the blood, smell the smoke and feel the pain of flesh that had been burned.

Hendrik looked westward. 'My memories of that morning have always been fuzzy. If Mandu Olda was there early, I wonder what he did during the attack?' Hendrik lowered his voice. 'It reminds me of the unexpected actions that occur when tracking. Sometimes I was looking for a leopard. I'd spend days looking into various bushes and trees. Then I'd give up and look for a certain bird, only to find the leopard lounging in the tree or under the bush.'

Flynn glanced at his friend. 'So, what you're saying is we need to stop looking in the bushes for birds that have flown away, and start looking for a leopard?'

'Something like that. Think of Mandu as a leopard. They're very stealthy animals. But leopards make a distinctive deep, guttural, roaring sequence. It sounds like someone hand-sawing wood. We need to listen for that call. Someone around here knew this bloke. Knew where he came from … and where he went.'

Chapter 7

The Man without a Name

Nelson Airport, South Island, New Zealand

Ric moved quickly, as if he were a player in a baseball game, sliding to catch a ball in left field. When Elaina started to collapse behind the back of the Land Cruiser, Ric raced over, his arm outstretched and putting his fingertips under her. He lowered her slowly to the ground, resting her head on his arm. Then he sat on the sidewalk by the truck, holding her.

Kiri kneeled and started rubbing Elaina's hands for several minutes, while John stood by the truck dialling a local family doctor they routinely used.

Elaina opened her eyes and looked up at Ric. 'Did I see …?'

'Yes, don't think about it anymore, Elaina. My mum will explain where it came from. But my father and I will take it away from here. No worries.'

'I told you I was a big baby. Even with my father being a doctor, I was never great about anyone getting wounded, or cuts, or blood …'

'Well … you did help me more than once,' Ric reminded her, looking into her eyes.

Kiri provided some water, and they both assisted Elaina in standing up. She looked around at the hillsides above the airport, deeply inhaling the crisp sea air.

'You'll have a chance to take it all in after we stop at our doctor,' Kiri said. 'There's our taxi.'

Kiri led Elaina to the car driven by a Sri Lankan man. 'Many thanks, Rehan. Did you bring the food we requested?'

Rehan held out a bag, still warm from his wife's kitchen. Kiri guided Elaina into the taxi and passed her the bag. 'Start eating, dear. We have a lovely ten-minute ride to the doctor.'

John had held the door as his wife got in the seat next to Elaina.

'You know where we'll be for a while,' John said. 'It will take us about thirty minutes to drive out and make the drop-off but we'll be back for the evening meal.'

~~~

Rehan deposited Elaina and Kiri at Dr Chen's office in Victory Square, a local community within walking distance of town.

Kiwis were all about walking. Sir Edmund Hillary, a bushwalker at sixteen, was on the top of Mount Everest at thirty-three.

In the waiting room, Elaina suddenly figured out why everyone was worried when she passed out. She turned to Kiri with a smile. 'Ahhh, in case you were expecting … I mean, if you thought Ric and I were … Well, you know what I mean.'

Kiri plastered on her most convincing smile. She was a psychologist after all. Easing over embarrassing moments were her forte. 'The word "expecting" has many interesting meanings. I have absolutely no idea what you were expecting. But you look fine now, and I thought it would be good to check things out. After this we can pick up some homemade carrot cake with New Zealand cream cheese. Later, I'll tell you the story of what you saw in the back of FJ-Orion.'

Elaina was keen to hear *that* story. She wondered how many human skeletal remains had gone for a spin in this family vehicle.

~~~

Site Manager's Office, Contaminated Waste Site, Longboat Island, Tasman District, NZ

'Not sure about the description for the skull in the site logs,' Thomas Murphy, the Site Manager, commented to the woman sitting across from him in the site office.

Outside, the intermodal shipping container looked like it had all the comforts of a mini-home. Inside it had all the charm of a morgue—with steel tables, two sinks, and sampling bottles stacked everywhere. The office was perched next to the contaminated industrial site at Longboat Island. It was the nerve centre of the site clean-up operations.

Louise McKenny, who had emigrated from Ireland, was the Operations Manager for the clean-up, including earthworks and sample-taking in all the identified cells of the excavations. The site was as complex as an archaeological dig, with the added danger of toxic chemicals rippling throughout. Breathing fumes was an issue, so traipsing around without an air-purifying respirator was forbidden.

'Aye, the log *is* a legal document. We've already recorded finding human remains. This is a crime scene now. And we've notified the police,' McKenny recounted.

'Let's wait and see what John Peters says happened. Trouble is, we don't know how old the skull is. Could be twenty or thirty years old or maybe a couple of hundred years. We're going to need some assistance,' Thomas said.

'Well, at the moment the skull's skedaddled off with someone,' Louise commented.

'We *do* have the record of where the skull was found—with photographs and coordinates. After we've put it back we can let the police deal with it. Peters can provide them with the details about its various travels.'

'It's moving around so much it should earn Airpoints,' Louise said.

'I can always count on you for a sense of humour, Louise.'

'Aye, I'm working six days a week at a hazardous waste site. If I go outside, I have to put on a Tyvek jumpsuit and a respirator. Who doesn't need a good sense of humour?' Louise turned back to her computer screen that was filled with the results of recent testing.

~~~

On State Highway 6 en route to Longboat Island, Tasman District

'Where did the skull come from?' Ric quietly asked his father, as if finding a skull in the boot of an FJ40 was like a cabbage head rolling out of a shopping bag.

They were travelling through Richmond towards Longboat Island.

John hesitated. The skull wasn't the only thing Ric wanted to know about. Kiri said Ric had been asking about his grandfather as well. The
~~~

details of his death. For John, that was too brutal. Too painful. Too horrendous. He didn't even want to think about it.

John decided to take the easier route.

He squeezed his eyes and cleared his throat, breaking the silence. 'We're headed towards Longboat Island on a mission. You remember Longboat Island. We're doing something for your mum.'

'Isn't there an industrial site out there?' Ric said.

'Yes, in fact that's about all there is. They were producing many chemical formulations to sell. They operated for years, then the plant went bankrupt and shut down about year ago. But I do … or rather I *did* know a person who worked on that site in a chemical engineering capacity.'

'What's the issue with the site?' Ric asked.

'Chemical contamination,' John answered. 'On a serious scale. High concentrations, right next to the estuary. There was a lot of product development at the facility. A fair amount of experimentation with new products. Some products—and maybe more than some—didn't turn out very well. My chemist friend complained about the lack of procedures and proper processing. He's … He dropped out of sight unexpectedly, so I can't chat with him about it now.'

'What do you mean, unexpectedly?' Ric asked.

John shrugged. 'He was there one day and then I couldn't reach him. No sign of him. He's now labelled a missing person. Most people lost interest in anything to do with the site after the facility was closed up.'

'Where did the skull come from?'

'Where the skull recently came from is easy to answer. I want to know where it originally came from and who it is.' John paused. *I have to know who it is*, he thought, gripping the steering wheel. He took a breath. He didn't want to tell Ric who he thought it was—his friend, who had once been Ric's old chemistry teacher from Nelson College, a high school in town.

John was never really sure if Ric thought of his chemistry teacher as a second father. During that period, there was an increasingly deep ravine that developed in Ric and John's relationship, and John had headed overseas for extensive periods. When Ric headed to University, his friend looked around for another job. He glanced at Ric and then described what he did know.

'After the plant closed, a major clean-up was funded. It's been much larger and longer than they anticipated. The skull was found on the site late yesterday during an excavation.' John flipped on the Land Cruiser's lights as dusk settled over Tasman Bay. 'These clean-up sites routinely have archaeological monitors working with the remediation crew. They help ensure that the crew doesn't dig something up that's sensitive and toss it aside.'

Ric nodded. At Victoria University in Wellington he had taken a few archaeology classes, until biology, chemistry, physics and languages dominated his schedule.

John elaborated. 'One of the archaeological monitors, a young man, was bothered about finding these human remains. His name is Tahi and he removed the skull from the site without permission. Your mum knows the family well. She managed to retrieve the skull so we could take it back.'

'Sounds like Mum. Get to the heart of something. Figure out what's right. Solve the problem.'

John smiled. 'I've heard that said of you as well, Ric. Our intention tonight is to get the skull back on site before the police bring in their specialist tomorrow.' But John's internal voice screamed out. *And find out the name of the person who ended up in a hazardous waste site.*

'Do you know the location of where the skull was found?' Ric asked.

'Everything is logged into the record with the GPS location. There's a digital image record. Should be able to get it back to where it was.'

Ric examined his father's profile. This was not the father he remembered. *His* father didn't bend the rules under any circumstance. Handling a piece of evidence from a potential crime scene and ferrying it back to the scene of the crime! Ric wondered if he'd been away too long.

They arrived at the site and pulled into the parking area near the site office. Ric watched John remove the covered box from the back of the cruiser, carrying it with extreme care, then followed him into the site office.

After the introductions, Thomas asked John, 'Do you want to come with us when we return the remains?'

John nodded. Louise went through the site induction routine covering emergencies, procedures, the emergency assembly point, and health and safety tips. They were sized up with protective splash suits, rubber boots, Viton gloves, a hard hat and an air-purifying respirator.

Of all the things Ric thought he'd be doing on his first night back in Nelson, this had certainly not been it. Sitting on the deck for dinner and sipping a Nelson wine … maybe! Returning a skull to a hazardous waste site hadn't been on the list. Then again, his life often seemed contradictory.

'We can head over towards the estuary,' Louise said. 'Ordinarily we need to be careful of excavators, trucks and front-end loaders that are moving around, but at this hour we're the only ones here.'

They trudged across the uneven ground, circumventing some of the open excavation pits. The site was broken up into fifteen-by-fifteen-metre squares within these excavation pits. Each half a metre layer of these squares was identified as a specific cell. The chemical products had been tossed, spilled or buried on site and ran like 'veins' to nearly six metres deep. The volumes excavated were much greater than expected.

'The skull's location was near that large pile,' Thomas said, pointing beyond two large mounds of soil labelled with the contamination level. His voice was distorted through his mask. 'The specific layer is covered with a tarp, which is secured to the ground.'

'I'll lift one corner if you can grab the other side,' Thomas told Ric.

The exposed layer reflected a partial excavation. Near the southern corner of the cell, wire markers with red flags showed the location of the 'find'.

Louise checked the logs and the initial digital images as John looked over her shoulder. He seemed particularly intent on the images of the original find.

Wearing gloves, John removed the skull from the box and gently placed it back onto the site in the exact location, as if he were returning a baby to its bassinette. He settled the skull in place. Spontaneously a sprinkling of lighter soil rained down from a ledge above. The lower jaw was slightly buried, as seen in the original image.

After he'd placed the skull onto the soil, John wondered about its origin. It was near the surface, somewhat shallow, maybe no more than a metre in depth. There was other debris below the skull that seemed relatively recent. It *could* have been an archaeological find, but in John's mind it had all the elements of a crime scene.

'It doesn't seem like it's been in the ground that long,' Ric commented through his respirator mask. 'Was there anything else found?'

'You mean like where is the rest of the body?' Louise asked, stating the obvious.

'Something like that,' Ric said.

Louise shrugged. 'A further examination is expected.'

After the tarp was laid over the top, they trooped back to the site office.

John was unsteady as he traversed the site. Missing person? he thought. I know who this is. They have all given up on you, Salvatore. But I haven't.

CHAPTER 8

THE CLIFF HOUSE

The Cliffs Road above Tasman Bay, Nelson, South Island
Heading home, they skirted around Rocks Road then upwards to The Cliff House, the Peters' home, staged in multiple storeys facing Tasman Bay. The house was cedar-sided with a green roof and sat on a promontory, blending into the native vegetation.

The sea covering Tahunanui Beach below the cliffs rose and fell with the tides. At various times it was like a blanket that was kicked off and fell away. At other times the sea was tucked up, snuggling the ridge of the shoreline.

Close by was Haulashore Island and a natural boulder bank (one of two in the world) that stretched thirteen kilometres long. The narrow bank held a countless number of boulders and the thin strip curved around towards the city. It was simply called the Boulder Bank.

Ric brought the luggage down the outside entry stairs. His old room was on the top level near the front door. His desk faced the lighthouse on the Boulder Bank. Every room in the house had a different view of Tasman Bay.

Kiri announced the menu when Ric ambled down two levels to the kitchen. 'Blue warehou grilled with baked potatoes and garden salad. Vanilla passionfruit swirl and carrot cake for dessert. Seem to remember you liked grilling things. The seasoned warehou is on the platter, waiting for your arrival to heat up the grill.'

Ric looked out the open window towards the deck where John was sitting with some papers and talking to Elaina. He was easily cruising through *The New York Times* crossword puzzle.

'I love crossword puzzles,' Elaina was saying, 'but I've never seen anyone complete them as fast as you.' She studied the puzzle over John's shoulder.

Kiri peered out the glass doors. 'She's made a friend,' she said to Ric.

'She can do that with anyone; it's in her nature,' Ric responded.

'A good trait to have,' Kiri said.

'It has its risks as well. She has a hard time spotting evil in anyone.'

'Do you think that maybe you see too much evil?'

'Says the psychologist to her son,' Ric replied.

'She's won you over, my son.' Kiri said. 'I never thought this would happen.'

Ric gave his mum a squeeze, thinking about the last year and a half. 'Yes, she has won me over, and then some.'

Ric's mobile went off. 'Business call,' he said to his mother.

He could see Steven Letterman-O'Brien's number on the screen. A former University of Southern California football player, Steven now served in The Observatory, a specialised ASIS operations centre in Brisbane. His new coach was Maximillian Oliver Williams, and his playbook was protecting the 'field' called Australia.

'Ric, Indonesian Intel has established contact with the Australian Government,' Steven said. 'It's part of a prescribed diplomatic and law enforcement process. Our ASIS team at The Observatory is being drawn into this. They have a video feed from the restaurant where the assassination occurred.'

'Have they identified the shooter from the feed?' Ric asked, tension rising in his voice.

'We've received two photographs taken from the video feed. They're poor quality. We had Kathryn, your friendly AI, take a quick look at it.'

'Did she identify anyone?'

'The photographs are inconclusive as to where the shot came from. I'll get right to it,' Steven said. 'The Indonesian Government isn't happy that you left the murder scene, much less the country. We're still waiting for the rest of the CCTV footage they claim to have. Oliver is stalling them, but they want you back there.'

Ric waited, as he could tell Steven had concerns that he wasn't stating.

'Whatever you do, don't go back,' Steven said. 'I'm telling you this as a personal friend. If the Indonesian Police find you there, it's a one-way ticket to an Indonesian jail, one you won't be leaving. I hope you're listening to me, Ric. This is not the time to worry about righting a wrong or correcting inaccurate data.'

'I hear you, Steven. I've thought about going back. But when I left the table, Patterson was alive. Who were the other customers? Has anyone talked to the kitchen staff? There was a group celebrating a birthday or something else. Someone carried in balloons.'

'We asked around where we could. We aren't in charge there. It's fortuitous you're not in Australia at the moment. Buys us more time. Oh, and Martin Moreau? You sent us his name. He owns The Blue Lotus Club in Jakarta. And he's a police and government informant, but he runs *info traffic* on a bustling two-way road. Informs the police *and* any government, while at the same time he works against them. The two blokes you met up with in Bali? They got caught in Martin's sticky flypaper.'

'I found that out the hard way,' Ric replied. So much for time off.

'As to the contents of the flash drive, there's a project underway to gather all the evidence on the Ambassador. He doesn't seem to know *his* assistant was recently assisting *us*. He's continued to expand his palm oil business on the Australian time and dollar. And your Bali visit has made it clear that you're a liability to him.'

'Steven, how do you always know where I am and what I'm doing?'

'We had you chipped when you were in hospital the last time,' Steven replied.

'Ohhh. And I thought that bump on my thigh was an insect bite. Talk to you later,' Ric rang off, smiling at Steven's droll sense of humour.

The wooden table with a view out over the sea was set for dining. Overhead, strings of clear LED bulbs were strung like a café in Paris. Candles glowed in glass enclosures.

The fish was fresh from a boat on the Quay and swam off the grill straight onto the plates. The salad and potatoes were doled out with freshly grated parmesan cheese and Italian parsley picked from Kiri's garden below the deck. The Neudorf Moutere Chardonnay was poured into chilled glasses that fogged up.

'To family, old and new,' John toasted, smiling at his new crossword puzzle partner.

The conversation drifted to the local Nelson intrigue.

Kiri thought of the phone call she had received that morning. The voice had been harsh, gravelly sounding, as if the man was gargling and talking at the same time. But what he'd said was more jarring.

'*Stop interfering. Stop talking to people. You stop or we'll stop you.*' The call ended with a click, leaving Kiri looking at her mobile.

'I received a …' Kiri halted mid-sentence and her dinner companions waited expectantly. *No, not now,* she counselled herself. *Not the right time.*

Instead, she updated Ric on the latest shenanigans of some local developers trying to build a housing development in the middle of unstable land not far away. She presented it with a light touch, in lieu of divulging the dark suspicions she had about the call.

'After the first heavy rains, the houses will have a toboggan ride down the slump to Rocks Road. Their new addresses will be Number 1 Seashore.'

'Why do they want to build on a slump, if it's that dangerous?' Elaina asked.

'A worldwide issue,' Kiri said, taking the conversation to higher, safer ground. 'Nelson is a small microcosm of what happens elsewhere; maybe everywhere.'

'Isn't the archaeologist that Ric knows coming tomorrow?' John asked, changing the topic, much to Kiri's relief.

All three heads swivelled to look at him.

'Well, yes, as a matter of fact,' Kiri said. She'd been planning to slip that detail to Ric later in the evening. 'The police are bringing in a forensics archaeologist to view the human remains at the hazardous waste site. You may remember her, Ric. Lenore? A British lass. She took some papers with you at university.'

'Lenore Peevy? L&P?' Ric asked.

'Yes. She's arriving tomorrow. She added forensics to her archaeology background. And she needs a lift to that hazardous waste site,' Kiri said. She dished out a piece of carrot cake with a heaping spoonful of vanilla passionfruit swirl, and gave it to Elaina, explaining, 'Ric nicknamed her after the iconic New Zealand soft drink—L&P.'

'Who *is* Lenore Peevy?' Elaina asked with interest.

'Oh …' Kiri was considering options on how she was going to further detail Lenore.

John cut in. 'She was one of Ric's groupies. She had a crush on him.'

'A crush?' Elaina asked.

'Yes, a minor affliction—like prickly heat.'

Kiri narrowed her eyes at John's comment.

'It lasted a year, maybe longer. She took up forensics to ease the pain of losing Ric,' John went on.

Elaina gave her most dazzling smile to John. '*One* of the groupies? Who were the others?'

Ric cringed, squirming in his seat, wanting to avoid any discussion about past romances. He switched topics by providing an overview of his friend Flynn, who was in Indonesia with an associate named Hendrik. He briefly touched on Flynn's attempts to find out what happened to his wife and child.

John and Kiri knew very little about Ric's occupation, but they were absorbed by Ric describing how Hendrik's tracking skills would be handy in the search.

'So, this Flynn and Hendrik are wandering around their old village near Jambi on the island of Sumatra? They're making a final check for any information?' John asked slowly.

'Not sure what they'll find.' Ric glanced over to Elaina, silently shaking his head relative to their most recent jungle adventure doing information-gathering.

John shrugged, stood up and then said, 'You ought to pass along the idea of checking Hindu or Buddhist monasteries near this Jambi locale. While Islam is the primary religion now in Indonesia, there was an ancient naval kingdom called Srivijaya many years ago. It brought Hindu and Buddhist influences to much of Indonesia. There's still a small population of each religion *and* they tend to be great observers.'

Elaina jumped in. 'Did you get Srivijaya from a crossword puzzle clue, Johannes?' she asked, carrying some of the empty plates away from the table. She had occasionally used his Dutch name and could see he liked it.

'Of course,' said John, following her from the outside deck table with more plates and almost tripping on the two steps from the lounge to the dining room.

'Drat these steps,' he muttered and continuing on to the kitchen. 'Crossword puzzles are the fount of all knowledge in a cryptic format. And it's the only time a newspaper asks *you* questions.'

'But you have to fill in the answers, and check if it's right,' replied Elaina.

'That's the fun part. No one cares if you cheat.' He gave her a spontaneous hug and they started work on the dishes.

Ric remained on the deck, long after his mother had given him a kiss on the cheek and headed upstairs. In Sumatra, his team had driven past a temple compound on the way to Flynn's village, but they had been in a hurry. They had also been too late. Almost two years ago, they saw the village smouldering in the distance.

He looked up the temple. Built in the 7th century, it was populated until about the 12th century. There had been a few Muara Jambi residents that Ric had seen in the distance. And there were other villages nearby.

He texted to Flynn and Hendrik.

Check out villages around Muara Jambi. Maybe even the Muraro Jambi Temple Complex. Pay particular attention to any Hindu or Buddhists still there. Mandu Olda could be a Buddhist name. And make sure you don't mention my name or location. Trouble occurred in Jakarta you don't want to get involved in. Travel with awareness. Be safe. Ric

~~~

The house had settled down, but it wasn't totally quiet. In his teens, Ric had lived on this hilltop above the sea, and memories of the creaks, groans and the wind clawing at the corners of the siding came back. There was a brisk southerly blowing outside, rolling up from the Southern Ocean and the Antarctic. The sounds were faded memories that sharpened with each new whisper. The southerly was wrapping its hands around the house and trying to make it dance.

Ric was in his bed at the top of stairs in his old room. Elaina was in the loft room next to his parents' master suite. He knew his father was a traditionalist about marriage. But he did wonder if Elaina was all right after fainting. Next travel vacation, he'd pack snacks to munch on. Though it wasn't every day a person found a skull in the boot of a truck.
~~~

He got up and swung his feet out of bed. He moved down the stairs, trying to be stealthy on the wooden floor, opened the door to the loft room and slipped inside.

'I thought you might be scared in the new house,' Ric whispered.

'I'm fine. But before you start scrunching down here with me, I'd like some more details on who exactly this Lenore is … other than the "radiant maiden" in Edgar Allen Poe's poem?'

'There's a chill out here, Elaina.' Then Ric lifted the corner of the down comforter and slid into bed next to her. 'As a solicitor, I'm sure you want me to state the case to you in great detail.'

~~~

'Kiri, what was that?' John said, waking up from a deep sleep.

'That was your son, Ric, sneaking down the hallway to make sure Elaina was okay.'

'Sneaking down the hallway? Why wouldn't she be okay?'

'Well, Mr Puzzle-Solver, why do you think I served passionfruit for dessert? Ric has the same reason as you, sneaking down the hallway at my parents' house when I brought you home, remember?'

'Ohhh, right. Passionfruit. Yes, I remember.' He smiled, putting his arm around Kiri.
~~~

CHAPTER 9

ASSESSING THE CHANGE ORDER

Jakarta, Indonesia

Francis had easily settled into his new job. It wasn't as difficult or entertaining as his 'elimination' responsibilities—he had various euphemisms for the other part of his life—though this job had required him to first eliminate the previous position holder.

He was quite proud of that hit. The dispatch came using one of his own designs, an assembled long pistol that fired two shots. Though he'd needed only one. The sitting target got 'the native treatment', as Francis described it, between two indigenous palm fronds in a crowded restaurant. And Francis had disappeared like smoked-salmon canapés at a fundraiser.

Ambassador Jenkins had accepted the fantasy of Francis's background. Jenkins wasn't concerned with the details. Francis passed everything with flying colours, except that Francis's flying colours were the skull and crossbones.

While on this job, he'd circle back to his elimination and disposal business. He had crafted his skill sets related to marksmanship and unique methods of eliminating pesky people for almost twenty years.

Four months ago, Jenkins had ordered an elimination job that became a reputational disaster for Francis.

When Jenkins used some trickster method to rescind his payment, Francis decided a personal visit to his customer was required, but not for a satisfaction survey. He was taking his time in a delicious resolution that would ensure he received the payment as promised, as well as retribution for the wrong that was done to him.

In the first few days of his employment, Francis managed to identify and map out the major information technology systems employed by this office. What was more interesting was Francis's discovery of a private IT system and its capabilities.

Sitting at Jenkins' massive mahogany and rosewood desk was once again a buzz. The desk was elegantly carved with several hidden drawers. Well, not hidden to him. Jenkins' ego had kept him from paying attention to anything Francis really did. The new accounting system that Francis created gave him some 'street cred' with Jenkins, who was oblivious to Francis snooping when he wasn't there.

'Now, here's an interesting document,' Francis said, evaluating one of the drawers. 'The Honourable Ambassador Jenkins is acting as a silent partner in the Nominex palm oil plantation and its expansion in the Jambi province.'

Looking at the numbers, Francis could see Jenkins had been dabbling in private business arrangements with local groups involved in the Indonesian palm oil trade. This while acting as a representative of the Australian Government!

He reviewed Jenkins' résumé. 'At one time an aide to the Minister for Foreign Affairs in Australia,' Francis said out loud. 'And now *the Ambassador*. Quite an enviable spot. A real bullseye.'

Francis realised that in Tasmania, Jenkins had been trying to use him as a janitor. 'I was supposed to clean up the problems and rewrite history.' He pulled down on his left earlobe, squeezing the end as he concentrated. 'Jenkins wanted the land. Cleared the land. Planted the trees.' Francis glanced at the time.

One interesting tidbit was that Jenkins had another private residence on the coast. Francis had found the complete files, plus real estate data and financing for the sale. The framed picture on Jenkins' desk looked like a store-bought decoration, but was the picture from the cover of the real estate brochure. The property was a place Jenkins kept secret, probably even from the Australian Tax Office. Francis loved secrets. It appealed to his inner nature of self-protection.

He finished up his fishing session. 'Mr Jenkins has an interest in expanding his influence in this region … but he's not interested in paying his bills.'

Francis spotted a Japanese puzzle box on Jenkins' desk. 'I love these.'

Japanese secret puzzle boxes typically have six sides with a hidden opening. They are graded according to difficulty, and often a series of sequential adjustments to the exterior of the box reveals the secret.

Francis manipulated the sides, until it opened with a loud click. Inside was a key with an address tag.

'Puzzle solved. Door opens,' he commented, noting the address.

Francis looked again at the framed picture. Must be the key to that house. *He* had never needed any key. But now he knew where it was. He thought again of the importance of paying for services rendered ... including any change orders.

'Puzzle solved. Door opens,' he sang. Then Francis turned off the lights in Jenkins' office as he slipped out.

Chapter 10

Findings in an Archaeological Find

The Cliff House, Nelson, South Island

Dawn had cracked the Nelson skyline open, and the sunlight poured in.

'What's that?' Elaina asked Ric as she heard scratching and clawing outside on the roof.

'A Tūī bird and probably seagulls tiptoeing on the top of the roof and rain gutter,' Ric kissed her head. 'It's early morning. Different birds, same wakeup call.' Ric pulled back the covers. 'I overslept. I'm going back to my room.'

'I'm not sure that you were sleeping that much,' Elaina said, smiling, and catching his hand.

Breakfast was on the deck with a view of the Tasman Sea. The sound of waves reverberated along the seawall next to Rocks Road. The ocean had been whipped up during the night of southerly winds and the waves were frothy. Waffles topped with Kiwi honey, butter and fresh strawberries were presented alongside poached eggs with bacon.

Ric carried made-to-order espressos, shuffling them out from the scullery behind the kitchen. The grandfather version of Ric's Surry Hills Rocket sat next to the open bag of Nor'wester roast beans from Christchurch.

'Are you two planning a date and place?' John asked Ric and Elaina.

'We're not sure of the timing,' Elaina said quickly, 'or the location.'

Kiri, the keen observer of facial expressions, saw the hesitation and a moment of reflection in Elaina's eyes. She put her hand on top of Elaina's and smiled at her. 'Are you thinking about your mum?'

'Yes, I was thinking she won't be there … for me. My mum, Saige Noelle, left Australia to help her parents in France. My grandparents had both fallen ill … and …' Elaina couldn't finish her sentence. That was the last time she had seen her mother. She concentrated on respreading the honey on her waffle.

Kiri watched silently, recognising some unhealed loss in this young woman. Unexpected and traumatic loss at a young age. Kiri tilted her head, wondering about her coping mechanisms. Elaina's use of yoga now made a lot of sense.

'Well, I'm off on a number of appointments,' Kiri said to John. 'And you, sir, have a date at the airport. Lenore is arriving on the early morning flight. Can you three pick her up and take her to the site?'

Elaina gazed across at Ric. John's term last night was a 'crush'. That could mean anything. And Ric had never provided an explanation.

'It was years ago,' Ric said to her, recognising 'that look'.

His relationship with Elaina had seemed to accelerate since they'd arrived in New Zealand. They hadn't yet set an exact date for a wedding, but meeting his family made it seem like the event would be the next weekend. And since they touched down in Nelson, Elaina had become enmeshed in a strange situation involving his family.

The easy way to handle that pressure would be his usual way—cutting and running, staying unattached. But he couldn't now. He didn't want to. Perhaps it was all fast-tracked because of how much he loved her.

There were two powerful opposing forces within him—increasing the pressure and urgency of everything. He was in uncharted territory … for him.

~~~

Nelson Airport, Arrivals Gate

When Lenore spotted Ric standing at the gate her face lit up, and Ric's stomach sank. No, she hadn't changed.

'Ric, it's been yonks!' Lenore slid her arms around him, moving in close and planting a kiss on his check. She held on like a lamprey eel, snuggling in while glancing at Elaina standing nearby.

'Is this your sister? I didn't know you had an older sister,' Lenore said, her short, brown-haired bob bouncing.

Elaina's face had been a blank mask, but suddenly her eyes sparked.
~~~

'Yes, it has been years,' Ric said crisply, pulling away. 'This is Elaina Williams, my fiancée.' He charged straight for baggage claim, leaving Lenore's warm welcome drifting like chicken feathers.

Elaina walked silently beside Ric towards where John was parked.

'It was a long time ago,' Ric said.

'Really? It doesn't appear that long ago.'

John assisted Lenore into the truck, unaware of the frosty atmosphere and more interested in a case he had read about in Wellington. He was focused on his own mission. He needed to know whose skull it was that he had gingerly carried back to Longboat Island.

As they headed out of the carpark, John asked, 'Is it true, Lenore, that you identified a dumped body by the thread count of the percale sheets wrapped around it?'

'Yes, but that was easy.' She beamed confidently at him. 'We had the DNA of an identified person to compare to. This skull is different. We'll know the DNA of the skull after analysis. But it's unlikely we'll have a match in our New Zealand DNA Profile Databank. If we don't, we've got to find something that directly relates to an identified person—a hairbrush, a toothbrush, a hat—and see if it's a match. It's possible, however, that we may never know.'

John's hands shook on the steering wheel. *No! I have to know if it's him!*

~~~

Site Manager's Office, Contaminated Waste Site, Longboat Island, Tasman District

Louise McKenney began Lenore's site induction moments after she arrived at the office.

'We've changed some of our operations since you were here last, Lenore. As a brief overview, we're excavating soil and other debris from four areas of the site. These are several potential areas of archaeological interest.'

As the induction continued, Ric asked Thomas about the products once produced on the site. 'You mentioned experimental products that were being formulated here. Do we know what those were?'

Thomas considered before answering, which made Ric wonder if he was about to receive a 'papered over' version. 'We don't know exactly. The
~~~

chemist who did a lot of the testing isn't around anymore. And there's no documentation on what they were experimenting with. That's one of the reasons we're careful on this site. There are heaps of unknowns that we're dealing with.'

Ric latched onto the comment about a disappearing chemist. He had grown close to his chemistry teacher, who also had an extensive commercial background. No, it couldn't be, he thought. Ric turned to his father, remembering the previous night's conversation.

John's face turned grey. 'The chemist's name was Salvatore Marino.' He seemed unheeding of Ric's obvious reaction. 'He disappeared over a year ago, shortly before the plant closed. Nobody knows where he went or what happened to him. They've been down this road when I first reported Salvatore missing. They didn't take a mitochondrial DNA sample from his mother, Arabella, because Salvatore was adopted.' His voice trailed off and he never once glanced at Ric.

Elaina sensed John's pain. She struggled to find the right words. 'Did you know him well?'

'Yes, I did. Very well,' John said. 'He was my first friend when I arrived in New Zealand. We both shared a chemistry background. We used to play poker with two other people here in town.' His jaw clenched. 'It wasn't like him to drop out of sight like that. Several years ago, Salvy brought his mother over from Italy. About a year ago, he moved her somewhere. Unsure where she is. More secure, he said. I understand she has signs of dementia. I'm not sure she even knows whether Salvatore has visited or not.'

Elaina glanced at Ric and could see his hand was stretched over both his eyes and his lips formed a thin, straight line. His left fist was tightly clenched at his side. Did Ric know this missing chemist? Why wasn't he saying anything?

Lenore had already noted the lack of DNA of the missing chemist. She was eager to get started, so she, Thomas and Ric headed out towards the mounds of pesticide-laden soil waiting to be processed.

Elaina and John stayed at the site office, and at Elaina's request Louise gave them a quick summary of the history of the chemical company, Parásita. She pulled out some old Parásita letterhead from the desk drawer, flipped a sheet over and jotted some notes with diagrams. 'I could show you around this part, but ...'

'Frankly, I don't want to put on a respirator again,' John told her. 'I have a scratchy throat and feel winded after last night's excursion to replace the skull.'

Elaina could see he was struggling. But there was something else going on between this father and his son. She pulled a chair over for John to sit with her.

Louise described how the soil was being tested and the samples then shipped out for further analysis.

At the outside staging area, the archaeological monitors had arrived and were cleaning their equipment to process some of the artefacts from excavated cells.

'We're heading to cell G-49 Level 2, Quadrant C,' Thomas said to Ric and Lenore as he pointed to a site map on his tablet. 'This is the area next to the cell that has the eel trap, which the monitors are documenting.'

The area had plastic barrier tape around it, and the large tarpaulin across the entire cell had been folded back in one section. Thomas pulled up the digital image on his tablet to cross-check. With 10,000 quadrants, cross-checking was a necessity.

Ric was still trying to hide his anger at his father's secrecy. Why hadn't he told Ric about his suspicions? Or the identity of the missing chemist? If it was Salvy … Ric forced himself to refocus his attention and scanned the area around the tarpaulin. There were a range of gumboot prints over the site. No one could tell the difference from one boot track to another.

'Can you help me lift the cover from this corner?' Thomas asked Ric.

As he'd done the previous night, Ric helped lift up the cover from one corner to expose the skull's location. Lenore held onto the other side, issuing bossy instructions.

'Be cautious about lifting the tarp. The least amount of movement can change the position of what's underneath. Take it easy! Careful!'

I'll be careful, all right, Ric thought. He obeyed her commands without a word.

The cover was pulled back from the partially excavated cell. On the southern corner in Quadrant C, the wire stakes held red flags which happily waved in the light wind, showing off the location of 'the find'.

Which wasn't there.

Lenore gazed around briskly, searching.

Ric closed his eyes. He was glad his father was still in the office.

Thomas looked at his tablet, checking the locale. 'I don't believe this! The damn skull is gone,' he yelled. 'What the bloody hell is going on?'

Chapter 11

A Night on a Bald Mountain

Contaminated Waste Site, Longboat Island, Tasman District

Lenore peered into the excavation. Forensics, like archaeology, often begins with recovery.

'All right, all right, a missing skull isn't going to help much. But I can start a preliminary assessment. There are likely further specimens nearby. Do you think someone has walked off with the skull?' Lenore set out a trowel, brushes, utility knife and tweezers near the flag-marked position on the now vacant soil.

'Any number of options,' Thomas said and he cannonballed into a few alternatives. 'We've had some locals who aren't supporting the clean-up. They often illegally trespass, then claim that their health is being damaged by the site. Though anyone living next to this chemical cocktail for the last thirty years is keen for the clean-up. Despite fences, a few midnight crawlers mucking around on the site treat it like it's a play park. It gives some people a buzz.'

Thomas left Lenore in cell G-49 and joined Ric to chat with the archaeological monitors. Thomas looked around, noting the youngest monitor was missing.

'Has anyone seen Tahi?'

The three monitors putting on their Tyvek suits shook their heads. Ric knew then exactly who had taken the skull. He texted his mother, suspecting she'd find out what had happened faster than anyone at the site.

~ ~ ~

John, Ric and Elaina returned to The Cliff House and found Kiri in the garage looking through a large collection of camping gear.

'I've already started to put together your lunch and camp dinners. You three are headed up Mount Arthur,' Kiri announced. 'That's where Tahi's friends and relatives think he is.'

The garage had been Ric's personal gear locker. At different points he had been interested in surfing, hiking, archery, weightlifting, karate and woodworking. Ric thought of it as an operations base, not just a garage. Kiri and John had added tennis rackets and golf clubs to the mix.

The walls were lined with steel and wooden shelving organised for the multiple kinds of equipment. One section was dedicated to climbing and bouldering with an array of ropes, carabiners, harnesses and climbing anchors. Another had cooking gear and several tramping stoves.

'Try my boots on,' Kiri said to Elaina, after handing her the tea bags, coffee and chocolate chip bikkies (Kiwi-speak for cookies) to shove into her bag. 'They should fit fine. I know we're about the same shoe size.'

Ric was looking at several older pieces of equipment that John had brought down from the rafters.

'Why didn't you tell me about Salvatore? Salvy was a friend of mine. Someone I turned to … when you weren't there.'

John decided to wait to answer Ric's question in detail. 'I really don't know the identity and am only guessing. Without the DNA or the skull, no one knows.' He switched topics. 'Some of this gear is from your grandfather. I've got a couple of stoves here that are at least fifty years old. Old brass models like Svea. Some of it is mine.'

'I never thought you liked going camping. I mean, we never seemed to do a lot of this, but Opa and I did before he died.' Ric was examining the camp stove.

'Your grandfather had better stories to tell than I did.'

Ric knew his father had never really opened up or been honest with him about his grandfather. And he sure didn't breathe a word about Salvy's disappearance. Salvy had become a de facto uncle when his father went overseas searching for Opa. How could he ever trust his father if he couldn't even be honest about this?

High up on a shelf, Ric spotted something he remembered from camping with his grandfather. Something he knew Elaina would like. He shoved it into a side pocket.

The four of them finished packing the bags with a combination of tramping and alpine gear from the shelves.

As John adjusted Kiri's Osprey pack to fit Elaina, he went over his personal mantra. *If this is what it takes to find my friend, I'm going to push myself up that hill every step of the way.*

In the kitchen, Kiri finished up the meal packs for them to take along. They were going for a short time, but she included reserve food. This was, after all, New Zealand. It could be bright and sunny one minute and in the next hour it could be snowing.

Kiri almost told Ric about the second call she had received that morning. She had no idea who was ringing, but she believed the caller was agitated—make that infuriated—about something. She couldn't figure out what it was.

You are going to get your family and yourself hurt. And you won't be able to recover.

It had been the same gravelly voice. Given her occupation, it could be a crank call.

Living in Nelson was like living in a rural community. It might call itself a city, Kiri thought, but it was cliquey and clannish. On many weekdays, only a few restaurants stayed open past 9 pm.

Sometimes, the vastness of a larger city muted the edges of living together. In a smaller town, where everyone knew each other, gossip topped even social media as an outlet of information.

Kiri shook her head and refocused on getting them out the door. She'd tell him when they got back. She gave Ric a nuzzle and he carried the meal packs up to FJ-Orion.

~~~

Heading to Graham Valley, South Branch Road and the Flora car park

Ric drove while John sat in silence. Ric thought the distance between them grew with each passing kilometre.

Lumbering log trucks bounced over the roadway with loud thumps. Their heavy loads were carved from the forestry blocks and bound for Asian processing plants. The early morning shift crews from the fish-processing facilities were headed home.
~~~

Before reaching Motueka, Ric turned southeast towards Dovedale and headed up towards Kahurangi National Park—one of the two national parks in the area.

'These rolling hills and small farms, grazing sections and vineyards are so green,' Elaina said, staring out the window. 'Sometimes my life in Broken Hill was an endless assortment of browns and tans. Sydney's palette is intermingled shades of grey.'

Mount Arthur's peak had patches of snow from an unexpected snowstorm. February was summer, but New Zealand's weather never played by the rules.

The macadam-sealed road gave way to a loose metal surface, then became a dirt track heading up into the mountains. To Elaina, the road seemed more like a goat trail along the cliff edges. They slowly crept up the last few kilometres to the Flora car park, Ric ensuring that at least three of the wheels always had some traction.

'What happens when there are cars coming and going on this road?' Elaina asked.

'It's the bigger vehicle theory,' Ric replied with a smile. 'If your vehicle is smaller, you back down.'

'Sometimes that's like life,' Elaina said, looking out the window at the rocky cliff and the valley some distance below.

~~~

Flora car park heading up to Mount Arthur Hut

Flora car park was the hikers' reward after negotiating the narrow dirt road and overhanging cliffs. They parked near the Mount Arthur shelter and checked out the trail logbook.

'Tahi's not logged in,' John said, looking at the page. 'Then again, he's probably not interested in anyone knowing he's here. Kiri talked to his family, and they knew this was his pāruru—his shelter place.'

'It's about four kilometres to the hut and more up to the summit,' said Ric. 'We'll take it easy, Elaina.'

'Don't worry about me,' she said, donning her pack and heading up the incline at a fast clip. John and Ric looked at each other and scampered to catch up.
~~~

The thick black beech forest towered over the understory of tree ferns. Then silver beech began to appear within the mix of ferns and mountain neinei trees. As they gained altitude and approached the Mount Arthur Hut, the tropical vegetation thinned out.

'Why are the trees so gnarled?' Elaina asked as they passed through one stand of trees that were twisted and crafted into tortured shapes.

'We're in the Roaring Forties. As a geologically "new" island nation, weather in the fortieth latitude is always roaring,' John responded. 'The storms coming up from the vast Southern Ocean can be formidable. There's not much between us and Antarctica. The trees reflect the weather and the soil.'

Ric continued, 'New Zealand is geologically active all the time. There's constant thermal activity. Hot pools, volcanic activity, eruptions. The mountains we're walking on are a catacomb of caves and fissures, with the upturned marble slabs almost forming a cathedral.'

'You're very fit,' John commented to Elaina as they moved along the trail. After the airport episode, he'd wondered if she would be ready for this. He decided she was intelligent, a good decision-maker and was game to try anything. Besides, she was a great crossword puzzle partner!

After one brief rest stop at the midway point and a nut bar each, they approached the hut.

The corrugated iron Department of Conservation hut was quiet and empty. A gabled steel roof hovered over the hut, creating a canopy around the front and north side. Benches, built to avoid rain, were tucked under the roof, awaiting customers. The roof captured rainwater which fed into a tank for dishwashing.

Inside the rectangular building, there were two stacked sleeping platforms, a dining table, wooden benches, a stainless-steel preparation counter, and a wood burner snugly placed in the centre of the wall.

'*Rough but cosy* the hiking blogs described it. Well, this is home for the night,' John announced.

'I'll bring in some firewood,' Ric said, heading to the woodshed and chopping area.

John loaded the fireplace with small slivers of wood and ignited them. The fire box warmed up, the flue joined in, and with a whoosh the fire roared away.

'Ric and I will have the top bunk,' Elaina announced. 'You can take the lower one, Johannes.'

'You have your choice on the menu tonight. We have a freeze-dried lasagne dish, or a chicken korma with rice,' John described.

'I'm thinking chicken korma,' Ric said, which was seconded by Elaina.

'Korma it is. Good choice.' John retrieved a bottle of Seifried's Sauvignon Blanc he had tucked outside for chilling and poured the wine into the three camping cups from his pack.

'I've got dark chocolate, chocolate chip bikkies and coffee or tea for dessert,' Elaina announced.

Ric sat on the bench, contemplating his father. This was a side of him he had not seen before. John was studying a map while the korma cooked. He had taken off his leather jacket and rolled up his long sleeves.

'The area where Tahi might be located is on a ridge above the hut and about an hour and half's walk away. The trail follows up a spur, but then there's a steep drop-off. There's been snow reported around there. Also, some scree piles and shale on the trail both above and below. In the morning, let's lay out our climbing ropes and slings, then bundle them to the outside of the packs. Anything we have to do is likely going to be jury-rigged.'

'Where did you pick all this up, Johannes?' Elaina asked.

'My pappa, Ric's grandfather, was a climber and tramper from way back. He passed it on to me. I joined the New Zealand Alpine Club and went through guide training, both with the Nelson group and down in Canterbury. We did some ice work and practised mountain rescues. I took Ric out when he was small.'

'I don't remember that,' Ric said.

Elaina could feel the unfinished business in the air between Ric and his father. John got up and brought the chicken korma over to the table, dishing it out. Then, after taking a deep breath, he made a proposal.

'We're in a small, cosy hut in the mountains. We have a fire, chicken korma, vegetables, Sauvignon Blanc and bikkies for dessert. I think it is time for a story. Do you know the storyteller Scheherazade, Elaina? I think the story I want to tell is best told in three parts.'

The firebox acknowledged 'Storytime' with a crackling hiss and a red glow.

'Ric has wanted to learn about his grandfather for several years now. And I admit I've been reluctant to tell him. Some of it is painful to me. Some of it will be painful to him.' As John topped up the wine glasses to begin, Ric unexpectedly got up.

'If you are finally going to start on this story, I might as well provide some atmosphere.' Ric pulled out a string of tiny white Christmas lights and the small battery that powered them, and put the string around the walls. The lights cast a cheery twinkling in the room. Ric thought the sparkle might aid in hearing a story that he knew had a dark ending. Even in the shadowed room, he noticed his father seemed tired after the hike.

'The overarching story is hard for me because it affected my life, my mother's life and ultimately Ric's life in ways that I don't even know about. But it starts on a historical note.

'Ric's grandfather, his Opa, came from the Netherlands. Early on, our family lived in the province of Holland. They were involved in trade since the days of the early sailing ships, with various land holdings and manufacturing—everything from shoes to cannons and muskets, including the black powder that powered them.

'My great-grandmother was the ultimate entrepreneur. The matriarch of the family. She married a seafarer, a captain, at an early age, as was the tradition in the family. Together with Opa's parents, they were quite formidable in the Netherlands.

'My father grew up in Amsterdam. He was well educated and did a stint in the Dutch Marines. Wilhelm met your grandmother at a dance in a public square in the Netherlands. She was Dutch, but of Scandinavian origin.

'When you see her pictures, she was beautiful. It's funny but I can see a little of her features in Elaina's face. Or maybe it's her spirit,' John said, looking at Elaina.

'Her parents ran a number of canal barges across Europe. It was love at first sight, but it brought together trade, manufacturing and transportation in one fell swoop. My father used to describe it as "*een pakketdeal*"—a package deal. But they loved each other with a passion that is hard to find.'

Ric and Elaina's eyes met. There was the faintest of smiles at the corners of her mouth.

'My mother had spent her life on canal boats, moving all over Europe, except for the times when she went to a formal school in a convent,' John went on. 'Her life was travel—different cultures and customs. She was excellent with languages. This is something I think Ric inherited.

'My father eventually became interested in foreign affairs and diplomacy. Because of his language skills, he went into the foreign service with the government.

'From his family's background, he was a good businessman, understood manufacturing and commerce. They lived in Amsterdam, but he was posted to a number of other locations. I came along and all was bliss.' John stopped for a moment and put his hand to his eyes, rubbing them as if something was in them.

'When I was growing up, Amsterdam was always such a vibrant city. It still is. Day and night, all year long, something's always happening. As I got older, becoming a young boy, I roamed all over the place.

'There were many cafés, restaurants, libraries, and art museums and galleries. It's often like living in a famous painting come to life. Almost every street, home scene and canal has been painted by one famous painter or another.

'To me, it was like a carnival every day. Music, dancing, shows, events. Everything was available to a young man growing up there. When I wasn't in school, I'd jump on any number of canal boats or freighters and travel with the crew from one place to another. We travelled with my father's postings around Europe. Sometimes I would attend international schools when we were away.

'Though my parents were affluent, they believed that it was a duty to look after others, to use what you had to help people who had less. It's something that Kiri and I drummed into Ric when he was growing up,' John added.

'That sounds like Ric,' Elaina commented, holding Ric's hand under the table.

'My father was always supporting people in the community. It's what drove him. He wanted to make a difference, to comfort people in need. Though sometimes he took risks. Often without describing these to my mother.

'I eventually went on to university and followed my interests in physics and chemistry. I was expected to take on the business. However, that's when I discovered I had a bent for seeing a different perspective on things. I took up engineering, and then moved into a creative, inventive role. Initially I maintained our business activities but, like my father, it was not a primary interest to me.

'And this is where the division starts. It became a sore spot with the larger Peters family. Those who were destined to inherit didn't want the pathway that had been chosen for them.' John looked directly at Ric as he spoke.

Ric sat there in the glittering of the lights with the fire still smacking its flames around in the background. He realised there was much he didn't know or understand about his father. Did he know him or his Opa at all?

'I'm a bit tired,' John announced. 'And since this story is in segments, and we are sitting on the edge of the Mount Arthur cliffs, I'm going to leave it now as a cliff-hanger.'

He got up from the bench, came around the table and gave Elaina a gentle pat on her arm. He stood for a moment behind Ric and then put his hand on Ric's shoulder. Ric closed his eyes.

Ric and Elaina went outside and stood under the porch roof. Unexpected snow gently drifted down, laying a patchy white blanket on the ground. They peered out into the darkness. The hut resembled a 1600s Dutch painting. A small glow of yellow light radiated through the glass of the hut windows; smoke from the chimney curled up, colliding with the falling snow. Rembrandt would have enjoyed the flood of light from the window and the brooding darkness of the shadowed forest.

Ric felt an urge to explain more of his side of the story, knowing Elaina would understand. 'My grandfather was the glue between my father and myself. More worldly, funny, and a risk taker. A *bon vivant* wherever he was. I found out about Opa's death when I was in college – or high school as you call it in Brisbane. Friends in the Netherlands first relayed the details and then my father left to find more clarity about Opa's death. But if he found anything out, I never heard about it. He simply wouldn't tell me.' Ric sighed. 'It was what started the ever-widening breach of trust. Our relationship changed, with Salvy helping fill a major gap during those years. I left home for university and several peripheral assignments. And as you know, my work is pretty near all-encompassing.'

They stood in the silence, Elaina letting Ric's words sink in. It was good to know more about him, even though the story was a sad one.

In the yellow glow, Ric cradled Elaina's head and drew her to him, kissing her on the mouth. Crystalline snowflakes drifted onto her head. Her lips were cold with the frost in the air, but warmed quickly. She placed her arms around his neck, embracing him and kissing back. John was asleep by the time they re-entered.

'We'll be warmer if we zip our bags together,' Elaina said. 'Friction, Ric. Rub one irregular surface against another and they produce heat energy!'

Ric smiled. 'Always was a fan of using basic science in human activities.'

Ric and Elaina settled into the one giant bag zipped together.

John, still asleep, turned around in his bag.

Ric had made a pillow using his puffer jacket, but Elaina put her head in the crook of his arm, her favourite spot. The hut was warm, the snow was drifting down, and all the lights were out. They could hear each other's soft, slow breathing. As Ric pulled her closer, the breathing speeded up.

The night was still and silent. But Ric's sleep was fitful and uneasy.

In the middle of the night, Ric thought he heard a scream. He got up, looked out the window, then went and stood on the deck. There wasn't an absence of sound exactly—he could hear the rustling of the forest leaves and whatever was crawling around on the ground—and he wondered if he had imagined the scream. Imagination was something he always guarded against. The peaceful stillness didn't seem all that empty somehow.

Chapter 12

Tracking Mandu: A Mind Full of Mindfulness

Jambi and surrounds, island of Sumatra, Indonesia

'What did you find out in Selat?' asked Flynn as he studied the maps on his phone. 'Did your friend say anything useful?'

'We're close enough to the Muraro Jambi Temple Complex that Ric told us to check out,' Hendrik responded. 'We'll look at a few places tomorrow. One thing my friend in town mentioned is that the police are checking certain male Australians who are roaming around. They have a blurry image of Ric in Jakarta. And there's someone named Martin Moreau, from Jakarta, who is fanning the flames.'

'So they don't know where Ric is now or what he does,' concluded Flynn.

'Not exactly. I was thinking that we may be looking for a leopard called Mandu who travelled this way, but we're going to be the cheetah and slink around. And you, Flynn, are going to brush up your Irish accent, so you are more Irish sounding than Saint Patrick.'

'Ta, I will, yeah.'

'If they're looking for Ric, it won't be long before they make tracks to us. We're going to browse, like a cheetah … in incognito mode.'

Flynn and Hendrik spent the night in a hotel tucked away on a side street of Jambi not far from the Batang Hari River.

Flynn had wanted to take a room in some outlying village. Hendrik knew better.

'It's easier to hide in the centre of congestion like the jumble of Jambi. Fish like schools of fish; wildebeests like herds of wildebeests. A predator is a risk-calculating animal. When they see fewer numbers, there's more opportunity to find a weak spot.'

'I get it,' Flynn acknowledged. 'But we aren't part of the herd of this community. We are foreign from our looks to our language.'

Both knew that O'Neill and Ackerman were names with a history and background as activists. They had talked at length about the possibility that if they were found and picked up by the police they could end up in jail based on some whim at the time. From there, they would pass through the Indonesian judicial system rapidly like logs going through a sawmill. The method of execution in Indonesia was carefully prescribed.

After midnight in some undisclosed location, perhaps a jungle clearing, Flynn and Hendrik would be bound, hands and feet to vertical poles. A black mark would be made over their hearts.

The execution team of twelve would load their rifles. Each of the twelve rifles had ammunition. Three rifles had live ammunition and the other nine had blanks. This was to assuage the guilt of the firing squad, so no one knew which one did the killing.

The commander of the firing squad would raise his sword, then drop it in silence. The intent was to avoid anticipation in the person being shot. But it never worked.

O'Neill and Ackerman both knew the process. They had no intention of going out like bullocks to the slaughter.

In the morning, they packed up their swags and headed towards Muraro Jambi. Flynn and Hendrik's village was near Jambi but neither had been to the temple before, though Hendrik had hiked near the edge of a temple compound once and seen a small group of monks.

His friend in Selat had provided a name. Asanga was a Buddhist monk living in the back of the compound of Muraro Jambi.

'How do we know that Asanga is going to be there?' Flynn asked Hendrik.

'We don't. This is one of those times you head out into the bush and look for a spoor … what you call a track or a scent, Flynn. You observe whatever you can, until you finally discover what you're looking for.'

'I don't want to end up *being the game*,' Flynn said.

'Remember this. Don't ever give up … no matter what,' Hendrik stated, then repeated more emphatically, 'Ever!'

The countryside unfolded as they sped down the slabs of grooved concrete sliced with irregular expansion cracks. The road periodically turned into dirt tracks sprinkled with brown water and mud-filled potholes, then back to concrete.

The view out of the open windows was a reoccurring scene of palm oil plantations. It was as if Andy Warhol had crafted a never-ending painting of repetitive palm oil trees. The trees differed with slightly varying colours of green and brown.

Plantation access roads had various warning signs advising sudden death should someone wander off the road into their confines.

Hendrik came off a main road onto a smaller, narrow road that led them … back in time. As one of the largest and best-preserved ancient sites in South-East Asia, there was still much work to be done at the Muraro Jambi Temple Complex. Out of eighty temples needing restoration, only a dozen had begun, while the remaining crumbling temples were waiting their turn, and bucket loads of funding.

The narrow road headed towards one side of the temple complex. A modest timber building was located outside of the reserve area with its own small compound. The two iron gates looked like they had been installed a century before and were rusted permanently open.

A main building rose off the ground on short pilings with several outbuildings off to the side. As the Land Rover drove closer, a man appeared in the dark shadows of the front entrance.

They got out of the car, with Hendrik taking off his bush hat. They both stood in the hot sun and dust, waiting.

A man in multiple layers of robes came from the shadows. Hendrik had learned long ago not to approach a man's house without an invitation. Flynn gave his first enquiry a go.

'I'm Flynn O'Neill and this is Hendrik Ackerman. We were at a nearby village, ah, nearly two years ago. The village that was destroyed … for the land. I lost someone … that … I wondered if I could talk to you, if I may?'

The old man nodded then spoke with a practised English accent. 'Yes, I remember that time. It was very bad for you.' The old man beckoned them to the porch. He entered the building and came back with a jug of tea and three rough cups.

'I am alone here right now. My name is Asanga. I am a Buddhist, but I am also not interested in leaving this Earth yet. Some don't see it that way. So, I must be careful.'

Asanga was a short man with a nearly bald head. He wore round, tortoiseshell glasses. When he smiled, which was often, his high cheekbones were prominently displayed, making him look even more pleased.

Flynn described his time at the neighbouring village and how he tried to develop local resources for the villagers.

'There was a battle for the land. The result was the destruction of our village and the dispersion of many people. Some died,' Flynn said. 'My wife and my young daughter … disappeared.' Flynn stopped. He never could seem to go further.

Hendrik took up the explanation. 'Flynn and I are trying to find a man named Mandu Olda. He came to the village before it was attacked. An Australian group had asked him to help and they arrived later in the day. We think Mandu may have tried to help the villagers escape.'

'Yes, I know of him. Mandu Olda. A good man,' Asanga said and paused. He looked carefully at Hendrik and then Flynn. He seemed to be evaluating how far he would go in conversation.

Asanga took a breath before re-entering the conversation as if dipping his bare feet in the water to test the temperature. 'Mandu *was* trying to warn people about the attacks. But they happened anyway. In the height of the battle, he brought a number of people here to safety because the village had been emptied. Some people the Australians took. Some died. Others were captured. Mandu was able to bring seven of them here. They came with him because they had nowhere else to go.'

'Seven!' Flynn said excitedly. 'Who were they? What were their names? Where did they come from?'

Asanga stopped and gave one of his smiles. His entire face participated. 'He didn't say their names. He got them away before they were hurt. There was an older woman from a village north of here. Two older sisters, and middle-aged man and woman …' Asanga hesitated for a moment, looked at them again. His voice changed tone as if he was saddened to provide unexpected news. 'And a younger man and his son.'

'Who? Was that all? Where can we find them? Can we talk to them?' Flynn was frantic. This was more information than he had ever heard, but not the information he wanted to hear.

Asanga answered indirectly. 'They had nothing when they arrived here. They were tired and hungry. Mandu promised each person he would get them to family or friends. He would get them to safety.'

The colour drained out of Flynn's face. His last hope of finding his wife and daughter had just slipped away.

'Why did they come here?' Hendrik asked.

'They needed help. There was nothing left of their homes or families. And most importantly, they were all witnesses.'

'Witnesses to what?' Hendrik asked quietly.

'Why, it's mass murder,' Asanga answered. 'They bore witness to what the killers had done. Their lives were in danger. They could not stay. They would be sought out and murdered, as others have been.'

Hendrik and Flynn absorbed this truth.

'Many of my fellow brothers have been taken. They have disappeared because they helped Mandu, or they saw things they shouldn't have seen.'

'Where did Mandu go?' Hendrik asked. He was already back on the trail.

'They took the older woman to her relatives in the north. Then they headed to the Kangean Islands, staying first at the Buddhist residence in Surabaya,' the smiling man said.

'Are the Bajau people in the Kangean Islands?' Hendrik asked.

'Yes,' Asanga agreed readily. 'The Sama-Bajau. They are the maritime people of South-East Asia. They live on small wooden vessels in these islands.'

'Are they also called the Sea Nomads?' Flynn asked.

'Sometimes they are called the Sea Gypsies or Nomads. The two sisters had relatives in the Kangean Islands. They all went with Mandu to deliver the sisters. The Surabaya Buddhist residence is few hours from the ferry terminal where they could travel to the islands.'

'Mandu had made a promise,' Flynn surmised.

'Yes, you are correct,' Asanga confirmed. 'He had made a promise, and he kept the promise.'

Hendrik had been thinking about the comment from his friend in Selat. 'Have you heard of a person called Martin Moreau?'

Asanga's eyes opened wide and he sucked in his breath. He turned to go, then said, 'There is no more that I can tell you. Except both of you need to be careful.' Asanga paused, then quickly added, 'Be careful who you talk to. You must be like one of most popular gods in Tibetan Buddhism. He has eleven heads and many arms. You must use your heads, with your eyes and ears, to see and hear everything around you.' He walked back into the building and closed the door.

Flynn and Hendrik realised that was as far as this man was prepared to go. But they recognised it was a warning to them.

This was a country where information-peddling had monetary gain, as well as life-and-death consequences. Asanga was not prepared to lose his life.

They got back into the Land Rover. Hendrik drove as Flynn stared out through the bug-splattered windscreen.

'Did you notice he never said where the remaining four were going exactly?' Flynn said softly. 'He only said where two were headed, and the rest followed along. He didn't say what happened to Mandu. We need to find out. I need to know!'

'The Kangean Islands can be reached,' Hendrik contemplated. 'Though travelling by car from Sumatra through Java would take a while. Two days by car maybe. We can go carefully and take backroads.'

Flynn turned to his friend. 'Faster by planes. Maybe even several planes, Hendrik. Yes. It's doable. Very doable. One of these people may know something. They could have some small piece of information.' He looked out the window again. 'I need to know!'

CHAPTER 13

WARRIORS ON THE MOUNTAIN

Mount Arthur Hut, Kahurangi National Park, Tasman District
The dawn's light in the eastern sky appeared laser-like across Mount Arthur, feeling its way down towards the hut, warming as it went. The light snow had left a blotchy white blanket partially covering the roof. Ric stirred inside the sleeping bag, not wanting to leave. *This is new. Warm and inviting.*

Ric had restoked the fire several times during the night. After the first cry, he thought he'd heard a whistle or some kind of other noise, not mountain related. He had peered out the window and several times opened the door, letting the chilled night air in, but unable to hear anything further.

From totally zoned out, Elaina switched on. 'What's for breakfast?'

'How about this?' Ric whispered, kissing her.

'Ric, your father!' Elaina pulled her clothes from the bottom of the bag and got dressed while in the bag.

'How do you do that lying down?' Ric asked wondering where his clothes had ended up.

'Carefully and quietly,' she whispered.

'Ahhh, are you two up?' said John, coming through the door and launching into a soliloquy. 'Breakfast is hot porridge with raisins, cinnamon and brown sugar. And, of course, coffee. Coffee is one of those things the Dutch didn't invent. Ethiopia and Yemen are still duking it out on that topic. But the Dutch did label it *koffie*. It's hot, if you are interested.'

Elaina came down the ladder first, putting her hand on John's arm. 'G'day Johannes. Beating Ric to the *koffie* is a rare day for me.'

After breakfast, they packed their bags and Ric suggested the route.

'We can start moving up the trail since the sun has softened the snow a bit. We will have to take care on the shaded parts as there will still be frozen icy patches.'

John concurred. 'While the snow looks firm, once it warms it might shift on the trail. Looks can be deceiving.'

Ric pondered his father's comment. Not only can looks be deceiving, but he still hadn't found out what happened to his grandfather and the reason his father had waited so long to tell him.

John was in the lead with Elaina and Ric behind. They followed a narrow, craggy pathway that moved up abruptly over sharp rocks and rubble with periodic snow drifts. The footing was loose and unpredictable. They moved slowly, planting their boots with care.

Twenty minutes into the walk, John stopped abruptly. 'That's funny,' he said.

Ric and Elaina came up behind him.

'Someone's dropped their walking poles on the ground. It looks like they threw them away,' John said.

Ric bent down. 'There are small depressions in the trail coming down, though snow has partially filled them in. But they stop here.' Ric pointed to the dents.

Elaina inspected the direction and walked carefully to the ledge of the narrow trail that was carved into the cliff. But the drop-off over the side was sheer. Several scrub brushes were barely clinging to the cliff face, their roots forced into cracks to survive. Elaina could see a lower part of the trail further down. It was a significant plunge from the level they were on.

'It's almost as if this part of the trail collapsed downwards,' Elaina said, then she grabbed Ric's arm. 'What's that?'

Ric turned his head, listening.

'It was like a rumble or scrape,' Elaina explained. 'Did you hear it?'

'Yes! It's close!' Ric answered.

Elaina moved to the side of the trail near the rim of the escarpment.

'Elaina, be careful—that snow mound is hiding the edge,' Ric warned, coming to her side.

'Down there!' she cried out, pointing.

Ric peered over the ledge. Within a crevice, someone was hemmed in by the craggy bushes, about twenty metres down the cliff face. One bush was holding the person in place, but barely.

They could see that a red bag served as a buffer against the snag. As they watched, the snag bent further; it seemed ready to give up what it had held in place. A lump of rocks slid downwards.

'He's going to fall!' Elaina's voice was insistent. 'The cliff edge is slipping!'

'Hey, down there!' Ric hollered over the side.

There was no response.

John scanned the body and then the cliff face. 'He's unconscious. We need to get a rope on him quickly, before he falls further.' He turned to Ric. 'Lower me over the side. We'll secure him with a rope. Then I can lower him to the level of the trail below.'

'No, *you* lower me. I don't want you going over the side like that.'

'Not going to happen, son. You're stronger than I am. You have the strength to control the ropes, if you brace yourself,' John said. 'We'll put a sling around that big rock above the trail. Then you can lower me on the rope using the rock as an anchor.'

Ric looked at his father, tall and thin. Suddenly he seemed too thin.

Elaina had been trying to get at least one bar on her mobile phone. She offered another option. 'I could go down. I'm not afraid. But frankly, I'm not good at knots.'

'We don't have time to debate this, Ric,' John said. 'Belay me down. I'll make the person safe with an improvised sling harness, then we can lower him to the next level. It looks about 50 metres, so the 60-metre rope should do it. Trust me,' John said with a pleading voice. He was asking Ric to do something he hadn't done for years. Trust him. 'We don't have time. If he's alive, we need to act now.'

Ric peered down the hillside. 'Elaina, try my phone. Call Triple One.'

Elaina started dialling while Ric grabbed his gear.

'We're approximately twenty minutes north of the Mount Arthur Hut on the trail to the summit,' John added as Elaina looked up and nodded.

Ric ran the sling around the large rock and set up the anchor point and belay device to control the rope, while John quickly got into his harness and grabbed the carabiners, slings and other gear he might need. Once John was attached to the rope, he could drop over the side towards the bush and crag that were holding the man.

On the phone Elaina called out, 'Dispatch confirmed.'

'Tell them there's some snow on the ground,' Ric said. 'The wind is a southerly at approximately five knots. The sky is clear for a visual landing.'

'You can control my rope from above,' John said. 'Once I get down there, I can improvise a harness around the person. Then we can work together on lowering him to the trail below.'

'I'll help you both,' Elaina said. 'I'm strong.'

Ric and his father looked at the slight woman standing before them. John nodded. They got back to the task of laying out the ropes.

Ric gazed over the verge. 'We've gotta *move*!' he roared out. 'He's slipped again!'

'We're ready,' John said, ropes in hand. 'Lower me fast! We need to secure him.'

Ric and Elaina lowered John's rope, letting it slip slowly through a carabiner attached to the anchor line loop. John's Prusik knots were ready as friction hitches if he needed them.

'Keep going … keep going,' John chanted as they put him over the side. He began to gently walk down the side of the cliff face. Small stones rolled beneath his feet.

'I've got a ledge coming up. I'll need to get over that,' he shouted back to Ric and Elaina.

Suddenly he missed a step. Part of the cliff face crumbled beneath his foot. He tripped, falling forward. For what seemed like seconds, John hung in the air resembling a deer being dressed out.

Ric and Elaina froze in position. They couldn't do anything but wait and watch. Elaina inhaled a long breath in anticipation.

As if in a slow-motion sequence, John regained his footing, then signalled upward. A universal sign. Thumbs up.

'He's okay,' Elaina exhaled. Ric's face was furrowed in deep concentration.

After about ten minutes, they had John alongside the crevice in the cliff face.

He shouted up, 'It's Tahi!'

Tahi was pressed into the crevice with the snag only loosely coupled onto the rockface. John carefully put a sling under Tahi's arms and secured his body to the Prusik knot with a carabiner. Once he had a safety line on the boy, he looped the larger sling around Tahi's waist and between his legs, securing it to the second Prusik with a carabiner. He left Tahi's backpack on him. Too difficult to remove, mid-air.

After securing Tahi, John tried to find a pulse on the boy's neck. 'His pulse is faint,' he called up. 'Irregular breathing and he's unresponsive. Take up any slack on his rope. I'm going to free him from the snag. Once he is free, you can lower both of us to the next level.'

Ric and Elaina secured John's rope and brought up the slack on the rescue rope. John pulled at the snag that was holding the young man.

The bush broke free, tumbling easily. Too easily. It fell down the face of cliff. Not much had been holding it up.

Tahi's body slumped down about 50 centimetres, but was firmly attached to the rope by the Prusik knots. Ric and Elaina held tight.

'Okay, together we're going to lower the boy and myself at the same time!' John called up the cliff.

'We're running out of rope,' Ric said to Elaina as they belayed the ropes together.

The young boy got caught on several small outcroppings and each time they paused, then started again slowly, with careful movements along the side of the cliff. John could see Tahi was injured badly from the gash on his forehead and his pants were ripped. If they hadn't gotten to him, he would have fallen down the steep cliff to his death.

Ric and Elaina stopped. They could no longer lower the boy. 'We're out of rope!' Ric yelled down to his father.

'Wait! I'll setup a belay and lower him from here,' John called back. 'Once we're safe on anchors, drop his rope over. I'll use it to lower him further,' John hollered up to Ric and Elaina.

John built an anchor with a cam and a nut from the gear he had, equalising the anchors. He called for the rope from Ric and Elaina. Using an Italian hitch, he lowered the young man down to the lower trail area. After landing the young man on his side, Ric and Elaina removed the sling and belay from the large rock, while John rappelled down the short distance to the boy.

'It's going to take us a little time to get down to you along the trail. Are you okay?' Ric shouted down.

'I'm Fine. I think he's coming to,' John said, putting his large hand on the boy's forehead.

Elaina and Ric gathered the gear and were soon out of John's vision.

Tahi stirred, looking up at the man with the blue eyes. 'My mother will be mad at me,' he said.

John paused, trying to figure out how to explain what he needed to do. 'You were trying to protect a warrior, weren't you?' He touched Tahi's bag. 'But now I need to take this off.'

'He *is* a warrior,' Tahi said.

'You may be right, mate. But I'll take care of him. I promise. Let's get you off this mountain now,' said John.

Ric and Elaina arrived with the three backpacks. John was now holding the bag that Tahi had worn. In the distance, they heard the whoop-whoop of blades beating the air as the rescue helicopter came up from Nelson.

John stepped over the remnants of the bush that had plummeted down, and its thin roots that had clenched to the rocks before releasing.

Tahi's bag holding the skull had been the buffer. Once more John's friend, whom Tahi had called 'a warrior', had been in battle.

Chapter 14

A Dark Knight

Above Mount Arthur Hut, Kahurangi National Park, Tasman District
Ric, Elaina and John stood adjacent to the emergency helo landing spot beyond the hut.

The pilot gently lowered the helicopter onto the emergency pad, a scattering of rubble cleared for landing. The pilot kept the blades rotating slowly. Hunched over, the two paramedics scrambled out of the helo, marching down the small incline carrying a stretcher.

John, Ric and Elaina had brought Tahi up from the lower trail with a temporary litter created from walking sticks and a space blanket. Together they had used their complementary backgrounds to triage the patient, secure his leg, check his vitals, and pass Tahi's condition onto the paramedics.

'Do you know him?' one of the paramedics asked as they strapped Tahi onto the stretcher, getting ready for the short trip to Nelson Hospital.

'Yes, his name is Tahi and he lives in Nelson. My wife has called in his details,' John said.

'Do you want a lift down the mountain?' the paramedic asked.

'Thanks, but our vehicle is at the car park,' Ric replied. 'We'll walk down.'

The helo's engines began to roar. Resembling a dragonfly, the helo lifted off and banked away. The thumping sound of the rotors waned, as it darted away from the Wharepapa—the Arthur Range.

~~~
~~~

The three went back to the hut where they had spent the night.

'Can we stop for a while?' John asked when they got to the cabin. 'I'm a little winded. And my glasses went down the mountain when I tumbled off the cliff side.'

Without John noticing, Ric took some of his father's gear and put it into his bag. The sun was sinking behind the mountains, snapping the shadowy edges of the afternoon into the landscape before fading away.

After some bush coffee and apples, they started back down the trail to the Flora car park. The fading light cast longer shadows and a golden glow lingered over the crags and stunted trees as they descended the hillside.

The carpark loomed ahead in the twilight, deserted except for one large black truck parked down an access turnaround some distance away. It was too far for Ric to read the plates, his habit for every vehicle parked near him.

The dirt road (the term 'road' being generous) was bad enough in the daylight, but now seemed like a cow's trail in the deepening gloom. Past landslides had thrashed the surface and heavy rains gouged the depressions into pits. Falling tree branches had done their bit to turn the pits into pitfalls. In the darkness it was slow going.

'I'm glad you're driving, Ric. All I can see is black fuzz,' John remarked from the back seat as FJ-Orion lumbered its way down the incline.

After fifteen minutes on the road, two dim lights appeared behind them. Ric checked the rear-view mirror. The black vehicle was barely visible, with its parking lights on. It was the SUV from the carpark. And now he wondered if it did have plates.

'Someone's following us. Is there a place to pull over?' Elaina asked.

Ric shook his head, quickly calculating the minutes he had been on this pot-holed gravel road and the probable hour left to get down the hill.

Even in the subdued light Elaina could see Ric's wrinkled brow. From her pack, she pulled the last of the bikkies out to share.

As they cleared a corner, made narrower by the rocky cliff above it, FJ-Orion proceeded onto a straight portion of the road.

The SUV trailing them accelerated. Now it was barely a metre behind their back bumper.

There was only blackness in the SUV. The angle of vision obscured the cab, so Ric couldn't make out who was driving or if there was a passenger.

John turned around. 'Who's driving like an idiot?' he demanded. 'Someone could get killed.'

Ric was beginning to think that was the intention, but he said nothing. He kept his pace slow and steady, refusing to be pushed to go faster.

'Make sure your seat belts are tight,' Ric warned his father and Elaina.

The truck backed off to about thirty metres and waited for a few seconds. Then it sprinted rapidly forward.

Ric maintained his speed. He remembered a slightly wider portion of the road somewhere up ahead.

The truck repeated the move—it dropped back and then rushed forwards. But this time it tapped the back bumper of the FJ-Orion, nudging the Land Cruiser enough to make it rock.

Elaina held the front bar on the dashboard.

John called out to Ric, 'Stop the car. I'll sort this guy out.'

'Not a good idea. Unsure how many there are. Not sure what they want.'

The SUV dropped back and then began its run up to the FJ-Orion. Ric tapped the pedal, flashing his lights. The SUV barely missed making contact.

The straight track was ending with a sharp bend in the road. Ric remembered the turn, followed by a straight away and a turnout midway down.

'You two do what I say. Don't ask why.' Ric was forceful, leaving no options. 'Get your hands on your seatbelts. Get ready to get out. There's a spot coming up. I'll do a quick stop on the side of the road. Move into the bush. Get out of sight.'

'Ric, no! NO!' Elaina shouted.

'Elaina, do what I said,' Ric demanded.

He entered the hairpin turn, tapped the brakes lightly, then accelerated around the corner. The wheels skidded to a stop at the broad turnout. He killed the lights. 'Get to the uphill side. Lie flat. Hurry!'

John and Elaina unclicked their belts and left the Land Cruiser, slamming the doors. Elaina grabbed John's hand and pushed him towards the side of the road. They climbed into the bush and lay down.

As they disappeared, Ric tromped on the accelerator. He headed down the mountain, turning his lights back on. The SUV came around the corner fast, barrelling down on his bumper.

On the side of the road, John and Elaina popped their heads up as the dark SUV raced past them, trailing a cloud of dust.

'Where's Ric going? What's he doing?' John was rattled and flustered.

'He's …' Elaina couldn't explain to John, but she knew it was what Ric instinctively did. This time, it was going to get him killed!

Ric increased his speed as he careered down the hillside. The SUV came up behind him. Two car lengths back, the chaser suddenly turned night into day with two million candle-power of off-road lights flooding the hillside. The intensity was blinding.

Ric tapped his brakes quickly, a red warning from the rear of the Land Cruiser. It was an unexpected move. The driver of the SUV stomped on its brakes, causing a fishtail slide. It slowed the vehicle down, which almost hit FJ-Orion broadside.

Ric downshifted and hit the pedal, still hugging the high side of the road heading into a hairpin turn. A shallow ravine was on the left of the roadway. Ric shot into a turn out, leaving the tail of FJ-Orion sticking out onto the road.

'Two can play this game,' he muttered.

He grabbed the handle of the spot beam in the overhead and swivelled it around towards the hairpin corner.

The SUV came powering down, handling the corner but not slowing down. Ric flicked the spot lamp on, laser-focusing the beam onto the windshield of the oncoming vehicle.

The driver was blinded by the light, but could see the tail of Ric's truck hanging out. His lizard brain reacted. He swerved to avoid hitting the parked truck and mis-judged the narrowness of the road. The SUV rocketed off the edge into space, four-wheels airborne.

John and Elaina had walked across to the edge overlooking the valley below. They couldn't see any lights or any cars.

But suddenly in the night air there was a loud, crunching sound. Then a bang! Metal hitting something hard.

Elaina screamed, 'Ric! Ric!'

She and John started running down the road, then stopped. A set of lights was racing back towards them. Elaina grabbed John's hand and they hunkered down in the bush.

The FJ-Orion stopped close to where John and Elaina were crouching.

'Get in. Let's get out of here,' Ric said.

They sped down the road and Ric pointed to the small turnout. The black SUV had gone up and over the road edge, slamming into a large rock in the lower part of the ravine. Even in the moonlight, they could see the truck was totalled. Two figures were outside the SUV on the far side of the rock. They were shouting at each other. One arm took a swing and connected with a head. The scuffle turned into a brawl.

Ric sped up.

'Shouldn't we help them?' John asked.

'I'm sure they'll have roadside assistance, considering how safety conscious they were,' Ric responded. 'I'll call the police.'

John sat in the back of the Land Cruiser, retrieving Tahi's bag that he had secured under the seat before his quick exit. He realised that minutes ago, one skull could have become four from a deadly crash on that mountain road.

John had taught Ric how to drive. He didn't remember teaching him to drive like this. What kind of world did Ric live in now? He wondered if he really wanted to know.

Chapter 15

Layers, not in Cakes

Outskirts of Richmond, Tasman District
On their fourth day in New Zealand, John treated Ric and Elaina to takeaway coffees from The Grape Escape as they headed back to Longboat Island. Lenore was meeting them at the site and asked if the skull had been carefully handled since it left the site.

'I didn't have the heart to tell Lenore the journey it's been on,' John said. Late last night, he and Ric had inspected the Land Cruiser and noted there wasn't too much damage considering its outing the previous night. Nothing a panel-beating shop couldn't easily tackle.

John's mobile rang as they travelled along a highway that had once cut through acres of strawberries and apple trees.

'Nothing at all?' John asked, after listening to the caller for a few minutes. 'A chunk of metal? Yes, yes, I heard that.' John paused. 'All right, thank you, Constable, for letting us know.'

John put his phone away, protectively returning his right hand onto Tahi's bag. 'That was the Motueka Police Station. They went to the locale we reported last night where the black truck had crashed. Nothing—well, apart from a chunk of metal. A crane? A tow truck? They weren't sure how it got removed. The constable reminded me that thievery of SUVs is very high on the South Island. Especially for parts. It could be a stolen vehicle. Maybe some kids on a joyride.'

Ric thought differently. That truck had been following them. And it tried to run them off the road. Why him? Why his father? Why Elaina?

~~~
~~~

Site Manager's Office, Contaminated Waste Site, Longboat Island, Tasman District

Thomas, Louise and Lenore were standing outside the office when Ric drove up.

'Quite the welcoming party,' Ric announced as he got out of FJ-Orion.

John carefully removed the black bag and its contents from Tahi's backpack and slid the red backpack under the seat. He wanted to put the skull into Lenore's hands without identifying where it had been.

'Considering what we have found so far, I am intrigued by what's in that bag,' Lenore said to John as he reverently passed it over, releasing his tight grip.

He whispered to himself, 'I hope it helps identify this man.' Aloud, he said, 'I heard you may have found some additional … items.' He gave Louise a surreptitious side look; she'd called him earlier that morning.

'Yes, yes! Come in for a cuppa and I can tell you what I've found so far,' Lenore said.

In the office, John, Ric and Elaina followed Lenore to the metal table where a white cloth had been spread on the top. She pointed to several plastic evidence bags on the table, all of which had been identified and labelled.

'They appear to be a full set of phalanges—the distal, middle and proximal phalanx for each finger, but missing the metacarpal bones below. This is the upper part of a human hand.'

Lenore took a magnifying glass out of a small Pelican case on the counter. She looked at the bones she had found. 'Absolutely human, no question,' she said. 'Funny, though.'

'What?' Ric replied.

'I think I see tiny lesions in the bone. Maybe it's the soil.'

Ric took the magnifying glass and viewed the bones. 'I see them. It's like a lytic lesion. There are little holes.'

'We'll get all these finds to the lab and properly examine them,' Lenore said. 'I'll be on a plane first thing tomorrow morning back to Wellington.'

Elaina stood next to John who was clutching the edge of the metal table.

Thomas added, 'We found these remains near the same place as the skull. The adjoining cell was much deeper.'

Louise picked up the thread. 'Yes, the adjoining cell had the beginning of an eel trap three levels below from where the skull was found. And some midden shells were in the walls above the eel trap.'

'So, the skull is relatively recent,' Elaina proposed.

The five scientists stared at her.

'Good on you, Elaina,' John said. 'Older artefacts like the midden shells and the eel trap are in the lower levels. The skull has been more recently placed there.'

'Correct,' said Lenore, keen for the attention to be back on her. 'There are a number of black layers of soil along the side of the cell. Likely it's charcoal from fires on what could have been the beach during that era. This might have been a food collection place, or a temporary area of gathering before moving on to another location.'

Thomas chimed in. 'The phalanges were put in bags yesterday, marked and tagged as evidence. We have to add this last, ah, item, which you all brought back.'

'With all this circumstantial evidence, this is a crime scene, Ric. But a crime scene buried, not to be found,' Lenore summarised.

'There could be more human remains in this area,' Ric said.

Lenore lowered her voice. 'I always thought you were a smart guy.'

Elaina completely ignored the exchange and picked up on Ric's comment. 'It seems there are only parts of a body here. Where's the rest?'

'Originally the entire body may have been buried on the site. Then the production plant closed down,' John surmised. 'When the site clean-up was announced, someone must have come and tried to move the body.'

Elaina contemplated the bones. 'A full-scale clean-up of the site would reveal what they didn't want anyone to find.' Her statement hung for a few seconds longer, like the low, damp air over a musty, wet field on a frosty morning.

'Anyone there?' a man called and came into the office. 'Hello, hello,' he said, coming over to the table. 'I heard all about the bodies that have been discovered on site. How many were there?'

Thomas started to reply, but Lenore took over. 'Whatever you've heard is likely incorrect, and I wouldn't go around repeating it.'

'Well, that certainly is a welcoming greeting. I'm Eric Roberts, TDC Environment here.' Eric was an import from the US of A and visited the site often. He stretched out an open hand to shake Lenore's.

While Eric oversaw the environmental monitoring of various sites for the Tasman District Council, he also coordinated the community outreach programme for local residents. He claimed his major role was to eat muffins and listen to complaints for most of every day.

'I'm here to snatch John. Have a minute to chat outside?' Eric smiled broadly and exited the trailer. John, Ric and Elaina followed.

Out of earshot, Eric continued, 'Something important has come up, John. Can we meet at the Old Stagecoach Pub if that works?'

'That's fine,' said John. 'We'll give the site folks and Lenore a chance to regroup, and we can have some quiet time.'

Twenty minutes later, two vehicles were parked at the Old Stagecoach Pub, said to be the oldest pub in New Zealand. It sat on a small promontory at the side of what was once a stagecoach road. Other pubs claimed they were the oldest, but the locals knew that this was the oldest establishment. Their grandfathers had told them so.

The place was decked out in white clapboard siding with two gabled windows that peered out like eyes checking the road for the latest stagecoach coming in. The wooden bar sat adjacent to the large fire. Over the years, the bar watered the passengers, and the fire warmed their legs. The road took them one way or the other. Only the brews and patrons had changed.

Eric had the appearance of a terrier—wiry in body, quick in his movements and speech. When he arrived from the States he'd studied the local government history, policy background and all the juicy gossip. There was some suggestion that he wanted to be buried in one of the Council flower beds when his time came. Some suggested that sooner would be okay, too.

Once they reconvened, Eric launched his objective. 'John, I heard you were around today. The benefit of a small town. You've been a gem in assisting with the outreach programme in the community. I'd like you to meet someone this afternoon—Cynthia Paxton. She's upset and needs some neighbourly guidance on selling a piece of rural property. Should she sell it herself or get an agent? Cynthia recently lost her brother, Bruce, who owned a property not far from Longboat Island. His wife, Margaret, died of cancer some months before Bruce.'

John explained to Ric and Elaina, 'About a year ago, after my friend Salvy disappeared, I started volunteering in the community outreach programme. I've assisted in a way that the Council often can't.'

'Exactly,' Eric said. 'The Council's been doing some research on disposal sites beyond Longboat Island. Parásita had bought or rented various properties in the area. 'Cynthia now wants to sell her brother's property quickly, but would like to talk with us while she's there. She mentioned that it's possible that someone from Parásita had wanted to buy the farm from Bruce a few months before he died.'

'Isn't Parásita bankrupt?' John asked.

Eric nodded. 'Parásita went bankrupt before the clean-up started at the Longboat site. Maybe it's a shell company or owned by several trusts. But it's still interested in purchasing that farm.'

'Purchasing it for what?' Ric asked.

Eric shrugged. 'Good question. Cynthia says that Bruce didn't want to sell even though it wasn't a productive piece of land. Some interested party is working through a real estate broker and says they want to the buy land for a housing development.'

Ric didn't like the sound of that. 'Do I have this right?' he asked. 'The farm is not far from the current hazardous waste site?'

'Yes, correct,' Eric responded. 'Bruce and his wife, Margaret, both died of cancer—

leukaemia. Bruce died from the exact same type of cancer as his wife.'

'Didn't you say Parásita rented property around the Paxtons' farm, as well as bought property?' Elaina asked.

Eric nodded. 'Yes. Bruce had some arrangement with Parásita regarding the storage of various items from their site. They've been storing materials and products on his farm, but I think they may have also been using the farm for disposal of waste. Similar to the waste they were disposing at the site. There's enough rumours around that make me wonder. Bruce's sister wants a quick sale to get rid of the farm. It's been in trouble for a long time. The place started having crop failures when Parásita began expanding. They had problems with the dairy herd, and had to get rid of the cows.'

Ric and Elaina glanced at each other. The dots here were getting easier to join up.

'John, the other reason I asked you to speak to Cynthia is she mentioned that over a year ago she spoke to a chemist. He was working at the Parásita site and told Cynthia to get her brother and his wife off the farm—that it wasn't good for them to stay on the land. Shortly after that, the chemist upped and disappeared.'

'Did Cynthia say the chemist's name?' John asked.

'Yes, it was Salvatore. Salvatore Marino,' Eric replied.

John's face went ashen. He put his hand up to his forehead, covering his eyes. He knew where this was headed. John wanted to focus on Salvy being missing … maybe even killed. Even so, John was astonished at the amount of sickness around that site. He knew the Paxtons weren't the only ones.

CHAPTER 16

'HERE, MIDDIE – GO FETCH'

Paxton farm, Tasman District, South Island

They left their unfinished coffees and drove straight out to the farm. Bruce's old black dog, Midnight, was running around the farmhouse, announcing the arrival of the two vehicles that came up the drive. She kept barking until her job was done and they were parked by the front door.

Cynthia Paxton came out of the house to meet them. 'Stop now, Middie. Everyone's here.' Cynthia was a small woman with pale blue eyes and a face with worry lines permanently etched.

After the introductions, the group went onto the front deck and sat in large wicker chairs, where John asked her to describe her conversation with Salvatore.

'He was nervous and insistent when he talked to me,' Cynthia said. 'He kept telling me that I needed to get my brother and his wife off the farm. Then Margaret died and I heard from him again. He was even more persistent, but wouldn't come out and say what was bothering him. I tried to reason with my brother, but the land was important to him. It was his life. But then it cost him his life, as it did Margaret.

'Several years earlier, they'd started having trouble with the farm,' Cynthia continued. 'First, the dairy cows had some type of sickness. They would fall over. Some got blisters on their mouths. They stopped calving. And when they did calve, the results were sometimes terrible. The calf would come out … deformed. Grotesque.'

Cynthia took a breath, looking out to where there were large patches of dusty land. 'Then the crop areas that Bruce had started began having problems. The crops withered and died. It was random, though. Some areas were okay, and other spots didn't grow anything. It was like areas were set on fire and then burned. There was dust everywhere.

'With all the failures, the costs for the veterinarian and other bills piling up, they got in deeper. When Margaret died, my brother's heart, as well as his body gave up.'

Cynthia wiped tears from her eyes. 'I saw my brother and Margaret put their hearts into this place and then die. If you could have seen what was left of my brother before he passed, you would understand. I want out of this place and to get away from here.' Cynthia started to cry, pulling a hankie from her pocket.

Elaina went over to Cynthia's chair, took her hand and held it.

It was so quintessentially Elaina, Ric thought. His mind flashed back to a few of the times he had come so close to losing her. He understood a part of what Cynthia was feeling.

'Did your brother have any personal papers?' Elaina asked, thinking of the legal aspects of selling the property.

'Sure he did. It's a mess, though, mostly in cardboard boxes.' Cynthia pointed inside. 'Towards the end he threw stuff in boxes. He was sick and couldn't focus any more, or even think straight.' Tears streamed down her cheeks.

'I can help you sort the boxes out and put them in order,' Elaina offered. 'We can separate out the important documents connected to the land.'

'Thank you. I'm lost here. It's too much,' Cynthia said, standing up.

'I'll go in with Cynthia and make her some tea,' Elaina said to Ric.

Ric spoke gently to Cynthia. 'Do you use any water from the tap here? I think this place is on bore water, right? Do you drink it or even wash your hands?'

'Margaret did and so did Bruce. Though I brought some bottled water this time.'

Ric cautioned her. 'Don't use any of the tap water. Use only bottled water.'

Cynthia came back out with a tea, while Elaina carried a large package. 'My brother left something addressed to Eric, and a John P. I suppose that's you two,' she said to John and Eric. 'I think he must have received it from Salvatore over a year ago.'

The package was wrapped in brown paper and tied together with red twine. It was wrapped like a Christmas package. The red bow lay across the addressee. *To Eric Roberts or John P.*

Eric undid the wrapping and found a blue, hard-bound laboratory notebook that had Salvatore's name on it. The title said *Data from Parásita* followed by: *Silent Night* – Lab book number 12 of 12.

Inside were copious notes, chemical formulas, observations and procedures. They were all written in flowing cursive and, in some cases, block lettering. The writing was with a fountain pen in black Indian ink. It resembled a cookbook with recipes. There were notations regarding LD50 and the 'side effects'.

Ric glanced over Eric's shoulder. 'LD50 means Lethal Dose for fifty percent of a test population. Wait, that's awfully toxic—that's got to be a mistake.'

'It's full of notations,' John commented. 'Looks like Salvy was working out something.' John took the notebook and turned the pages. 'Eric, would you let me go through this first?'

'Yes, you probably have the chemistry background. Mine's a little rusty,' Eric replied. 'Cynthia and the dog are coming over to stay at our place. So, I want to get them settled in.'

As John closed the notebook, Middie barked again. Ric stood up, thinking someone was coming up the drive, and went down the porch steps.

The dog ran out from an unpainted barn with a large stick clenched lengthwise in her teeth. She ran up to Ric, wagging her tail and dropped the stick, wanting to play fetch.

Ric bent down. Then took a better look at the stick. It wasn't a stick. He took out a bandana from his pocket to pick it up. It was a bone—a femur, bleached and white. Unmistakable. On one end was the head and the greater trochanter, and at the other end the lateral and medial condyle. It was in remarkably good condition, despite Midnight's teeth marks. Ric knew the origin. 'It's human,' he affirmed out loud.

Everyone on the porch froze and gaped at Ric, holding the bone with his bandana. The only exception was Middie, the border collie, still wanting to play fetch. She was circling around and barking, waiting for Ric to throw the 'stick'.

CHAPTER 17

WHISPERS IN THE BOATHOUSE

Paxton farm, Tasman District, South Island

Ric was the first to take action.

'Middie came from the barn. We need to check it out.'

John had slowly stood, grasping the wooden railing. *I don't even want to think about what this is.*

'Eric, can you stay here with Cynthia? And Elaina—'

Elaina cut in. 'I'm coming with you.'

The barn was dark and dank. Shafts of light slipped through slats in the unmaintained walls like sweeping spotlights. An occasional roosting bird flittered up into the loft, knocking dust and cobwebs loose. Neglect was written into every nook and cranny. The barn told the story of a once proud man whose farm had slipped into ruin and disuse.

There were no sounds, but an oppressive and sweetly, sickening odour that permeated the barn. Not earthy or musky. It was sharp, something that could be tasted all the way down one's throat. It made Elaina gag. She grabbed Ric's hand.

Ric knew the odour. It was hard to forget, once experienced. Cadaverine. An organic compound, a diamine. It was a colourless liquid produced by the putrefaction of rotting flesh.

'It's coming from over here,' Ric called out to his father. 'Elaina, stay where you are. The dog's been digging over here in this corner next to the foundation. It's pretty strong here.'

John could see Elaina was feeling sick. He felt dizzy himself. As he started to back out of the barn, Elaina came over and offered her hand. Together they staggered back out into the sunlight.

Elaina's stomach was churning. She could taste the bile welling up. She leaned over and vomited onto the dirt.

'I'll get some water from the truck,' John said, hobbling over to FJ-Orion.

Ric explored the location of the dog's digging, the strongest part of the odour. He could see several bones where Middie's paws had dug a hole. They did not seem like 'clean' bones. It looked like some residue tissue remained. He took out his phone, called Lenore and then the police. If she got to the site before heading back to Wellington, it might speed up the next steps.

Ric remembered Elaina's comment. They had tried to move the entire body, but had missed parts. This wasn't an archaeological anything. This was a murderer covering their tracks and not doing it very well.

John and Elaina stood in the fresh air. John had fetched water from the truck, but Elaina was still gasping. John was pale and rested his hand on the side of the barn.

Ric emerged back into the light. He could still smell the cadaverine on his clothing and in his nose. He took a small jar of lip menthol from his pocket and jammed some into his nostrils, trying to kill the odour. Coming closer to his father and Elaina, he could see they were both woozy.

'What happened? I couldn't deal with it. The smell. The bones.' She grimaced.

'Nobody can deal with it, Elaina. Nobody ever does. No matter what they say.'

The three paused in the sunshine. Ric passed the jar of menthol to his father and Elaina, then eased them both to a rough-cut bench sitting by the barn wall.

'It's more human remains, Pappa,' he finally said. 'I think this might be related to the skull that was found. And maybe the bone fragments on the clean-up site. If so, the body may have been buried in at least two locations. Maybe more.'

John knew what Ric was saying. But it wasn't about science, forensics, testing or any specific examination that was to come. He knew what he felt.

It was the same feeling he'd had when he first saw the skull. Then again today with the phalanges. Now here on the farm. He knew where

Salvatore Marino was … or at least some of his parts. Proving it would be another thing.

He had to help his friend now. He hadn't helped him when he needed it.

'Lenore texted she'll be over,' Ric said. 'I've notified the police, and they won't be far behind.'

They walked back to the porch where Eric sat with Cynthia. When Ric finished talking, Cynthia pulled her legs up to her chest and put her arms around them, rocking and crying. John reached over and patted her on the shoulder.

For Cynthia, the sale of the farm would have to be put on hold until the police were done.

Elaina had been sitting on the steps, deep-breathing, and now stood up. 'Eric, I've been thinking about Salvatore's mother. If it was possible she had dementia, you might call around to all the facilities that care for older people. Perhaps she is somewhere not far away.'

She turned to Ric. 'I'll pack up the papers in those boxes I saw in the hallway. I can go through them later to see if there's anything that might help Cynthia.'

'I can help,' offered John, but he remained seated.

Ric put his hand on her shoulder. 'You don't have to do all that work. This isn't the vacation I planned. I wanted to reveal the New Zealand that *I* knew. I've got you stuck into something that's unravelling all around us.'

He gazed sadly at the green hills behind the Paxtons' brown farmland. 'It seems like a common occurrence with me. If you … want to reconsider my proposal, I'll understand.'

Elaina gasped and shook her head. 'Are you crazy? After what we've been through? No! You're stuck with me. Besides I like your arm too much. And your million-dollar kisses. And no one makes espresso like you. Sorry, you're on the hook … forever!'

Holding up her left hand, she added, 'I've still got my glow-in-the-dark ring and I'm not taking it off.'

Ric focused on her blue eyes and smiled. She never failed to amaze him. He leaned forward and kissed her on the cheek. 'I'll help you get the boxes together. We can set up everything in the sunroom of The Cliff House. Let's try and give Cynthia a hand in moving her gear to Eric's car.'

Lenore arrived shortly thereafter. She conducted a preliminary examination.

'It's definitely some sort of burial,' she said to Ric as she came out of the barn. 'What's with the teeth marks?'

'Oh, that was Midnight, the discoverer of the burial site. She brought me the femur in her mouth,' Ric replied.

'Great. Anything else that the dog may have gnawed on?' Lenore asked.

'Not that I know of.'

'It appears like a hasty burial. It's shallow, irregularly dug out, done in a hurry. Not that well packed when it was backfilled. I think they tried to put something over it,' Lenore said.

'I agree,' Ric concurred. 'Some bones are clean. Others … aren't. Maybe they used some lime. And there's no clothing or anything else.'

'I noticed that as well. I'm going to do another quick assessment now, then start in earnest on this site tomorrow morning. Ric, if you have a hankering, why don't you come out to the barn with me?'

I doubt that would occur, Ric thought.

The police arrived and began placing tape and markers around the barn and securing the area. They took everyone's details and some initial statements.

Ric, Elaina and John gave Cynthia a hug. Carrying the blue, laboratory book, John spoke to Eric as they headed to the car.

'This meet-up started as part of the community outreach programme. But you and I now know this is so much more.'

~~~

The Cliff House, Nelson

When they returned to The Cliff House, Kiri gave them thirty minutes to get ready for dinner out. They all realised it was better to get out and have a change of scenery, something that might help to dispel the horrors of the farm.

Grabbing her purse, Kiri found Ric on the lower deck talking to Flynn or Hendrik.

'With Mandu's background, he's going to stick to Buddhist monasteries or related locations. Pick overnight accommodations with two exits, preferably in opposite directions.'
~~~

Ric nodded to Kiri. He knew he'd promised Elaina and his parents he would take total time off here—but he kept excusing himself to take Flynn's or Hendrik's calls. He looked up information for them and chased down leads they came up with. It was like being a virtual ringleader for a live high-wire act. He just wasn't inside the circus tent.

~~~

The Boathouse, Nelson waterfront

The Boathouse Nelson was originally built as a rowing shed by enthusiastic rowers in 1906. During Saturday nights from the 1940s to the 1960s it became a popular dance venue, and a band played to a packed hall. While the dances and the menus changed over time, the sea view from the hall did not. In the high tides, the waiters rolled up their pants legs as the floorboards occasionally got wet!

The wooden building sat like a dowager on spindly legs and concrete piles, suspended above the churning waters of the harbour. In a small city, it was one of the few restaurants that faced the sea, with aromatic and tangy food and premium liquor brands—a magnet for both discerning diners and desirous drinkers.

The building had been repeatedly bashed by storms and high water from the Tasman Sea and the Southern Ocean but was always repaired to continue its century-old activity schedule.

'I'll drop everyone off and park FJ-Orion,' Ric said as he stopped in front of the Boathouse, delivering John, Elaina and Kiri to the front door. He watched Elaina, wearing a black dress he hadn't seen before, walking arm-in-arm with his parents.

Ric remembered Elaina's worry before they left Sydney. She'd thought his parents would judge her. Well, the jury's verdict was in: 'Definitely for the Defendant.'

'Let me order the drinks while you get the table,' Elaina said, squeezing Kiri's arm. John and Kiri were led to a table directly across from The Cut, with a frontal view of the harbour entrance out to the Tasman Sea. The close seating of The Boathouse fulfilled the region's requirement to hear a few other conversations splashing between the tables and the bar.

Elaina went to the bar near the reception area, sat on a stool and looked at the options.
~~~

'A bottle of Cloudy Bay Marlborough Pinot Noir and two sparkling mineral waters, please,' Elaina said to the barman. She pulled out her card, waiting for the card reader while watching a lean man who'd entered and looked her way. The man sauntered up, trying to negotiate the planked floor as if he were on a ship at sea in heavy rolls, rocking back and forth.

If 'four sheets to the wind' was extremely drunk, thought Elaina, this man was at least six sheets. Maybe more.

He wore a black shirt, and his black hair greased back as if he was keen to recreate the 1960s, complete with tight jeans and oversized rings. He came up and put a hand on her shoulder.

'Ernest Bennett,' the man slurred. 'I never forget a face. I think I met you at the music fest up on the hill. I'm Ernest, remember?'

'I beg your pardon?' Elaina said, looking at the pink-faced, tipsy man.

'I'll find us a cosy seat and buy you a drink and we can talk about your blue hair and the music,' Ernest stammered on.

'Sorry, you've mistaken me for someone else,' Elaina said.

Ernest squinted at Elaina and tilted his head. 'You're right. You're right. I love black. Black dress. Black truck. Black pack. Black jacket. Black pants.'

The barman came over with the card reader, and read Elaina's face as well. 'Ernest, find another spot to dribble on,' he said.

Elaina clicked her card, nodded to the barman in thanks and glided off to the dining area, catching up to Ric as he pulled out her chair.

'I can barely keep up with you three,' Kiri said. 'I'm forever grateful for you tramping up Mount Arthur and rescuing Tahi. But the new discoveries at Bruce Paxton's farm are alarming. Years ago I met both Bruce and his wife. Sounds like things will be difficult for Cynthia.'

Elaina described the paper-sorting she had started. 'There's lots of confusing data in Bruce and Margaret's paperwork. I found a copy of a letter from a real estate group called Pinnacle Property and Investment Company. They had a cash offer for the farm. It notes some of the problems with the farm, but the cash offer is substantial. The odd thing is the offer is clipped to a note that is addressed to "Dear Mr B – Confidential." It said: "We've made the offer and are waiting for the recipient's response." I think the handwritten note was mistakenly given to the Paxtons.'

'Eric mentioned someone wanted to buy it,' John said.

'Yes, but the offer was on the same stationery used at the old Parásita site. I saw some of the old stationery and envelopes because Louise had recycled it for scratch paper.'

'So, the chemical company wanted to buy his farm,' Ric said. 'We know they used some neighbouring land, like the Paxtons', for storage.'

'But this particular offer is dated *after* Parásita went into receivership,' Elaina said. 'They were in no position to buy anything, given their financial and legal circumstances. And why would they want a run-down farm for such a high price?'

'They either wanted something that was there, or something buried there. Maybe something they didn't want anyone to know about,' Kiri surmised.

Loud voices reverberated in the hallway behind her, and she turned her head to listen, eavesdropping on the talking. She recognised the gruff tones of one of them. It was the voice on the phone! The two men seemed not to care about their grumbling being overheard as they stood in the entryway of the eatery.

Elaina noticed Kiri's clenched hand near her plate and the two men entering the dining area.

Ric asked a question he had been pondering. 'I know Parásita was focused on agricultural and industrial uses, but what other chemical compounds were they concocting?'

No one got a chance to reply.

Ernest Bennett and Odell Rodmen had negotiated a path to the Peters' table. Odell, the alpha wolf, butted in.

Odell was short, with a partly balding head interspersed with greying tuffs. His skin was grey, and his stomach sagged with a pronounced midriff paunch. He resembled uncooked liver wrapped in grey gaberdine slacks, with the pant legs rising high above the tasselled golf loafers. His sidekick, an Elvis wannabe, wore black as if it was a political statement. They hovered behind Kiri.

Odell's gravelly voice rumbled and growled across the table. His breath reeked of stale beer. 'Why are you always interfering with progress and plans? Why do you stick your nose into other people's business? Always complaining. Always talking to people,' continued Odell. 'You aren't going very far. If you're going at all.'

'All right, Odell. We've had enough of your floorshow for the evening.' John stood up and towered over the other two.

'You aren't doing anything to us, Dutchy. Sit down,' Bennett snarled.

Ric had had enough. 'You have two choices,' he said, looking directly into the eyes of each one. 'Exit quietly or exit headfirst out the window.'

'Ha, he doesn't get it,' Odell said to Bennett. 'Have your dinner. Have two. I know who will eventually profit, no matter what you do.'

The barman had spotted the duo and started over. He was a part-time bartender and the rest of the time pumped iron at the gym. They shuffled away, faces flushed with anger.

Elaina had been watching Kiri during this interruption to their meal. The normally superbly confident psychologist had seemed ice-bound onto her chair. Her face was blanched, and her eyes stared forward.

Kiri thought, I know now it was Odell on the phone. She had heard stories about him in her practice. Odell was a drunken lout, a complainer who always agitated. Was he capable of more? She knew if she told John and Ric now they would go out the door after Odell. A fight never solved a problem. Her guidance for conflict resolution would go out the door with them. She would sit them both down tomorrow and tell them. They would make a plan.

Elaina was skilled at recognising moods that people brought with them to yoga. What she saw was fear in Kiri's face. Then a flash of anger.

Chapter 18

A Kiwi Jurassic Park

Jurassic Park #1, Marlborough Sounds, South Island

The Peters clan, including their newest, soon-to-be member, Elaina, were up early. John had two waffle makers pumping out Dutch waffles and a pan of apple slices cooking on the stove. Ric was pressing the espresso machine to perform. He cranked out double shots in rapid fire and transformed them into flat whites, long blacks, lattes and mochas.

While they were breakfasting on the deck, Terence Nigel Thompson (TNT or Terry to his friends) came up from the house below to say hello and have an espresso.

Kiri thought she'd have time to tell her family about Odell, but now was not the time with TNT at the table.

'Knew the coffee would have improved since Ric arrived,' Terry began, obtaining a shrug from John and an oblique smile. 'I'm headed to my place in D'Urville Island for a few weeks. How about an overnighter on the island in the next few days? I can pick you up with our boat any place you like. Come and enjoy the solitude.'

The island's Māori name was Rangitoto ki te Tonga, which meant *red heavens look to the south.* As the northernmost island of the Marlborough Sounds, it rode easily in the waves from the Southern Ocean.

Marlborough Sounds and Nelson were both labelled as Top of the South Island, though there was always a friendly competition on which region made the best wine or which had the most sun. Sunshine was an important commodity in New Zealand.

D'Urville Island had an area of almost 150 square kilometres, which was greater than the size of San Francisco. It sported a resident population of somewhere over 50.

John thought that the island's irregular and convoluted coastline was much like several of its residents. 'Doesn't Reid Baxter live there?' he asked. 'Do you know him?'

'I wish I didn't,' Terry answered. 'He's one of the vermin they haven't eradicated from the island yet.' Terry was a man known for being blunt. 'Though the Department of Conservation routinely uses 1080 poison drops to control pests. Speaking of poison, I think he was a partner or something with that old chemical company on Longboat.'

'You don't enjoy Baxter's company?' John pressed on.

'You know Scrooge in *A Christmas Carol* by Charles Dickens? Baxter could star in *any* production. Only he never gets any ghost visits. And he never changes.'

Ric remembered the name 'Mr B' that Elaina had mentioned in connection to the Paxton offer. If he owned or partially controlled the hazardous waste site, it could have been him.

'You like him that much?' John asked.

'"Let me count the ways", to quote Elizabeth Barrett Browning,' Terry began. 'Baxter's generally mean and cantankerous. He's miserly. He'd take the pennies out of his own dead mother's eyes. He thinks he's a barrister and a businessman, yet he's not good at either. He looks for ways to up-end the court system and finagle any business deal.'

'Tomorrow we can come,' Kiri offered, moving the conversation forward. 'We're headed off to Cable Bay this morning and then on to a place near Moetapu Bay. Another neighbour has a bach in Mahau Sound.' Kiri turned to Elaina. 'What you might call a holiday home in Australia.'

'I can pick you up by boat from Mahau Sound tomorrow,' Terry suggested.

'That would be fine, but I've got some things to take care of tomorrow afternoon,' John said. 'After the over-nighter at your place, I'll collect them from French Pass.'

Kiri gazed over at John and crinkled her brow. His smile said *I will tell you later* in the unspoken language that couples sometimes invent.

With FJ-Orion loaded up with their gear, they shot through Nelson and headed north on Highway 6 parallel to the meandering Boulder Bank that sheltered Nelson Harbour. They turned off to Cable Bay before Hira.

The road snaked along through a green valley heading to the bay where the first overseas cable link connected New Zealand to the rest of the world. After the cable install, telegraphic messages to Europe suddenly took a mere four days, instead of the usual six months for letters.

~~~

Archery Range, near Cable Bay, South Island

John drove into an adventure park located off the main road.

John's friend, Jannick Hansen, ran the archery range for the local club. A portable trailer held a variety of recurve bows and quivers of field tips for target practice. Two baskets contained arm guards and gloves for drawing the bows.

Kiri sat at the table under a large fig tree behind the firing line. Ric, John and Elaina lined up with Jannick who gave them the safety briefing and said he'd call out the movement to and from the targets.

After the first round, Jannick walked them down to their targets. 'That's pretty good,' he commented to John and Ric who had managed to group their arrows in the three rings closest to the bullseye at the 50-metre range.

They moved to Elaina's target which was clearly another story.

'How long have you been shooting?' Jannick asked her. All her arrows were competing for the centre of the bullseye.

'A while,' Elaina replied. 'I started in Australia in Broken Hill and then did more during high school in Brisbane. My father thought it would strengthen my muscles, something like weightlifting.'

'I don't think I've ever seen spacing that tight before—certainly not here,' Jannick said. 'Maybe in a European competition, but that was a long time ago. Would you be interested in moving to targets that are further out?' he asked her.

'Sure,' Elaina said.

Jannick shifted the three archers to another range, set up with the targets further back. As the three archers were conversing, Jannick went to his four-wheel drive and pulled a long case out of the back seat, bringing it to the table where Kiri was sitting. He opened the case, took out a cloth sack and removed a recurve bow from the cloth protector.

Jannick returned to the firing line and handed the bow to Elaina with mutual respect.
~~~

'This is not your average target bow,' Elaina said, recognising the workmanship.

'Well, I think it's safe to say that you're not the average archer either,' Jannick answered. 'Maybe you and the bow go together.'

Elaina placed the bow in her left hand, held her arm out straight and pulled back on the string as a dry fire. She slowly relaxed the bow string to its starting position, getting a feel for the tension and flex of the bow.

'This isn't a bow—it's a work of art,' Elaina commented to Jannick.

'It was handmade. Used at the Olympic Games and other places. Try it.'

Elaina stood with her feet apart, her left shoulder to the target, bow in her left hand cradled between her forefinger and thumb. She gently loaded an arrow, pointing it down to the ground, then lifted the bow in the direction of the range.

Her left hand tightly closed around the bow grip. As her right hand drew the string and arrow back, the arms of the bow flexed backwards. She brought the arrow and string alongside her cheek and sighted down range towards the 70-metre target.

She stood there, not moving a centimetre, frozen in position like a Greek sculpture.

For Ric this was captivating. How could he know this woman so well … and not know her at all?

Elaina released the arrow with a twanging sound and it streaked down the range. With a loud swat report, it hit the target in the bullseye. Outer edge. And this was her ranging shot!

The next four shots all fell within the bullseye—not as tight as at 50 yards but still in the bullseye.

'That was quite some shooting,' Jannick said as they were leaving. 'Any time you want to come out to shoot, let me know. I'll set it up. The range is yours,' he said, smiling at her.

'My father used to say that archery is about Posture, Patience and Persistence. I usually manage only one of three these days,' Elaina responded with a laugh.

~~~
~~~

Havelock, Marlborough Sounds

After packing up, with FJ-Orion chugging around the curves, John announced they were passing through Havelock, the green-lipped mussel capital of the world, according to the locals.

Elaina laughed. 'You're kidding me—a green-lipped mussel capital? I can't imagine looking at anything that has green lips, let alone eating it!'

'These New Zealand mussels would be offended at your refusal,' Ric said. 'They have their own raving audience that comes to Havelock just to eat them.'

'Let's at least stop for a takeaway espresso and chicken pies at Ray's Place on the main road,' said Kiri. 'No green-lipped pies there,' she jested.

The interior of FJ-Orion soon smelled like chicken pies and coffee. John announced, 'Our next stop is Moetapu Bay next to Mahau Sound. That's where Richard's place is. It's called Jurassic Park Number 1.'

Ric was thinking about Richard's amusement when they had chatted on the plane. 'Is this Richard Hornwell?' Ric asked, knowing Richard was a popular male name in New Zealand.

'Yes. He's an Air New Zealand pilot who lives not far from us in Nelson, with some property out this way.'

On the plane, Richard had figured out Ric was the son of his neighbour. In New Zealand, Ric often felt there wasn't six degrees of separation; it was more like two.

'I want to know, what is Jurassic Park Number 1?' Elaina asked.

'Richard's bach on Mahau Sound,' Kiri explained, 'is about five acres of jungle fronting a scenic shoreline. He's been planting natives for many years and John claims it's the perfect setting for any remakes of Jurassic Park. That's Jurassic Park Number 1. His house in Nelson is Jurassic Park Number 2. Richard and John allege they have seen dinosaurs around both these places. They have yet to reveal the wine they were drinking.'

~~~

Jurassic Park #1, Marlborough Sounds, South Island

Arriving at the top of the driveway along the Mahau Sound and travelling down the jungle-laden driveway, Elaina was on the lookout for at least a brontosaurus.
~~~

The Jurassic period of palm trees, cycads, ginkgos and tree ferns had been replaced with the Kiwi version of nīkau palms, black tree ferns, kawakawa, five fingers and rangiora plants. Same array of green colours, same variety of polished and waxy leaves, same dampness, same carpet of dense underbrush, same heavy rain.

'Elaina is glad New Zealand doesn't have any snakes,' Ric observed to his parents. 'But in this locale, they'd be massive.'

In front of the property, a collection of ancient, sunken river valleys were now filled with ocean water. The forested hills rose steeply from the sea around an intricate coastline of sheltered inlets and sandy bays.

Elaina spread two yoga mats out while Ric and John set up one tent on a flat piece of grassy land next to the bach.

John built the fire while Ric dusted the chicken with smoked paprika, salt and garlic. The chicken breasts were on a grill balanced on four rocks after the fire had died down. Corn, costumed in aluminium foil, was roasting on the side.

Richard appeared with freshly baked bread and wearing his JP#1 attire. He had swapped out his crisp pilot's uniform for coveralls and gumboots. Gumboots were requisite attire for every Kiwi. Elaina had seen people wearing them in the supermarket and when headed to the cathedral. John had set her up with her own green pair while in Nelson.

As the afternoon light sprinkled gold on the water, Kiri joined Elaina for her first session of yoga before dinner.

Elaina stood on one of the mats on the grass overlooking the glimmering sea. She faced Kiri, looking at the green backdrop of Jurassic Park, and started with an introduction.

'It is often said that a Warrior's Pose helps with hip flexibility and increasing fortitude.'

'I could use a dinosaur's dose of that,' Kiri said. Elaina caught the edge in Kiri's voice.

'Warrior Pose is one of the most powerful poses in yoga. It helps to strengthen the arms, shoulders, thighs and back. It's named after the warrior Virabhadra. In yoga, he symbolises a spiritual warrior.' Elaina grinned at her yoga class of one. 'The three forms of this pose always help me to discover both strength and humility. After doing these poses, I feel I can face life with greater courage and determination.'

Kiri tried to imitate the pose Elaina was demonstrating. 'Perhaps I should incorporate yoga into my counselling practice. I know a few people whose ego stands in the way of humility.'

'Think of Warrior 1 as a "giant step forward". Step your left foot forward, your knee then bends at ninety degrees.' Elaina came over to Kiri, putting her hands on her right heel. 'Your back heel stays grounded on the mat. Try and turn your toes to about forty-five degrees.'

'You've got me into this position, Elaina. I wonder if I will ever get out,' Kiri said as Elaina helped her with the pose.

'Inhale and reach your hands up above your head.' Elaina guided her hands up Kiri's arms. She felt Kiri become relaxed with the pose.

'Warriors may build strength with this exercise, but I hope it teaches me balance,' Kiri said, feeling as if she was going to fall over.

'Like most things,' Elaina said, 'inner strength and balance comes from enhanced focus and willpower.'

Kiri nodded, trying to remember to breathe deeply, spotting the crescent moon appearing in the twilit sky.

After a 30-minute session going through all three warrior poses and a gentle relaxation at the end, Kiri sat up, putting her hand on Elaina's arm.

'Thank you for my first-ever yoga session. I feel refreshed and ready for any tyrannosaurs coming my way.'

Elaina hesitated, then asked, 'I noticed last night when those two men came to the table, the man named Odell startled you.'

Kiri *was* startled. 'I must be losing my touch. Usually I can mask surprise.' She paused. 'I've received two phone calls from a man with a gravelly voice. It was terrifying.'

'I take it these calls didn't start with "Kia ora".'

'No,' answered Kiri. 'In the first call he said: "*Stop interfering. Stop talking to people. You stop or we'll stop you.*" In the second call he said: "*You are going to get your family and yourself hurt. And you won't be able to recover.*" It was Odell. I know it was him. Why is he making these threats? I'm going to tell John and Ric before we leave here. I need to figure out the right words to say.'

Elaina caught the tone of Kiri's voice. It was softly beseeching her to remain silent for a while. Elaina nodded. 'I can help you when you decide to tell.'

Kiri squeezed her hand. 'Two warriors who may not know what they are getting into.'

Dinner was around the campfire on the edge of the grass before the cliff edge dropped off to the sea. The moon was a sliver, so the stars had taken over the night's performance. Naming the constellations was the opening activity.

After identifying Orion the Hunter, the Southern Cross, and a discussion of the *aurora australis*—an upcoming natural light display, Richard announced a mystery guest he had invited.

'I heard from the jungle drums that your "family activity" has been looking into that old factory site on Longboat Island. I know a man who used to operate a digger there.'

'Yes, our "family activity" this week is trying to help a few people relative to that factory site,' John answered. He didn't bother explaining that one of them was almost certainly dead.

'George Taylor is someone you need to meet up with. He was telling me that he did a lot of work for that Parásita group. He dropped out of circulation about a year back. He said it was to keep himself safe.

'I ran across him camping in Jurassic Park one weekend and listened to his story. I told him he could camp here any time he wanted. He travels around the Sounds and Golden Bay as if he's Marley's ghost. Though sometimes he heads down the West Coast "trying to stay off everyone's radar".'

'Great,' said Ric. 'We have Scrooge to look forward to tomorrow and now Marley's ghost appears tonight.'

'He ought to be along shortly. George isn't a fan of phone calls and only texts.'

Richard launched into his transition of the land with the native plantings. The Jurassic period had stretched about 56 million years. Richard's transition was clocking in at 25 years.

'Kiri and John, I'll bring you two palms so you can plant them in your atrium area,' Richard promised.

He was about to list the wildlife in Jurassic Park when George's camper appeared in the gathering darkness shrouded in a low fog, as if he were indeed Marley.

The ancient campervan moved down through the overgrown access road. As the tyres gyrated over the metal-sealed drive, the van creaked and groaned like the sound of heavy chains pulled along a surface. To complement the van's arrival, in the distance they could hear the grunting of a large feral pig rummaging through the forest for roots.

George was medium height, but his thick boots made him seem taller. From the sun, he was tanned like leather and sported a grey, stubby beard, a floppy leather hat, and shorts with a singlet. Winter or summer, that was his 'relax-in' outfit.

In his early life, George had been a hunter and fisher and ate what he caught. Pigs, deer, goats, the occasional smaller mammals were on his menu, plus fish of any kind. His life was outdoors, hunting things that were edible.

His wife understood that and always released him out the door with boxes of biscuits in tins. When the biscuits were gone, George came back like a homing pigeon, except carrying venison, pork loins and smoked fish, which filled the chilly bin. He stayed until he needed to restock the freezer. But his wife had died five years previously and he had since taken up digger duties on the South Island.

Kiri created a plate of supper for George, and Ric added another chair around the campfire. The flames were stoked up with driftwood from the beach. Richard provided cold beverages from the small fridge in the bach.

Between bites, George began his narration.

'I suppose this is probably my moment of redemption. I'll tell you what I know and probably should have been telling people sooner. But now's as good a time as any. I used to do some prospecting on the West Coast, got handy with equipment like diggers and front-end loaders, trucks and the like. Started doing bits and pieces for the crowd down at Parásita, excepting it was called something else then. Don't remember what. It got to be Parásita when that fellow Baxter took over.'

'You mean Reid Baxter?' John said.

'Yes, that's him. He's a real piece of work. Pardon my language, but a real wanker,' George said. 'They used to make many products, mostly for farming, some for tree plantations. But they expanded and shipped lots of things overseas. A lot of different chemicals were made around then. Drums, sacks, cans, bottles were moving in and out of that place all the time. Baxter wanted to expand the production and speed up all the processes.'

'What chemicals were they using to make the products?' Ric asked.

'I don't remember all of that stuff,' George said. 'It came in barrels that had skulls and crossbones on them. Lots of labels. Red, orange and yellow warning labels. Stripes and symbols. They were using it to make things that you would spray or dust on crops. Even to kill a variety of animals, and for all I know shipping it out for killing more than that. But after a few years they were making something else there, too. New people came in. Wasn't really sure if it was all commercial products.

'At first there was a fellow there that used to run around in a white coat like in the chemist shops. He was trying to understand what the agriculture products were doing to the ground. He'd try them out on plots of land to see what the stuff would do. He never seemed happy. Always yelling at Baxter to stop this or stop that.

'They were trying to find new kinds of things for farming and for tending livestock, and Gawd knows what. I wasn't too close to what they were doing. It was pretty technical, and the chemist and maybe one or two others were trying to get them to stop, to not mix the products, or make them stronger.'

George shook his head. 'They didn't seem to listen to him. I do know they killed some of the local livestock a fair few times. By accident, they said. It seemed a bit daft. They were trying to help the land and they ended up killing things. I know because I had to bury them. They wanted lime spread onto the carcasses, too. You know something's up when they start spreading lime all around like that,' George added.

'Then the chemist left one day all of a sudden. About a year ago. That lady doing the books took off, too. She was a fair dinkum of a woman, if I do say so,' George said. 'Quite the looker. Her name was … Tamara. No, no, no. Toni? No, that's not it. Tessa! Tessa Bright. Don't know why she left. That Reid Baxter at Parásita said that the chemist fella and she ran off together.'

George took a bite of his dinner. 'The chemist was a decent chap. Treated me like a person. He enjoyed fishing, like me. Reid said he took some of their documents and information to sell somewhere. But I didn't think so. The chemist even told me to be really careful when I was handling some of the bad batches. Made me wear all that safety stuff,' George explained.

'What do you mean bad batches, George?' John asked.

'When I first was there, they would do these runs of small batches of sprays or dusts. Wanted to figure out how to make them up. Then the tests were tried on crops or animals. Sometimes it didn't work out—a batch would go bad or fail. The disposal was another department. They had to get rid of it. Sometimes they even dumped it because it wasn't the right colour for sales.'

'Where did it go?' Ric asked quietly.

'Depends. Sometimes it got backfilled into the property. Sometimes it got dumped into the estuary behind Longboat Island. The only fishing tip I'll ever give out is not to fish or catch anything and eat it from *that estuary*,' George sneered. 'On the other hand, there's pretty decent fishing up near Murch and in Golden Bay.

'Sometimes we took the bad product out in trucks with a small digger piggyback. We'd bury the barrels or sacks,' George continued. 'Usually at night.'

'But where?' John asked, now sitting on the edge of his camp chair.

'Everywhere!' George threw his hands up in the air. 'Some of it was in steel barrels. Some of it in plastic barrels. It was waste. Some of the locals took it because Parásita paid them to be able to dump it. Nothing grew in those spots after that.

'Mate, can't remember all the places and I'm already sticking my neck out here with this confession,' George said. 'One thing I know is Baxter is not someone to mess around with. I'd like to help, but I'm already on the run.'

The fire crackled as the gloom of the night deepened the shadows. This had been Marley's moment.

'I didn't say anything back then but I'm telling you now. Still, I'm staying clear of Baxter and those other lowlifes that work with him.'

'Odell Rodman and Ernest Bennett?' Ric asked.

'Sure as the sun's coming up tomorrow,' George said. 'They're like twins. Odell is the wealthier one—the other wishing he was. Both are dangerous and used to getting their way. They have powerful friends to make that happen. And they don't stop because you ask them nicely.'

Elaina looked across the fire at Kiri who nodded. They, too, were playing with fire.

The friendly, roaring campfire burned down to a glowing mound. Native owls started calling in the trees—sounding like they were singing their own name. 'Morepork, morepork, morepork.'

George retired to his campervan. Richard ambled off to the large utility garage where there was a sleeping area, a wood burner stove and an old tractor. John and Kiri slipped into Richard's bach while Ric and Elaina were opening the zippers of their tent.

In the middle of the night, Ric woke Elaina up. 'Come on, I want to show you something.'

Feeling the coldness of the midnight air, Elaina slipped on some black yoga pants and her puffer jacket and followed Ric outside who wore a black T-shirt and shorts. They headed up the hill with minimal light on a small pathway. Ahead was a row of rocks surrounded by native bush in dense hedges. But the rocks and bushes didn't seem to be grey or green. They were alive with small lights like someone had decorated the side of the hill with fairy lights.

Elaina was half asleep and trying to figure out what she was seeing. 'Did you bring those fairy lights again, Ric?'

'No. Guess again.'

'Sequins?' she asked.

'Glow-worms.'

'Worms?' Elaina said loudly.

'Who goes there?' a stern voice yelled out.

Ric and Elaina were rooted to the path. Ric quietly slid Elaina behind him.

From the moist and humid darkness, George Taylor emerged with a rifle across his arm. The rifle was his constant companion in his paranoia of being scared.

'A few more steps and I would have been arrested for manslaughter. You two shouldn't be out and about at this hour. Go back to bed and do what you're supposed to be doing,' George muttered and he headed back up the hill. But turned again to shout out, 'And don't wear black when there isn't any moonlight!'

Ric hustled Elaina back to the tent, but she paused near the opening.

'And here I was worried about snakes!' She unzipped the fly of the tent and dove in.

Chapter 19

Tracking Mandu: Alive, Alive, Oh

Jambi, Sumatra enroute to Surabaya, Java, Indonesia

For many years, the number of islands that made up the country of Indonesia was hotly contested, ranging from 13,000 to 25,000. In the 20th century, Landsat satellite images helped lock in the number at 17,508 … at low tide.

Flynn and Hendrik were flying from the third largest island, Sumatra, to the most populated island, Java. The east coast city of Surabaya in Java was the jumping-off point to reach the Kangean Islands via the ferry terminal at Sumenep.

'Flynn, we're keeping a low profile in the airport,' Hendrik cautioned. 'Pretend you're invisible.'

'Ya, ya, I understand,' Flynn said. 'Stop acting the maggot.'

'We don't want to be picked up here. It wouldn't be good for either of us.'

'Especially if we are tied to the same pole,' Flynn replied.

'Look at us, Flynn. Both of us look rough as guts, like we've been dragged out from a dust bin. Carrying our duffels like two Australian swagmen. We don't look like all these tourists with their wheelie bags.'

'All right, boyo, I'll behave, but you can buy the coffee this time.'

Hendrik wandered to the first café in the airport.

The young server rattled off, 'Do you want regular milk or plant-based? We have almond, coconut, oat and rice milk.'

'I said black coffee,' Hendrik said. 'Do I look like I take bloody milk in my coffee, whether it comes from a cow or a plant?'

'So that's a no, sir,' was the reply. But the server remained upbeat. 'Could I interest you in upgrading that black coffee to a latte or maybe a mochaccino?' the young man enquired. 'Oh, and do you want the eco take-and-keep cups, recycled paper or the porcelain "for here" cups?'

'Black coffee ... two.' Hendrik signalled with his thumb and finger, European style. 'In takeaways. Or, I takeaway my order.'

'Yes, sir. Right, coming up.'

The server looked at Hendrik, who was standing tall at the counter wearing his French army field jacket, and decided to the fill the vacuum created by the lack of conversation with some conversation of his own.

'Man, you've got some drip going on there with that jacket. It really slaps. Did you get that on Etsy?'

Hendrik was having trouble maintaining a low profile, let alone a conversation with this kid. 'No,' he said. 'I ripped it off a dead terrorist in Africa. I was cold. And it was lekker—very nice.'

Hendrik figured the kid thought he was making it up.

Surabaya, Eastern Java, Indonesia

Surabaya was a bustling city of ten million people crammed together like bees in a honeycomb, with every member hustling from one congested cell to another. The congestion seemed to intensify in the heavy rain that filled the streets.

From the airport they hired a taxi to take them to the Buddhist residence that Asanga had mentioned. The driver skimmed through the city as if the streets were a waterslide.

Flynn and Henrick had packed light, but they knew about the weather in Indonesia and pulled out their Tasmanian rain jackets. While Indonesia had almost double the rain, Tasmania had oilskin jackets for the bush. Not much got through those jackets, even in a storm.

The taxi dropped them at a large commercial building, a former fabric factory that had been refurbished into a residence for monks, a Buddhism learning school, and a scenic spot for visitors ticking off 'Buddhist centre' on their bucket lists.

The building had a small Buddhist icon out front, making it less pretentious and less of a target. Leaving the taxi, they found the door of the monastery and waited with the rain rolling off their oilskin jackets.

Once inside the building, they repeated their enquiry six times, seeking anyone who knew of Mandu Olda. Finally, they were directed to an older monk who had lived in Surabaya for thirty-five years.

After entering the small plain room with a single mat on the floor they asked the older man the same question. 'We wondered if you know of a man named Mandu Olda who came here. Perhaps with others some time ago.'

The monk smiled, four of his teeth missing, and bobbed his round, shaved head. 'Come with me,' he said. He led them to a covered building with one open side. Several stumps served as stools. The rain poured down in front of them.

Arranging his orange robes, the monk was the quintessence of calmness and serenity and looked like he had lived at least a century … maybe two. Hendrik hoped that buried in that calmness and serenity there were some answers.

'I am Bodhim. I can see that you are seeking some information.'

All three of them performed the ritual dance of trying to get information without giving much away. In Indonesia, the dance was often performed with many veils and many veiled threats, which sometimes ended in a deadly finality.

Bodhim confirmed that almost two years ago, Mandu had passed through and stopped at this monastery overnight.

'How many people were with him?'

'Six.' Bodhim held up six fingers, then added one finger. 'And he made the seventh.' Two of them were sisters and were going to Kangean. That is the main island in the group. They had relatives on that island. Four were going to continue on.'

Flynn was desperate to wring any small piece of information about the group going on. 'Who were the four? The ones going further?'

The monk tilted his head in concentration. His brow wrinkled and he tucked his hand under his chin.

'I do not remember,' he said with a smile. 'I remember the sisters because they were returning home.'

Hendrik had been worried about anyone trying to track them. 'Do you know if there has been anyone here looking for two Australian men?'

The rainfall on the iron roof was deafening.

'You should go before they ask us again,' Bodhim said. 'I have the luxury of old age and a poor memory.'

The warning was clear. Their exit was swift. Flynn and Hendrik had no option but to talk to the two women on Pulau Kangean. From Surabaya, to get to the ferry terminal was a few hours' travel. They opted for a car hire with a driver and were dropped off at the terminal in Sumenep. As they waited in the pelting rain, they provided an update to Ric. No matter what the time difference, Ric served as their personal sounding board and was more useful than Artificial Intelligence (AI) as a strategist for guiding advice or multiple options.

At last they could see the boat en route.

The fast boat to Pulau Kangean wasn't fast enough for Flynn. He paced the deck and looked as though he wanted to leap in and take over the wheel and throttle from the captain. It took another four hours to get to the island, with the rain pounding the aluminium deck until, midway across the Bali Sea, it began to let up.

Pulau Kangean, in the Kangean Island Group

The Bajau are a significant part of the various ethnic groups in the Kangean Islands. Flynn and Hendrik connected with a driver of a small vehicle. He took them to a congregation of boats that were packed in like sardines, pressed against the southwest coastline of Pulau Kangean, the largest island in the group. Two oversized houses on stilts jutted out into the water, serving as meeting houses for the nomadic tribes in the area.

As they got closer, they could see that the larger buildings had been damaged by the recent storm. The houses had parts of their roofs missing. Some of the smaller boats around it had been driven up on the shore, grounding their hulls into the mud flats. Debris was scattered around both the stilt houses and the boats.

A group of men and women were outside, trying to collect the roofing, pieces of cloth, siding, anything they could fit into baskets and shawls and carry away by hand. Children, always up for a change of activity, were enlisted in gathering what was left.

'Let's chip in, and then find these sisters,' Flynn suggested. They set their bags aside and bent down, gathering what looked usable.

'I can see they were planning some type of celebration,' Hendrik said, looking at the red paper wrapped around a stack of boards he had assembled. 'I'm guessing a wedding.'

'Do you ever turn that tracking mode off?' Flynn asked.

'Not when it relates to my survival … which is typically 24-7,' Hendrik replied.

The decorations on the boats and two buildings had been blown off and were scattered amid the debris. The area was a shambles.

Hendrik joined a group of men moving several boats that had grounded, pulling them back into the water.

Flynn was enlisted in replacing colourful flags and pieces of bright material that were attached to the 'wedding boat' and other boats that would participate in the ceremony. He was impressed how they used any small piece of aluminium foil, plastic wrap, string or ribbon to make it festive.

The Irish are celebrators at heart, friendly and engaging and well known for their singing and dancing. Flynn couldn't resist coming up with a song. His version of *Molly Malone* sought to include any audience immediately available, and he captured the attention of the Bajau with the chorus:

Alive, alive, oh,
Alive, alive, oh
Crying, 'Cockles and mussels, alive, alive, oh.'

By the time Flynn had run through the song several times, the children were repeating the verses while the adults chimed in on the chorus. Very few had an idea of what they were singing about, but it mattered little as the melody had an addictive pattern.

The afternoon sun sank lower and two men helped in the reconstruction of the buildings and the boats. Flynn was encouraged to sing whatever he wanted, and he ran through a repertoire he hadn't thought about for years.

There was no question of where they would eat that evening or stay that night. They were invited to the next day's wedding, which had been postponed. Some thought the storm had created a space for these men to arrive.

As the evening meal of squid and sea cucumbers was being prepared, a small group of the village elders gathered around Flynn and Hendrik in the newly repaired meeting house.

One of them spoke crisp English and translated the remarks from both sides.

'You are welcome here because you sought first to help us … even if you came to ask us to help you.'

'We have lived in an Indonesian village in Sumatra,' Hendrik explained. 'And we know the hardships that the Bajau face upon the sea and on the land.'

Flynn asked his perennial question with the hope that someone knew something. 'Have you heard of a man named Mandu Olda? We believe he came here two years ago. And he brought with him two of your relatives.'

The eldest man, who had listened carefully, signalled he would speak.

'Yes,' he said. Then louder, 'Yes, he was here.' His English had been taught to him by his granddaughter and he wanted to demonstrate his knowledge.

After waiting a few minutes for more, Flynn replied, 'Thank you. Thank you for telling us this. Originally, I was hoping my wife and daughter came with Mandu. Now, I wonder if Mandu or the others knew about them.' He was trying to phrase this carefully, worried his Irish accent might skew the translation.

The elders looked perplexed. This was knowledge they did not know.

The two sisters were summoned, and the translator resumed his duties.

'Four others went off with Mandu. A man and wife. A man and his son,' was the older sister's response.

They spoke broken English, and the translator was working overtime to translate what each of the sisters was saying, as they continuously talked over each other. Flynn repeated that he was looking for his wife and child.

'No young woman. No girl child,' one of the sisters finally got in. 'With Mandu, we travel fast. After dark. There were always the police.'

Flynn felt like a dagger had pierced his heart. It was confirmation that there was no young woman or child. He closed his eyes, seeing the fire, smelling the smoke, hearing the screams.

Wait a minute. There were still four witnesses who might have seen something. They observed what happened at his village. They might know something and know where Mandu went. He had to go on.

Flynn and then Hendrik made several attempts for further information. The sisters had been more knowledgeable about the man and wife than the other two.

'Where did Mandu and the four people go from here?' Hendrik asked.

The elder held up his hand again.

Henrick waited for the translation. But the elder pointed out towards the sea. Hendrik and Flynn both looked out at the sea, trying to figure what he was pointing at.

The translator finally explained, 'They go to Bali.'

All the Bajou men nodded and smiled.

There seems to be a missing piece, Hendrik thought.

'Did you take them there?' he finally said. To him, tracking was half looking plus half thinking and 100% analysing them both together.

'Yes,' the translator said. 'Mandu wanted to go to Brahmavihara-Arama. A large Buddhist monastery. It is the closest area to us on Bali.'

'Shap shap,' Hendrik spoke in Afrikaans, signalling agreement. He figured the translator meant one of their ships travelled from Pulau Kangean through the Bali Sea to the northern coast of Bali.

Flynn knew that was all the information they would glean. One more seed to plant and water, if they could get to Bali.

It was a special honour to be part of the pre-wedding festivities. They ate with the families of the wedding couple, as the children played by jumping off the boats into the water. It was their jungle gym, conveniently attached to their living quarters.

Later in the evening Flynn and Hendrik were given a place to sleep in one of the boats. Four of the children were rousted from their small pallets to provide room for the two men.

The wedding started in the morning and included ritual festivities that Flynn and Hendrik tried to participate in. When the wedding couple wanted another round of *Molly Malone*, Flynn became the spontaneous wedding entertainment.

They left to catch the ferry, still hearing and participating in the singing as their small vehicle headed up the rugged hill.

In Dublin's fair city
Where girls are so pretty,
I first set my eyes on sweet Molly Malone,
As she wheeled her wheelbarrow
Through streets broad and narrow,
Crying, 'Cockles and mussels! Alive, alive, oh!'

On the ferry back to Sumenep, Flynn could not push the image from his mind of a burned-out village with the ashes from the bodies of his wife and child. Being among the now-married couple and the young children had brought back memories of what he once had.

Flynn could feel the small hands of Diah on his face. He could taste the kisses of Gemi. He had had it all once. He'd now gone beyond the edges of grief into the lake of remorse.

He looked out the open window of the ferry towards the Bajau village they had left. All he wanted was to find his family.

'Alive, alive, oh! Alive, alive, oh!'

He put his hand over his eyes, the tears flowing out.

Hendrik saw the tears and could feel Flynn's pain. He knew Flynn was thinking about the fire at the village—the fire that almost engulfed him as well.

Chapter 20

More Blood-sucking than Scrooge

Jurassic Park #1, Marlborough Sounds

Ric heard the birds chirping early. He wasn't sure he'd slept that much. There was something about sleeping outdoors, all the fresh air, being in Richard's Precambrian forest, and the sounds of nature during the night.

Scratch that. Being there with Elaina. He had not been interested in sleeping, no matter how many hours were needed for a restful night.

They got up and stoked the fire with fresh driftwood. After a quick cup of filter coffee (Ric couldn't believe he was drinking it), they headed down to the sandy beach below and went for a swim.

The cove was secluded and sheltered by rock heads at either end. They hadn't brought their swimming togs, but decided to shed their clothes. They draped them over a tree branch and dove in. The water was cool and clear. They swam back and forth across the face of the beach with the swimming becoming a race to see who was first. Ric caught Elaina, somewhere in the middle of the cove. He kissed and held her, until he spotted George fishing on the edge of the water.

'We'd better head back before we become the floor show.' Ric pointed towards George, who nodded and waved.

Coming up the long path from the beach, Elaina could smell the aroma of bacon cooking and Kiri looked up, announcing the breakfast menu.

'Fried duck eggs this morning with sourdough toast, orange marmalade and Canadian bacon.'

Ric dug out the Italian roast coffee beans and began hand-grinding them. He had calculated how to make an espresso using a stove top coffee maker on the coals.

'I've got some smoked trout in my chilly bin and some venison sausages,' George offered up.

Breakfast was leisurely at JP#1 as if it was a land that time forgot. 'I realised you don't get mobile reception here, Richard,' John said.

'Yes, it's a convenient excuse to avoid the constant stream of messages, and having my eyes constantly glued to a screen. I like looking at actual scenery, instead of *screenery*.'

'You're right. The blue of the sea and sky and the luscious green in all the vegetation is therapeutic,' Kiri agreed. 'Between the yoga and the lack of communication, I've decided Jurassic Park is less distraction and more attraction.'

However Kiri thought it was time to explain the messages she had received. She steeled herself and detailed the two threatening messages and her suspicions that Odell had made the calls.

'I know you've been trying to give me time to find the answers to what has haunted me for a year, Kiri,' John said after she'd finished. 'But I'll be damned if I'm stopping now.' He balled his hand up. 'It's good to know these men believe their calls will make me stop. But years ago I was fearful about something.' John glanced fiercely at Ric. 'I could have taken some action, and I didn't. This time I'll see it through.'

To Ric his father's response was vague and unsatisfying. He wanted a direct answer. Ric sensed that his father's fear related to something about his Opa's death. But now was not the time to press him.

He decided to redirect a question to his mum. 'Do you think Odell is anything more than a coward making threatening phone calls?'

Kiri glanced over to the shimmering water, then back to Ric. 'I don't know him well enough. And I can't rely on what people say when they are gossiping.'

Ric looked around at them all. 'We have to be aware that this could escalate. Someone's out there who doesn't want us to know. And they want to scare us off. But they may try more than that.'

The group was sombre as they packed up.

'I'll drop the three of you off at the Mahau Sound dock for Terry's pick-up,' John said, putting the last of their gear into the FJ-Orion.

George said his goodbyes, crinkling his eyes at Ric and Elaina, then shaking his head. 'The land of discovery, indeed!'

'What made *him* so amused?' Richard asked.

'Must have been the glow-worms,' Ric answered.

They left Richard polishing his red tractor, getting ready for some trenchwork he wanted to do before the rainy season.

~~~

Mahau Sound's dock to the Blood-red Sky of the South (D'Urville Island)
Terry pulled up about ten minutes after they arrived at the dock. They boarded his boat and headed up Pelorus Sound towards D'Urville Island.

'The island is about an hour twenty from here,' Terry announced. 'Life jackets are under the seats for you to put on. Sit back and enjoy.'

The cruiser was modern. It had a deep-blue hull with a semi-elevated flying bridge. It cruised in and out of various sounds, past small coves and beaches, some of which seemed like the perfect setting for *The Hobbit*.

They left the outpost of French Pass on the point and crossed the deeper water until a long sandy beach was seen edging the island. Terry's house was set back from the beach on a rise above a cove. His wharf stretched out into a bay where a gaff-rigged sailboat, a rowing scull and two kayaks waited at the end.

If Richard's place was a bach, short for bachelor, this was an extensive house for a multi-generational family. The building was constructed with various sections of steel, cedar and stone sitting under a series of skillion roofs.

Inside, a massive fireplace showcased large boulders that ran to the top of the roof. The patio was adjacent to the living area, which was supplied with accordion doors to open during good weather. Large windows allowed every drop of sunlight to shine inside.

'I've got your rooms upstairs,' Terry said. 'Kiri, you're up on the left at the top of the stairs. It's a view of the headlands and cliffs out to sea. Ric and Elaina, you're on the right overlooking the beach down the coast.'

Terry's idea of sleeping accommodations varied from John's.

'Dinner's around seven pm. And since Joan isn't here, I'd be happy to have as much help as possible. I've got some fresh fish and crayfish that we can grill.'

~~~

'Thompson, this is Reid Baxter,' the phone call began. 'Have you given any more thought to my offer? I promise a good price for you. I'll be generous.'

'I like it here, Baxter. I always have. My family had this place for three generations and I don't intend to sell. Thanks for the offer, but no.' Terry finished the conversation with military precision and then hung up.

'Reid Baxter is very persistent man,' Terry said to Ric and Elaina. 'I think he wants to buy the whole island. By the way, you have an invitation to visit him if you want. Go if you want to hear a monologue from a nasty narcissist.'

~~~

Cornhill House, Baxter's Residence, D'Urville Island

Ric and Elaina walked down the beach and up towards Baxter's property tucked back into the hillside. They had one objective. Find out exactly how he was connected to the Parásita site.

The residence was impressive but garish in its architectural statement, starting with a Gothic window looming in the front. The structure wasn't about complementing the surroundings—more pushing back against the natural environment with a strong impression of ego, authority and security.

Further off to the right was a large flat area for a commercial-grade helo pad, complete with lead-in lights and appropriate markings.

'Nice touch,' Ric commented as they walked towards the house.

A large black mastiff started with a low growl and then kept up incessant barking.

'Easy, easy,' Ric said to the dog that was bent on protecting the Lord of the Manor. It continued to bare its teeth while advancing.

Elaina stopped. She opened her hand and made eye contact with the dog, slightly averting her head downward. The dog moved slowly towards her.

'Elaina, be careful. I don't think he's being friendly,' Ric said.

The dog came to Elaina and sniffed into the air. She maintained a gentle stance and it began to wag its tail.

'You'd better stay with me, Ric. I don't think he likes you,' Elaina said with a spring in her step.

They walked up the steps onto a main porch overlooking the cove. The door was open and the dog walked in front of them.
~~~

'Hello, Mr Baxter,' Elaina called out into the interior as she entered the house. Through an open door to a den on the left, they noticed a large table holding a model of a multistorey building with various residential configurations around it. There were papers, photos and maps all over the desk. Another box, maybe two, sat under it. Elaina did a few charades gestures to Ric about checking out the room and he gave her a thumbs-up.

'I'm to your right in my observatory,' came a cryptic voice from the inner confines of the house.

They entered and found Baxter sitting uncomfortably high atop a bar chair at the end of his spotting scope. It was a perch from which he could see the entire cove, the length of the beach and Terry's house, as well as out to sea.

An ideal spying spot. Ric figured that was why the door was open; Baxter had been watching them for the past ten minutes.

'Come in,' he said with a somewhat off-kilter smile. 'Sorry about the dog—I forgot to chain him up.'

If he saw us coming, opened the door and beckoned us in, why wouldn't he have chained up the dog? Ric thought.

'That's okay—he's quite friendly,' Elaina said.

Baxter opened his mouth to respond and closed it again. He'd get rid of that dog like every other creature—animal or human—that didn't measure up to what *he* needed. It was all about him, all the time.

'I'm Ric Peters. This is Elaina Williams.' Ric began the exchange, which was almost like a medieval joust.

'Peters? Are you related to John Peters?' Baxter seemed to squinch his eyes to narrow slits and Elaina thought he looked even more like Scrooge than she'd imagined.

'Yes, he's my father,' Ric replied.

'John and I go back a long way. We've been on both sides of many issues in this region. But rarely on the same side,' Baxter said, with what appeared to be his version of a smile. 'And what do you do, my dear?' he asked, taking in the tall, confident woman in front of him. She reminded him of …

Elaina knew he was sizing her up. 'Oh, I'm Ric's friend, who came along to see the island.'

'Well, my dear, you're welcome here any time,' Baxter said. 'Any time you want. Name a time.'

Ric reflected on Baxter's comment. He wasn't trying to be neighbourly; he was a predator. His father had said that Baxter had health problems. Perhaps he meant it was his mental health. Ric could see this man was aggressive, ignored boundaries, and would not take no for an answer. Baxter's language raised big red flags to him. He'd check the side room, but wouldn't leave Elaina alone for too long.

'Do you mind if I use the lavatory I saw on the way in? A little too much coffee,' Ric asked.

'You should have a doctor examine that,' Baxter responded with a crotchety laugh.

Ric started towards the front of the house, but turned into the den for a brief peek at the building model with maps spread around it. Baxter definitely was a man interested in land and construction. Ric went closer to the table, snapping photos with his phone while he tried to remember everything he was seeing. There were several boxes shoved under the table of older looking pieces of paper. He bent down to thumb through those.

'Does he have that problem often?' Baxter asked, directing his attention to Elaina.

'I don't know. I sure hope not,' Elaina responded with a very large smile that turned into a giggle. She was having a hard time staying in character. Deep breath, Elaina, there is much to be gained with a narcissist.

'You are friends with Peters and Thompson?' Baxter said, probing.

Elaina had a practised repertoire from word-duelling with her uncle and her father. And she could tell this man had several favourite topics.

Elaina spent the next fifteen minutes talking about Baxter's house, his helo pad, his boats and Baxter's endless stash of toys that she had seen on the way there. She delved into his history and likes and dislikes, of which he had many.

'I know the helo pad seems extravagant, but I can jump into a helicopter and be in Wellington in a matter of thirty minutes. I get around to anywhere I want to go.'

'It sounds so, so exciting,' Elaina said brightly, a sparkle in her voice, while wondering what was taking Ric so long.

'You should visit me sometime, Elaina. As a matter of fact … you have an open invitation, my dear … any time your heart desires. Give me the word and I can have you picked up anywhere you want and have you whisked out here.' Baxter grinned, focusing on her chest for a few long moments.

'Well, that sounds amazing,' Elaina responded, beginning to feel slightly uncomfortable. Ric certainly wasn't included in *that* invitation. Baxter had obviously ignored the plastic glow-in-the-dark ring on her finger.

'It's best if you come and spend a few days. It gives you a chance to sunbathe on the beach and the cove. There are hiking trails all over and the house is verrryyy comfortable. I have quite a movie library and a mini theatre here. *Any time* you want to come out,' Baxter said again.

'Thank you … unbelievable,' Elaina said, measuring her words.

'Here's my private mobile number.' Baxter passed Elaina a card.

Ric returned and Baxter sat upright on his stool.

With Ric's encouragement, Baxter launched into his business interests and the changes in the Nelson area, as well as all the development that was happening. Almost every deal was waiting for a skilled negotiator like him. Baiting a narcissist was easy, but Ric sensed it was time to leave.

'Thanks for the quick visit, Mr Baxter. We appreciate your time,' Ric said, taking Elaina's arm. 'I think Terry has something lined up for us this afternoon.'

'No trouble, and please call me Reid,' Baxter responded.

'See you soon, Reid,' Elaina said.

As they walked out the front door, Ric gazed at Elaina. 'What do you mean "See you soon"?'

'I had to keep him distracted while you were taking your time checking out a single room,' Elaina answered briskly.

'A single room with lots of material, and I was very curious,' Ric answered.

'Okay, next time I'll be the curious one and you can talk to Baxter,' Elaina said to Ric. 'You can bat your grey eyes at him and see what he does.' She fluttered the lashes of her blue eyes rapidly.

Baxter sat back in his tall chair. What a delightful conversation, he thought.

He readjusted himself in the swivel chair, swung the spotting scope out towards the sea and the headlands, then changed the focus and swung the scope towards the Thompson house and down to the beach. He spied his two recent guests marching down the beach and followed them with the scope, increasing the focal point.

She's photogenic, he thought. Very intelligent. And athletic, like someone out of a fitness magazine. What a remarkable woman.

There were a few small characteristics that reminded him of the other woman who had come to see him at his office about a year ago. Tessa Bright was on a mission then, but left with blood on her dress.

Chapter 21

The Value of Antiques

Just over a year ago, Longboat Island, Tasman District, South Island
Reid Baxter visited Longboat Island and the production plant almost every quarter. This coincided with the accounting cycle. He was always very fond of viewing places where the money was being made. For years, the production plant churned out chemicals for agricultural fields and industrial applications. For a while, those uses *were* a big money maker.

That was before various chemicals were turned into illegal drugs for public consumption. The chemicals themselves started to have an intrinsic value for humans. Forget helping the tomatoes. Humans were helping themselves.

Five years ago, the plant had run full bore on two shifts with fifty people. At that time, the volume of production required a regulated lab. He could never remember why he agreed to adding a lab on at the plant. *A dumb decision, so obviously not mine.*

Reid insisted on a well-outfitted administration building on the plant grounds. He was a director after all, and put money into the plant. Well, not his money really.

Pictures of the early history of the plant and more modern works adorned the walls of his office. Off to the side, a small, locked liquor cabinet was opened often for entertaining fellow directors, sympathetic foremen and, of course, visiting inspectors. That was in the days before all the health and safety nonsense set in. He bitterly rued the time when operations started to become difficult. *No, not difficult, it became impossible.*

Outside, it was always dusty with the smells of chemicals and products being produced. He had an air-purifying conditioner installed so he could keep the windows closed.

The laboratory next door to the administration building was a nightmare. When he went in there he almost always started gagging. The chemist would walk him around the work tables and lab equipment, explaining the products that had failed. The chemist told him they were shipping off the failed products to France—the 'go-to' country for incineration, but it was expensive.

Baxter created a separate division for disposal. He spent over five years trying to figure a better way to deal with the waste from the plant production. When the production plant site was chock-a-block with bad batches, they expanded to burying the failures all over the district. Spending more money on the process was not an option and sending it to France was costing a fortune.

Then he finally found a rather simple solution for the lab. Outsource the chemist. A small task and endless freedom.

The plant happily went bankrupt after he had edited the annual report for that last year. It was more science fiction than fact, but he was out of it. Let someone else deal with the clean-up.

During the plant's last year, Baxter and several others had looked around for other opportunities rather than agricultural chemicals. Around that time an older process was reinvented. The manufacturing of methamphetamine became viable. The result was a more potent, more plentiful, and more affordable version of an addicting drug made from a combination of carbon, hydrogen and nitrogen. Importantly, to Baxter, it didn't need a lot of lab equipment. It could even be made in a rubbish bin. Disposal of waste was easier. Consumer goods became clandestine goods.

That fitted in perfectly with the property designs he had in the region.

Generate cash with drugs—lots of cash. Invest in property—including cliffs, hillsides and near rivers that flooded. Buy cheap land—with the illegal money. Sell cheap—to get clean money.

There was always a Greater Fool Somewhere. If groups could do this in other countries, why not New Zealand?

~~~

Flashback, Baxter's office, Top of Trafalgar Street, Nelson

Tessa Bright's mission to his office at first seemed fortuitous. Tessa was the bookkeeper and had come up from Longboat Island to see him in Nelson.
~~~

He thought she had been flustered when they were working on the final annual report. The facts and figures had been manipulated to present a totally misleading picture of the company's financial actual performance. A colourful fantasy relative to the actual operations. He wasn't. cooking the books—this was flambéing them with a hot flame. Maybe Tessa had come over to tell him again that the numbers weren't right.

He'd been sitting in his Nelson office, nestled in a large leather chair behind his desk. The desk was cluttered, but had a vintage headlamp he had bought in the Nelson Market that was mounted next to another vintage car part—a long tube that had a dipstick in it for measuring oil. The dipstick was a steel rod with a pointed end. At the other end was a loop handle to grab when needed.

It was late afternoon. He remembered it had been winter and dark outside.

Tessa Bright had buzzed to his floor and he let her in. She was in her late thirties and served as a pseudo-office manager at the plant. She had taken over the books—accounts payable and receivable—coordinated orders, administered the growing fiasco of health and safety rules, and answered all emails and messages. She had started shortly after that chemist, he recalled.

He had no problem remembering that she was a knockout. Beautiful brown hair and brown eyes. She wore dresses all the time. Very feminine. She had a soft, alabaster complexion and the right amount of lipstick.

'Mr Baxter,' Tessa said shyly at the door.

'Tessa, come in, come in. And please call me Reid. You've made quite the journey to come and see me in Nelson, young lady. You need more of a social life.'

It was a delight that they were alone together in his office. An unexpected pleasure. He had often thought she would be an interesting diversion.

'I apologise, but I needed to ask you something,' Tessa had begun.

'Absolutely. Have a seat. Do you want a quick drink?' Reid had asked. He had an extensive liquor cabinet in this Nelson office. He took out two glasses.

'No, no, thank you. I have to get home and I'm not drinking.' Tessa sat down, smoothing her brown and blue dress and setting her tan clutch bag beside her. She nervously crossed and uncrossed her legs, finally putting her brown shoes together, trying to still her thoughts.

Baxter poured himself a Scotch. Neat. He tried several avenues of conversation with little response. He was used to women who fawned over him, because he was rich. And they knew it, because he paid them handsomely.

'So, what is it that you want?' Baxter asked, disappointed and ready to get back to finalising the closure he planned for the Longboat Island plant. He had shut down most of the operations in the last months.

'It's about Salvatore Marino,' she answered.

'Salvatore? Now, we've had this conversation before,' Baxter replied.

'Well, you said you sent him on an important task down to Christchurch. He hasn't been back for two days. I don't know where he is or what's going on,' Tessa said. Her face was crimped and sweat broke out on her brow.

'Ah, well, why the concern? He's a grown man, Tessa,' Baxter said.

'Yes, I know, but he told me he'd be back yesterday,' Tessa answered. She had been agonising over Salvatore's disappearance. No one knew where he was. She hadn't known what to do and decided to come and see Reid Baxter.

Besides sharing the lab facility with Salvatore, she had personal knowledge that Salvy was supposed to be back by now.

'Well, not to worry, Tessa. He had some business to take care of. Maybe he had a medical problem, or perhaps it was his mother. I don't remember which.' Baxter response came quickly.

'I would have known, Mr Baxter. He told me he'd be back,' Tessa said firmly, looking straight at Baxter.

He squinted his eyes as he liked to do. Lizard-like. Thinking. *This is more than a casual relationship*.

'He's taking some time off. Stop worrying about it,' Baxter told her.

'This is not like Salvatore.' Tessa knew Baxter was lying and she knew her visit had been a mistake.

'Miss Bright— ' Baxter switched to formal address ' —I have explained the situation with Salvatore. You need to go home.' His anger was rising.

'I'll go, but I'm going straight to the police,' Tessa said, picking up the clutch bag she carried in.

'Police!' Baxter said, walking to the door and closing it. 'Sit down, Tessa. Let's talk further.'

He came to the front of the desk and drew the dipstick out of its case. 'I'm always fond of vintage items. Have you ever seen one of these?' he asked, showing her the entire length of the stick from its looped handle to the pointed end. Perfect for what he intended right then.

Chapter 22

A Brochure Moment

Cornhill House, Baxter's Residence, D'Urville Island, South Island

Yes, Tessa had been quite the little beauty, Baxter reflected as he watched Elaina walking down the beach. He peered at her through his spotting scope. The woman was young and had real spark. Almost like the other one.

'Too bad it has to go this way,' he said out loud. Baxter had a way of stirring things up. And his solution was very mobile … in a slip not far away. Malcolm Sloan had been there a few days ago, cleaning up the boat for use when needed. Baxter always had some deliveries to make.

He grabbed his mobile, dialled, and eventually the call was answered.

'What are you doing, Farmer in the Dell? Pick up your phone when I call you. I have something I want you to do.' Baxter was impatient and drummed his fingers on the table while giving his instructions.

Along the beach near the Thompson's residence, D'Urville Island

'Do you think Reid Baxter is spying on us from up there?' Elaina asked as they walked back to Terry's house. 'He seems to revel in knowing everything that goes on here.'

'Elaina, don't get too caught up in this. Humans see a lot of connections that aren't really there. That's the part I love about you. All that passion and curiosity.'

'About that curiosity. What did you find in the den?' Elaina asked.

'Reid did have some kind of directorship at Longboat Island when the plant was in operation. I'll show you the images I took of the desk and the papers and photos under the desk later.'

He caught her hand and turned her towards him. 'If he's looking, let's give him something to look at.'

After a few minutes, Terry walked down from the patio to meet them. 'I didn't want to interrupt,' he said. '*That kiss* was like one of those brochure moments. You know. *Come to New Zealand. Visit the Sounds. Fall in love.*'

Elaina smiled. 'We tick those boxes.'

'You chaps need a break? I've got the rowing scull down at the dock. Oars are inside with the life jackets. Or there are kayaks if you prefer. A nice gentle day. You're at slack water now. Go for a glide. It's a great relaxer. There's lots of bird life around the heads. Make an afternoon of it.'

'I'm game,' Elaina said. 'Some relaxation and communing with nature seems idyllic.'

Ric thought about Terry's 'brochure moment'. Glancing at the jagged inlets rising above the stilled aqua blue water, he figured a small rowing boat added to the scene could only improve the optics. He looked back at the water. 'Thanks, Terry. I guess you're right—we can't get into too much trouble paddling around out there.'

Wharf, near the Thompson's residence, D'Urville Island

Ric and Elaina tramped down to the wharf. The boat was a classic wooden clinker design with a wineglass stern. The hull was dark blue, the interior trim was oiled timber and its name was *Clinker2*. Ric checked the oars and life jackets and saw bottles of water and cups in a small compartment. A boathook rested along the keel at the bottom of the skiff in case it was needed.

There were two sets of oars and two rowing positions. Elaina sat closest to the bow behind Ric, both facing the stern. They shoved off from the floating dock and cut the water with the wooden blades as they rowed out past the heads. It was still and quiet except for the birds that provided commentary on the possible menu for their teatime.

'Make sure you're rowing to keep up,' Ric said.

'Are you insinuating that because I'm behind you and you can't see me that I would not keep up?' Elaina protested, though she had her oars up and was looking at the lush jungle onshore.

Terry had offered relaxation and she was going to make the most of it.

While communing with nature, Elaina noticed a cruiser that had come up from French Pass and was approaching fast from the south. She put her oars back in the water.

Ric spotted the eight-metre cruiser skimming towards them at high speed. Even from a distance, he could hear the two outboards grinding away. He turned to see Elaina fixated on the vessel. She had stopped rowing, unsure of which direction to go.

After a few minutes, the incoming boat had increased its speed and was beginning to plane. It was heading directly towards *Clinker2*.

'The boat's bearing down on us!' Elaina hollered.

'Let's head back towards the beach. Row towards the beach now.'

The cruiser was built for high speed. The outboards, pulsating in the water, were cranked up to the maximum redline. The propellers created a foamy wake. It wasn't passing them. It was aiming straight for them.

'Ric, it's coming up pretty fast!' Elaina called back.

'I know, I know,' Ric said with worry in his voice that wasn't missed by Elaina.

That boat wasn't out for an afternoon cruise; it had a deadly assignment. The boat was on course to run over the top of them. Their afternoon paddle was less a brochure moment … and more a decapitation.

Chapter 23

The Likelihood and the Consequences

Admiralty Bay, off D'Urville Island, South Island

The vessel was on them within seconds. A collision was imminent.

'Hold on!' Ric yelled, staining while pulling the oars. The boat roared by, barely missing their bow. It kicked up a spray of water over them, leaving a heavy wake that rocked the *Clinker2*.

Elaina was soaked. The rowboat had taken on water and she grabbed the two cups from the small compartment, frantically bailing, trying to empty the water in the bilge.

'It's one person driving. He's wearing a fisherman's hat with a strap,' Elaina screamed. 'I can't get this water out fast enough!'

'That was no accident!' Ric called out.

The cruiser executed a Williamson turn—arcing out to the right, completing almost a circle, and then coming back on the left, headed on a reciprocal course.

'Ric, they're coming back!' Elaina joined Ric in rowing hard towards the beach, but it was still too far away.

The vessel was definitely targeting *Clinker2*. At dead centre, it would cut the rowing boat in half.

'Elaina, keep rowing towards the beach!' Ric shouted. 'I'm going to try and turn our direction again.'

Elaina glanced back at the cruiser. It was approaching even faster than before and she dug her oars in, but the water was choppy from the wake.

Plan B, Ric decided. He reached down and picked up the boathook.

The cruiser was now only twenty metres away.

'Elaina, get down low. And hold on!'

As the cruiser closed in, Ric stood in the rowboat, left foot forward, right foot a large step behind. He leaned back, his right arm holding the boathook, his left hand straight in front for balance. He flung the boathook like a javelin; it flew through the air towards the oncoming boat and crashed into the short windscreen in front of the wheel. The metal tip hit with a whump, cracking the glass.

Barely missing *Clinker2*, the cruiser veered off the collision course. The turbulence of its wake flipped *Clinker 2* over and Elaina went under the water.

Ric fell in the other direction. He came to the surface, searching for Elaina, but couldn't find her.

'Elaina! Elaina!' He dived underwater and looked under the rowing boat—a common death trap when a boat flips.

Seeing nothing underneath, he went back to the surface and grabbed another breath of air. Seconds matter if someone's drowning. He couldn't see her. He went back down. No Elaina.

Ric came to the surface. She wasn't there. He swung his head around. Nothing.

The moment seemed time-warped and endless.

Then he heard something.

Elaina had resurfaced on the other side of *Clinker 2*. She was treading water and seemed confused. Ric saw her and grabbed her under her arm. He started swimming with a steady sidestroke towards shore.

'Elaina, are you okay? Are you hurt?' Ric asked in puffed breaths between his towing. His heart had gone into overdrive, his muscles revved up as the blood flowed to his limbs. He harnessed all his swimming power to get her to shore.

'Yes … I'm okay. The side of the boat … hit my head when it … when it tipped over,' she panted out.

In shallower water, Ric helped Elaina ground her feet in the sand and she stood up, pushing her wet hair back from her face. Tears were close, but she pushed them back too.

'Is that boat coming back?' she asked, spluttering.

'I think I hit it with the boathook,' Ric said. 'They're off in a new direction. Though they're circling, so they may be coming back for another try.'

'No, look,' Elaina said. 'It's still circling.'

The cruiser continued in a broad arc to the north of them. The arc turned into tighter circles with no sign of the driver.

Ric insisted Elaina sit for a minute on the sand while he swam back to rescue *Clinker2*. He pulled it into the shallower water and flipped it.

As she sat on the shore, Elaina shivered, trying to calm herself, not wanting to show Ric how terrified she'd been. She summoned some humour from deep inside.

'I liked the rescue, Ric. And being towed back to shore. We'll have to try that again.'

'Not until tomorrow,' Ric quipped. He held out his hand to her. She put her hand in his.

Ric had thought he could keep her separate from a dangerous life and thus be safe. But even his 'real life' seemed like rickety footbridge. His goals seemed at odds with reality, which kept tension high and the stakes taut.

'I have to tell you Ric—you looked like you were in a Warrior Pose when you threw that boathook.'

'Elaina, to be honest, that was the first pose you taught me. It came in handy.'

They picked up the cups, water bottles and life preservers that had drifted ashore. After securing *Clinker 2* to Terry's dock, they watched as the cruiser moved in concentric circles further out to sea. Ric thought that the boathook might have gone right through the window and … He decided not to worry about that possibility right now.

When they got back to the house, Ric and Elaina explained to Terry the near miss on the waterway—but that they had retrieved the *Clinker 2* and all equipment.

Terry got onto his mobile and helped them file a police report with a description of the boat that Ric and Elaina had seen.

'This is crazy. People in the Sounds aren't like that,' Terry said. 'And where did this boat come from? It's no boat that I know of from around here.'

Kiri came down the stairs, and they told her what had happened.

'What is going on here!' Kiri was outraged. 'This has got to stop. You could have been killed out there. Who was driving that boat?'

'We didn't see the driver. But you're right—he was aiming right at us.'

'We could've both been badly hurt,' Elaina said. She didn't want to say the word 'killed', but she shivered all the same.

Terry realised the gravity. 'I'm so sorry for all of this—I was expecting this to be a nice getaway for you.'

Kiri sat in silence, a heavy dread settling over her like a shroud. A few days ago a vehicle on a winding road had tried to force the FJ-Orion off a cliff with her family inside. Today, a vessel tried to run Ric and Elaina down in a narrow channel. She mulled over the second warning: *You are going to get your family and yourself hurt. And you won't be able to recover.*

She knew all about the psychology of misinformation, but now she realised the threats were real, not just intended to create fear. Was it related to John's year-long quest to find Salvy? She wasn't sure.

Kiri decided she was going to confront Odell herself. Since he was making the threats, maybe he knew who had driven the boat. This had to stop.

~ ~ ~

With morning dew still on the grass, Terry was up watching the news in his den, while Ric was in the chef's kitchen.

'Eggs, toast, marmalade, and espressos from the Bezzera machine,' Ric said, handing Elaina and Kiri their warm plates. Elaina was describing Ric's use of Warrior Pose as a strong javelin-throwing position.

Terry came from the den with his mobile phone and handed it to Ric. 'It's a follow-up on the boat battle yesterday.'

'Mr Peters, this is Detective Inspector Hamish Parkhurst with the Wellington Police District.'

'Hi, what can I do for you?' Ric answered picking up on the Detective's British accent and wondering why Wellington was responding to the report instead of the local Nelson police.

'This is about an investigation that we're conducting regarding the boating incident you reported last evening. The incident that occurred off D'Urville Island?'

'Yes. Someone tried to run us over while we were out in a rowing boat,' Ric said. 'They capsized our boat. It wasn't a careless accident. They steered directly towards us. Twice.'

'Yes, I understand, Mr Peters. Marine search and rescue were alerted to a boat circling not too far from the area of your reported incident.'

'We saw that,' Ric replied, waiting to hear what happened.

'It was an eight-metre cruiser with two large Mercury engines. The boat originally had a glass windscreen,' the detective said.

'That sounds like it.' Ric knew investigators often used half-truths to get further information. He had effectively used this type of interrogation himself and knew the rules.

'A passing boat did manage to come along side and render assistance,' the detective continued. 'They found an individual on the deck of the boat with a bloody hat. He was bleeding from a head wound.'

'I mentioned in my report that I tried to fend the boat off. The boat was trying to run us down,' Ric countered.

'Yes, Mr Peters. It appears that while fending them off, a boathook became dislodged from your hands and ended up hitting the small windscreen in the cockpit. It struck the driver,' Parkhurst said.

'Not sure what happened to the boathook,' Ric said cautiously.

'We've been trying to identify the man. He was semi-conscious when the rescue boat came alongside, then he developed some sort of amnesia,' Parkhurst said. 'The volunteer rescue boat took the boat and the man to French Pass. He subsequently abandoned ship, so to speak.'

'That's unfortunate,' Ric replied. He could tell there was more to this story, and waited.

Parkhurst yielded. 'There was a wallet on board. And several sets of different prints. The name Malcolm Sloan was on the Australian driver's licence.'

Ric waited again for the punchline, which was seconds away.

'Mr Peters, Malcolm is wanted by the Australian authorities in New South Wales,' Parkhurst announced.

But Ric thought it sounded more like a stage line than quoting from a report. And why did he use an escapee's first name?

'He was convicted of a murder. He was tried and under sentence, but he escaped before imprisonment. Had some kind of help to get him out. That was a year or so ago.'

'What's he doing here?' Ric asked, curious about Parkhurst's answer.

'In hiding. And he did a good job of it until your altercation with him,' Parkhurst continued. 'But he's abandoned the boat and likely he's back in hiding somewhere. Your statement said that you didn't see him clearly.'

'He was running us down at the time,' Ric pointed out.

'I understand. I'd like to put some photographs together and have you review them in case you can remember anything further. With a Ms Williams who was with you at the time.'

'Sure, that's no problem. We both can have a gander,' Ric answered. Parkhurst appeared to need some assistance and Ric was willing to give it. But there was something else odd about the conversation. 'Do you know where Sloan was living or working at the time?' Ric asked.

One pass in the boat might be an accident. Twice was deliberate. This guy must have been from the local area, Ric thought. Unlikely the boat driver came from a long distance in that boat. But risking extradition to Australia and a long prison sentence? One thing was clear. The driver wasn't in the water as a holidaymaker. Something was off about the entire description.

Ric had another thought. Was this driver connected to Odell, Bennett or Baxter?

Parkhurst interrupted Ric's reverie. 'Probably hiding in some remote spot. Could be around here or any other crevice in New Zealand. There are plenty of those. Will let you know when the photographs are ready for viewing. Tell TNT, I mean Mr Thompson, that we'll have to hold onto his boathook for now,' Parkhurst added. 'Oh, and a friend of yours, Jack, says to say "G'day".'

'Got it,' Ric said. Now he knew something was off. Why was Jack McMasters, his Alice Springs fairy godfather, talking to a Wellington detective?

Chapter 24

Debt Collection Service

Rocky outcrop, north of Jakarta, Indonesia

Francis had been schooled in the importance of paying one's debts. He had inherited this from Norman, his father, along with his Cockney accent and receding hairline. Norman had been a lorry driver who had a passion for keeping up with one's debts. He didn't worry about a credit score but *did* stress out when a payment was missed. He didn't like owing anyone or anyone owing him.

'Neither a borrower nor a lender be, Francis,' Norman would say. Francis liked to talk to himself and quote his father now and again.

Francis knew it was a quote from Shakespeare. But his father would have picked that up not from the bard, but in his favourite pub—*The Hamlet Pub*. The pub believed in prompt debt repayment.

Until his job as assistant to the Ambassador, Francis had never been face to face with the man who'd bought a murder—make that two—on the island of Tasmania. However, with his customer service visit, Francis had learned a variety of different secrets that Jenkins had squirrelled away on his office computers. Those secrets were interesting, but Francis was tiring of the constant bark-bark-barking of orders, most of which he ignored. His recent discovery of Jenkins' coastal estate had been very useful.

Francis figured this was a nice day for his *Day of Reckoning Tour* to settle accounts. 'Nice like chicken and rice,' he repeated several times.

He approached the estate in a small, rented car.

'Yes, it's certainly impressive by all standards,' Francis commented. He was an excessive commenter on life since he often held life or death in his hands.

He stashed the car in the steamy tropical forest adjacent to the house. The estate was set back against the hills above the azure sea which pounded the coastline. The house jutted out from the headland with a 180-degree view of the coast. Sumptuous green jungle continued behind the house, as if it was held in a soft green glove, then black cliffs shot up, intensifying the jungle.

The gates were solid and impressive, hinting at a drive that twisted and turned up and out of sight through the jungle landscape. The swanky property was walled and fenced, with CCTV cameras abundantly placed near the entrance and along some of the fence lines. Vegetation was thick right up to the walls, in some cases obscuring the areas under surveillance.

The levels of the house were stepped back from the cliff edge, hugging the contours of the shore. It resembled layers of flying saucers that had crash-landed in steps up the hillside.

It was difficult to find a clear space to observe the whole house. Evaluating from a distance was hopeless. There was certainly no clear line of fire. This would require a closer range. That meant an entry onto the property.

'There are a couple of options here,' Francis announced. 'Let's check for security and dogs as the first order of business.'

Security was lax near the grove of palms surrounded by a massive growth of bamboo. The bamboo was tall and thick, with a gap where two walls met. Camera positions on either end were blocked by the vegetation, creating a dead space.

'Good as Robin Hood!' Francis concluded.

Eyes on the compound revealed that there were no onsite guards or security personnel. And no dogs. Perhaps the man who sounded like a dog didn't like competition.

One of the great things about Indonesia is that it is close to the equator. Francis squinted at the sun. 'Don't have to wait long for the sun to go down.' Francis headed to the gap in the bamboo.

Under the cover of darkness, with the lack of surveillance coverage and the thickness of bamboo, entry was easy. 'Bright and breezy,' Francis murmured.

In the darkness, he felt he was standing in the wing of a theatre, waiting for his entry onto the stage. He had dressed in black and was carrying his gear in a small backpack.

He worked his way down the slope until he was in line with the uppermost level of the house. There were a series of bedrooms, each with a commanding view of the sea.

All the lights were on in the house, and there were no curtains or blinds to obstruct the views.

A large deck dangled out from an opulent suite. The fencing was both decorative and designed to keep anybody from getting into the house. But a gate at the far end was easily picked and Francis slinked through.

Still obscured by the landscaping, he could see Ambassador Clarence Jenkins barking at a young Asian woman. Her skimpy black nightgown was designed to reveal every sensuous curve through the thin black material. The old man was waving his finger at her.

Suddenly he slapped her face. The smack knocked her down on the bed. Jenkins slithered out of the room pulling the door closed. The Asian woman sprung up, trying to open the door. Then pounded on the door while crying. She was trapped.

Francis inhaled. *That was uncalled for. Bully. Bastard. Attack dog.*

The man not only sounded like a dog, he was far worse than a wild dog. Overly aggressive.

Wild dogs feed opportunistically. They eat whatever is easiest to obtain. If they are hungry, they scavenge and will eat live prey. They will eat roadkill, dead livestock, and scraps from rubbish tips. Jenkins was as opportunistic as they come.

Francis shook his head. *I have no choice.*

He had previously thought of this weekend as merely a scoping exercise. Maybe taking action a few days or a week later. But Jenkins exhibited an extremely high bite-risk. After all, for wild and aggressive dogs there was only one option—euthanasia.

Action was needed.

He often had to act as a behaviour consultant. He had read all the files in the office. Jenkins had spent years demonstrating high-level bite behaviour.

Francis went back into the dense jungle behind the verandah. Removing his backpack, he pulled out an automatic, ensured that the silencer was secure and removed the magazine. He depressed the first shell with his thumb checking it. Francis put the magazine back into the weapon and pulled back on the receiver. The first shell was rammed into position.

I am ready.

When it came down to it, there were certain cases where there was no other viable option. And, Francis concluded, when a person does make that hard decision, they deserve everyone's compassion and support.

Francis entered the open screen door with his weapon at the ready. Jenkins was in the library and turned around quickly and angrily. Perhaps he thought it was the woman, that he had somehow left the door unlocked and she had gotten out of the bedroom.

Jenkins squinted, sceptical of the image he was seeing. Staring down the barrel of an automatic was not how he'd intended to spend his weekend.

'What do you want?' Jenkins said, his voice shaking while examining this decrepit small man with the wispy hair.

'You owe me my fee. I'm here to collect. Paying your debts on time is important.'

Jenkins gaped at the man again, realising he was the new office assistant. Could this also be the man he'd hired as a gunslinger? *That man* was slinging the gun *at him*.

He converted from a sceptic to a believer.

'Ahhh, I have cash here. I can pay you,' Jenkins was talking rapidly and almost unintelligible.

'That's a start,' Francis said. Though he still wasn't going to 'outsource' the euthanasia.

Francis waved the automatic at Jenkins, who compliantly opened a wall safe concealed behind a small cabinet.

'This is all I have here. It's in euros,' Jenkins said.

Francis nodded. 'I'll take those boxes as well.' He recognised several watch boxes with Breitling labels, as well as some Patek Philippe boxes.

'That's not part of the deal.' Jenkins knew the prices he'd paid for the watches. 'The cash is enough.'

Jenkins moved back towards his desk, littered with papers he never took to his office.

'Yes, but you must pay for cheating and that's the price,' Francis responded. Then he remembered the girl.

'Why did you slap that girl?' Francis wanted to know.

'She's nothing. Why does it matter to you?'

Francis sputtered, saliva dripping from the corner of his mouth. He knew this attitude from his schooldays. Being called 'A Nothing' meant 'Something' to Francis.

'You keep her locked away here, don't you?' he asked.

'It's for her own security,' Jenkins lied.

Francis lowered the barrel of the automatic and shot Jenkins in the knee.

Jenkins screamed then crumpled onto the desk, clawing at the papers as he fell to the floor. Writhing in pain, he clutched his knee. A bullet to the knee is one of the most painful wounds that can be inflicted. Excruciating didn't even come close in describing what Jenkins was feeling.

'People aren't NOTHING! You're a BAD dog! You're DANGEROUS to others! You won't EVER learn!' Francis was yelling, something he rarely did. 'You told me you were looking forward to a long weekend. It's going to be more restful than you ever expected.'

Francis aimed again, announcing, 'Wild and aggressive dogs have no place here.'

The shot was fast and accurate.

'*Last breath before your death*,' Francis sang.

The blood around Jenkins body pooled from the residual pressure of the pulsing vascular system. Blood dripped down from the 9mm hole in the side of his head and spread across the floor.

Francis glanced at the papers on the desk. Stock certificates. Deeds of property. Trust documents. A recent travel itinerary and several passport photos—two of which Francis recognised.

'Very helpful, Ambassador Jenkins,' he said. He was always respectful of the dead. Especially when he had caused it.

Francis was careful not to get his shoes bloody as he took the backpack off and slid his weapon inside. He walked to the safe and removed the watches and several stacks of Euros, leaving some for the woman.

He padded back through the house, stopping at the master suite and unlocking the door without opening it. He called through, 'Go to the safe in the library. You have been paid for services rendered. You need to leave this island and never come back.'

He retrieved the car from the undergrowth and headed back to Jakarta. He was feeling peckish.

Yet while the various dining experiences had been interesting here, he simply could not take another dish with MSG. He wanted to get back to where he could control what he ate. Especially the salt content.

And now he knew where Ric Peters was. He had never been to New Zealand and was looking forward to it. That country had an excellent reputation for serving wholesome food.

Chapter 25

What You Give Away

French Pass, across from D'Urville Island, South Island

John was waiting on the other side of French Pass, parked near the wharf and adjacent to the Beachfront Villas.

He listened carefully to Ric's summary of meeting Reid Baxter.

'Well, while you folks were enjoying Terry's hospitality, I checked with the police and the Council for any information, news or updates on Salvy. Nothing. As you all know, I strongly feel that Salvy's disappearance is somehow linked with Tessa Bright.

'But not in the way George described. I believe that skull found at the Longboat site is or rather was Salvy. Where Tessa is now is anyone's guess. Perhaps the bones found at the Paxton farm could be one or the other, or maybe both.'

Ric was starting to understand how close his father had been to Salvy, and how hard his disappearance must have been for him. The discovery of the skull had 'unearthed' more than the ghostly features of human remains.

Ric, Elaina and Kiri provided a three-part summary of their 'enjoying' time with Terry.

'We're wondering who owned that cruiser that almost ran Elaina and me down,' Ric said. 'The police in Wellington seem to believe the driver was an escapee from Australia.'

Elaina summarised their visit to Reid Baxter. 'While Baxter is well into new development, Ric found some references to his directorship on Longboat Island. I'm researching those now to see what Baxter's interest is. Early indications are that he held title to that land and the surrounding area in some type of New Zealand trust that was set up to obfuscate his ownership.'

'One document under the desk seems odd to me,' Ric said. 'Reid had purchased about ten used containers and shipped them to a remote location down the river from the town of Riwaka. That's way out in the countryside. I have a friend in the US who used to clean up hazardous waste sites. He found a number of sites like this that were used for illicit drug manufacturing.'

'It is an option,' John said, and Ric nodded.

'I'd like to know if Odell and Bennett work directly for Baxter, or whether they have skin in the game too,' Kiri pondered.

She thought about the threats, and John's determination to know the answers to what had been bothering him for over a year. Her husband had invested a lot of energy and emotional empathy into finding Salvatore. He'd probably never be at peace if they stopped now so they'd better get a clear understanding on how these men were connected.

Kiri glanced at Ric and Elaina. The higher the stakes, the greater the knowledge gained. Her psychology background told her that breaking points were coming. But how far could they go before someone got hurt?

~~~

Saturday market, Nelson

They left the wharf, passing the hills and valleys studded with ferns and rata trees beaming under the blue sky. John recalled the locals saying this area was 'gobsmackingly beautiful'. Despite his efforts to learn Kiwi expressions, he had never understood the proper way to use that one. It seemed somehow related to smacking one's mouth.

As the road twisted and turned along the coast, Ric's mobile buzzed again, luring his attention like a fish to a baited hook, making him glad his father was driving. It was another call from Indonesia.

'Got it, Flynn. That's fits with what we know. A warning to you both. The Mobile Brigade Corps (you might hear them called the Brimob) were very active in East Java when I was there. They were monitoring what they determined were "hot spots". There were rumours of disappearances on both political sides. Be cautious even when you're stopped for the night. If you're travelling at night, there will be roadblocks. If you have to ditch everything and leave—don't hesitate.'

Ric hit the home button and tried to casually slide the mobile into his pocket. In the rear-view mirror, Ric could see the disappointment in
~~~

his pappa's eyes. His mother turned and eyed Ric with a wrinkle in her forehead. Elaina stared out the window, her face a reflection of concern in the glass.

This was supposed to be a family outing. Now Ric was answering calls from Indonesia.

The tension fused them together like contact cement. No one moved or talked. Ric's preoccupation with the search over 7000 kilometres away was fuelled by his own guilt of what he had done. That guilt was eating away at the connection he was trying to form with Elaina and his family.

The FJ-Orion rumbled onwards over the sealed roads with its six-cylinder diesel chugging away.

To create a break, John stopped in downtown Nelson and they all dashed into the Saturday market, which was still thrumming in the Montgomery car park. Everything from Dutch *oliebollen* to possum-fur slippers was on sale. Swiss braided bread, handmade jewellery, knitted wool jerseys, wood-turned bowls, raspberry jam and greenstone necklaces were all sold from individual stands. Rain or shine, the stall owners turned out, and so did the rest of Nelson.

As he wandered down the crowded aisles, a familiar voice made Ric turn.

'Ric, I am so glad to see you!' Eric said, bursting out from the crowd. 'I've got some news. I've found the mother of the chemist, Salvatore Marino, who used to work at Parásita.'

'Where did you find her?' Ric asked.

'It was Elaina's idea. I got a list of care facilities that treat dementia and started calling around,' Eric said. 'A friend of a friend knew Salvatore's mother. Everyone knows everyone around here. Don't ever put a meringue Pavlova in your shopping basket or you have guests for dessert. Anyway, she's in an assisted care unit in Golden Bay. I called and made an appointment to go up and talk to her tomorrow morning. Want to come?'

'Elaina and I can come,' Ric responded while spotting his father further down the aisle.

'Choice,' Eric replied. 'The nursing staff says that she hasn't had visitors since her son left. She has dementia ... more or less. They thought it would be good for her to have bona fide visitors from the local Council.'

'I'll meet you there,' Ric said.

'Sweet as! Takaka on the main road. GlenEden Care, past the community gardens. Ten am.' Eric glanced to the end of the aisle. 'Going to get some *oliebollen* before it's sold out.' He hastily disappeared into the maze of people between the stalls and small pop-up stores.

'Fancy a drive to Golden Bay tomorrow?' Ric asked Elaina who had bought some liquorice and chocolate for her father, Edward, and a pottery tea mug for her Uncle Max.

'Is it really golden?' Elaina asked.

'It's about as close as you'll get to golden. Eric has located Salvy's mother through your suggested research on dementia care. It's possible we might find something out about him. I'd like to do this for my father, but more or less incognito, in case it doesn't pan out.'

'I thought incognito was your middle name, Ric?' Elaina quipped.

'After the meeting we can stay on the coast at a place I know. It's quiet and quaint.'

'How do you know so much about quiet and quaint places to stay on every coastline?' Elaina asked.

'I read a lot of travel guides.'

'I bet you do. With whom?' Elaina asked.

'Only you, my darling. Only you,' Ric replied with a smile and a kiss. 'And we'll take a nice, long walk on the beach.'

'I think you're attracting me with a nature activity to get me on a quiet beach at night,' Elaina said.

'That occurred to me,' Ric said. 'But I'm exposing you to night-time wildlife and expanding your experience with the natural world.'

'You do that every night,' Elaina parried, as Kiri strode up.

Kiri was gushing over her cloth bag filled with avocadoes, cauliflower and red potatoes. John was off buying Swiss chocolates and Dutch edam cheese.

'We saw Eric, who has found Salvy's mother in Golden Bay. We're off in the morning to see if she remembers anything. I'm only telling you, Mum. I don't want Pappa to worry about the threats and actions now escalating.'

'What can I do to help? How can we keep everyone safe as we go through this?' Kiri asked.

'Be aware of your surroundings and whose around you,' Ric said. 'You folks stay at home. Make sure a couple of neighbours know you're there. Don't go out unless it's necessary. Especially at night. Tell Pappa you want a cosy night at home.'

Kiri nodded. 'All right, son. Will do.'

~~~

They had dinner on the deck, watching the sun go down. Ric and Elaina got sleeping bags and jackets together for an overnight run to Takaka in the morning. They put their gear into Ric's room and Elaina noticed an old Colt archery bow and a quiver of arrows alongside his bed.

'I got it out for you, in case you want to practise,' Ric said.

After grilled salmon, roasted potatoes with coriander, and baked cauliflower with parmesan cheese, they sat around the outdoor table listening to the water crashing against the seawall down below.

'I owe you another part of your grandfather's story, Ric,' John said, swirling a Scotch around in his glass.

'This sounds like a good time for Elaina and me to tidy up the kitchen,' Kiri said, raising an eyebrow to Elaina. She knew Ric never really trusted John. If her husband and son were ever going to resolve the chasm between them, both of them had to be honest with the other.

After they left, Ric stood on the deck waiting. He still didn't see how his Opa's death related to him.

'Your grandfather, my father, was an interesting man. However, his death was traumatic, so much so that my mother never recovered. And I was in Australia during his last few months … and didn't know exactly what was going on.' John was forcing himself not to tear up, which always happened when his thoughts went down this track. *I could have found out … if I had taken the time.*

Ric could see his father wasn't the same man he remembered. That man always seemed to be made of steel, unwavering, unbending, and not very revealing about anything.

'Our history in the Netherlands and other parts of Europe goes back several centuries.'

'Opa once said our crest had sailing ships, cannons and crosses, as well as roses on it. As a kid, I always hoped we had pirate ships in a fleet.'
~~~

'Well, your grandfather was an entrepreneur. The family was involved in various businesses, largely related to trading and manufacturing. At one point this included cannon- and musket-making, of all things. Then both agriculture and several art dealerships became a focus. It changed every fifty years or so.

'From seagoing ships, barges and cargo, we set up small trading posts and warehousing on various trade paths between countries and regions. By the time my father became the head of the family, a lot of wealth had been accumulated. Initially, he was intent in making it larger.' John paused. 'Then something happened. My father took a trip to Africa. This was to scope out additional opportunities.

'He fell in love. He was in love with Africa. I can't explain this exactly. But many years later, it's what I feel about Australia. As an immigrant, you seem to savour a different landscape than the locals might see or experience. Africa to him was like a spell. Do you know what that's like, Ric?'

Ric had been looking at the Tasman Sea. 'I know what it's like with a person,' he said, glancing towards the kitchen. 'What was it that fascinated Opa?'

'He loved the large expanses, the people, the tribes, and especially the children. But also the animals that inhabited that continent. On the flip side, he saw the conditions that many lived under. In some areas there was great poverty and abuse. Constant warring. Local and natural resources disappearing and leaving nothing in return. At some point he decided he didn't want to be part of the problem. He wanted to be part of the solution.

'He started investing heavily in small businesses there, helping the locals establish trading connections. He offered his services to the Netherlands Government to advise on diplomatic missions. He had some type of role within the Dutch Foreign Affairs.'

'I remember when I was in high school we didn't see him as often,' Ric said.

'My father spent longer stints in Africa. But he poured more of the family funds into starting schools, funding health care, setting up sanitation systems and improving drinking water. There were rumblings among family members, but they didn't know the larger extent of it.

'The last time I spoke with him, we had a bad connection. He kept saying, "Whatever you give away, you keep forever. Whatever you keep is lost."'

Ric turned to his father. 'Why did Opa stay in Africa? Why did he stay in a place that was dangerous for him? And why didn't you get on a plane when you thought there was a problem?'

'You're right, I should have. I made a million excuses not to go. I will answer this. But not now.' John got up and walked away.

Fifteen minutes later, Kiri and Elaina returned to the deck, surprised to find it empty. Kiri shrugged and brought a bottle of sherry out. She sat with Elaina, gazing out across the Tasman Bay and watching the lights turn on one by one.

'I was thinking about an Aesop fable that relates to John and Ric,' Kiri said.

'*The Tortoise and the Hare*?' Elaina asked.

'No, *The Farmer and his Sons*. I'm so grateful that they are talking. Two strong sticks standing together are a lot better than ones set apart.'

And she hoped they stood together long enough before one of the single sticks broke.

CHAPTER 26

IS GOLDEN BAY … REALLY GOLDEN?

Nelson over Takaka Hill to Golden Bay, Tasman District, South Island

They left The Cliff House early, carrying two thermoses, one of Kenya bold black tea for Ric and a thermos of jasmine green tea for Elaina. In a hamper were Kiri's scones with marmalade and honey, along with some apples picked up from the Nelson Market.

As they travelled, agricultural land was replaced by grazing animals, then forestry overtook the countryside, along with native tree ferns that gave way to sparser vegetation.

Ric noticed a blue truck behind FJ-Orion that had seemed to tail them since Tahunanui. It felt like it was ghosting them, but to Ric it was visible. As they got into Motueka the blue truck turned and disappeared, so he relaxed.

They passed through 'Mott' (its nickname) and then Riwaka. FJ-Orion started up the snake-like curves ascending Takaka Hill—the gateway to Golden Bay.

The hill was an imposing chunk of lime and marble formations. The pock-marked surface led to massive caverns. Chimneys and sinkholes were discovered when animals fell out of sight, sinking into the earth. In the region it was known that anything could be hidden in this hill … and often was.

'Wondered if you ever get carsick, Elaina?' Ric asked. 'Takaka Hill has 257 bends or turns in the road. Some of them are 320-degree hairpins. There's a debate on whether the road is unforgettable or unforgiving.'

'They say carsickness can depend on the driver. So this ought to be a test of your skill as much as my stomach.'

'You know I like a challenge,' Ric said, concentrating on reducing the sway of FJ-Orion, which did not want to cooperate.

As they continued to edge their way along the steep incline, Elaina looked at a map on her phone. 'Is this a hill?'

'This is New Zealand. We're the land of the Long White Cloud. Sir Edmund Hillary used the South Island as his test site for his climb on Everest. Marble Mountain is Takaka Hill's local name.'

Ric declared fifteen minutes later. 'Eureka!'

'You found gold?' Elaina asked, recalling a miner's expression.

'No, that's the name of this bend in the road—Eureka. It's not far from a turnoff to Ngarua Caves. Pretty sure they have a café with coffee. We could get a coffee now and catch the caves on the way back from Takaka. The caves weave their way under this mountain, and you have to be careful. There are many sinkholes around the place.'

With coffees in hand, they drove past Eureka Bend and headed down Takaka Hill. The Māori name of the area was Mohua. The bay swung around like a long-curved blade with Farewell Spit forming the end of the blade. The giant sandspit was about twenty-six kilometres long. From the top of Takaka Hill, Golden Bay looked like the Shangri-La described in *Lost Horizon*.

'My grandfather and I camped and hiked on a portion of the spit once. It was the last time he and I were together,' Ric said. 'And when Opa was gone, Salvy stepped in. He encouraged my love of science and, of course, chemistry. There was one time when the SciTech Expo was held in Nelson and I wanted to split water using electrolysis. It was the single occasion when Salvy, my father and I worked together in the garage. It was like Salvy was a coupling between us. Oddly, my pappa seemed more relaxed. He seemed to trust me and treat me as part of the team, the way Opa and Salvy always did.'

Elaina hoped Ric would continue, but he seemed instead to concentrate on street names. She didn't want Ric climbing back into the dark recesses of his memories. She knew what the reality of those memories had done to him. They had come close to ending his life.

~~~
~~~

GlenEden Care Retirement Village, Takaka, Golden Bay, South Island
They pulled into GlenEden Care before 10 am.

Eric showed up with his normal high-speed bustle. They went inside, identified themselves and were led out to Salvatore's mother.

Arabella Marino was sitting under a kōwhai tree in the garden in a wheelchair. Julie Clark was the staff nurse for Arabella and she would remain during the interview as an advocate.

'Arabella, you have some visitors,' Julie said, gently waking her.

Arabella gazed up with tired eyes, focusing on Ric.

'Salvatore … Salvy, where have you been?' she said slowly. 'I'm so glad that you came to see me again. I missed you so much, my son. I missed you.'

Julie glanced at Ric. 'Arabella's recognition of anyone drifts in and out,' she said.

'Hi there, Arabella. I'm Ric.' He spoke in his quiet, sympathetic tones.

'I'm fine, Salvy. They love me here so much,' Arabella answered.

Ric realised he could correct her a hundred times and it would not change what she was thinking. For the moment, Arabella believed that she was seeing her son again.

'Arabella, this is Elaina, my future wife,' Ric said in a low voice.

Arabella focused her weak eyes on Elaina and her face. 'She is so beautiful, Salvy. She's like an angel. I can see angels sometimes and they're like her. It's nice you're marrying an angel.'

Elaina took Arabella's hand and held it gently. The conversation turned towards what her son was like and what he liked to do.

Arabella fingered her shawl. 'Well, you always liked fishing, Salvy. You always told me "a river runs through it". You told me to remember that. I've said it over and over again. Near the River Styx. We're going across the River Styx.'

Julie whispered to Eric, who was trying to deduce where the conversation was going, 'I think she's talking about those famous paintings. She says the River Styx a lot. And crossing over. She repeats these over and over again. It seems to keep her calm and happy.'

'Thanks, Julie, I was trying to suss it out,' Eric responded.

'Arabella, why do you like the River Styx so much?' Elaina asked.

'Because that's where Salvy likes to go. That's where Salvy's going. He loves the Styx.'

Julie smiled at Elaina. 'Maybe it's the transporting soul thing. She liked attending various churches around here too.'

'Do you think she's talking about death?' Elaina asked. 'In Greek mythology, the River Styx is where the ferryman Charon transports souls into the underworld.'

'Well, it could have been a Greek river,' Julie said. 'There are so many Greek names for places in New Zealand. Mount Olympus, Acheron. Pandora. Oh yes, and Sphinx. I can't remember them all.'

'Are you a friend of Salvatore?' Arabella asked Ric.

'Yes, I am,' Ric answered in his new position as friend. 'And we're keen to learn more about him … as a friend.'

'Are you going to the River Styx with Salvy?' Arabella asked.

'I sure would like to go there,' Ric answered.

'Salvy always likes the fish there. Big fish,' Arabella said.

'Where is the River Styx, Arabella?' Elaina calmly asked.

Arabella turned her light-blue eyes towards Elaina. 'It's where the river runs through it, my angel. Before it moved. That's what Salvy did. Because the river ran through it.'

Ric was trying to piece Arabella's words together. Part of it seemed real and part seemed like a fantasy. He couldn't sort out which was which. But there was something in what she said. It was like a code and he needed to break it.

The conversation drifted in and out until Julie thought Arabella was tiring.

'Can we take a picture of us together?' Ric asked Julie.

'Yes, let's do it inside in her room,' Julie said, wrapping the pink shawl around Arabella and wheeling her along the pathway. At the end of the hallway was a single bed and a stuffed chair with homey decorations surrounding them.

'Salvatore brought several items here from their family home. She likes sitting next to this table,' Julie said.

On the small wooden table a DVD box was arranged, along with a profusion of framed photographs.

Ric took a few photos of the room, and then a selfie of all of them together.

'Say "Yoga",' Elaina said, and they all chorused the word while Ric took a photo.

'Can we take another?' Arabella said. 'I like pictures.'

'Say "Mocha",' Elaina said, and they chorused again.

'I'm sleepy,' Arabella announced and closed her eyes as her head fell forward.

'Apologies, but we need to stop now,' Julie said. 'She's tired and probably needs a lie-down for a while.'

'Will she remember us?' Elaina asked.

'No, sorry, she won't. Today she was fairly talkative, but it's pretty unclear what she is saying,' Julie reflected. 'She saw her son about a year ago. And I know she really misses him. Thank you so much for talking to her,' Julie said, patting Arabella's arm as she dozed in her chair.

'I'm off to a friend's housewarming,' Eric announced.

'We're off to the theatre,' Ric replied, and Elaina looked at him quizzically.

~~~

'The theatre, Ric? A little early in the day, don't you think?' Elaina asked, grabbing his arm as he bent it to lead her to FJ-Orion waiting in the shaded lot.

'You give me challenges in driving, Elaina. This one is for you in the category of entertainment.'

They hadn't noticed the same truck from their early morning drive was parked down the road on a cross street.

Ric drove into Takaka and parked outside the Wholemeal Café.

Elaina clapped her hands. 'It *is* a theatre!' she said, entering the large two-storey building. 'How glorious to eat among the old-time stars.' She took in all the posters on the walls.

'Quite famous here, mainly because it's the first place in the entire region that had an espresso coffee machine. My mum use to drive over that hill to get a coffee, as well as lentils, beans, soy milk and tofu. She was always trying out whole earth recipes on us. You're going to love this food. It's natural, healthy and organic.'

'Is that what you think of me?' Elaina asked in mock surprise.
~~~

'Well … I do see you as natural, healthy … and okay, at night very organic.' Ric got ready to pay for the meals they had selected from the display cabinet.

Elaina stopped and gave him a kiss. Astrid, who had keyed in their meal items, paused to watch the embrace before totalling the bill.

'How's that for organic?' Elaina said, picking up two of the four dishes while Ric lifted up the other two.

The next customer in line had seen 'the warmth and passion' and noted what that couple ordered.

'I'd like to change my order to whatever they were having,' the customer said.

Astrid shrugged and changed out the items.

'Ric, why do you think Arabella mentioned the River Styx?' Elaina asked, sitting below a poster of Humphrey Bogart. 'The River Styx to her seemed different than the connotation of the Greek myth.'

'She definitely had several themes going on,' Ric replied. 'To me, it seemed she was trying to remember something. She had practised saying it to help her remember.'

'What if it's random and doesn't mean anything?' Elaina asked.

'In that case, we had a chance to cheer up someone who hasn't had visitors in a while. And she did enjoy the selfies. Yoga or Mocha included.'

'Those are words that end with an "a". And that makes you smile?' Elaina savoured the zucchini quiche.

'Is that an attractive proposition for you?' Ric asked.

'More than you can imagine,' Elaina replied.

'Oh, I have quite an imagination,' Ric said.

They finished lunch and walked the town for a short while and then were on their way north towards Farewell Spit.

~~~

Tukurua Road Bungalows, Golden Bay, South Island

They found Tukurua Road, a small rural road that led them to the sea.

'We are now officially holiday-makers,' said Ric, after checking into the forty-year-old cottage that hadn't changed much in the intervening years.

The small cabin fronted onto the golden sands stretching out along the bay. The main room contained the lounge and kitchenette, with a
~~~

sleeping loft set in the back. The wood-burner stove looked original while the deck in front looked new.

Ric took a call from Lenore while setting out the ingredients for the evening meal.

'I'm betting my career that there's a match of the skull and all the bones we've found at the Paxton's,' Lenore reported to Ric. 'I don't know why the head and part of a hand were over at Parásita and the rest of him was over at the farm, but I'm pretty sure this is one set of human remains. A male.'

'Was there any damage to anything you've examined?' Ric already knew what she was going to say. He'd been looking for confirmation since he first saw the skull.

'There seems to be some skeletal damage where the neck was. Perhaps blunt force trauma. Can't be sure, of course, until I'm back in a proper lab. I'm packing this all up and will be taking it over to Wellington by air tomorrow.'

'So we still can't connect this to the missing chemist, Salvatore Marino?' Ric said.

'The one who disappeared?' Lenore asked.

'Yes,' Ric confirmed.

'Well, if it is him there's a good chance he was helped along with his disappearance,' Lenore said. 'And to answer your question, we'd still need a DNA source that a hundred per cent confirms his identity and that source must match the human remains we've collected. And by the way, I've checked for dental records, but there's nothing there.'

'Got it,' Ric acknowledged.

'Otherwise these bones will be classified as unknown. As soon as I'm back in Wellington I'll start putting this all together at the lab. Why don't you come over tomorrow? You'll get the latest data I can give you.'

Ric looked over to Elaina. 'Ahhhh, I'll text you back. Want to check out a few things.'

'One more point. If this was a murder, then the person or persons may still be around in your area. They won't be exceptionally happy that what they buried didn't stay buried. You need to be careful, understand?'

'I thought the same thing,' Ric replied. 'I'll text back in a while. Thanks, Lenore.' He clicked off and went to join Elaina outside gathering wood.

They worked together to chop and stack wood for a night-time fire.

After the sky shifted colours and the sun decided enough was enough, Ric finished the dinner.

Fresh seared snapper lay next to the vegetables and rice. A chilled bottle of Old Coach Road Nelson Chardonnay was pulled from the tiny refrigerator. They set a table for two on the deck and lounged in the early darkness.

'All right, since I'm the camp counsellor for tonight's activities, the next event is a long walk on the beach.' Ric provided Elaina with a torch and her puffer jacket and guided her down the path.

'There's nobody and nothing on this beach,' Elaina said.

'Sometimes looks can be deceiving,' he replied.

Ric continued guiding them until they could hear a large party in the distance.

'Wow, that is one noisy racket,' Elaina said as they walked further. 'What have they had to drink?'

'Oh, maybe a smoothie with some small fish, or squid, maybe even anchovies.'

'Do they cook the fish first?'

'I think they eat it raw.'

'Yikes! Those people must be filming a horror flick,' Elaina said as the noise got louder. 'Are you sure they want us to join them?'

'Absolutely,' Ric replied, coming close to a series of sand dunes.

He swiftly and adeptly executed a sweeping movement with his leg curling around both of Elaina's legs and lowered her gently to the ground while supporting his weight.

'What was that, Mr Peters!' Elaina protested, trying to squirm loose.

'Well, Miss Williams, that move was an "Osoto Gari". It's a gentle sweep take-down often found in Judo. I took you down … you might say … to get a bird's eye view of the little blue fairy penguins that come ashore at night. They are the world's smallest penguin weighing at about one kilogram.'

'Penguins? All that clatter and gurgling was made by birds!'

'That's what I love about you. You're such an observant solicitor,' Ric said.

Golden Bay's little blue fairy penguins had clambered ashore in droves. They were marching up the beach, heading for their nesting areas and bedding down for the night.

They stopped occasionally to gaze at the two figures (mammals?) in repose on the sand that were also bedding down for the night. At least that's what it appeared like from the penguin's vantage point.

The arrival of the penguins near the sand dune went unnoticed.

CHAPTER 27

THE THIGH BONE'S CONNECTED TO THE LEG BONE

Tukurua Road Bungalows, Golden Bay, South Island

During most of the night, the penguins invaded the beachfront unobserved, but not unheard. They screeched and yelled while padding around in the shrubbery, until they eventually tired. In the early morning hours the 'horror-party' noise subsided.

Before midnight, Ric had moved the biology lecture to the cottage for a hot shower and used their sleeping bags to cover the loft bed. The fire roared in the wood burner for an hour, then melted into a red glaze behind the small glass window.

Rain began as the penguins quietened down and created a pelting patter against the glass window facing the sea.

Early in the morning Ric and Elaina packed, and picked up an espresso and mocha at the Wholemeal Café. As they headed back to the car, Ric received a call from Eric, and he clicked the speaker phone button.

'Hi, Ric. I've got some confusing news.'

'What's up, Eric?'

'I got a call from Julie at GlenEden. As Arabella's nurse, she's pretty watchful. She mentioned someone showed up at the care facility yesterday after we left. The man said he was related to Arabella and was checking on how she was. He wanted to talk with her, Anne, the receptionist said.'

'Talk about what?' Ric asked.

'He said it was a private family matter. He wanted to have a chat with her … alone,' Eric replied.

'Alone? Why?'

'That's what Anne questioned. She told the man she needed to see some identification and he hesitated. Gave her a line about getting his wallet from the car. But he never came back,' Eric said.

'Doesn't sound right.' Ric remembered the blue truck he'd seen behind them coming out of Nelson and disappearing somewhere around Motueka on the other side of the Takaka Hill.

'Eric, could you tell Anne and Julie to keep an eye on Arabella? She has no family locally that I know of. It was her son, Salvatore. Do you think you could get a description of the man? And his car, if either of them saw it?'

'I'll try to get the description, no probs. And will tell them to check anyone who comes to visit. Julie confirmed someone would always be in attendance for Arabella.' Eric rang off.

'That's odd,' Elaina said. 'My solicitor brain wonders who would be interested in Arabella, but doesn't want to identify themselves.'

Ric added, 'I didn't mention it before, but when we were coming here yesterday, there was a blue truck behind us until Motueka. I didn't see them after that. It wouldn't be that hard to shadow us to Takaka Hill and then figure out where we were headed. Then, it could have been a local.'

'But why us?'

'Maybe it's who we were going to see,' Ric continued. 'If they know Salvy isn't around anymore, then it could be something that Arabella might have?'

'Do you think Arabella is in any danger? Would they harm her? And what would Arabella have? She certainly doesn't know about Parásita. She has no idea her son is gone.'

Ric was quick to respond. 'Finding out *who* it was could pinpoint whether they were after information about Salvy, Arabella … or us.'

'Or all three,' Elaina concluded.

~~~

Top of Takaka Hill, Tasman District, South Island

As they reached the crest of Takaka Hill, Ric cleared his voice. 'I … ah … want to take a quick trip to Wellington to meet up with Lenore.'

'But I didn't bring a change of clothes,' Elaina noted, looking at Nelson Bay through the windscreen.
~~~

'Ahh, I was going to drop you at The Cliff House on my way to the airport. I'm running a bit late for the flight.'

It felt like the temperature had dropped twenty degrees in FJ-Orion. Ric was sure icicles had formed inside the cab.

'Elaina,' Ric said softly, 'my mum's been wanting to take us … to take you to the Nelson Cathedral. It's a historical site in Nelson. Maybe today's a good day to go.'

'You're going to Wellington to meet up with one of your old flings and I'm going to see a stone cathedral … with your mum?' Elaina spent the rest of the journey staring straight ahead.

Ric dropped Elaina off at the top of the driveway, waving to his mum as he took off. Though he'd tried to work it through with Elaina during the drive, no angle he pursued cut through the chilled air. He supposed if the roles were reversed and Elaina was meeting up with an old boyfriend he'd find something else to do.

No, he wouldn't! He'd stick with her as if he were welded to her side. No matter who it was or what they wanted to do. Ric got on the plane, and texted her for the twentieth time.

~~~

The Institute of Environmental Science and Research, Forensic Scene Investigation Unit, Forensic Lab, Wellington, North Island

'Your lab smells like someone dumped a bottle of antiseptic bleach in here,' said Ric, pulling on the blue gloves that Lenore handed him in the brightly lit laboratory. He slipped on the white coveralls over his clothes and added the booties.

'The night cleaning overdid it on the hypochlorite. Don't sneeze.' Lenore was in 'her space, her element' and enjoyed commanding people about. Especially Ric.

She guided him to her section where the human remains found in the Nelson region had been carefully set out.

'I wanted to catch you up with some of my findings and get some background information from you. Can't say the site personnel, or your father for that matter, were particularly forthcoming,' Lenore began.

'Let's hear what you have.'
~~~

'I've done a preliminary reassembly of the remains. I've got most of the pieces of what we found in place. There were a couple of erroneous bone fragments that weren't human.'

'That's to be expected, considering where everything was found.' Ric examined the fragments.

'I've photographed and tagged what we have. There are a few smaller bones missing, but we do have most of the large bone sections,' Lenore summarised.

'What are the general measurements as far as height and the basic structure?'

'I have some preliminaries. Another forensic team member is checking my data,' Lenore responded. 'A male. I estimate he was of medium height 180 centimetres, so 5 foot 11 inches. Not buried long. About a year. European. And not Māori, African or Asian. But I want to emphasise, we have no idea who in this entire country these bones relate to.'

Lenore moved to some specific bones set out on the lab table. 'I've confirmed there were lesions or pock marks on the phalanges. Notably the hands.'

'Little pits in the hand bones?' Ric confirmed. 'Whoever this was may not have realised at first how toxic the material was that they were handling.'

'Yes. It looks like some sort of chemically induced deterioration. It appears chronic rather than acute exposure. We're running a few more tests. And another thing—the skull that was found is a pretty good fit for the top of the spinal column.' Lenore pointed out the requisite items.

Ric could tell she was enjoying herself.

'I've done a preliminary DNA analysis, which reflects they belong together,' Lenore concluded.

'So, all from the same male.'

'Yes, and the back of the skull reflects a severe blow. This was an intentional bash from the angle and impact area. I don't think he knew what or who hit him. The skull only had soil from the site.' Lenore then pointed to various other parts of the bones displayed. 'But these bones at the farm had soil from both the site *and* the farm.'

'Someone moved some of the bones from the site to the farm. After he was dead,' Ric surmised, remembering his father's and Elaina's theory from the site.

'Correct,' Lenore nodded.

'Have you checked for RNA?'

Lenore's eyes gleamed, and she launched into her spiel for lab visitors. 'The RNA analysis is always interesting to me. It can tell us things DNA can't—such as which body tissue or fluid is present at a crime scene.'

'And did you find anything leading to possible suspect?' Ric asked.

'Well,' Lenore said, 'not yet. But there's something else you ought to know. And for that you can buy me lunch at the Mojo, a Wellington waterfront café, and get ready for a lengthy lunch. All these bones make me hungry.'

Chapter 28

Divine Intervention

On the deck of The Cliff House, Nelson, South Island
'Kiri, I'm so sorry to be blathering on about my insane, jealous moment.' Elaina was still tearful but at last was able to control her emotions. 'What is it about Ric that does this to me?'

'You're in love with him, Elaina.' Kiri shrugged noting the gloomy sky. 'Frankly, men can be totally insensitive about a woman's feelings. They have no concept of things that hurt women.'

'Ric has saved my life in more ways than one. And what he's trying to do is help his father unravel what happened to his friend. How can I be so insensitive?'

Kiri took her hand. 'Trust me. You're not. Let's go downtown and get some of that carrot cake. And a coffee. You have to taste Nelson, to get to know it. At least before it rains.'

'I feel starved,' said Elaina, smiling. 'My treat!'

Café, Top of Trafalgar Street, Nelson, South Island
Elaina and Kiri sat close to the Tonga Bay granite steps that led up to the tall grey Nelson Cathedral.

'This cake is so good,' Kiri said. 'I feel like licking my plate!'

Elaina laughed. 'I thought of that myself.'

'Do let me take you into the cathedral,' Kiri offered. 'It's like a stage set for a movie. The marble structure is the Modernist Gothic Revival style. With today's dark sky, it looks like the Empire State Building meets Notre Dame, doesn't it? The majority of marble came from a range near Takaka. It took them forty years to complete this building.'

As they looked at the steps leading to the cathedral, Kiri quickly put her hand on Elaina's arm firmly.

Elaina knew something was wrong. Kiri was immobile looking at two men headed up the steps. Her usual calm face was spooked. Her eyes wide. Her mouth a grimace.

'It's urgent we find out where those two men are headed. It's unlikely they're going there to pray or take in the architecture.'

They climbed the rare granite steps and passed the well-manicured gardens.

Elaina noted another man, who looked familiar, had also entered the cathedral through the left door.

'We need to follow them,' Kiri whispered.

Elaina nodded. Whatever Kiri was fearful of, Elaina needed to stick by her side.

They waited a few seconds and then entered the right door which opened up into a cavernous space almost three storeys tall. They moved to the right into a darker passage that led up the side of the central nave. Benches were placed all the way up the nave to the transepts.

Giving time for their eyes to adjust to the darkness, they could see the first two men seated. The lighting seemed to be off. Even with the multiple stained-glass windows, the long alcove was in deep shadows. Kiri and Elaina moved closer, still hidden in the layered darkness.

In a pew about eight rows up from where Kiri and Elaina were standing, two men sat as if in prayer. 'That's Ernest Bennett and someone I don't know,' Kiri whispered.

Odell Rodman came up from the left aisle and sat behind the two men, so he could easily talk to them. This was not a discussion with God. This was a discussion about gold … or the Kiwi equivalent.

Kiri and Elaina moved around a large pillar that vaulted up into the vast darkness of the cathedral's ceiling. They crept along the far right wall to get within listening distance of the conversation.

In a secluded alcove in the wall of the church, a votive candle stand had a series of candles arranged on tiers, and several were already lit. Blending into the locale, Kiri and Elaina became busy at the candle stand.

'We probably need this,' Kiri whispered to Elaina, each lighting a candle. Then Kiri continued, 'Do you remember two of the men sitting in the pews over there?'

'Yes. I believe we saw them at the Boathouse café,' Elaina said.

'Ernest Bennett is in one pew. Behind him is Odell Rodman. I think Ernest Bennett is one of Rodman's flunkies but I'm trying to figure out how they all relate. I don't recognise the other man in the seat by Bennett.'

Rodman began in his gravelly voice, which reverberated in the open space. The acoustics were excellent for a rousing rendition of any Christmas carol or hymn, but the men were chanting their frustrations instead.

'I understand, but we need to keep a low profile. There's a lot of complaining about all the development that's happening in Nelson. We can focus on buying the low-value land.'

'Who cares what people think?' the man said. 'There's always someone trying to stop progress. They'll get bored and find another cause. Ignore them and they'll go away.'

'Malcolm, you don't get it.' Rodman was shaking his head.

Elaina closed her eyes. Where had she heard the name Malcolm recently?

Bennett raised his voice, oblivious to his locale. 'You and that idiot Baxter must have dreamed up that crazy idea to run those two people over.'

The man sitting by Ernest shot back, 'I just work for the guy. And come to think of it, so do you.'

Elaina's eyes opened. She grabbed Kiri's arm, her fingers pressing tightly. She whispered furiously, 'That man by Bennett must be Malcolm Sloan. Maybe he was the one in the boat that tried run us down. We need to go to the police. How do we get out of here? Fast!'

Kiri looked behind them at the long passage to the exit door. 'We can't leave now—they'd see us. We have to wait a bit. Get behind this pillar. We'll slip out quietly after they've gone.'

Rodman continued, 'We're making a lot of purchases in the region. There's buying and selling everywhere, and not just property. We don't want to risk *any* of that.'

'Besides, things are buried on so many properties that even we can't keep track,' Bennett said, but the other two men skated over his comment.

'In a backhanded way, we're making an offer regarding some farmland in the Red River Valley,' Rodman said.

'They should sell before the river *does* start turning red.' Bennett laughed.

'Shut up, Ernest,' Rodman hissed.

'What does he mean "turning red"?' Sloan asked Rodman.

'Nothing, he's an imbecile!'

Bennett shrugged it off.

'There's a little delay,' Rodman said. 'The new owner is a relative, a sister. She wants to sell and get rid of the place. I'm waiting on the details. I think we can grab it up pretty quickly. She's not the farming type, and besides, ironically there are problems with the land. We're trying to get the agency to move on it.'

Bennett piped up. 'Once it's bought, we can start pushing the plans through.' He glanced at Rodman.

'Ahhh, yes, pushing. You two are always good at pushing things around.' Malcolm said. Something had triggered a memory.

'Listen, Sloan, we need to keep everything out of the spotlight until the deals are fait accompli,' Rodman said.

'A what "plea"?' Ernest said with a blank face.

'When a deal is done it can't change. You're a dummy, Bennett.' Rodman's gravelly voice crackled.

'Out of the spotlight is exactly where I'm going,' Sloan said. 'I'm in it for the money like you. But I'll pass along our meet up.'

'I don't want any stickybeaks getting into our affairs,' Rodman concluded.

With that, Rodman pushed himself up, gazing around like a jackal licking its snout after feasting on some carrion.

When he started to leave, Kiri pushed Elaina further into the darkness of the alcove. Elaina exhaled a slight gasp.

Rodman peered around in the darkness. 'Schoolkids,' he said out loud. 'They should keep them out of this place—they have no respect in here,' he said to himself and traipsed through the left door, uncaring that he had conducted business in a church. The two other men followed, ambling slowly like choir boys leaving practice early.

Kiri peeled herself from the wall in the alcove. She was shaking, but held back until Bennett and Sloan had paraded out of the cathedral.

'We need to get the police onto what we heard, Kiri. They will likely not believe we found the man they were looking for in a church.'

'We could tell them it was divine intervention,' Kiri responded, heading into the sunshine. She marched them towards the police station a few blocks away.

~~~

Mojo Café, Wellington Harbour, North Island

Ric was on his second espresso of the afternoon by the time Lenore arrived in a hurry.

'Sorry, trying to get away without being seen by the boss,' she said.

'Well, you've aroused my interest so that's a good start,' Ric said. 'What's the info I "ought to know"?'

'Arousing your interest is what I'm all about,' Lenore murmured.

'You know where I stand on that point, Lenore.'

Lenore sighed and plunged in. 'You know that story about the woman who was also missing from this factory, either before or after the chemist?'

'Yes, I believe I've heard a few details,' Ric said. He wondered if this was case information Lenore was revealing.

'I thought it was important that you know the police have issued another call for any tips on her whereabouts. Her name is Tessa Bright. They have a bee in their bonnet about getting any new information on her. And this is someone who has been missing over a year.'

Ric figured the information was of interest, but Lenore had wanted him out of the office so she could pressure him. Lenore 'wanted him', full stop.

'Humph. Well, that *is* interesting,' Ric said. 'Better grab a cab to catch my flight.'

'Ric, you can book another. I selected this restaurant because of its name, Mojo. It's magic. Why don't you stay a while? We can make a night of it.'

Ric realised he was walking down the centre of a two-lane highway. While he still needed information from Lenore, he was already previously engaged. 'I've mentioned my commitment to Elaina before.'

'She's not wearing a ring, unless you call that plastic band an engagement ring,' Lenore huffed.

Ric got up, 'It glows in the dark.' And he grabbed the bill to pay, leaving Lenore frustrated with her mojo.
~~~

~~~

Interview room, Nelson Police Station, South Island
'I've been telling you, Constable Cox, that this man we saw at the cathedral is wanted by the New Zealand Police, as well as the Australian Police.'

After filling out forms and twice providing a ponderous explanation of their visit, Elaina and Kiri had been shown into a small anteroom to have a chat.

'Well, we certainly appreciate your reporting a missing person who was in the cathedral. A lot of people who go there think they are missing something.' Cox smoothed his hair back, thinking this young woman was quite attractive. And the older one wasn't half bad either. He flashed his brightest smile.

'We think this was the same man who almost ran Elaina and my son down in the Marlborough Sounds,' Kiri said, recognising stonewalling. She tried a more direct cracking of the veneer of Cox's face.

'Yes … yes. Boating traffic this time of year is a steady stream of splashing water on other boaters and swimmers who want every bit of the Sounds to themselves.'

'Mr Cox— '

'Constable Cox.'

'All right, Constable Cox, you must know that there were two people who went missing from the Parásita site about a year ago. This could be related,' Elaina persisted.

'Yes. Mr Salvatore Marino was reported missing by a friend, a Mr John Peters. The woman was reported missing by her former employer, Parásita. The current conclusion is that they ran off together.'

'But what about the skull that was found at the Parásita site?'

'No one knows who that is yet.'

Elaina and Kiri exchanged glances.

Elaina stood up and extended her hand. 'Thank you for your time, Constable Cox.'

Outside, Kiri shook her head. 'Like water, some people seek the path of least resistance. This guy should be lighting lamps in Nelson. He's been gaslighting us for the last half hour.'

'That was very profound, Kiri. You even sound like Ric.'
~~~

Kiri smiled. 'Thanks. Talking of Ric, we need to fill him in on what we've heard.'

After they left, the Constable dialled a number on his private mobile. He wondered what the weather was like at Cornwall, D'Urville Island. Likely it wasn't as cloudy as Nelson.

CHAPTER 29

ROCK OF AGES

Nelson Airport to The Cliff House, Nelson

Ric had arrived from the Nelson Airport and he and John had dinner ready when Kiri and Elaina came in. Kiri insisted they wrap it up for an outing to the Boulder Bank. Seared teriyaki chicken, roasted capsicum, Spanish onions, kumara and carrots that had sizzled on the grill were ladled into four meal containers. The basmati rice was dosed liberally with nutmeg and saffron to provide the base. With a fresh sourdough bread loaf in one bag and hot herb-seasoned olive oil for dipping, they were off in FJ-Orion to the east of Nelson.

After walking on the Boulder Bank for fifteen minutes, they found a spot where previous boulder-browsers had created a circular stone encampment on the sand. The dinner was unwrapped and the bread appetiser started with the sound of the waves slapping the shore as 'their' warm-up.

Ric opened the conversation. 'What do we know?' He thought he sounded like a friend of his, Professor Scott, who had a habit of asking penetrating questions. Ric quickly summarised what he had found out from Lenore.

John was nursing a cup of hot Kenyan bold tea with his meal. 'So, from Ric's report I feel that my friend Salvy had parts of his body hidden in two places—at the Parásita factory site, which is now being cleaned, and on the nearby farm.'

'Pappa, for a long time you've thought the skull was Salvy,' Ric said pointedly. 'If so, you're right that other parts of the same person were at the farm.'

'Yes, but I didn't want you to be biased or prejudiced with something I told you. You had to find out on your own,' John said, further emphasising the value of more than one line of investigation.

Kiri summarised another facet. 'If John believes the location of Salvatore is more or less firm, the mystery of Tessa still remains. Therefore, they didn't run off with each other, as the—*Breaking Gossip*—in Nelson seems to report.'

'That's correct,' John confirmed. 'Salvy was always dedicated to his mother. He's not one who would have just up and run off. But they did work together and it's possible that Tessa was a good friend, or maybe …'

Everyone waited for John to finish that sentence, but he never did.

'While Salvatore's human remains may all match up, we really don't have a method for positive identification to a person,' said Elaina, pondering the next step. 'And there isn't a DNA source so far. If some item with a positive ID existed, Lenore could do a comparison.'

'They've been down this road when I first reported Salvy missing.' John elaborated. 'As I mentioned, Salvatore was adopted, so there's no DNA connection.'

'Did you check for something that Salvy wore, or a hairbrush or anything like that? Where did he live? What happened to his things?' Ric asked.

'When I figured out something was amiss I went to his apartment, but nothing was left. Someone had packed everything up. There was no trace of where his furniture, clothes, books or anything had gone.'

'Someone, or a group, was keen to make his presence disappear. The reason could relate to the hazardous conditions that Salvatore had found at the site,' Kiri added. 'George said Salvatore was pretty vocal about what he thought.'

'If Salvatore was talking about the very negative results and then people started dying, someone may have wanted to bury the evidence … any way they could,' Ric said. 'Do you think there's a cancer cluster study of the area?'

'I'm interested in that question too. I'm happy to look at any data available,' Kiri volunteered.

'And I can help on that one,' Elaina said.

'Pappa, I know you had a cursory look at Salvy's lab notebook but we need to go through it more thoroughly.'

Elaina then related their recent candle-lighting experience at the cathedral. 'One thing I picked up was that Odell Rodman is somehow involved in the purchase of the Paxton farm.' She explained how Constable Cox had no interest in pursuing Malcolm Sloan.

Ric said, 'But Detective Inspector Parkhurst in Wellington certainly *was* interested in Sloan. I'll let him know about your Cathedral visit, and what happened when you tried to report your observations to Cox.'

Elaina posed a question to the group under the studded southern sky. 'Do you remember when Ernest was at the Boathouse restaurant?'

'How could we forget?' asked Kiri.

'Ernest said something that's been on my mind and today I think I figured it out. That night, he was dressed all in black. He said to me, "I love black. Black dress. Black truck. Black pack. Black jacket. Black pants." I thought he was talking about how he liked to dress, but now I think he was talking about me. I was wearing a black dress that night. But then, I believe he rattled off what he likely saw while sitting in the black truck at the Flora car park. Black pack. Black jacket. Black pants. I wore those on the hike down from Arthur's hut and Ernest could have seen me in the Flora car park. If so, he may have been in the truck that tried to chase us down.'

'Agreed. And he connected it up when he saw you at the Boathouse,' Ric said. 'Another thing to pass on to Parkhurst.'

'True to a puzzler's brain,' said John. 'More than likely Odell was the other person in the truck, since those two are always roped together like they're in a three-legged race.'

'So, in reality,' Elaina said, 'the threatening messages they gave Kiri weren't empty threats. This group turned them into reality. First, coming down a mountain, and secondly, using a boat. What's next?'

'I can't answer that,' Kiri said, 'but there is something I want to mention and need Elaina's help. I've been meeting Kevin, a little boy. His father drives a disposal truck around the region. Yesterday, I heard from Dave Bower, the dad, about something he did, and he needs some advice.

'About a year ago he had a contract with the demolition company to periodically pick up the waste material and haul it to the scrap or the recycling centre. One of the loads had some computer equipment—some to be dumped and some to be recycled.

'His son is home-schooled because of bullying. Dave thought the computer equipment he was supposed to dump could be put to use. So he took the computer and some of the equipment home to his son. He's feeling uncomfortable about it now because of something on the computer and he wants to know what to do.'

'Where did the computer come from?' Ric asked, worried about what the child had seen.

'Parásita,' Kiri said softly.

Elaina quickly responded. 'I'm happy to meet with Dave and chat over the issues. New Zealand and Australia law have similarities, and I can give him some suggestions to help ease his mind.'

They all were contemplating a young boy being bullied in school, as well as whatever it was he saw.

At that moment, the skies above them lit up in shimmering lights of pink, red, green and purple.

The Boulder Bank was pitch black and away from the lights of Nelson, so it enhanced the *aurora australis* effect.

'Wow, what's that?' Elaina exclaimed, as the sky transitioned from its appetiser to bring out the main course of emerald green, then swapping it out for acid green, transforming moments later to a streaky pea green. For a few seconds the still seawater resembled a toxic green soup.

'Solar winds that pass through the atmosphere and react with Earth's magnetic fields,' John explained.

'In Brisbane, you may not have seen the Southern Lights,' said Ric. 'They make the sky light up like a multicoloured fluorescent light tube.'

'Forget the technical stuff, guys. The auroras are like seeing glowing rainbows at night. Like we are living *in*, not just watching, a technicolour sky,' Kiri added. 'We have some of the best views of these in New Zealand.'

Elaina responded, 'All I know is you folks produce an extraordinary finale to a great location. Don't know how you're going to top this tomorrow.'

John didn't want to tell Elaina that in some places the rare auroras were considered a bad omen and could be a sign of anger from the gods.

Chapter 30

Nelson Nightlife and Hotspots

After leaving the Boulder Bank, Ric dropped his parents off at The Cliff House. He was keen to show Elaina the 'Nighttime Nelson' and wondered if they'd find anything open. Elaina wanted to drive, so after his parents waved from the front door, Ric got out, grabbing his baton from underneath his seat and got back into FJ-Orion.

As the trusty navigator, a new feeling for Ric, he directed Elaina to one of the few pubs he figured would remain open on a weekday past 9 pm.

The street had a collection of drinking establishments called night-clubs in various advertisements, but was really a few pubs and a number of family eateries. Social life for people in Nelson was often more active at the senior bowling club than downtown at night.

'I'll drop you off at the front,' Elaina said to Ric. 'Last time you dropped me off, I ended up having to listen to a drunken Ernest Bennett. I think parking is around the back.'

Elaina was determined to submit more evidence in building her case of competence. She knew Ric was afraid she couldn't take care of herself and always had an urge to protect her. 'I'll park the truck this time. *You* get our drinks,' she said, turning the tables on him.

Ric laughed. Trying to make a good-faith gesture that he did trust her. He got out with his baton. Pubs would be pubs, after all.

Elaina driving FJ-Orion was another surprising move on her part and he wondered what would be next.

The alleyway next to the pub was narrow and not well lit. Elaina carefully drove FJ-Orion down the alley and turned left into the car park. She swung wide, then backed the Land Cruiser into the tight parking spot.

Two motorcycles rummm-rumbled in and motored to the opposite side of the car park in a darkened area. The riders switched off their headlights and sat back on the bikes.

Elaina locked the doors and headed across the car park towards the alley.

The men got off their bikes and moved towards the carpark. As Elaina was passing a parked car, they came out in front of her.

'Hey, chickie-babe, what ya up to?' the shorter, fatter man said.

Elaina ignored the comment and walked on. She scanned for anyone else in the car park, but it was deserted.

'That's not nice. We're talkin' to ya,' the taller one with wide shoulders said, tugging at her and pushing her back towards a car.

'I'm going to the pub. Let me pass,' Elaina said, trying to make her voice stronger. But she felt vulnerable.

'Hey, we'll take ya,' one of them said. 'Show ya a good time. Ever ride on a hog, baby?'

Elaina knew confronting them wasn't going to do anything and she tried to move around the two bikers.

The tall one punched the other in the shoulder and said, 'Hey, Graeme. This is her and I saw her first.'

'Don't worry, Ian, there's enough there for two. We can share.' Graeme laughed.

'Someone's waiting for me,' Elaina said, edging closer to the alleyway, thinking she could run.

'You need to be polite, luv. Maybe you should go back to Australia where you came from.'

Elaina stopped. 'What are you talking about?' How did they know where she was from?

'Poking your nose around here, you might get hurt,' Ian sneered.

Ric had waited long enough for Elaina to park. He left out the side door directly to the alley way and walked briskly to the car park. There was no sound of an engine. No lights. He heard loud voices around the corner.

'Now, chickie-babe, we're gonna go for a little walk over behind the stairs,' Graeme said. 'It's private back there.' He grabbed one of Elaina's arms. Elaina screamed and Graeme attempted to shove his plump hand over her mouth.

Ian grabbed the front of her shirt, trying to rip it open. He slammed her against Graeme, so she was sandwiched between them.

'Elaina!' Ric yelled into the dark as he cleared the corner at a dead run, his heart pounding hearing the fear in her scream.

Ian looked up. 'This ain't none of your business, mate. It's between me and my girlfriend, so bugger off!'

Graeme was still trying to put his fingers over Elaina's mouth.

She bit down on his fleshy index finger, yielding an instant response.

'Ahhhhhhhh. You little … Ahhhh … She bit me again.'

Ric hit Graeme full tilt and he spun around. Ric cocked his elbow, smashing it into Graeme's solar plexus so his breath puffed out with a whoosh. Graeme bent over, unsure what hit him. Darkness clouded his vision and he fell. Out cold.

Elaina had lost her balance and dropped to the ground.

Ric shoved Ian, who lost his momentum and stumbled into the back wall, hitting his head. Then Ric grabbed Elaina's arm, pulling her up. 'Run to the light. Into the pub. Now. And don't stop!'

Elaina hesitated and Ric cried out, 'Go, now!'

She pulled her blouse together and hurried down the alley to the side entrance.

Ric stood looking at the two attackers. Graeme was on the ground, still out from the frontal assault. Ian was holding his head, with blood dripping down the side.

Ian saw his mate was down. He pushed himself from the wall, running for his bike. Ric jammed his foot out into the biker's path, toppling him. Bending down, he grabbed Ian's T-shirt, bunching it together, pulling his head up and punching him.

'Who told you to do this?' Ric lowered his voice and repeated the question. 'Who told you to do this?' he demanded, shaking the man and then pushing his face on the gravel. The pressure of the stones into his skin forced an answer.

'I don't know,' Ian muttered.

'Who told you to do this?' Ric said roughly. He tightened his grip on the man's shirt, chocking his air off until he started to gag.

'We had a picture of her!'

'Where is it? Where's the picture?' Ric ordered.

Ian dug into his jacket pocket. Ric seized the biker's wrist as it came out of the pocket with a knife. He twisted it back until something snapped; the man yelled out in pain and dropped the knife, which Ric kicked away. He dug into the biker's pocket himself and pulled out a crumpled picture of Elaina. He knew where it was taken! D'Urville Island. And he knew who'd taken it.

Ric pressed Ian's head back down onto the gravelled surface, making a crunch that sounded like sugar-coated breakfast flakes. He knelt down, yelling into the man's ear. 'Wallet!'

Ric raised his knee and the man rolled sideways, pulling out a large wallet on a chain. Ric ripped the chain from the pants and put it into his own jacket pocket.

He leaned onto the man's chest again, clenching the man's shirt, yanking the stubbled face next to his.

'Remember my face. I know who you are now. If I see you around her ever again … If I see your mate around her ever again, anywhere close to my family, it will be the last thing you see.'

The man tried to focus on Ric's face. But the pain in his head was overwhelming. His eyes were red. The blood coming from the side of his head continued to flow. With the pain in his shattered wrist, his thoughts were incoherent.

'Do you understand what I said?' Ric pushed harder on his chest.

'Yeeesss,' the biker panted out, his chest heaving.

Ric reached into the small of his back, pulling out his baton, flicking it to its full length.

He walked towards the two motorcycles, knocked out the headlamps of both, then slashed his baton into the petrol tanks and side panels. He pushed the crumpled bikes over with fuel spilling onto the ground, then collapsed the baton again and tucked it away.

Ric turned towards the side door of the pub and stopped. Elaina stood under a single overhead light, casting her face in shadow. Her shirt was ripped at the top, her arms red where they had grabbed her. There was ruddiness across her cheeks.

Ric was so angry, adrenaline coursing through his veins, and he had no way to turn it off. Anger had gotten the better of him. Not a good thing. He took two deep breaths.

'Elaina,' he said gently, 'we need to go to The Cliff House and pack. We can't stay here where there is any chance someone could hurt you. Let's get on a plane and get out of here.'

The light above flickered, seemingly a flash away from going out.

Elaina knew his response was out of character. Ric was a solution developer, always able to formulate a plan. But an attack on *her* switched off his logic and switched on his anger.

'What about your parents, Ric? What about them being here with all these threats?'

Ric put his arm around Elaina. 'We'll have to leave it to the police.'

She remembered Kiri's face at the Boathouse and said, 'Years ago, when I was younger and on a playground getting shoved around, Uncle Max told me something I'll always remember. "Don't get mad," he said. "Get even."'

Ric blinked. She was right. If he left, his parents would be in danger. Perhaps grave danger. And it was likely they couldn't deal with the magnitude of the threat he felt was there. He needed to find whoever was out there and put a stop to it. He had to do this.

And he knew how.

Chapter 31

Marble Mountain

Near the summit of Marble Mountain, Tasman District, South Island

In the early morning light, Tyler Nowland did the final check on his abseiling gear and cave communications. He wanted to practise with his new harness and repelling rack. The combo would help control the speed for abseiling down the rope. He loved the feel, especially the smell of new gear. He was thinking of starting a YouTube channel to talk about it.

He stood above the ground that was riddled with both caves and sinkholes. Waiting. He wasn't very good at waiting.

Avalanches, landslides and sinkholes in New Zealand were dangerous for both skiers and climbers. As a 17-year-old, Tyler was probably more a spelunker looking for the adrenaline rush. The rest of the team were serious cavers—exploring caves from a conservation or biological viewpoint.

The caves and sinkholes on Marble Mountain were a natural attraction for him. Some of the holes were called bottomless. To him, that sounded 'cool'—both figuratively and physically.

He was working in a group of five. They were on the third week of putting down stages into a sinkhole that had recently been rediscovered during a brush clearing. The proverbial rock dropped in the hole had drifted out of sight. No one at the top could hear a *ka-plunk*, so they figured it was deep.

His group had put down two rope lengths of stages from the surface. The top anchor point was installed with steel bolts drilled and glued into the rock. Their lives hung on it.

Tyler made a last-minute check of his headlamp, then checked his harness and rappelling gear, including spare Prusik knots, locking carabiners, screws, hammer, bolting gear, cordless rock drill and spare batteries. He was taking down the third stage of rope into the sinkhole. His task was to secure the rope at the bottom of the second stage and build the anchors into the rock for the repelling station at the third stage. The ropes went down in stages since the hole was so deep. No one wanted to run out of rope near the bottom. The objective was always to be able to come back out.

Check done, he went over the wide mouth of the sinkhole, dropping into eerie blackness. The only light was the beam from his headlamp. Descending to the first stage was no problem. He stopped at the anchor point that made up the stage two rappel. Then clipped his harness to the anchor bolts before releasing himself from the first rappel rope.

The second stage had parts of the sinkhole that protruded outwards. Tyler manoeuvred past these, walking down the side of the hole, then out over the protrusion and going back down again. His rappelling rack was acting up, not gripping the rope like it should. He thought about aborting and coming back out to see what was going on.

Suddenly, the rack slipped on the stage two rope and he careened into the blackness. His headlamp hit the wall and extinguished. He tried arresting himself. He grabbed onto the rope with his gloved hands. The rope slipped by. He was nearing the end of it. The dead end.

Panic surged in his throat. The end of the rope whipped through his hands and the rack. Then he free-fell. Almost four metres.

Whirrr. Thump. Smash.

Tyler was no longer falling to the bottom of the sinkhole.

He'd thudded onto a small outcropping of rock and was now lying on coarse gravel. He felt around in the darkness.

The firm ground extended out from where he had landed to an edge. The sheer drop then cascaded down into blackness. The ledge appeared big enough to support him. For a while. Until help came. Hopefully.

Tyler took a deep breath. At least he was still alive.

His leg hurt and he had hit his head on the way down as his helmet ricocheted against the rock wall. He began searching for his cave radio. The crew had dropped a cave radio wire down the sinkhole to facilitate communications with the surface team. *Where is that radio?*

There was a strange odour in the air. Faint … but off. Sweet … but not pleasant. *What is that*? His headlamp wasn't working so he took his glove off and felt around. Was that … a foot?

It felt like a leathery foot. Weird like rawhide. *What is that?*

He tried the headlamp again. It clicked on.

A face stared at him from out of the blackness. An image like the one painted in *The Scream*.

'HELP!' he screamed. He was unable to get his eyes off the grimace. 'HELP! I'm in trouble,' he hollered again. His voice didn't seem to go anywhere.

On the surface, the four members of the team thought they heard shrieking. It came from inside the sinkhole. No one was sure it was Tyler, but that didn't stop Bob Lambert.

'Get set up on the rope.' Bob was the senior safety officer. 'Something's happened.'

Within half a metre from where Tyler propped himself up, a human body was partially sitting on the stone outcropping. Leaning against the wall. Tyler couldn't stop looking at it.

The eye sockets in the head were deep and empty. The mouth was open, forming an elongated 'O'. The lips were dried and cracked, still coated with lipstick that had turned black. The jaw hung loose. The hands seemed to be up around the ears. Dusty brownish hair encased part of the skull, with some of the hair worn or torn away.

The apparition was dressed in brown and blue material, crumpled and heavy with dust. Was it sitting on something? Tyler didn't want to touch the thing. It was tan. He couldn't tell what it was.

The legs extended towards him. What remained of one foot was clad in a brown shoe with a bow. The other foot seemed bent in an impossible direction. It had no shoe and the dried skin appeared as a brown pelt. The frozen, crumpled face was begging him for help. It seemed to have been screaming when it died.

Tyler frantically searched his pockets. *Where is that radio?* He felt it in his leg pocket. Pulled it out, switched it on.

'Help me. Help me,' he screamed looking at the face. 'Please! Please! Something's down here.'

'What is it, Tyler?' Bob asked. He was the senior climber in the club. His voice radiated calmness; he was soothing, comforting, controlled. He had seen or been involved in many alpine mishaps during the past thirty years.

'It's … it's got a dress!'

'What are you saying, Tyler? Is there someone down there with you?'

'It's … It's … I think it's a woman. It's wearing a brown … or blue dress. It has feet and arms … and a shoe.' His voice was wobbly, and the transmission faded in and out.

Okay, that's a first, Bob thought. 'What is she doing down there, Tyler?'

'She's dead. She's dead and she's all dried up.'

Bob closed his eyes. *He's too young to see that.*

'Okay, mate. I understand. You'll be okay. We're coming to get you. Follow your training. Stay calm. Stay cool.'

Bob turned to the three other members of the team. 'Arnie, get down there. I think Tyler's on the second stage. Maybe below. Go slow. Be safe. Christie, you're the safety. Watch Arnie's descent. Talk to Tyler. Darrell, get the larger first aid kit from my truck. I'll get the police and cave rescue mobilised. Arnie, once you're in, let us know if Tyler needs an assist to get out of there.'

Bob called the police and followed up with the cave rescue team. They would helicopter to the location of the sinkhole. Bob once had a similar experience to Tyler's. He had found a small child in a sinkhole on a mountain close to Christchurch. As he'd been responsible for getting the child out of the hole, he kept singing the same song over and over again. It always calmed his nerves. The words of the song *Amazing Grace* came back to him now. 'I once was lost, but now am found'.

In this case, Bob thought, *someone was found and is coming home, but too late.*

~~~

The Cliff House, Nelson

John was shaving, something he liked to do. His mobile rang, requiring to be answered. Something he didn't like to do when he was shaving. He let it ring. Kiri picked it up and listened for a minute. Then she asked the caller to hold.

Kiri popped her head around the bathroom door. 'It's Derrick Potter from the *Nelson Daily Telegraph*. There's something he needs to ask you.'

John turned off his shaver and took the call.
~~~

'Kia ora, Mr Peters. Hope you remember me. I worked with Brad Marshall and I know you both were working together on a missing person case. Salvatore Marino.'

'Yes, we were,' John said.

'You've probably heard some rumours about a woman that Mr Marino supposedly ran off with?'

'I didn't know the *Nelson Daily Telegraph* was now publishing rumours as news,' John said.

'Well, this bit of information isn't a rumour. One of the spelunking groups has found a body in a sinkhole up on Takaka Hill.'

John's breath went out with a whoosh.

'It was near the Endless Fall on Takaka Hill. A young lad was climbing in the sink and fell onto a broad ledge. He found some human remains there.'

John couldn't seem to catch his breath. 'Could they … did they identify who it was?'

'It was fairly easy,' Derrick said. 'The remains were pretty much intact including a dress and a shoe. And there was a clutch bag. Inside was a driver's licence and lipstick, some lists and a comb. The remains were tentatively identified as a Miss Bright.'

The name hit John like a stomach punch. 'Tessa Bright,' he said faintly. 'She went missing. About the same time as Salvatore.'

'Yes, correct,' Derrick said. 'The rumour was that she and Salvatore had gone off together. At least that's what her employer said. I guess the police bought into that. They stopped investigating shortly thereafter.'

'I suppose there will be an investigation now,' John said.

'Absolutely. Especially since the Wellington Police are involved.'

'Wellington?' John asked.

'Yes, they believe it's related to something else they're working on.' Derrick switched gears, loading up his question into firing position. 'Of course, I know you never bought the story of them running off together. But I did wonder, do you have any other information you can provide?'

John didn't hesitate. 'I can give you a direct contact name at ESR. It's likely Lenore Peevy will be involved in this investigation.' He wasn't above using any pressure point he could to help accelerate the process.

He had a chemistry background after all. Catalysts make reactions go faster. Increasing the reaction progress was exactly where he was going.

~~~

(1 year previously) Flashback, Nelson City to Takaka Hill, Tasman District
Odell remembered the night he got another call and task from Baxter. He was out having a drink at the Vic Rose, a brew bar on Trafalgar Street. Baxter called late at night. He sounded clipped and out of breath. Thinking back, for once Baxter sounded scared.

'Get up here, Odell, right now! I'm in Nelson at my place.'

Baxter's place was his little sanctuary on the fifth floor of an office building he owned at the top of Trafalgar Street. Right around the corner from The Vic.

It was Baxter's hidey hole—part residence, part office.

Baxter had called and Odell came over quickly. Like he always did. But he was more than a foot soldier in Baxter's army. He parked in the alley behind the building, and used the back entry.

It wasn't pretty. Tessa Bright was lying on the floor. There was a small hole in her throat, in the soft tissue of her neck, a visible dip sometimes called a jugular notch. Her eyes were closed. She had bled onto the rug.

Baxter stood as if he was in a glacier. Icebound. There were scratches on his face.

'What the hell?' Odell said. 'Is she alive? Do you want me to get her to the hospital? Better get her there soon. This one isn't going to last long.'

'No! NO! Get her out of here,' Baxter screeched. He sounded like a bird with a siren call. One scratch on his face dripped blood.

'What happened?' Odell asked.

'She … She was … asking too many questions about that chemist! Get her out of here.'

'Salvatore? What was she asking? What did she know?' Odell implored.

'Get her out,' Baxter repeated his call, over and over again, as if his neural network had short-circuited.

'Okay. Okay. But this isn't going to be easy.' The rug was bloody. He wrapped a sheet around her.

'Get her out. Take the rug,' Baxter ordered.

Odell had never seen Baxter so terrified.

Tucking the rug around her, Odell finally lifted both the rug and body. He got her down in the private elevator and then into his ute. There was blood everywhere. Someone else could clean it up.
~~~

Baxter told him to dump her on 'the Hill'. He knew where Reid was directing him. Everyone said anything could be hidden on this hill and often was.

He pulled up in the carpark at the top of the hill.

She had been beautiful. Even then. In the blue and brown dress and shoes with a bow. She seemed smaller than he remembered her, when she was working in the lab office.

Odell carried her to a sinkhole he knew of that was off the beaten path and overgrown. He pushed away some scrub brush that he could re-layer. He removed the sheet and carpet to take back to the truck.

He picked her and her bag up and dropped her into that awful black hole. Like she was so much waste.

Odell watched her fall out of sight. He thought she had smiled at him as she was falling.

Chapter 32

Something's Fishy

The sunroom, The Cliff House, Nelson

The sunroom was a large room next to the front entry of The Cliff House. The bright Nelson sun had made a reappearance to stream in through the French doors.

Elaina and Kiri sat at the large rimu table and focused on investigating a possible cancer cluster. They spread all the data they had gathered from the Paxton farm, health reporting, newspapers and online sources. Like most businesses on the planet, funeral homes and newspapers had moved their obituary business online.

Elaina put together a spreadsheet and started with Bruce and Margaret Paxton. She and Kiri looked for any deaths in the past ten years that had an address within 50 kilometres of the Parásita site. Kiri was on the mobile asking friends if there were other individuals who had fallen sick.

Ric and John across the room reviewed Salvy's lab book. The technical data was extensive, with notes and results that Salvy had highlighted. Some of the compounds being manufactured at Parásita were easy to formulate, but when applied to vegetation or pests they were persistent and deadly … sometimes very deadly.

Towards the end of the lab book, Salvy had started what appeared to be a diary. Names, dates, places. What the company and people were doing and what he was seeing. He was a thorough diary-keeper, recording details in a factual, straightforward way with clear observations, and noted thoughts and feelings.

'I wonder what the other eleven laboratory books recorded … and where they are?' Ric pondered. 'If he journalled the details as he did in this lab book, it would be devastating to some of the people he mentions here.'

Kiri and Elaina methodically searched, as well as picked up data from a number of incidents. Being a health professional, Kiri had a lot of contacts. Elaina kept uttering 'Eureka' when she spotted something.

Ric and John were recruited to the women's health data team. By noon they had established a rough pattern of incidents, which Ric plotted on a digital map. The dots were pink and labelled with the same or similar cancer as the Paxtons', and formed an ellipse around the site, thin at the ends and branching out east and west in the middle.

The Paxton farm was not far from the epicentre of the ellipse.

An unusually high number of the same type of cancer occurred in this group of people. Looking at the dates they'd gathered, the deaths were not quick.

Elaina sat back in her chair and said, 'I saw a sick room in the back of the Paxton house. I think it was for Margaret. The bed was turned around facing the valley and fields. The bedside table still had a stack of bandages and dressings and a number of painkillers and other drugs. The room had a lavender smell from a large lavender plant on the floor. There was a man's reading glasses and books in a bump-out window. Maybe Bruce spent time reading to her.'

After several moments of silence, Kiri spoke. 'It was very painful for her. She had wanted to stay alive a year to see the red blossoms on the pōhutukawa tree. But she didn't make it.'

John looked up from his phone where he had been calculating the math. 'This cancer cluster has an eight-fold increase over the number of cases that might have been expected in this area.'

'Given the data, and what we know about Parásita, this needs to be investigated by the authorities,' Kiri said.

'And at least two people died who'd worked at the plant,' Ric added. 'They may have been trying to prevent further exposure.'

'The plant's been demolished. Remediation is underway. Are people going to chase after the details of all this?' Elaina asked.

'Murder is still murder,' John said. 'At least two people were potentially killed.'

'And maybe more,' Kiri added.

~~~
~~~

Tahunanui Beach, Nelson

In the early afternoon, Ric decided a break away from the sunroom to get actual sun was needed. He drove Elaina down Bisley Avenue to Tahunanui Beach. The seashore had white sand and was both long and exceptionally wide at low tide. Even at high tide, Tahunanui still maintained a sizeable swathe for beachgoers to sunbathe, set up umbrellas, walk on the shell-laden sand, float on rafts, or sit and look out to sea.

Ric and Elaina were lying on the beach in a rare moment of 'doing nothing'.

'This feels strange,' Elaina said, looking at the occasional mum running after a swift child or elderly man heading to the water to become more wrinkled.

'And on our ninth day here, we have time to ourselves,' Ric said.

'I keep thinking of that place Arabella talked about,' Elaina said. 'A river where Salvy would go to fish. If both of them went there, there could have been some place for them to stay. A small cottage or hut. If we could find it, perhaps we could get some of Salvy's DNA on a hat, toothbrush or something else he used.'

Ric rolled on his back. 'His apartment was packed by someone. Not Arabella. But someone in a hurry.'

'Let me see the photos you took in Arabella's room. Not of us, but the table by her rocking chair.'

'I thought this was our few hours away from screens.'

'Only two minutes,' Elaina said.

Ric went to the car park to collect his phone and stopped for two ice creams from a truck he remembered during summers in Nelson. Mr Whippy was still doling out ice creams from his rolling truck business.

Returning to the beach, Ric's ice cream on a cone was almost gone. Elaina's chocolate ice cream in a cup was surprisingly still intact.

'Mr Whippy? The ice cream man was named after what I'm eating from this cup!' Elaina's expression reflected that of a child with an unexpected pleasure.

They sat in beach chairs under the cabana and scrolled through Ric's mobile until they came to the images he had snapped in Arabella's room. One image included a DVD sitting by a collection of picture frames. *A River Runs Through It* was the movie's name. While DVDs were less plentiful, they were still around, especially in retirement villages.

'I still don't understand what that DVD title means relative to a hut,' Elaina said. 'Though Arabella said it a few times. Nor do I get the River Styx reference.'

'Clearly the hut would be pretty soggy if a river *did run* through it,' Ric said. 'Hey, look at this one.' He fingered the image to magnify a photograph on the table. 'The edge of this photo has horizontal boards. Is that a hut? I reckon it's a wooden or log cabin perched on this knoll,' Ric said. A meandering river was below it.

'Enlarge the image of this,' Elaina asked. 'Seven months ago I was looking at so much CCTV footage my eyes needed drops every few hours. I didn't want to blink and miss something.'

Elaina looked at the images again. 'I wonder if the River Styx could be related to actual sticks. I've been thinking of something your mother said about Aesop's fable and sticks. Maybe Arabella wasn't talking about the River Styx of underworld fame. Perhaps she was taking about the construction of the cabin. Sometimes in people's memories they use a different combination of names to help them connect things.'

'Well, come to think of it,' said Ric, 'there are different companies in New Zealand that rescue logs from rivers. Logging and milling native forests was an early European industry in New Zealand. Now they call this "River Recovery" timber. Salvy may have built this cabin out of logs from that nearby river. Maybe Arabella even saw it being built.'

'Let's get back to your house and a bigger screen. Besides, I think it's going to rain.'

Elaina slipped on her windbreaker. Ric felt a few drops on his face and looked at the clouds that were dark across the Western Ranges.

Their 'doing nothing' had lasted an hour.

~~~

The sunroom, The Cliff House, Nelson

John, Kiri, Ric and Elaina clustered around the screen looking at the images. All the photos seemed to focus on the trees and river more than anything else. Likely Salvatore had taken the photographs. John spotted a bench with two cups and a pink shawl on the bench.

'For Salvatore and Arabella,' Elaina said, remembering the shawl Arabella had worn at GlenEden Care.
~~~

They scanned all the photos which didn't reveal much. There were edges of the cabin's exterior and two photos showing what they now realised were the cabin's interior. Two were river photographs and one photo showed freshly caught fish.

One photo was of Ric, who had clicked the reverse button. 'Whoops,' Ric said, looking at a selfie. 'Now that's a suspicious character.' His audience of three laughed.

'We can go to the Council this afternoon and see if there's any registration of property in Salvatore's name,' Kiri said.

'Going to grab my rain jacket,' said John.

'And relative to Elaina and me,' Ric said, 'we've gone fishing.'

All Things Fishy, fishing store, downtown Nelson

Rain had started pounding the Nelson streets in a relentless pattern. Elaina pushed through the door of the fishing and hunting shop off Trafalgar Street while Ric parked. She was immediately confronted by a 175-kilo stuffed boar positioned near the front door. Large, protruding tusks pointed outwards to welcome customers.

The walls were lined with racks of rifles and a centre section was filled with fishing gear from rods and reels for fly fishing, to deep-sea fishing equipment, to tackle for surf casting.

At the sound of the door opening, the attendant at the counter had lifted his face of frozen boredom, erupting into a plastic smile.

This shapely blonde gracing their shop was dripping wet. Her light shirt was clinging to her body. Gill looked down at his worn, dog-eared magazine. Had he wished her into being?

He had to admit it was a welcome change to the burly, scruffy crowd that typically shuffled through the door. They wanted traps, ammunition and oversized waders. She must be in the wrong store.

'The boutique shop is next door, ducks,' Gill chirped from his bastion of the front glass counter loaded with ammo. 'Though I'm happy to help with any sunnies or sunhats we have here.' He didn't really want this wet woman to leave too quickly. He was eyeing the way her shirt clung to her, while he pointed to a display of sunglasses on top of the counter.

Elaina knew a cheeky smirk when she saw one. She viewed the vast store and saw cabinets filled with rifle scopes and knives.

'I need a high-grade rifle scope,' she stated with utmost confidence. 'Where can I browse?'

Gill did a double take and directed her towards the side display cabinets. 'Do you need any help, luv?'

'No, I'm fine, I'll have a squizz,' Elaina shot back, smiling.

Gill returned to his centrefold of a large boar hanging by its haunches, ready for field dressing, while a woman in a bikini was touching the hairy skin and somehow smiling.

Elaina was walking around, intently inspecting the various rifle scopes, when she felt a familiar hand on her shoulder and smelled a cologne she recognised. A very soft and delicate kiss landed on her neck.

'Hello lass, I noticed you inspecting rifle scopes and was immediately attracted to you. Can I help you in any way? Are you interested in daylight scopes or perhaps something involving the latest generation for night vision?'

Elaina turned and put her arms around Ric's neck and kissed him as they stood between the pump-action shotguns and large-bore hunting rifles.

Watching, Gill accidently knocked his Yeti tea mug off the counter, sending its contents splashing across the floor lino. Who the heck was this guy? Did his boss hire a new salesperson?

'Let's get to this,' Elaina said to Ric. 'I have studied the rifle scopes enough. Let's cast our way into fishing.'

They returned to the counter and started in on Gill, who was sponging up his tea.

Ric always had a Mission Objective. This time it was: Find some possible rivers that matched the pictures.

'Hello, Gill,' said Ric, looking at his trout shaped nametag. 'The missus and I are looking for some bonny fishing spots. I have a wee list here of some options. And a picture of a river that looks like a *braw* place. Let's have a wee blather on some options.' Ric showed him Jack McMaster's fishing spot list.

'This is a pretty extensive list,' Gill said, scanning what were all of his favourite fishing spots listed on the sheet. How did this Scot get a hold of the list? 'These places are good, but are out of order. The couple at the bottom are better than most of these others.'

Ric knew when he was being fed a line (and not for fishing). The store's name was appropriate. Gill's story was fishy. Gill was really saying the top of the list was the better fishing rivers, just as Jack had arranged them.

'What about this picture?' Ric asked, showing Gill the print he had of the river by Salvy's fishing shack and the recently caught fish on a line.

Ric could see Gill's eyes widen. Gill recognised the river. 'Those are really large browns, really large,' Gill said. 'I've only seen that sort in the Aorere River, Golden Bay.'

Then he realised he had given away something. 'Wait! Wait. I was wrong. You only find those out in the Owen River areas near Murch. Try there.' Gill licked the lips of his synthetic smile.

Elaina was reading Ric's normal poker face. She saw the tell-tale signs of Code Red.

'Thanks for your help, Gill,' Elaina said. 'Come on *bràmair*, we have to dash to the knife sharpener shop now.' Elaina tugged Ric towards the door.

Gill made no move to return the list of fishing spots which he had transferred further down the counter.

'Oh, and the list, please,' Elaina said to Gill, who handed it back slowly.

'You didn't say if you wanted a scope,' Gill pleaded with Elaina. 'I can do you a deal. Mate's rates.'

'I need to check my Remington barrel mount first,' Elaina offered as she got Ric out the door.

Heading back to FJ-Orion, Ric simmered down. 'Check the barrel mount? You don't own a rifle … that I know of. What do you want with a scope?'

'You never know when I'll be going bear hunting,' Elaina replied.

'This is New Zealand. We don't have bears.'

'It applies to boars as well,' Elaina said.

Chapter 33

Lock and Forget

Storage Unit #31, Nelson

The steel door of the storage unit groaned as Ernest pulled it back. The contents were packed to use the maximum capacity of the two-car garage size unit. Nothing much had changed since he had stuffed it all in there.

Ernest remembered the sudden phone call from Reid Baxter twelve months ago. Baxter had ordered Ernest as if he were an entire squadron in the New Zealand Army.

'I've got a job for you, Ernest. Get this done now.' The man had no concept of the time anything took. 'Get to that chemist's apartment. Salvatore Marino. Clear it out. Leave nothing. Did you hear me, Ernest?'

Of course he had heard. Baxter had been shouting to him on the phone. Ernest had turned down the volume to preserve his eardrums. Fellow was flipping crazy.

Baxter always treated Ernest as if they were in some kind of high-intensity war-fighting scenario.

All he was supposed to do was empty this bloke's apartment. But no one had been 'deployed' for that assignment except him. Ernest finally had to get Odell to help with the couch and bed. Who else was supposed to be lifting all this stuff?

Baxter ordered people about like he was in command of dozens of personnel. For this task, with the two of them, it took three days to empty the apartment and move it to the storage unit.

Now, after a year of all the stuff in storage, he received another directive from this very demanding man who thought he was some type of Officer-in-Charge. Baxter the bigot.

'We need to start emptying that storage, Ernest. Start with the boxes of paper. The easy stuff. Find a place to burn them.'

Ernest was fuming. He had other things to do. Besides it was raining!

Baxter didn't care that the boxes with paper were in the back of the unit. Ernest knew what had happened to the chemist. Odell spent enough time bragging about how he had an edge on Baxter. Why else did they empty the chemist's apartment? Who trusted what Odell or Baxter said anyway?

Getting rid of the paper meant either taking it to the tip or to some field where he could burn it. There was a friend's farm near Cable Bay. He could mix it with their agricultural burn-off. He grasped that Baxter was trying to erase the chemist's things, like he did Salvatore himself. 'Burn everything! No trace ever!'

Ernest pulled out a trolley from the hallway at the storage facility. After manoeuvring out some furniture, he accessed the boxes he knew were in back.

He looked inside the boxes where Salvatore had kept a lot of files, photos, receipts. A person's collected life. Now it was rubbish.

He lifted the first box from the storage unit. Getting it to the ute was a disaster. The rain was pouring down and the box became soggy in his hands. He put in two more boxes, each sagging by the time he got them in.

'Damn rain,' Ernest said. 'Forget this. I'll get these boxes to the farm and try again tomorrow for the rest.'

7 pm, Sheep farm at Cable Bay

Ernest headed out to Cable Bay and met up with his friend, Jerry, who was leasing the farm to graze sheep. Jerry invited Ernest in for a beer, which turned into two, and then Ernest lost count. By eleven pm, Ernest had given up on trying to wait until the storm had cleared. The storm was holding onto Nelson with a vice grip. The boxes could stay in Jerry's den until he had time to get back there.

Before he left Jerry's, he checked his phone and found he had received a text from Baxter two hours previously. The text was clear. Another order to be obeyed.

Get out to that property above Rocks Road. Check all around. With this rain and all the landslides, I want to make sure this land remains in place. I have plans to sell it soon.

Ten minutes after Ernest deleted Baxter's message, he received another text from Odell emphasising he needed to get down to the property right away.

Ernest looked at his mobile. What do they think? I'm on a 24-hour call service?

He was headed to his home on the other side of Richmond, so he could check the property above Rocks Road on his way. He had a flashlight somewhere in the ute.

Midnight, Nelson Storage Unit #31

At midnight, the caretaker at the storage facility did his final round. This rain was downright the worst he had seen. He stopped by Unit #31.

It always happened. Someone was in a hurry. They closed their secure door but forgot to use the lock. Then they'd come running to the office saying someone broke into their storage unit.

Alistair took out one of the office spare locks and clicked it onto the storage unit. The owner would have to come back to him and establish his identity and ownership before he'd take the site's lock off.

Alistair looked at the sky. The rainclouds were kissing the ground and were so thick with moisture that water was pouring out of every downspout.

'Going to be the worst one ever,' Alistair said out loud.

Chapter 34

Number Three on the Hit Parade

Auckland, North Island, New Zealand
Francis landed at Auckland International and quickly passed through security. He was travelling light with one check-in and his rolling bag.

He breezed through the immigration check with one of his Australian passports. Despite never having been questioned or stopped, he was ready. There was always a first time for everything.

Retrieving his luggage was a breeze. He loved answering the simple questions about not having tuberculous and not visiting Africa recently. He never carried food from the airplanes, he told the biosecurity staff.

If they only knew that various weapons could easily be broken down, and innocuous looking parts, equipment and supplies carried in.

Francis walked to the domestic terminal briskly in the clear, crisp sunshine of Auckland. The air was so clean it hurt to breathe. What a place, Francis thought, after the congestion of Jakarta.

His brain was doing somersaults in the chilled air. He felt almost giddy.

Francis was now focused on another clause within his contract. Not that he had any remaining clients on this job. He had killed them both. They broke the rules. And to top it off, they had stiffed him on the payment. They both became 'stiffs' by their own actions.

They had failed to read the fine print on Francis's contract. 'Failure to pay will result in termination of all conditions.' They didn't understand that *termination* included them.

He had time for a scone and a quick cup of tea before he made his connection through to Nelson. He looked at the airline magazine for New Zealand. It was nice to be able to balance a business trip with pleasure.

All clients needed to respect *Duty of Care*, Francis concluded.

Until death do we part
This is the end
And not the start –

'I'm so chuffed to be here,' Francis said to himself, ready to bite into his buttered scone.

Central Business District, Nelson

The hotel was white, a two-storey, cookie-cutter building on the edge of Nelson's CBD. Inside were plastic lamps and shades and polyester bed linen. The small balcony overlooked the car park.

Exactly the way Francis liked it. Killing was a private business. All of his equipment was ready and he had included a pair of night-vision binoculars if needed.

Tahunanui Beach, Nelson

Francis drove to Tahunanui Beach and parked his car near a statue of Captain James Cook. The Cap'n had no hat and the seagulls were currently fighting for the perch on top of his head. Someone had removed his bronze sword, so fighting back wasn't an option.

Turning off the motor, Francis heard a pitter-patter on his roof. Raindrops smacked into his windscreen as the sou'wester slammed into Nelson.

The rain was being pesky.

He stepped out of the car and tried to focus his spotter scope towards the house on The Cliffs. The Peters residence was easy enough to find.

This recon was to familiarise himself with the area and locations, especially access. He always scoped out his terrain before a kill.

The house was on a cliff face overlooking the Tasman Sea and the coast below. Cedar siding, green roof and glass rails with extensive decks marching up the hillside. It was surrounded by plenty of cover—thick native bush on two sides.

The rain was hampering his recon. It was hard enough doing his line of work, but when the weather didn't cooperate it was too much of a struggle.

'I hate rain,' Francis said. 'I hate rain almost as much as bullies.'

Chapter 35

Changing Pressure

2 pm, Lambretta's Café, Nelson City, South Island

The rain had intensified. Ric found two rain jackets in the back of the Land Cruiser. His father was always prepared for Nelson's variable weather.

'I'm treating you to a coffee because you were very good at restraining yourself back there, while Gill was blatantly lying to you,' Elaina said.

Ric smiled. 'It's always the first reaction to a list or a photograph that counts for a courtroom examination. Though practised liars can lead you astray. In this case, the location of Golden Bay is logical.'

'I wouldn't think it's the only place around here where that particular fish would be found,' Elaina said.

'No,' Ric agreed. 'But Gill was focused on the type of fish and the look of the river. I think he's probably fished there. And he sure didn't want to let go of Jack's list.'

'That's what you think, eh?' Elaina said. She knew what Gill had been focused on. Fishing was a secondary interest.

'I'll see if I can match the electronic version of the image when we get back to The Cliff House. If not, I know some people with better equipment who have friendly AI,' Ric said. He glanced up at the dark sky. 'The rain seems to be settling in.'

The streets were emptying; at the same time the stormwater was flooding out of the drains. Several bubbled over, their capacity outstripped.

Ric looked at the time and dialled Hendrik's number. 'I've tried getting a hold of Flynn and keep missing him,' he said to Elaina.

She had been watching the rain slide down Trafalgar Street as if it was a waterfall. Elaina felt increasingly marginalised and kept at arm's length. She thought that Ric was trying to balance all the tasks at once.

'Is everything okay with you?' she asked, reaching across the table and touching his sleeve.

Ric gave her a vague shrug, then added, 'All good.'

She leaned back. Did he really trust her to help him?

She decided it was time for a break. 'I'm supposed to meet your mum at the top of Trafalgar Street. She's carpooling to town with a friend. A group of them were planning to do something. Not sure what. By the way, she and your father didn't find any property in Salvatore's name. Maybe he had a trust, or it was in someone else's name …' Elaina was ticking off options.

'Better take my father's rain jacket too,' Ric said, assessing the weather. 'Put it over the one you're wearing because yours isn't waterproof.'

'But you'll get wet,' Elaina protested.

'I've been wet a lot of my life. Besides, I'm wash and wear with drip dry,' he said, planting a kiss on her cheek and hustling off to meet his father.

Elaina met up with Kiri, who'd arrived in a friend's car. 'I dropped my friend off for an hour while we meet up with Dave Bowers and his son at Miyazu Japanese Gardens. There's a Pondside Pavillion that is quiet and way out of the earshot of anyone.'

'Sounds mysterious,' Elaina said, getting into the vehicle.

Nelson was a sister city with the Japanese city of Miyazu, and the park was a little slice of Japan. A small bamboo 'forest' was interspersed next to short bridges and planks over reflective ponds with a series melodic cascades trickling down. There was a sense of serenity and calmness amid the cherry trees that Kiri thought was a perfect atmosphere, given the hint of what was coming.

They found Dave out of the rain at the Pondside Pavillion, a miniature tearoom. A small boy with large glasses sat beside his father, his jeans cuffs rolled up above his tennies. He wore a Superman shirt.

'Hello, Kevin,' Elaina said, bending down to eye level. His glasses were thick and bi-focal.

'I found something bad on the computer.'

'What did you find, Kevin?' Elaina asked softly.

'Some angry people. People were fighting. The old man was hitting a man in a white coat with a shovel.'

Elaina and Kiri looked at each other, astonished at Kevin's unexpected story.

Dave further described what Kevin had seen. 'This is what I hinted to you on the phone, Kiri. Kevin found a few video files on that old trashy computer that I picked up from Parásita. But he didn't know what they were. And he didn't tell me until I told him I was thinking of getting rid of the computer.'

'The old man in that movie scared me,' Kevin said, his eyes wide behind the glasses. 'After a while, another man came and dragged the man on the ground away. His white coat had red on it.'

Kiri cut in. 'It's best we don't discuss that here. We'll take a look at it, Kevin. You did the right thing by telling us. And I'll be seeing you soon at our usual meeting and we can talk about it quietly. You can tell me everything. You can always talk to me about what you feel and think.'

Dashing over to an awning, Kiri and Kevin looked at the carp in the pool.

Elaina provided some specifics to Dave. 'For the moment I'm your attorney and what we're talking about is confidential. Get everything that you have into a box and get it to Kiri's. I'll make the arrangements and make sure it's taken care of. And you don't have to worry about Kevin. Kiri's on his side and she's the best, Dave.'

Maitai River, Nelson

Ric picked his father up in FJ-Orion and they drove to the river's height measuring gauge. The Maitai River was typically a lazy river that ambled through Nelson, originating from the Maitai Dam located in the hills above the city.

A family friend and local environmentalist, Lance Stewart, was in coveralls and a high vis vest walking back from the river gauge.

'It's already past historical highs, and we've just started into this storm front.' Lance had to raise his voice over the tumbling noise of the Maitai flowing by the gauge. 'People are coming down to the river to watch it increase in size, while some are already bailing out their basements.'

'The Council's Emergency Management team is stacking sandbags by the houses along the river,' John reported.

'It's hard to get people to stay away from the river,' Ric said. 'Humans are addicted to the precarious.'

'Most of the weather sites say this is a 100-year flood event,' Lance replied. 'Though *now* it could mean every other year.'

As the three men stood in the rain, two teenagers on inner tubes blasted by on the Maitai torrent.

Lance watched them barely hanging onto their tubes and unable to control the direction or speed they were travelling. 'I have a meeting at the Council. Can you two check the Maitai swimming hole upriver? Make sure no one else, especially kids, are up there.'

'Is the swimming hole still in existence?' Ric asked his father.

'You mentioned "Humans are addicted to the precarious",' his father answered. 'That's probably *times ten* for kids.'

Swimming hole, Maitai River

They drove further up the river, noting with each kilometre how the river was broader and faster. The access road to the riverwalk was flooded. They parked on a stretch of elevated land. John handed Ric a pair of gumboots and they sloshed towards the swimming hole. Two young boys in boardshorts were racing towards the water with inner tubes.

'Stop. No, no!' John yelled.

The older of the two stopped. The younger boy hit the water while running, trying to surf with his tube.

Like a stunt movie sequence that went ghastly astray, the younger boy was knocked off when he entered the water. He grasped the side wall of the tube, trying to hold on.

Ric raced towards him, leaving the gumboots on shore as he dove in. The boy was hanging onto his tube, but he was trapped into a circulating vortex in the bend of the Maitai. Hefty branches and chunky debris were rapidly being swept downriver.

Ric slammed into the flow with his practised Australian crawl. In the shallower bend, he managed to grab the tube that had caught on a tree snag. On the other side of the tube, the young boy was screaming as the water began to flow over his head.

Stumbling and tripping over the boulders in the river, Ric edged around the tube. He frantically flung his arm out, grabbing the boy, then clasping his hand. The inner tube wasn't waiting for rescue and broke loose from the snag and Ric's hold. It bounced down the river, disappearing under the massive pressure of the flowing water.

'Look Out! Tree!' John had spotted a stubby tree branch barrelling down the river further up and angling towards them.

Ric clawed across to a standing tree now engulfed by the flood waters. He anchored his feet and shifted the boy to face the trunk. Ric wrapped his arms around both the trunk and the boy. The branch swung around the tree with the momentum of a waterfall unleashed, and one limb cut across Ric's back. He felt the laceration tearing his skin, but he wasn't about to move. The boy was pressed against the tree and crying. The swish of the water on the other side of the tree changed the projectile's direction and it slid away down the river.

John flagged an Emergency Management vehicle that was headed in the opposite direction. The truck came back down the street and John waved his arms.

'We've got to get a line to them!' John roared as they drove up and he pointed to the two people clinging to a tree in the centre of the river.

'We can jury-rig a weighted safety rope to hitch onto the tree,' one of team bellowed through the increasing rain.

On the third try, the safety rope overflew the tree trunk and branches and wrapped around the other side. Ric secured the rope to the tree and cinched it tight noting the line was still chafing against the tree. Debris coming down the river periodically snagged on the rope.

'You have to hold onto me tight, okay?' Ric told the boy. 'Tight as you can!'

'I'm scared!' the boy cried. 'I'm really scared!'

'We're together. You and me. You focus on my face. Okay?' Ric shouted. The flood waters clawed at them.

The young boy trembled, his eyes filled with terror.

'I'm Ric!'

'I'm Tommy.' The boy spluttered and gasped as the water splashed over him.

Ric took his belt and looped it around the safety rope, securing it at the end, and put his arm through it. They started moving across the expanse of tumbling water using his belt as an impromptu loop. The rain bombarded the river; the shoreline became invisible as racing water continued to rise.

'Hold on tight, Tommy!'

Ric slipped on a boulder, falling into the river, submerging himself with the boy. They both came up, spitting out the soil-laden water.

'You okay?' Ric raised his voice over the water's roar.

'Yes!' the boy said faintly.

John and the Emergency Management team were holding fast on the safety rope.

Ric and Tommy made the halfway point. A large log roared by, smacking against the rope again. The log broke free, barely missing Ric.

'We've got to get to them!' John shouted.

Ric was within striking distance of the shore. The river's flow momentary eased off as the water had been transformed into a thick slurry of silt, sand and boulders. Debris from the upper part of the river relentlessly battered the line. Rocks and boulders pelted Ric's legs.

Suddenly the safety rope snapped near the tree. Ric grabbed the slack rope end and his belt loop. He doubled up the safety rope and made a non-slip loop that he placed around Tommy under his arms.

Ric called out, 'Haul him in!'

The men on shore heaved on the rope, wresting the boy into the shallows and scooping him up. They rushed Tommy from the river's shoreline and got him to the emergency vehicle, wrapping a blanket around his shivering body.

Ric couldn't stand up anymore. He was tired, out of breath and his muscles were burning. Another surge from the river and Ric could no longer fight back. The water whisked him away.

'He's gone!' John got into FJ-Orion and turned the vehicle around. The road was now flooded as the river continued to rise. The Land Cruiser ploughed through the water, which started to come into the cab. The vehicle had a snorkel for high water but there was a limit on what it could do.

Ric was swept along with some debris and it piled up at a bend in the river near the Queens Gardens. He was closer to shore but could not lift his arms anymore. He felt like he had done seven hours of high-intensity workout in the last thirty minutes. He was close to a tree branch, but couldn't move to free himself. Ric's head was visible above the dark chocolate water and the level was rising fast. Waves splashed over his face while he held his breath.

He felt a firm grip on his shirt collar and arm. Then the grip began to hoist him, slowly dragging him out of the deep water and closer to the surface.

'Ric, stand on your feet if you can! I can't pick you up. You're going to have to push up with your legs!' John yelled at Ric, desperately trying to hold on to him as the water clawed at Ric's body.

Ric concentrated, planting his legs on the rounded stones on the riverbed. Slipping back once, he managed to push himself up again. John tightened the grip on his son's shoulder and arm, hauling him backwards towards the shoreline. In a narrower channel, the water rushed harder, but a bend in the river created a sandbar where the water slowed. Four local residents on the right side of the bank formed a human chain, holding each other's hands to help Ric and John ashore.

Ric and John collapsed on the ground, panting. Ric coughed up dirty water, and then surveyed the damage. Considering some of his escapades, not bad. A nasty gash on his back. Scratches on his arms. He was more concerned about his father. John was waterlogged and out of breath.

For the last few days, Ric had pondered his relationship to Salvy. In the past Salvy had been close to Ric, more inclusive, more interested in what he was doing. Was this the father he always wished he'd had? He couldn't remember.

But today, working with his pappa, saving Tommy, along with searching for any information about Salvy, had wound up bringing him and his pappa closer—small bridges over their wide differences.

A photographer snapped some pictures of thc two exhausted men on the lawn.

'I'll get the first aid kit in the truck in a moment,' John gasped.

They lay in the grass with the rain pelting down, protected by umbrellas from the emergency team that had rescued them.

'It's good to have you home, Ric,' John said, puffing. 'I hope you are enjoying … your vacation. And that we've built in enough adventure for you.'

His father's droll humour had returned.

They patched each other up with antiseptic, and dressings for Ric's chest and back. Paramedics checked them out as a precaution. Ric shed the remainder of his torn, sopping clothing and changed into a pair of coveralls and gumboots. John did the same. They got into FJ-Orion and moved further up the river towards some homes where people were sandbagging garages and front doors.

Ric caught sight of Elaina, who was shovelling sand into bags. Kiri's plan to meet up with friends had shifted to everyone helping the homes along the Maitai River that would soon be hit by high water. While Elaina shovelled, her hair fell down into her face. She repeatedly had to push the plastered strands back from her wet cheeks.

Somehow with her wet and muddy clothes, the gumboots a size too large and her rumpled hair, Ric thought she looked irresistible. What was it about Elaina that in her most stressful moments, he seemed to love her more? He didn't get it. And even his biology background couldn't explain it.

Everyone who could come from the surrounding areas was out putting up plywood barriers over doors and moving sandbags into position. It was an assembly line.

In New Zealand, during any type of emergency, people had two choices. Help someone who could be affected; but if you're affected, try the best you can to dig your way out.

'Can you use a hand?' Ric asked Elaina as he walked up.

She smiled at him. 'I'm so glad to see you. I was worried. What happened to you? Where are your clothes?'

'A lot of questions from my solicitor,' Ric responded. He used his wet bandana to wipe a little mud from her cheek. 'I was in some water and my other clothes got wet. My father and I changed into coveralls. And it's raining.'

'Your mum and I were recruited to put sand in the sandbags,' Elaina said.

Ric glanced to where hundreds of sandbags had been deployed. Most of the crew had moved further upriver.

'I think you've covered this side of the river. Why don't you do the rest of the river now?' Ric smiled.

Elaina stepped back, picked up a fistful of mud and let Ric have it squarely in the chest.

'I don't take any prisoners,' Elaina said. The second clump was already in her fist when Ric lunged forward, mud still on his chest from Elaina's first hit. He held her arms at her side.

'You're lucky you have fast reactions,' Elaina teased.

'Maybe you're slow,' Ric said, releasing her hands and headed towards FJ-Orion.

The second shot of mud hit him in the back of the overalls. 'You've forgotten. I do have a love affair with bullseyes.'

'And I'm forever going to watch my back,' Ric said, coming back and squeezing her shoulders.

They finished the sandbagging and headed home.

~~~

Marcella's near The Cliff House, Nelson

They approached The Cliff House, spotting an elderly woman who stood in her driveway, her grey hair plastered down and rain jacket askew.

'What's going on at Marcella's?' John observed.

Marcella was at the top of her drive, trying to lay out sheets of black plastic with the help of several neighbours. The rain kept pouring down and the wind was picking up again. The driving rain made the plastic fly around like sails on a luffing sailboat.

The thin sheets were coming apart where they had been taped together. One couple was attempting to tie lines on the corners of the sheets while Marcella and two men were holding the slippery plastic.

'My roof's leaking,' Marcella said to Kiri as she and John got out of FJ-Orion. Her wrinkled face had lines of desperation etched across it. Her small house was the oldest on the street and her corrugated iron roof had never been replaced. 'Everything in the house is getting wet,' she said.

'Dinner's delayed,' John said to Ric and Elaina. 'Ric, can you get those salvage tarps we have in the rafters of the garage? They'll work better than these pieces of plastic.'

Ric's body ached and burned as he moved up into the garage rafters. He started dropping the massive tarps down to the garage floor. Elaina, Kiri and John dragged the tarps onto the drive and took them to Marcella's house. The neighbours were redeployed and set up extension ladders by the leaking roof.
~~~

Ric and John climbed onto the roof as the rain continued unabated. Several neighbours hefted the heavy tarps up. Elaina and Kiri went inside Marcella's house to empty buckets.

'The winds are picking up,' Ric said to his father. 'Let's tie these off as soon as we can.'

'The forecast isn't improving, as they hoped. It will get worse tonight. And more rain in the next twenty-four to forty-eight hours,' John said over the din of the rain and wind.

After an hour of manhandling the tarps, they were arranged over the major leaks and tied off. One of the neighbours, a skilled sailor, put his knot-tying expertise into practice. Elaina and Kiri left the 'Secure the House Project' to make dinner.

Marcella checked the atrium in her house. 'It's down to a trickle, John. I think your tarps have done their magic.'

'Keep the buckets out,' John told her, 'but the tarps should stop most of the water. If it gets worse, call me.'

'Thank you, John. And your son. Good to see you, Ric. It's hard to keep up now that I'm alone.'

John put his arms around Marcella. 'We're here for you, always remember that.'

Ric watched his father with Marcella. How come he couldn't remember this man in his dreams or in the memories of his youth? It had always been his grandfather. The man with the grey eyes like his, who taught him how to box, how to ride a motorcycle, how to spot a liar and how to shoot. He hadn't learned much about how to trust.

CHAPTER 36

AFRICA UNWRAPPED

Garage, The Cliff House, Nelson

Ric and John worked together putting the garage back in order. As Ric finished with sweeping, John cleared his throat.

'The third part of the story I've wanted to tell you is not long and not very complicated. But it's also not pleasant. It made a large impact on your mother … and me. Your grandmother never recovered from it.

'I know you've wanted me to open up and be honest with you about your grandfather. But in my mind I wanted to protect you from the painful truth. So I'll try to be clear, Ric. The conflict between honesty and protection fractured our relationship. It created a distance between us. The truth will likely raise the stakes.

'Ten years ago, my father was travelling in Central Africa for the Dutch Government. He received instructions to assist Dutch nationals in trouble. A number of men, women and children were caught between several warring groups. This was fuelled by local warlords with longstanding grudges, a variety of political groups, and gangs of marauders. In Africa, things are either extraordinarily simple or impossibly complex. Each group began exchanging gunfire with threats that became more intense. Local police were non-existent.

'The Dutch nationals, along with some children from a nearby school, ended up as hostages. That turned into a ransom demand. It was unclear which group was in charge, or if there were more than one group making the demands. But it was clear that they would start executing the captives. The men would be killed, and the women raped or worse. The militant groups competed in their threats, which drove the groups into an increasing crescendo of angry hatred.

'Your grandfather went to the supposed leaders and sought clear terms of a ransom. He had a guide and translator who'd contacted the group to start a negotiation for the hostages' freedom and a passage to safety. Your Opa wasn't armed. He was convinced that the groups simply wanted valuables in exchange for the captives.

'The negotiation went on for too long—from days to weeks. Finally, there was agreement on an amount. The leaders insisted on gold. Arrangements were made to bring the gold in and the hostages out. Your Opa even managed to convince the captors to let the women and children go on the guarantee that he would remain until the gold arrived. Red Cross workers and missionaries led them out of danger.

'But the gold didn't arrive. There was some hold-up—both in time and theft. Travel in rural Africa is always convoluted, never on time, never has a schedule or a specific route. The gold simply never arrived. The group felt betrayed by my father. They had my father in their camp and took out their anger on him. It was more than a passing emotion. They wanted to cause harm and violence. It was evil intent.' John stopped; unsure he could continue.

Ric waited. Here it was – the brutal honesty of what had happened. Now he wondered if he really wanted to know. After years of conjuring up scenarios, and with vague, cloudy answers from his father, the truth of what his grandfather had experienced was perhaps something beyond his worst imagining. Ric took a breath, then offered a prompt. 'And …'

'They peeled his skin off. Piece by piece. Centimetre by centimetre. Over four days. They sent pieces of him out with a few of the men who could still walk. They recounted his death in ragged breaths, unable to express in words their horror at what they saw going on at that camp.'

Ric closed his eyes. So, this was it. The reason he was never told. He was in high school, just before entering university. They didn't want him to know. To have it in his memory. To scar his life. To keep him from going down the same direction as his grandfather … and the path he ultimately followed anyway.

Tears streamed down his face. His father took a hankie from his pocket and handed it to Ric.

'We were told that he had died. There was no discussion about the return of his body. It would have normally ended there, but it didn't. My father's friends near Pretoria headed into the area where my father had gone.

'A group of men, six in total, got together. Some were professional trackers; the others were hunters. They found the gang or bandits, whatever you want to call them, after a few days. They retrieved my father's remains.' John stopped for a moment to collect himself. 'What was left … was recovered. And then cremated. They brought my father's ashes out and sent them back to the Netherlands. I never asked what happened to the men who did it. I never wanted to know.'

John stopped his narrative as tears began to spurt out. Ric passed the now wet hankie back to his father. John wiped his eyes, caught his breath and continued.

'My father believed that good faith and a person's word were important in changing the world. But it shattered my faith in everything. And most importantly, I never wanted you to follow in my father's path. There was always too much risk. In the end, I think you are now in deeper than he ever was.

'What happened to my father has never left me. I think I could have done something … And I didn't.'

Ric stared wordlessly at the rain. He was having a hard time thinking of his grandfather in that camp. Like camps he had been in. Like camps he had tracked.

For years, he hadn't trusted what his father always said about his grandfather when he learned Opa had died. And now he knew why.

Father and son sat in the cold garage, listening to the rain. It was painful for both men to imagine Opa enduring such torture. Together they were reliving his loss.

John had tried to shield his son from the horrifying details of his father's death. And his own lack of action. Ric could feel the dynamic had shifted. His father's efforts to care for and safeguard him would likely be something *he* would do … for his own child.

Finally, John walked over and briefly laid his open hand on Ric's shoulder. 'I think this is a Scotch night. Don't you?' He stepped out of the garage, heading towards the front door.

Ric looked around the garage, packed with equipment that his grandfather once owned. Once used. Once valued.

That last Golden Bay camping trip was up near the 26-kilometre Farewell Spit. He realised farewell was used to express good wishes on parting. Somewhere, sometime, he would have to find a way to view the parting of himself and his grandfather … not as a departure but as a good memory. They had sat near their tent at the small holiday camp beside the sea at the base of the spit. They had swum and kayaked, talked and laughed. At low tide they walked close to the resident seal colony at Abel Head.

Ric realised the power of choice over his memories.

He closed the garage and went into the house for a shower. He turned the nozzles up, hoping the water would wash away his thoughts about Opa's last hours. He removed the bandaging from his back. The bleeding had stopped, but he winced trying to pull off the sticky tape from the laceration. It felt like he had been through a vegetable spiraliser and then pounded with a meat-tenderising mallet. The adrenaline was gone; the pain was in its place. But less pain than his grandfather would have suffered.

Kiri had started the Lady Kitchener wood burner in the dining room. In the shower, Ric could feel the wood burner adding heat to the water through the wetback coil. The shower room was filled with steam and he could barely see through the dimmed overhead light. The shower door opened quickly and shut.

'Oh, I'm sorry,' Elaina said. 'I thought you had finished. I'll come back when you're done.'

Ric's arm quickly shot out from the hot water and grabbed her as she was turning to leave.

'This saves water and it's faster,' Ric said.

'I'm very much into water conservation,' Elaina replied.

She knew Ric had been up in the garage talking with his father. And looking at his face, she recognised that something had transpired well beyond anything that had passed between them in the last few years.

For Elaina, there was a strong parallel, even an echo, of the dynamic between Ric and his father. She wasn't going to let *their* relationship wind up distant and aloof, so they couldn't find ways to solve divisive issues.

She wasn't about to give up on this man who was extraordinarily complex, and at the same time singularly caring. Elaina remembered techniques from her yoga notebook on the many ways to concentrate on being gentle, soft and calm.

~~~
~~~

After everyone turned in for the evening, Elaina slid under the down comforter to ward off the chill. Was this summer? She heard the door creaking as it opened slowly.

Without turning towards the door, she asked, 'Are you coming to check on how I'm doing?'

'My father did say that I should check on everything and make sure it's shipshape with the approaching storm.'

'All right, Skipper,' Elaina said. 'Welcome aboard.'

In the stillness, Ric told her about the death of his Opa. He spoke in halting fragments.

Elaina could see it was affecting him now, maybe would forever. He'd learned a truth he'd wanted to know for years. And it was his father finally trusting and opening up to him that made the difference. It meant finding a common bond in the pain, and Ric and his father could reflect on the man they'd both loved.

It was one of the few times that Ric had let Elaina into his most inner thoughts. It seemed to progress their relationship, deepening it. He trusted her with this story and his hurt. And she helped him by offering some solace. To her, it felt like the fusion energy that powers the stars. It was an intense and deep cauldron of trust between them.

The rain hit with a vengeance later in the night. The barometer had been dropping as another low-pressure system skirted into the Tasman Sea. A new front with high winds and rain struck the Nelson-Tasman area and along the west coast of the South Island.

The crew in the Loft Room didn't notice the change in barometric pressure.

Chapter 37

Tracking Mandu: A Tasty Morsel

South of Surabaya, island of Java, Indonesia

Ahead, Flynn and Hendrik could see a black police truck. Ric had warned them about this. Flynn pulled their truck further into the undergrowth over several piles of coconut husks, edging their vehicle between two palm trees with leafy fronds. The truck couldn't be seen from the road, especially in the dense vegetation.

The previous day they had left the island of Palau Kangean, passing back through Surabaya on the island of Java. They'd spent the night at a small tourist encampment with several bungalows. Ni Luh Suardika ran the guesthouse with her family. It wasn't far from the car ferryboat to Bali that they would take at noon. Early in the morning, they packed up and went out to get fuel. They were headed past their accommodations when they noticed a police vehicle on the road nearby.

'Cut through the jungle and park behind the bungalows and the main house. We need to see what's going on with that police vehicle,' Hendrik said. 'We're not leaving Ni Luh in the lurch because of us.'

Close to the first bungalow, they heard a voice talking in mixed Indonesian and English. A man was being asked, 'What are you doing here? What is your purpose here?'

Flynn and Hendrik came round behind the main house. Ni Luh was outside the back door to the small kitchen area, hiding behind a stand of palms.

'Shhhh,' Ni Luh whispered to Flynn who reached her first. 'We must be quiet. Those men are police.'

Ni Luh was terrified of the police and their many different units, which often seemed interchangeable. Each police group considered themselves an 'elite part' of some 'special' force.

'They came asking about any foreigners staying here. They were looking for two men. They are going into the bungalows and checking on everyone.'

Hendrik peered through the vegetation. There were two policemen in black pants tucked into leather boots and black shirts. Black berets sat jauntily on the sides of their heads.

'How long have they been here?' Flynn asked.

'About an hour or so. They started going through the bungalows about twenty minutes ago,' Ni Luh said.

Hendrik had noticed the large police truck was deliberately parked on the main road near the top of the drive, partially blocking the road so that no one could easily drive out.

'Do you have any petrol or spirits?' Hendrik asked Ni Luh.

'What are you going to do?' entreated Flynn.

'While I'd like to be putting chicken on the braai, we have to get their minds on something else. So, a little barbie, as they like to say in Australia.' Hendrik smiled.

Flynn had never been an advocate for anything other than open discussion and healthy negotiation for an agreed-upon solution. But he had seen the coconut husks that had been tossed into a pile on the roadway. He knew where Hendrik was going.

Besides, they needed to get to the car ferry dock, which was forty-five minutes beyond the police truck.

Ni Luh showed them a petrol can in a shed further back from the house.

'Stay inside for about an hour. Don't come out,' Hendrik said to her. 'Flynn, are you coming with me?'

Flynn nodded. 'Grab your shillelagh and let's get at this.'

Bending low, carrying two small containers, they moved back up the road towards the entrance, past the trucks to the small mounds of coconut husks.

Hendrik splashed the petrol across the husks and lit the edge of one of them. 'A fire won't burn much, but the smoke should be enough of a distraction for us to head towards Bali.'

'Plus keep the mosquitoes down for the evening,' Flynn observed.

They scurried back through the jungle to the kitchen and waited.

As they were examining the last bungalow, the two police caught sight of the flames flickering through the underbrush. The coconut husks were now gleefully engulfed in the bonfire, burning hot and then quickly dissolving into a red ember glow.

By the time the police had gotten water buckets to the site, the mounds had smouldered into ashes.

Flynn and Henrick edged around the side to the front courtyard. Flynn got into the driver's seat of their truck while Hendrik crouched down in the back seat.

Flynn turned right, noting the police barely glanced at the single person in the vehicle, still busy stomping on the last of the ash.

Twenty minutes later, Flynn's curiosity got the better of him.

'Do you think they were looking for us, Hendrik?'

'I don't know. Animals in Africa are always interested in us. We are all part of the food chain, although we aren't the tastiest morsel. I use the cautious approach. Create a diversion. Avoid confrontation. It's safer than butting heads and often more effective.'

Flynn looked at his mobile. 'Grand. We have a couple of days left before we fly out of here to Oz. We've still got four people to find. One of them may have seen Gemi and Diah on that day. One small glimpse, so I know they made it out of our house before it caught fire.'

'Well, Bali is radically different to Java. Maybe the 'wild life' on Bali will also be different,' Hendrik added.

Chapter 38

An Old Stick in the Mud

Flood warnings issued by Nelson's Emergency Management continued throughout the night, along with cautions about landslips and obstructions. Driving in the storm was only for emergencies. Evacuations had started from the flooded homes along the Maitai River. Several slips had occurred in the region, including a major landslide along Bisley Avenue coming up from Tahunanui Beach.

The garage door grumbled and rattled as it rolled up at two in the morning. Ric woke up, gently shifting Elaina's head from his shoulder. She let out a soft murmur of protest, then went back to sleep.

Ric padded to the upper hallway that opened into a two-storey atrium glass wall. It had a direct view of the native garden below and the garage window up above. A dull white light from the garage cast a glow on the garden. *Who is in there?*

He dressed quickly, slipped on rain gear and exited the front door. The garage was open. The rain hadn't relented—the drains were overflowing and the iron roof sounded like kettledrums in a jam session.

Someone was moving down the side of the hill from the garage. Not far away was a large swathe of land, well known for its past slump activities. The person on the hillside was wearing a head torch which glowed in the distance like a firefly. From the occasional splash of light, Ric could see they were wearing yellow rain gear.

Ric swapped out his already soaked tennis shoes for the gumboots he had stashed in the garage. He picked up a head torch from the gear shelf and headed down the slope, moving carefully towards the light. The ground near the fringe of the slump had become a quagmire of mud, fine silts and flowing water.

The rain had cut deep erosion paths in the hillside, which were made worse by recent earthworks in the area. A property owner had removed the vegetation and attempted to re-contour the land. The slushy mud became its own gigantic wave, flowing down in spurts towards the houses below that fronted the state highway.

The headlamp light was being ferociously whipped around, casting small beams through the wind and rain, which assaulted the hillside with no remorse.

Ric arrived at a major crevice in the hillside where a fissure had forced the land to release its hold on several tonnes of soil. A large portion had slipped down the hill. It felt like he was walking on a mud avalanche as he took one exacting footstep at a time. He held onto to the scarce plants and trees still rooted in the soil, at least for the moment.

Coming over a rise, he careened down the hill, slipping and skidding, finally stopping before a former dirt trail. The trail was now a continuous mud ooze of slime. The back of the man with the yellow rain slicker was ahead of him.

John Peters was knee-deep in mud, and was using his hands to clear the slush away from a person's head and upper body so the man could breathe.

'Pappa! Pappa, what are you doing?' Ric yelled.

John looked up. His face was smeared with streaks of brown. 'Ric, help me get this damn idiot out of this muck!'

The person was up to their chest in the mud. John's slippery fingers were losing their grip on the man's clothes!

'If this gets much more above his chest … we won't be able to get him out!' John spat out his plea, trying to communicate while the wind stole his words.

Ric knew burial at chest height was the death zone and could lead to suffocation.

'He may have hurt his leg … or arm! Can't tell. He's in a lot of pain!'

As John turned, he lost his balance, falling into the river of mud himself. Ric grabbed at his father's yellow rain jacket. His fingers clenched his father's arm, then shoulder, and Ric managed to pull him out towards the edge. The storm was unceasingly intense. Nature had struck back.

'You sit there, Pappa. I'll go alongside. With the both of us, I think we can get him up!' Ric pointed.

The man in the mud burial pit seemed to have lost consciousness. Or he was zoned out with fear.

John nodded. 'Pull slowly … but steadily. It's like a snow avalanche. And it's sucking him down!'

The rain was harsh. Inflexible. The flow of water around them was rising. New water pathways flowed through the soft soil and underbelly of the increasing slump. It felt like the entire hillside was moving. Silt and debris-laden water continued to cascade over some of the sharp angles, with large chunks of land breaking free and heading down the hill towards Rocks Road. Ric could hear sirens on the roadway below them.

A howling emerged from the mud as John and Ric pulled together. A high-pitched shout and then moaning. In the darkness and rain, with mud caked on the face, they hadn't seen who it was. The silt and mud began to release Ernest Bennett from its sucking embrace. One arm was freed from the grip of the cement-like soil.

'Look, we have his arms out! What the hell is Ernest doing in the slump?' John coached Ric to pull Ernest's arms and his chest, unshackling him from the bonding action. For a brief moment John clutched at his own chest.

With Ric applying constant pressure, the rest of Ernest's body slid out, though he was barefoot as his gumboots were left somewhere in the mud slide.

'Let's get him to the grass and out of this,' John said. 'There's something wrong with his arm.'

Ric triaged Ernest quickly. With the wild wind, raging rain and the mud swirling around, he couldn't tell if Ernest was breathing. Then he felt it. Ernest still had a pulse.

'Prop his head back,' John said to Ric. He cleared Ernest's mouth and airway, then despite Ric's protest, John leaned over and began mouth-to-mouth resuscitation as the rain beat down.

After several minutes there was a low groan, a cough and Ernest vomited up water.

Ric watched as his father functioned manically. There's something going on with him. Why is he touching his chest?

'Pappa, let me take it from here.' Ric rolled Ernest to his side to expel the excess water. 'We've got to get him out of here. I think this whole hillside is slipping. Let's sling him out somehow.'

'We can tie our rain jackets together at the sleeves. Make a kind of cradle.'

Ric nodded. His father was not the Constant Gardener. But definitely the Constant Inventor. They made a makeshift sling out of the jackets. Ernest was still breathing as they put the cradle around him. Slowly they lifted Ernest up the hill, following the now waterlogged trail. Halfway up another part of the hill—a mud slab—cut loose and headed towards Rocks Road, crashing into a house below. The hillside was collapsing. They kept bearing towards the upper edge.

The pace was slow and tiring, and the storm unabating. After thirty minutes they could see the outline of The Cliff House garage.

'Let's get him near the garage and under the eaves. The ambulance can come down the driveway,' Ric said. He had hefted Ernest up the hill for the last half of the haul. His father was struggling to breathe. Ric got Ernest to the bottom of drive and went back to help his father up the steep cliff. In the garage, he pulled out a camp chair for John to sit by Ernest.

'Don't move. I'll be a minute.'

Ric ran down the entry steps to the front door.

Years ago, his father had bought a ship's bell and installed it by the front door. Ric rang the bell, which clanged loudly, then he opened the door and called out, 'Mum! Elaina!'

Elaina was up the stairs first, with Kiri following.

'What's happened?'

Ric was covered in mud, brown slime from his hair to his gumboots. 'Make a call to Triple One! Ernest Bennett was trapped in the mud. Pappa went to get him out.'

Ten minutes later an ambulance arrived. Ernest's body and clothes were smeared with mud from the hillside, but he was alive. As the four of them waited in the garage, Ernest was hoisted onto a gurney, given oxygen, then transported to hospital.

'This has been a very long evening. Or perhaps a jump start to an early morning,' John announced, still sitting in the camp chair.

'I can't believe we got him up here,' Ric said, putting a hand on his father's back. His father had seemed to sluff down into the chair with the same whooshing sound as the hill collapsing around them a short while ago.

'All right, you two, we need to get out of this garage' Kiri directed. 'Elaina, I'll get John into a shower and you and Ric—' Kiri looked over at John.

John's smile became quizzical, his face slackened, and as he stood up he weaved. His lined face winced with pain and then he let out a grunting moan. John began to cough and sputter. Blood came out of his nose. And he collapsed.

Kiri and Ric each caught an arm. Elaina didn't need direction; she was dialling Triple One.

'We need another ambulance. Yes, same address.' Elaina described the emergency and the need for urgency.

Ric helped Kiri place his father on a mat over the concrete cement floor. As his father lay there, the blood continued to run. For a moment Ric's mind seemed to frost over. Then he went into automatic rescue mode. He layered a wool blanket from the camping gear onto his father and raised him slightly off his back.

Kiri's face was taut and her mouth firm. She muttered, 'Hurry up! Hurry up! Where's that ambulance!' Then in a strained voice she said, 'Elaina, can you please call Emergency again?'

The ambulance finally arrived and picked John up. Kiri rode with him to hospital, her hand clutching John's.

Ric stood in the driveway, tears falling, indistinguishable from the rain streaming down his face. 'I was just beginning to know who he is,' he said. He stared at the concrete where his Pappa's blood had pooled. The storm pummelled the red stream and washed it down the drain.

CHAPTER 39

TRACKING MANDU: WATER, WATER, EVERYWHERE

Bali, Indonesia

Arriving on the island of Bali from the ferryboat, 'wild life' is exactly what Flynn and Hendrik found. The island of Bali is almost an exact opposite of Java. The overriding difference is the number of Australians and New Zealanders who vacation on Bali, making it a holiday hot spot. 'Hot' applied to both the weather and the liberties available to the vacationing consumer.

The religious orientation was different. The development was different. The feel of the countryside and look of the people were different. And there was a huge party scene prevalent on Bali.

The Bali police were interested in the 'wild life', but in a different way than the tourists. They knew that Bali was an international amusement park and one of the 'cash cows' of Indonesia. Its contribution to the Indonesian economy was significant. The police on Bali had become the security patrols to keep the tourists safe, happy and, importantly, continuing to spend money. Opportunistic criminals (including drug dealers) who preyed on holidaymakers were the main police target.

The Blue Light Patrol first spotted Flynn and Hendrik coming off the ferry. They weren't exactly dressed like tourists, and they didn't exactly act like tourists. They didn't ask anyone for directions. They didn't check their phones for the weather. They didn't stop at a tourist spot to eat. The patrol noted the licence plate of their SUV and circulated it for further investigation.

Denpasar is in the southern end of Bali and has an array of beaches for every water sport, colourful local markets for souvenirs and photo-snapping, restaurants and bars in and out of the water, and even a turtle conservation centre for the environmentally minded.

It's the fun spot where most tourists go. Some never leave, and then depart on a plane, having 'seen' Bali.

However, Flynn and Hendrik did not head to Denpasar, the largest city.

Flynn and Hendrik turned left after exiting the ferry terminal, aiming for the north shore and the Buddhist monastery Brahmavihara-Arama. While Surabaya's monastery had been built to blend into the area and culture, Brahmavihara-Arama was built to stand out, looking like a remnant of the 13th century, although it was a product of the 1970s.

Arriving at the four hectares of land, Flynn took in the numerous meditation rooms, libraries and gardens that were layered up the hillside.

'Bit of a contrast from the Jambi compound,' Flynn commented, gazing at the colourful decorations, Balinese ornamental carvings and bright orange roofs with numerous Buddha statues.

'And this one has a doorman,' noted Hendrik, eyeing the tall Buddha statue beyond the entry. They entered the monastery, walked past an imposing set of red gates and up to the doorman. The large statue's hand looked like he was indicating '*Stop*' with his open palm.

In reality it was a sign of peace, benevolence and protection. They went right in.

They had no problem finding monks at the site. And since Bali's tourism depended on Australian and other tourists, Flynn and Hendrik's accents were easily understood. They were directed to the Dharmasala room, a space used for giving lectures. A younger monk had. concluded his lecture on *Finding the Perfect Heaven*.

As the attendees were getting up off their mats and filing out of the Dharmasala, Flynn plunged into his soliloquy on why they were there.

'Of course I've heard of Mandu Olda,' the young monk said with an Aussie sounding accent. He was gathering his notes from a small stand. While his head was bald, his eyes were blue and his accent wasn't local. Hendrik realised this monk *was* from Oz.

The Australian monk was also talkative. 'I wasn't here when Mandu arrived about a year and a half ago. I was travelling from Sydney, via Auckland up to Bali. I had stayed in a small town outside of Auckland for a few nights. It was in a Buddhist monastery in the Forest Tradition. I almost missed seeing Mandu. But we overlapped a day here on Bali and we chatted about what each of us was doing. So I did hear all about your village, Mr Flynn. I am very sorry for you.'

The ever-focused Hendrik zeroed in. 'We know that Mandu brought four people with him to Bali. There were originally seven that he rescued from our area. Do you know what happened to these people? Perhaps they are all here on Bali?'

'I definitely know the two people that remained in Bali. A water engineer and his wife. He is quite famous in our region for his technical skills in the water management systems. Water distribution is very important on Bali and is part of the Subak system.'

The Aussie monk seemed to have studied this in depth. Hendrik wagered he was a university kid testing out alternatives. 'Wasn't the water system part of the Hindu religion at one time?'

'Yes, it was, Mr Hendrik. It's still administered by temple priests. The water engineer's name is Dasur Almat and his wife's name is Ida Agung. He has even come here and lectured in this room about the Subak system.'

'Where is he now?' Flynn asked.

'Not far away. In a town called Gobleg near one of the Subak water system regions.'

'And the other two people? We understood there was a young man and a boy.'

'Sorry, I don't know much about them. I think Mandu said he was taking them to another island in the north, but I don't know which one. Did you know there are 17,508 islands here in Indonesia?'

'We've heard,' said Hendrik while thinking they had two days before heading back to Australia. Time for one quick pass through one spot somewhere else … and that was it.

~~~

Towards Gobleg, near the Subuk Water System of Catur Angga Batukaru, Bali

Gobleg was about an hour from the coastal town of Banjar. Coming down the hillside from where the monastery sat, they stopped at a local
~~~

guest house for food. Their meals for the past two weeks had been the same: rice, local vegetables and chicken, when it was available. Flynn thought it was chicken, but he wasn't always sure. At least one time he thought he had eaten snake.

'This doesn't look promising, does it, Hendrik?' Flynn asked, thinking he really had nothing to return to, except an empty house in Tasmania and his dog, Charlie.

'Looking forward to some different tucker, Flynn,' said Hendrik, eyeing the current dish before him and wondering about the colour of the 'chicken'. He would eat the odd African animal but at the mentioned of Flynn's dog, he put his fork down.

'You liked taking care of Charlie, didn't you?' Flynn asked, pushing the meal away.

Hendrik's head snapped up. 'Stop talking like that, Flynn. Charlie's a downright good dog, but he's not *my* dog. Let's get back on the road,' he said. 'Too much time in one spot.'

From the monastery on the northern coast, Hendrik and Flynn travelled on the two-lane road up from the main highway and into the mountains, making a gentle climb past rice fields and patches of vegetables, along with fruit orchards.

The topography towards Gobleg was a rich tapestry of green fields and natural lush vegetation. Small villages, farms and clutches of dwellings were strewn across the landscape. Mangoes, bananas, guavas, avocados and papayas were plentiful. It was February in Bali—the growing season.

Hendrik pulled into a compound off a side road not far from the main village. Dasur Almat and his wife, Ida, had a modest house and massive garden. Vegetables, fruit trees, native plants—a botanical garden with a trickling waterfall nearby.

A man with a scythe approached them from the garden. He had paused in cutting the grass, but the scythe remained in his hand.

Flynn decided another approach was necessary before he got to his request. He was running out of options for information. He needed someone's memory of what happened at his village.

'I understand you're an expert in water,' Flynn said.

The man paused, then put the scythe down. 'Who is asking me this question?'

'My name is Flynn O'Neill, and this is Hendrik Ackerman. We used to live near Jambi in Sumatra.'

Dasur decided to answer since the man asked about his favourite topic and at least this foreigner knew where Jambi was.

'Water is sacred here. The Goddess of Life. We have a system here in Bali that helps control the water. It's an ancient and intricate irrigation system. It plays a pivotal role in our agriculture and cultural heritage.'

Hendrik saw where Flynn was going. 'Yes, I've read about this system too. It started in the ninth century, and it's still used today. The water system and the fields are connected to temples. Is that right?'

'You are very knowledgeable,' said Dasur, eyeing Hendrik suspiciously. Even in Bali the police were always watching.

'Yes, there are Temple priests who practise Tri Hita Karana. They keep an eye on the timing and coordination to control water flow.'

Dasur invited them to his porch. His wife brought tea and the real conversation began.

'I have been to a place near your village. I was there to help the area set up their water system. But in the end it didn't happen. The people who attacked those villages were not interested in water. Not for the villages. Only for the palm oil trees. We escaped with the help of a man named Mandu Olda. Do you know him?'

'Yes,' said Flynn. He was relieved he didn't have to mention Mandu himself. 'I'm looking for two people who were in my village at the time. I'm searching for my wife and child. I was hoping you might have seen them when you were leaving. Or perhaps the other two people with you, the man and the boy, might have seen them.'

'When we left, we were hiding most of the time,' Dasur said. 'Travel was difficult. There were police patrols everywhere. We did stop at several places. One was a monks' house next to a Buddhist Temple site. Another time, we stopped in the Kangean Islands near western Java. Then we came to Bali. Mandu had made a promise to me. He promised my wife and me that he would bring us home.'

Flynn was an emotional wreck sitting in the sun on the sweltering porch. Was this it? Was this the end of it? He waited for more.

'I remember the two sisters very well. We were all very scared at the time, but I tried to offer comfort to them. The other two people that you spoke of travelled with us to Bali,' Dasur said. 'There was a young man and a young boy. I don't know if the boy was a relative of the man or a friend. The man was very protective of the child. Always holding his hand. Always putting his jacket over the child when it rained.'

'Did the child have a name?' asked Flynn, his voice trembling.

'Everyone was frightened. We rarely spoke. We were terrified at what we had seen and what we were trying to escape.' Dasur shuddered, even now remembering the fear of being in hiding. 'Mandu was worried about reprisals for any of us who witnessed what happened in the villages. I am sorry that I do not have all the information that you want. I worry each day that someone will come up the drive. That they are looking for us and not to simply talk like you have done.' Dasur wiped his brow.

There was a long pause in the conversation. There were no words that Flynn could say. No more questions he could ask.

Hendrik helped his friend to the rental vehicle. They would get to Denpasar and take the first plane out of Bali. Maybe heading back to Australia was their best option. It was really the only option left.

CHAPTER 40

KNOWING IS TRUSTING

Elaina grabbed Ric's arm. 'Ric, we need to get to the hospital to see your father. I'll drive, get in.' She hit the ignition, and the glow plugs in FJ-Orion warmed up and the engine fired on the first crank. Ric sat in the passenger seat, numb and still cold. He had stripped off the muddy clothes and donned a pair of coveralls. Elaina negotiated the long drive and onto the street, en route to Nelson General Hospital.

Dawn had come and gone unnoticed. The sky was still dark and filled with massive rain clouds, but the rain was subsiding. It had already broken hundred-year-old records. But there was always an opportunity to break another record the next time. Not to be outdone by the rain, the Maitai River had exceeded historical flood levels and also set a new record.

A State of Emergency had been declared for the Nelson-Tasman region. Hundreds of homes evacuated. Lives disrupted. People cut off from families, stores, schools and the rest of New Zealand. Rocks Road, a major arterial road, was closed and slips dotted the landscape. Nelson slowed down with the pace of passing one road cone after another.

The impact of what was going on in the world outside the emergency waiting room was unknown to the three people … still waiting.

'Hi, you're the Peters family?' A doctor finally appeared.

'Yes,' Elaina said instinctively. 'I mean they are …'

'We are,' Kiri corrected Elaina, patting her knee.

The doctor pressed on with the update. 'Mr Peters is resting. We have him on oxygen and medication. He had a ruptured blood vessel in his sinus. I'm being cautious about this. We're going to run some more tests this morning and we have him stabilised. We need to keep him here overnight and ensure he stays calm. Do you know if he was doing anything strenuous before this happened?'

No one said anything, then Ric spoke. 'He's probably overdone it for the past ten days or so.' Ric filled him in on their activities.

'Well, that certainly is an uptick in cardio exercise, as well as the stress levels. It may have been the trigger,' the physician said. 'If you'd like, I think you *should* see him for a moment.'

The doctor's last comment was a warning bell in Ric's head. Kiri picked it up as well.

The intensive care unit was in subdued light—never day and never night. Time stood still and was measured by heart monitor blips, the sound of intravenous warning signals and respirators pumping.

John was lying slightly elevated with supplemental oxygen delivered through two soft prongs placed in his nose. A drip feed from an IV bottle was attached to his arm. His chest was strapped up to monitors. Ric noticed his blood pressure was low and his heart rate and respirations were higher. His heart monitor blipped along.

John opened his eyes, started to speak. He closed his eyes for a few seconds, then tried again. 'Ric, you have to find Salvy's cabin. I have to know. Was that his skull? Was that his body buried at the farm? I have to know … Please, Ric. Do this for me before … ' John stopped and closed his eyes.

For the last year, Ric had no knowledge that anything had happened to Salvy. The lack of communication between him and his father extended to brief chats without content. Coming to Nelson had brought one discovery after another. The skull that his father had so carefully handled might have been a man they both had tremendous respect for. Each discovery created a personal connection and riveted Ric's focus.

A few days ago he could see that helping his father was a way to earn his trust and confidence and maybe stitch up their broken relationship. He felt *now* their future could ride on him finding Salvy's cabin.

A young doctor came to check John.

'He's stable, but very tired. We'll keep on oxygen for a while. He really wanted to see you and he's somewhat of a persistent man. I'd say a little stubborn.' The doctor grinned.

'Of course he is,' Kiri said, relieved that John was stable. 'He's the original Dutch boy holding his finger in the dike.'

CHAPTER 41

REALITY IS WHAT YOU ARE LOOKING AT

The Cliff House, Nelson, South Island

With John in the hospital, Kiri came back to the house to get a few things, then she'd return.

Elaina made a breakfast of blueberry pancakes and brought it to Ric and Kiri at the dining table where they were studying maps on their mobiles, as well as cross-referencing two hiking maps.

'What do you think Ernest was doing down in the slump during the deluge?' Ric asked his mum. 'He was insane to be out there. Alone. Unprepared.'

'Ernest and that other character, Odell Rodman, are involved in real estate purchases and development all around the region.' Kiri paused, thinking. 'Possibly Odell sent Ernest to check and see if one of their properties was still there.'

Elaina added background details. She had researched Ric's photos taken of documents from the box at Baxter's house. 'Most of the properties aren't in their names but set up with some complex arrangements and held in trusts. I think Reid Baxter is the majority shareholder for a large number of them. The properties are in varying stages of development, with roads, housing and utilities being planned.'

Kiri continued. 'And if that land is slumping, on a cliff, or near a river? It doesn't matter, as long as they can off-sell it, and the initial purchase was relatively cheap. Odell, and maybe even Baxter, probably wanted to know if there was still something to sell.'

Ric was pondering why his father went out to save Ernest. 'I think Pappa must have heard something in the middle of the night. Then when he went outside, he must have seen Ernest moving around. If he hadn't gone out, Ernest would have taken up residence on Rocks Road with the rest of the mud and debris.'

'Like father, like son, pushing the boundaries,' said Elaina. 'I saw the photograph with the story of the boy in the Maitai. The inner tube incident and the rescue.'

Ric shrugged. 'As the doctor said early this morning, we were seeking an uptick in the cardio. By the way, Elaina, I want to show you another photo. This image is from Hendrik when he was in Tasmania.' Ric shared the photo of the 'quirky man' with Elaina. 'Remember our day on the beach at the Bay of Fires?'

She glanced at the photo of the man. 'Yes, I remember *that* day!'

Kiri looked up from the map of Golden Bay. 'I was thinking that your father's like the Dutch boy who stays up all night despite the rain, cold or slagging mud. He thinks he can delay any impending disaster. But he is human … like the rest of us, Ric.'

Elaina could see Kiri was good at sentences with two meanings. She turned her focus to the maps. 'Do you really think Salvy's cabin is in Golden Bay, like Gill mentioned yesterday?'

Ric answered her. 'Gill is one source. I checked a programme that uses AI to analyse the images in the photograph. It examines the shadows cast by those images.'

'You make this stuff up, don't you, Ric! Shadows? Why shadows?' Elaina asked.

'The AI assesses the height of objects, and the length and position of shadows that are cast by the objects. It considers the sky or background in the picture. I found matches in two areas along the Aorere River.' Ric pointed out the meandering river slithering around thc Wakamarama Range in Golden Bay.

'The thing about AI,' said Kiri, 'is that it can't capture all the choices that humans routinely make. Sometimes we make wrong choices that turn out all right. And it sure doesn't have passion for what it's doing, like you two do. And with that, I'm off to the hospital. Please keep in touch.'

Elaina looked at the map where Ric was headed. The Southern Alps were one of most rapidly rising mountain ranges in the world. It was a collision of tectonic plates, like a head-on of two trucks on the interstate highway. The collision forced the mountains upwards. Earthquakes, tsunamis, and geothermal activity and volcanic eruptions were all in a day's work in New Zealand.

Ric would be traversing a remote wilderness where help, hospitals and helo pads weren't necessarily available. He looked again at the two options of where Salvy's picture could have been taken. For him, it was better odds than some of the journeys he had travelled in the past.

~~~

Wagon Wheel Inn, Takaka, Tasman District

They rolled into Takaka mid-morning and parked off the main street. At the café, they didn't have to tell Astrid what coffees they wanted. This was Takaka, after all. Everyone knew everyone else's business and, of course, their coffee preferences.

Despite the unexpected travel over Takaka Hill, they were noticed by a man in a blue truck across the street from the café.

At the nearby Wagon Wheel Inn, sipping her takeaway coffee, Elaina signed in and chatted with Helen at the front desk. Ric moved the gear into their room. As he made the second trip in from the Land Cruiser, he thought he saw the blue truck across the street in a driveway.

Ric's mind was ticking off options. Was the blue truck from Takaka or from Motueka? But he didn't see the truck when he headed back out for the last of their gear.

Elaina had two phones that could be used as hot spots for data and communications. Ric had charged up a wireless device for his laptop. They had backup devices for boosting the net if needed.

Ric rented an upscale Personal Location Beacon (PLB) that he would carry with him, accessing two-way messaging, which he figured he could use. It had interactive SOS alerts, which he hoped *not* to use.

Helen at reception kept peering round the corner as they moved things in. They were such a nice couple. Why did they need all those gadgets? What were they up to?

All sorts of mischief and mayhem flowed through her mind, fuelled by an immense imagination and nightly reading of books related to crime-solving and romance. She always loved the line, 'Police suspect foul play'. She was on the lookout for any foul play in Takaka.
~~~

She wondered if this couple were like those movie people that came through every once in a while. The ones who filmed risqué movies on the beach and in the mountains. Hopefully this young woman hadn't fallen on hard times and this was how she was earning money. After all, Helen ran a respectable and clean operation.

In the room, Ric flicked on his beacon and within seconds the blip appeared on Elaina's screen. The map system could be extended in all directions and covered the area where Ric would be.

'The beacon will broadcast my position continuously. You can use the programme to track me,' Ric said.

'Gee. You should wear one of these things all the time,' Elaina said, her eyes wide.

'Yes, I could do that. It certainly is an option. On a more serious note, if there is an emergency, call Triple One and then call this number.' Ric flicked Elaina a text. 'Tell the person my name, your name, the location and the nature of the emergency.'

'I don't want to be a widow before I'm married.'

'Don't worry, you'd have smarter guys knocking on your door in minutes.'

'I have a smart guy!' Elaina replied. 'He's engaged to me!'

'I wish I was smart enough to figure why Salvy's place doesn't show up on the satellite images close to where the GPS says it should be. I ran the analysis several times and then went back and did it manually.'

'Satellite images are not always up to date. The cabin might have been destroyed, burned down, flooded over.'

Ric finished getting his gear together. He gave Elaina a kiss on the back of her neck, as she sat in front of the equipment and computers.

'All right command centre, I'll be checking comms with you to ensure everything is okay. I'll ask front desk for transportation to the Aorere River.'

He first asked Helen to keep an eye on Elaina.

Helen nodded. Okay, cancel the risqué movie scenario. This guy really likes her. 'I pegged you two as an item. I usually have a dinner break at the Wholemeal Café. I'll take her with me. Do you need any help where you're going, young man?' she asked.

'No, I'm okay,' Ric said. 'On the other hand, I could use a lift to near the Aorere River.'

Helen's mind went into overdrive. A love-struck couple escaping entanglements? Another husband or wife? A forbidden love? No parental consent? Scratch. They're older than that. The possibilities however were endless. And this was happening at her hotel. "My partner can take you."

Soon afterwards Franklin, Helen's partner, slipped into his Land Rover with Ric and headed towards a trail head on the Aorere River.

In the blue truck, parked down the road from the Roots Bar, the conversation to Cornwall, D'Urville Island, Marlborough Sounds was brief.

'I'll stay on him. He's heading out of town towards the south. Do you want me to pay the girl a visit later on?'

The voice on the end simply growled, 'Not now!'

'Okay, I'll focus on him. That Land Cruiser is still there. She isn't going anywhere without him.'

The caller rang off.

~~~

Trailhead, access to the Aorere River, Golden Bay

At the trail head, Franklin exchanged mobile numbers with Ric.

'If you need a pickup, let me know,' Franklin said.

On the way back, Franklin passed another vehicle heading up the hill. He raised his index finger on the steering wheel and the driver on the other side of the road did the same. He usually saw that same vehicle come into town about once a month and head up this way.

Franklin routinely received some brown trout when the nomadic driver travelled back out after a few days. The brown trout caught in this area were generally the largest fish in Golden Bay. He was already thinking of how he was going to grill them.

Ric paced himself as he trudged up the trail. He had several hours of slogging ahead of him. The trail was connected to a national park system that meandered into the mountains.

His first target area was south along the Aorere River, where the trail passed close by private property. There were areas that had been washed out with small slips and blockages.

Within an hour he was climbing through combinations of forests and fields as he worked his way up through mountain meadows and valleys.
~~~

This was gold country, the site of many previous digs and sluicing operations. The river was running high with see-through blue water. The afternoon waned with the shadows growing. He could imagine Salvy down by the river, casting for fish.

An hour later, he came along a stretch of the river that ran straight, then curved angling off. Ric texted a position check with Elaina. She spotted him on the programme and noted that his track and position were fixed on the screen.

You're close to location No 2, she texted back. *Do you see anything at all?*

Spot on with the GPS calculations. But reality doesn't match photo. Maybe on the wrong side.

Reality is what you're looking at now. Careful crossing the river.

I'll work something up and keep dry.

Ric went closer to the river at a point where it narrowed. Remembering what the Emergency Management team had done at the Maitai River, he tossed a line across with a grapple. It stuck in a tree, and he pulled it taut and tied it off. The line dipped as he scampered across, pulling his pack on a loop behind him.

When he looked around, it still didn't seem correct. He reported in.

Don't see anything. I should be on top of this. The river is on my left now.

You'll find it.

There's a short trail on this side. Looks like a small saddle for a broader view.

The saddle was up a scree pile of loose material and several larger rocks next to the river. He climbed to the top and looked back towards the point he had calculated on the map, then pulled up the beacon ready to text Elaina … and stopped.

He could clearly see the rifle and scope aimed directly at him. Targeting his head.

Ric lowered the beacon to his waist. A man stood directly above him on a rocky ridge. The 270 Winchester pointed at Ric's head, as if he were the black silhouette on a shooting target.

Odell Rodman leered down at Ric, licking his lips. Nervous. An animal gone mad. He had a large wound on his forehead that hadn't healed.

Ric remembered the dialogue with Detective Parkhurst. He realised it had been Odell in the speedboat in Marlborough. And whoever Malcolm Sloan was, likely Odell had found his ID somewhere.

Ric scanned for potential cover. There was none. He was in the open. A tactical mistake. Maybe his last. Exposed high ground. Excellent target for Odell.

The river was to his left—a sharp drop-off from the scree pile. He'd probably not survive the fall onto the rocks and water. The tree line was too far away.

Rodman had a steady bead on Ric. This was it.

As Ric turned to check below, the scree gave way beneath his left foot.

Rodman squeezed the trigger.

A microsecond after, a separate shot rang out. Dust kicked up near Rodman's foot. Rodman stumbled and fired again.

The scree continued to slough off.

Another shot cracked in the still air.

Ric was on a death slide down the slope towards a sheer drop-off. Rocks and a tumultuous river waited below.

He couldn't grasp anything to slow his fall, or even try to dig his feet in somehow. Panic stabbed through his guts. He was sliding to his death and he couldn't stop.

Odell staggered sideways. *Where the hell were those shots coming from?* Missing a step, he dropped his rifle at the top of the ridge and it slid down the loose material on the side.

He tried hobbling over the rocks, but kept losing his balance. A fifth shot echoed.

Damn, that missed my leg! Who else is out here? Someone who's a good shot.

Odell moved diagonally across the hillside, coming back to the trail. He couldn't even see Ric at the bottom of the scree pile.

Maybe he's buried underneath it? Good riddance.

He'd move on to target number two. The woman in the Takaka hotel.

He shuffled back down the trail.

Ric had landed next to a larger rock just above the river and came to rest on his back. His pants were ripped, his hands bleeding from strips of missing skin.

There had been five shots, two from Odell and three from somewhere else. His ankle was beginning to swell and stiffen. He needed to work out a plan to get himself up.

'Anything broken?' a voice yelled down from the top of the ridge.

Ric looked up. Marley's ghost had reappeared. 'George Taylor! What are you doing up there?' Ric shouted.

'I'm the man holding the rifle that stopped that dirty mongrel from plugging you,' George replied. 'He wanted to drop your carcass in the water. I was making myself useful.'

George stood on a cliff above him. Behind George, Ric sighted the roofline of a small building. It wasn't next to the river as depicted in the photo. It was higher and set back. His position at the bottom of the scree had given him a different perspective.

'Probably could use a rope down here, George,' Ric yelled.

George put his arm through his rifle, slinging it over his shoulder, muzzle down, and disappeared from view.

Ric waited a short time, and a rope flew over the edge and down beside him.

'It's tied off to a tree. Can you get up by yourself,' George asked, 'or do you want to me to come down and carry you?'

'My ankle's knackered, but I think I can get up to you,' Ric answered, shouldering the pack that had fallen down the scree with him.

'Reckon you're bigger than anything I've ever carried out of the bush. Except maybe that buck deer. Now that one was a beaut. Take your time there, Ric. Sun's not setting for at least twenty minutes.'

At the top of the scree, Ric hauled himself over the edge. He readjusted his small backpack and limped over to George.

George reeled in the line and looped it up, alpine style. 'You're not going anywhere tonight on that leg. We're hours away and darkness is coming.' George had evaluated the weather, the time, and distances with one look around.

Ric was having a hard time standing with his bashed ankle. 'We might be able to stay in that place I spotted. It's up from the river, on that promontory.'

George looked around. He wondered if the recent stress had affected Ric's memory. 'There's no hotel here, Ric.'

'That fishing shack behind you!' Ric replied, pointing to the top of the hill.

Finally spotting the roof outline, George asked, 'What's a fishing shack doing up there?' It was well camouflaged in the trees.

'I think they moved it,' Ric said. 'Piece by piece, or maybe using a sledge.'

George and Ric slowly climbed up the hillside and crested to a small meadow and a grove of trees.

'Well, Bob's your uncle,' George said, looking at the foundation and the way the cabin was affixed. 'There's a farm somewhere in Golden Bay with Clydesdale horses. Must have come up a forestry road somewhere and used the horses. They hauled it up and out from the river's edge.'

'A river runs through it,' Ric muttered.

'Well, maybe it used to,' George said, putting his hand on the cabin. 'Sweet as … but I need a cuppa.'

The cabin was square with a gabled roof, windows, outside benches, and the door Ric had seen in the original photograph. His mum had said that AI can't capture all the choices that humans routinely make. AI hadn't accounted for the human desire to move the cabin and the satellite imaging that hadn't caught up.

'I reckon the key to the lock is probably out back somewhere.'

George ambled around while Ric took in the view. Then he looked at the sign above the door.

Made from Logs and Sticks from the Aorere River.

Elaina was right. Arabella wasn't talking about the River Styx. She was recalling the sign above the door.

'The key was near the dunny! I can find a house key every time,' George announced, glancing at the sign.

The lock clicked open on the first try.

Ric stood on the threshold. His ankle was throbbing. He was hungry and tired. But this was the mission he wanted to complete for his father.

'Push the door open, lad,' George said.

Ric did as he was told, and it creaked as it swung inwards. Light filtered in through dirt-stained windows.

Cardboard record boxes lined the back wall with labels on the lids, block writing identifying their contents.

There was a small wash basin, with a shaving kit, hairbrush, toothbrush, a glass, and a bottle of Barber's Bay Rum to splash on after a shave.

Ric had their sample. Any one of these would produce the DNA needed for comparison. He set his bag down. Next to the Barber's Bay Rum was an envelope addressed to his father. 'To my friend John Peters from your friend Salvatore Marino.' Ric put the tan envelope into his pocket. It was perhaps the most important thing in this hut because it was addressed to his pappa from Salvy.

The boxes along the wall contained details of the waste disposal from various sites. There was significant disposal from the factory at Parásita that occurred both on the plant site and on neighbouring properties like the Paxtons'. But there were also several records of chemicals sent to the newer production site in the countryside.

Near the bed was another box marked Logbooks. Ric hobbled over and popped the lid off. The eleven lab books sat inside. He pulled out Number Eleven, sat down in the wooden chair near the wood burner and began to read. Ric now understood Salvy's dilemma.

'The owners of Parásita knew what they were doing to the people around the area,' Ric said, looking up.

'Of course they knew,' George said. 'But they sure as hell weren't going to stop.'

'These boxes and lab books expose everything they were doing.'

'Well, lad, we'll spend the night here and you can tell me all about it,' George said. 'I'll get the fire going. I've got a brace of rabbits in my pack. There are some greens out back and some wild berries.'

Ric checked his beacon. He texted and didn't receive an answer. He tried his mobile. No answer. Another text. *Where is she?*

It would be hard, if not impossible, to make it down the trail in the dark. He needed to get strapping on his leg, or he wouldn't even reach the trail. He tried calling again. And again. There was no answer.

Ric suddenly realised that if Odell knew where he was, he would also know where Elaina was. *What have I done?*

Chapter 42

Night Crawlers

Wagon Wheel Inn, Takaka, Golden Bay
Elaina couldn't reach Ric on his mobile. He hadn't called in when he was supposed to. Then Ric's beacon seemed to shut off. She could only message. She left eleven messages.

Had the beacon malfunctioned? She watched on the screen as the beacon had moved swiftly down the mountain. It wasn't the mountain trail. It was an erratic downhill race towards the Aorere River. Then it went dead. She tried every form of communication she could think of. What could she try next?

~~~

Leaving the Aorere River and travelling to Takaka, Golden Bay
Odell scrambled down the trail. He had his pack and headlamp, but had lost his rifle on the hillside. It was dark when he got back to his old blue truck and headed towards Takaka. He was tired and dehydrated, sweating, dirty and sore. The loss of the rifle could be explained. Someone had stolen it. He would report that right away. Truth was not something he ever felt inclined to use.

Everything was unravelling … too fast. He'd had a clear shot, but Peters slipped on the hillside. Someone had shot at him instead. More than once. Who the hell was that? Peters *had* seemed to be trapped in the rockfall. Or maybe he drowned in the river he was headed into. Either way, Odell had other things to do.

He drove slowly. Not the time to get stopped by the coppers. He had two unfinished tasks to take care of. Two things to tie off. Then it would
~~~

be over. No one would be able follow what had happened. All the snooping would be finished.

With each kilometre that passed, Odell got madder. He slammed his fist into the dashboard.

Whether or not Peters is still alive, I'm going to make sure she's taught a lesson. And if he's alive, it'll be something he'll never forget. Neither would that little bitch.

And then there was the mother.

Wagon Wheel Inn, Takaka, Golden Bay

Elaina heard a light tapping on her door. No voice or hello, just a light tapping. She grabbed an iron figurine from the fireplace mantel and went to the door. The chain and safety latch were in place. Her heart was pounding. This wasn't Ric.

~~~

Salvatore's Cabin, Promontory above the Aorere River, Golden Bay, South Island

There was something in Ric's mind. Something that kept coming up. Some small detail he had overlooked. Then it clicked.

The blue truck.

He believed he saw the blue truck again earlier when he was unloading their bags. It was possibly the third time he had seen it. Twice is perhaps coincidence. Three times? Not likely. It had to be Odell's truck. Who else would have been tailing him? How else would he have known that he had gone up the Aorere River?

And his gut feeling was that Odell had set out several objectives. The first objective was to tail him. *Trust your gut, Ric.* If Odell missed out on that 'opportunity', he'd be out to get Elaina. And he knew exactly where she was. He had been across the street from the Wagon Wheel Inn.

Ric pieced this together as he sat in Salvy's cabin. He glanced at the boxes. How could they carry out the boxes? George's camper was likely at the trailhead. They'd have to find another way to get the boxes down. He thought of all this in microseconds. He didn't have time to waste. He had to get down that hill. Ric looked again at his phone, willing a text from Elaina to appear.

Nothing. No connection.
~~~

Odell was out there, but where? Only one logical direction. He had left the Aorere River and headed back to Takaka.

'George, I can't stay here,' Ric said. 'Odell took two shots at me. He knew I was here. He saw me unload our bags in Takaka. He knows where Elaina is. He'll go after her. I have to leave.'

'Now, you don't know that exactly,' George said, getting ready to skin and dress out the rabbits.

'George, you don't understand. I should never have brought her to New Zealand. There's been one incident after another. We should have left as soon as this started happening. I've got to get down the hill and back to Takaka. I need to see if Elaina's okay.'

'Ric, your leg's had it. It's swelling up bigger than an elephant's,' George said. 'You can't walk on that. And how are we going to find our way back in the dark? You're going to damage that leg permanently.'

'It doesn't matter. I have to get down to the parking area, George. Where your camper is.'

'Well, once we get there, if we make it, we're still going to have to get back to Takaka.'

'No, George. My beacon isn't working, but when we're in range I can call Franklin on my mobile,' Ric said. 'I can let him know. He can protect Elaina. Let's go. I can't sit here—I have to get back.'

George took a breath. Ric stood up and hobbled to his bag.

'Ric, it's going to take us hours to walk to the parking area. Odell has a big start on us.'

'Help me get this leg bound up. I see that walking stick hanging by the door. Let's get out of here,' Ric pleaded. 'Odell will go after her. I can't wait until tomorrow. I have to move.'

George looked at Ric. Nothing was going to change this man's mind. He'd thrown reason out with the bathwater.

'Okay, okay, we'll bind up your leg with tape from my bag. Let me find something for a splint,' George said. 'But I'm going with you. At least we have two rifles, thanks to your shooter.'

He found the tape at the bottom of his bag, and two slats for makeshift splints in the woodpile.

Ric tried walking in the cabin with the stick. It was painful, but he could do it. One step at a time. They needed to get going.

Ric started another text as they were getting ready. 'What was that?' he said. 'The rumbling. Did you hear it?'

'I heard it,' George said. 'It's probably Odell. He's the only one around here. Suspect he wants to check to see if you're dead. And if you're not, give it another go. He probably figured out that there's forestry roads around here. They crisscross all over the back country.'

George picked up his rifle and checked the magazine to make sure he had several rounds ready.

The rumble became louder and clearer. A vehicle was definitely approaching across the meadow behind the cabin.

'It's coming closer.' Ric grabbed Odell's rifle off the table.

George doused the cabin oil lamp and looked out the window. It was pitch black. The noise was very loud now. They couldn't see what was coming from the drop-off below.

Ric opened the cabin door in the darkness and stood to one side.

George raised his rifle, pointing the barrel towards the sound of the oncoming noise. His finger was next to the trigger, ready for when the vehicle stopped. Odell was not welcome this night. Or any other.

The vehicle dropped into lower gear, wheels spinning as it shot across the meadow. It was making a beeline towards them, bouncing over the ruts.

George's finger moved to the trigger, his eye sighted down the barrel.

The vehicle rolled, slowing down.

The door of the shack was open. The two men stood with their rifles in the darkness.

CHAPTER 43

TOTAL MISMATCH

Flashback, earlier that evening, Wagon Wheel Inn, Takaka, Golden Bay, South Island

'Kia ora, dearie. It's me. Helen.'

Elaina went to the door and peered through the privacy hole. It was Helen! She didn't see anyone else. She opened the door and Helen stepped in.

'You need to come with me right now, dear,' Helen said breathlessly. 'There's a man that Franklin's talking to back at reception. He's a short man with matted hair, very sweaty. A sweaty bad guy. He said he was supposed to meet his girlfriend here. I knew you weren't his girlfriend. I also knew he wasn't very nice. And not a great outfit. You've got to come with me now,' Helen repeated. 'Things don't really occur as in murder mysteries … except for when they do.'

Elaina grabbed the mobile phones, and shoved the computer and tracking equipment into a bag.

'We're going around to the back of our residence,' Helen said. 'You can stay in our parlour until we get rid of this guy.'

A man was shouting in reception, his voice instantly recognisable.

'His name's Odell,' Elaina whispered to Helen as they snuck behind the building. Helen was well into her mystery mode, looking around and watching for any moving shadows.

'She's about this height.' Odell motioned with his hand to Franklin. 'Blonde hair, long legs, blue eyes, really pretty face. She came in tonight. She's here waiting for me.'

'I understand,' Franklin said. 'She's blue-eyed, long legs and a really pretty face and she's … your girlfriend?' Franklin asked, using his own dramatic flair. He had told Helen they should take up drama with the local Takaka theatre group.

'What's that supposed to mean!' Odell said loudly. 'I know she's here. Let me see your check-in screen.'

'Can't do that, sir. It's not legal,' Franklin said.

'A quick look. Come on now,' Odell demanded.

Helen walked behind the reception desk. 'Franklin, call the police. Jeffrey's on duty. He'd like nothing better than to arrest someone.' She used the strongest voice she could channel, as if she were on stage projecting to the back row of the theatre.

'No, no, it's a misunderstanding. I'll give her a ring and we'll be fine,' Odell said.

'I doubt any girl with that description would be waiting for you,' Franklin said, hoping this would end the scene.

Odell left, more furious than when he came in.

Franklin and Helen shifted the sign to 'No Vacancy' and went back to their quarters where Elaina waited.

'Girlfriend indeed. You'd never go with someone like that. A total mismatch of characters!' Helen said.

Franklin had a suggestion. 'We've got to get you out of here, before he comes snooping around again.'

Listening to Odell, Elaina had pegged him as angry and violent. 'Can I get up to the trail that you took Ric to?' she asked urgently. 'This guy is crazy. I need to get out of here. He could come back! But will you both be okay?'

'*We* can deal with him.' Helen loved tension in any scene. She was sure she was quoting a movie script from some gangster movie.

'Ric's vanished from the monitoring equipment I was using. But I can show you on a map where I last picked up his signal along the river.'

'Ahhh, there's no direct route. It would take hours to walk in and it's too dark now,' Franklin said.

Helen was the consummate mystery-solver. 'There're a million logging roads in those hills Franklin. Got to be one close by.'

'Hmmm. Think there's some roads that went up in the back country. Could be close to the place he was headed,' Franklin said dubiously. 'Hasn't been used for years now. Probably washed out in places.'

'Franklin, you go up with her on the road and see how far you get. Can we use that FJ40 you have out there, dearie?' Helen asked.

'Absolutely! Let's go.' Elaina was focused on getting away. She had to put her fears into her pocket. She needed get up to Ric. Was he okay? Where had Odell been before he got to this hotel? Why wasn't the beacon working now?

Franklin brought FJ-Orion around to the back.

'I'll drive.' Elaina slid behind the wheel. She was determined to drive as fast and far as she could, no matter what. Road or no road.

Posture, Patience, Persistence, she coached herself.

Franklin jumped in beside her and gave directions that Astrid at the Wholemeal Café had provided. She was a mountain climber and knew the back country. They were headed to a forestry road higher than the trailhead.

At a turnoff that Astrid suggested, a narrow dirt pathway went into the trees and started to climb up the mountain.

'Be careful, take it slow!' Franklin pleaded as he held onto the dashboard passenger bar and wedged himself into the seat. True to his prediction, the road was sometimes there … and sometimes not. FJ-Orion grunted, groaned and climbed with the headlights bouncing as they peered through the darkness.

'I'm going to call Helen before we get further out of range.'

Franklin dialled the number and when Helen picked up he put the phone on speaker so Elaina could hear.

'He came back, sure as sugar is sweet. It was a rerun,' Helen said. 'Jamie was here. He enjoyed tossing him out the door. What a performance. The creep wasn't happy and took off.'

The driving was difficult. They crossed over two branch tributaries to a river. Franklin and Elaina had to work on road-clearing when one small tree blocked the road. There was one wrong turn and then the road evaporated.

'I hope the tyres can negotiate these large ruts,' Elaina said. She tried not to think of changing a tyre out in the forest.

'We're on the last part, if I remember rightly. It's pretty much straight up there.' Franklin pointed towards the top of the hill.

Around one am, FJ-Orion made use of an old road that was rough but passable. Elaina and Franklin rounded a sharp bend and entered a broad mountain meadow. Up the hill, under the trees, was the fisherman's shack. Light flickered in the windows and then suddenly went out leaving only the stars in the moonless sky. The smoke they had seen now blended into the pines and native trees around the shack.

'Turn your lights off, Elaina. We don't know who's in that cabin.'

Salvatore's cabin, promontory above the Aorere River, Golden Bay, South Island
Ric and George waited on either side of the darkened door.

Their rifles were aimed at the vehicle that was rolling towards them in total darkness.

George whispered, 'Should we fire a warning shot?'

Ric shook his head. Sweat trickled down his neck. His leg was throbbing.

'If it's Odell, be prepared for him to fire first,' Ric said, listening to the wheels crunching over the ground.

The vehicle stopped.

Ric lifted his rifle, aimed. His skinned hands burned on the rifle barrel. He gripped harder, remembering the slide down the scree, the fear that he was about to die. Odell would pay for that.

Wait! In the diminished light of the moon and stars, he recognised that vehicle! His heart thumped harder. He hobbled out from the shadows, rifle down by his side.

A woman's voice rang out. 'Posture, Patience and Persistence!' Elaina shoved open her door and jumped out, running towards Ric and throwing her arms around him, hugging him tightly. In the darkness, she didn't notice he was wincing.

Salvatore's cabin, promontory above the Aorere River, Golden Bay, South Island
At the sound of Elaina's call, George was quick to take his finger off the trigger and lower his rifle.

Ric embraced Elaina, nestling his head against hers. 'George could have shot you. I could have shot you. We didn't know it was you out there.'

Franklin unravelled himself from the passenger seat. 'Well, that was quite the stock car race,' he said. 'Maybe even a demolition derby. Rather unbelievable that we made it.'

George wasn't expecting a hug from Franklin, but Franklin seemed overjoyed to be on solid ground.

'I guess we're sleeping in my tent tonight,' George said.

'Tent it is,' Franklin said. 'Hope you don't snore.'

Ric didn't want to let Elaina go. 'Please tell me how you got here. And why you're here. I thought Odell would go after you. Back in Takaka.'

'He did, Ric. It wasn't easy.' With the tea poured, Elaina described Odell coming to the hotel and her determination to get up the hill.

With their last cuppa, Ric related the moment he saw the outline of the cabin. And what he had found over the front door. He avoided describing the gunfire exchange with Odell.

'I bet Salvy brought Arabella here using that old forestry road where I came up. Arabella was correct in parts of the message she wanted to tell us,' Elaina said. 'Like a scrabble game where all the words are interconnected. In her mind, her phrases all meant something.'

The fire died down, and Elaina picked up Ric's jacket to stay warm. As she put it on, her fingers found a small hole through the lower hem. A perfectly round perforation. She showed it to him, sticking her finger through.

Ric looked at the coat, and simply said, 'Oh yes, Odell was around here. He missed. Thanks to George providing some distraction.'

Franklin cleared up the cups. George stood up, getting ready to set up a tent outside.

Ric had been rubbing his ankle as Elaina related her story. He was thinking about Odell.

'Franklin, one quick question. Was the last time you saw Odell at the Wagon Wheel Inn?'

'Yes.' Franklin nodded. 'He went out the door in a huff.'

Ric paused and slowly spoke. 'And you didn't see where he went?'

'We didn't see him after he left. But Helen said he came back later.'

'About what time was that?' Ric asked.

'Well, let's see. We started rolling about ten pm and arrived here around one.' Franklin glanced at his wristwatch. 'Helen saw Odell a fair while after we left, probably around eleven.'

Elaina reached her hand out and put it on Ric's leg. His face resembled an ancient stone statue labelled as *Fear*. It was a look Ric had when something terrible had happened. His eyes opened wide and his eyebrows arrowed down.

Outside the wind shifted direction, almost as fast as Ric's plans to stay at the cabin.

'How could I be so stupid?' he said. 'If he couldn't get at me, and he didn't get at you, Elaina … there's still one person he can harm. And he could do a lot of damage.'

Elaina's mouth opened. 'Ohhhhh nooo!'

'Mum!' Ric said. He tried to dial Kiri's number.

No reception.

CHAPTER 44

THE SUMMIT

Near the summit of Marble Mountain (Takaka Hill), Tasman District

Odell slammed his truck into the parking area by the caves near the summit of Takaka Hill, skidding to a halt. There was one particular sinkhole he remembered well.

It wasn't a conscious decision. He felt pulled to the area, like a magnet pulling the metal of his truck.

He couldn't pass by without the place reaching out to him, tugging him in. He knew what was there. He knew what he had done and what was waiting for him in that deep, dark hole.

Baxter's police source had called him recently. The police were full-on looking for Tessa Bright. Why now? Over a year later? He'd thought that event was long forgotten. Why had the police looked back over their shoulder to this particular missing person? One of many.

'She'd better not be discovered, you old codger,' Baxter had hissed over the phone. 'You had a big part in all this.'

It wasn't all on *his* gumboots. Odell knew Baxter was knee-deep in the cow dung.

Odell sat in the carpark. Lights off. The hill was dark. The sky was lit with so many stars it seemed to have no room for more.`

He wondered if she could see the stars from that hole.

First it had been Salvatore. Baxter had killed him and ordered Odell to bury him. He had dug a hole on the site that had been slowly closing down during the previous few months.

But Baxter had forgotten about the CCTV surveillance systems that were installed at the plant. Including the lab. Everything was on Baxter's orders.

Before the lab was dismantled, Odell had grabbed the sequence and used his phone to capture the images of Baxter with the shovel and Salvatore tumbling forward. Every once in a while, he'd watch those crucial minutes. They'd flicker across his phone screen—sharp and clear. A 'short' clip. Award winning. And Odell had this entire scene of Baxter digitally stored. It was his lifetime warranty.

He'd never go to jail … or even down some hole to never come back. It was all on Baxter's orders. He never knowingly assisted anyone.

He was getting cold in the car. Should he get out? Go look? What was the point? The point was … that it still ate at him. Gnawing away on him like a greedy dog chewing a beef bone.

The last twenty-four hours had been a disaster!

He had to forget about it. He needed to drive away.

Odell reached under the dash and pulled out a small bag. He popped two of the white pills from the plastic bag and swallowed them down with water from a grimy bottle on the floor. He got the pills from one of Baxter's cohorts out in the countryside.

He looked at his watch. He had an appointment in Nelson. Maybe he couldn't get at Peters, or that bitch of a girlfriend.

But there was someone left. Someone he could get at. A way he could hurt all of them. Something that would be long remembered.

~ ~ ~

The Cliff House, Nelson, South Island

It was four-thirty in the morning and Kiri couldn't sleep. She stepped out on the deck. Yesterday, coming back from the hospital, she had watched a group of waka or outrigger canoes glide towards Tahunanui Beach.

The Māori traced their origins back to ancestors who migrated in voyaging waka from their Polynesian homeland. Sometimes a waka had a side pontoon or two hulls which provided the balance against the sea voyage.

Kiri had been on a long voyage in the last ten days. She had tried, as she always did, to find balance. Keep things together. It seemed that Ric and Elaina might be close to finding something that would help. But those moments had happened before. The end of the journey often turned out only to be the beginning.

The Cliff House seemed too quiet … almost foreboding. She stepped back into the lounge, then up the two steps to the dining room.

Gusting winds from a southerly wrapped their fingers around the eaves, trying to pull the cladding off. She heard every creak and groan. Every little noise was magnified in her mind. *Come on, Kiri. You teach this to your clients.*

She was uneasy about the large cardboard box that Dave Bowers had delivered last night. Dave had finally gotten around to looking at the 'men fighting' that his son had seen on the computer. It was more than fighting, Dave had recounted, shaking his head.

'And the trouble is, I know the older man in the video clip. It was Reid Baxter. He had hit the man in the white coat and the man had fallen to the ground. Blood all over. And then another man came in to clean it all up. Odell Rodman. My kid shouldn't have seen that. What kind of dad am I?'

Kiri had spent 30 minutes working Dave through a quick counselling session, and he agreed to set up some additional sessions working alone and then alongside his son.

'You and your son are resilient, Dave. I can teach you some methods you can tap into, so that what you tell yourself helps you work through all this. Be compassionate to yourself,' she remembered saying.

The house creaked again as the temperature dialled down. Ric and Elaina were in Golden Bay. John was in hospital. Kiri was doing that which was hardest … waiting.

The doctor said John would be home in the morning. That was now a few hours away. Ric and Elaina were another story. She hadn't heard from them.

She realised that what they were uncovering was information that could have dire consequences. If Ric found what John had requested, events could unravel like a ball of yarn tumbling across the floor. This information could drive some people to desperate acts.

Not to mention the large cardboard box that sat in the scullery, a few metres away. If Baxter or Rodman knew there was evidence sitting in a box at The Cliff House … she didn't even want to think about it.

Kiri felt a chilled breeze that danced down the stairs into the lounge. She tried to remember if she had inadvertently left a window or door open up at the top of the house. Her mind was frazzled.

She didn't want to go back to bed, but she stepped into the hall at the base of the stairs and looked up.

Everything seemed secure. Earlier everything seemed shipshape from the ship's bell at the front door on down. Fantasised Events Appearing Real? FEAR, Kiri thought.

She went back into the lounge to rescue her liquorice-and-peppermint tea. She wanted to retrieve her phone to check her messages.

There was another 'creak' out in the hall.

She turned towards the door and the cup slipped from her hand, shattering on the floor. Tea spilled across the rimu wood.

Odell stood in her dining room, wet and dirty. He looked like he'd rolled down a muddy hill. He had a few scrapes on his face and his hair was matted and dishevelled. Had someone given him a thrashing? His arm was stretched out like he wanted to shake hands. The automatic had a long barrel, and the barrel opening was her focal point.

Kiri had wanted to meet Odell in person. Face to face. Find some answers. Be careful what you wish for, she thought.

She waited for Odell's next move. A tightening of his trigger finger. There was no way out of this.

Chapter 45

FJ-Orion Carrying Gold

Flashback, 2:00 am, cabin by the Aorere River, Golden Bay
'I'll help you get to the car, Ric. I can drive. Have you heard from your mum?'

'Still no reception. You'll have to drive, Elaina. My leg's better, but still sore.'

'What are we going to do with all these boxes?' Elaina asked Ric.

'George is going to bring his camper up the logging road and he and Franklin will load the camper and ferry them to Nelson.'

Elaina helped Ric slowly walk to FJ-Orion.

Ric carried the small chilly bin of samples that Lenore would use for DNA testing. It was what his father had asked him to do.

Not far from the cabin were extensive goldfields from the 1880s. Salvatore's personal items and the boxes he had stored were now more valuable than the gold of long ago. Ric needed to get them into the right hands to ensure Salvy's efforts had value in the end.

'This seems strange,' Ric said with a crooked smile, sitting in the passenger's seat.

'We'll be down the mountain as fast as we can,' George said, standing by the truck's window.

'I think I've got enough samples for the DNA that Lenore wanted,' Ric told George. 'But later, if Lenore or the police need more, you can lead them in.'

George tapped twice on the side of FJ-Orion and they were off.

On the way down to Takaka, Elaina suggested, 'The only road up Takaka Hill runs by the Wagon Wheel. The sooner we get the samples into Lenore's hands, the faster she can start.'

Ric caught Elaina's gist. 'There're some private pilots that operate from the airport in Golden Bay,' Ric said, reaching for his mobile. 'When I have a signal, I'll get Helen onto that. We can do a quick drop-off. I want to get to Nelson as fast as we can.'

They paused at the Wagon Wheel Inn for a few seconds where Helen stood waiting her arms outstretched. Briskly they offloaded the sample materials in the chilly bin. The lid was sealed shut.

'Here's looking at you kids.' Helen cradled the chilly bin.

Elaina didn't stop the engine and they were off. With little traffic around, she increased their speed up the hill.

In her show-stopping play, Helen carefully carried the samples and stopped at the local aero club. Like the movie Casablanca, the plane was warming up by the time she met the police constable at the Takaka Aerodrome. The Cessna, carrying Constable William Telemark and the samples, was outbound for Wellington.'

Flashback, 3:00 am, Marble Mountain (Takaka Hill), Tasman District, South Island

On the hill, Ric tried again to reach his mother. It went to voice mail.

'It's early in the morning. Why can't she answer?' Ric and Elaina were already cresting the hill and heard from Helen that the Cessna had taken off.

'You once asked if Golden Bay was really Golden,' Ric said quietly. 'I made a promise to my father when he was in the hospital. And I believe, in Golden Bay, we found the proof he needs to help identify his friend.'

He tried his mum again. It went straight to voice mail.

'One hour from here,' Ric said, looking at his phone and Elaina's speed.

Elaina focused on driving FJ-Orion as it groaned down the Takaka Hill on its way back to Nelson. Ric dialled Lenore and put her on speaker phone. It was before dawn, so Ric waited for Lenore to pick up.

'Hellooo?' Lenore voice was groggy. 'Oh, Ric. Sorry for the delay. Good to hear from you, I've been sleeping in the lab— '

Ric cut her off. 'Elaina and I are heading back to Nelson. I wanted to let you know Constable William Telemark is en route with the samples from the Salvatore's cabin. Can you process them as soon as you get them?'

Lenore clicked into gear. 'Absolutely, Ric. I'll send a car to the airport now.'

Ric provided the details of Salvatore's cabin and that there was a person on standby if she needed more samples. 'Well, Lenore— '

Lenore interrupted, 'There's some other news. Is Elaina there with you? This is a little hard.'

Elaina raised her eyebrows. 'Yes, I'm here too, Lenore. Go ahead.'

Lenore paused then took a breath. 'As you know, I got the remains from the cave find. The ones we tentatively identified as a Miss Tessa Bright. I've done a preliminary examination and have reconstructed what I could. There's a lot of tissue that's intact. It's almost like a mummification process because of the cave's conditions.'

'We heard about that from my father,' Ric said.

'Ric, she … she …' Ric could hear Lenore on the other end of the line choking on her words.

Ric and Elaina glanced at each other and waited.

'Ric, she was pregnant when she died. She died from the impact hitting a ledge,' Lenore said, pronouncing each word carefully. 'She had an injury to her throat. It looks like an inflicted puncture wound when she was alive, not from the fall. There is blood residue in parts of the skull. I think she may have been alive and bleeding when she was tossed into the sinkhole … and the foetus was intact.'

There was silence in the car.

Lenore broke in. 'Got a text. Your constable will be here soon.' She disconnected.

'So, if she was pregnant,' said Elaina, 'who was the father? And who wanted her murdered?'

Ric redialled Kiri. No reply. 'I called the police yesterday and asked that they do a welfare check. I'm calling them again.'

~~~

The Cliff House, Nelson

'Odell, what do you want?' Kiri asked, examining the man before her. Odell looked erratic. Ragged. He was breathing rapidly. Mentally unstable. He was insane … or was it something else?

She was alone, with his gun pointed at her. Her phone wasn't in reach.

'What do I want?' Odell said with a smirk on his sweating face. 'A beautiful woman should never ask that question. It could get her into trouble.'
~~~

Kiri looked around for anything she could use to protect herself. Nothing in the lounge. She glanced at the fireplace … the fireplace! If she could ease around the dining table, the fireplace tools were in the corner. Good God! The cardboard box in the scullery!

'Anyone else here?' Odell demanded.

Kiri remained silent.

'I asked you a question!' Odell said in a low, threatening tone. 'You're not answering. It means you are alone.'

Kiri could feel herself beginning to shake. 'What you're saying doesn't make sense to me.'

'It's funny to think that you spawned Ric Peters. Maybe bad genes,' Odell said.

'You are not being clear,' Kiri said, knowing he wouldn't register anything she was saying.

What was clear was that Odell was coming apart. She eased herself towards the fireplace. Odell moved closer to the steps leading from the dining room to the lounge.

'Not to worry. I've taken care of Ric and his friend,' Odell said, sneering. He was enjoying this. He felt like he was a cat playing with a mouse. Knocking it around, before he'd bite off her head and eat it.

Kiri could tell Odell was lying. She watched his eyes. He was sweating while standing there. His speech was animated, his hands jittery. He flicked his arm around, the gun wavering.

She tried to move out of his line of fire.

His speech was slurred, his eyes dilated. 'You're going to be joining them.' Odell raised the gun higher. 'Except I'm going to take care of you slowly. I want you to feel the pain.'

Chapter 46

Plant Delivery

Around the corner from The Cliff House, Nelson

Captain Richard Hornwell finished getting into his uniform. White shirt with shoulder boards, sporting four gold stripes. Gold wings above the pocket, black tie. Nelson was still asleep at 5 am. Richard was a methodical pilot and his time clock was always set to his next flight. This flight was leaving at 0700, and he needed to be there on time to get ready.

Richard walked down to his truck and remembered the two plants he had promised John and Kiri when they camped out at JP#1.

He threw his uniform jacket and travel bag into his truck, grabbed the two potted ferns he had sitting by his walkway and headed down to The Cliff House.

He could see the airport in the distance and saw a blue truck parked near the overlook. It wasn't one he recognised and knew it hadn't been there late last evening. Richard noticed things out of the ordinary. It was a quality he encouraged his pilot trainees to develop.

The driveway down to The Cliff House was steep. He took smaller steps on the incline, cradling the two prized ferns from JP#1, and reached the front entry steps. He wondered why the door was wide open at this hour.

He stood in the doorway, holding the ferns and peering in. There was a light at the bottom of the stairs. A loud male voice was talking. Almost yelling. And it didn't sound like either John or Ric.

Richard quickly put the plants at the entry and started down the stairs, stepping softly. He got to the first and then the second landing, and headed towards the main lounge.

A man was standing in front of Kiri, who was clearly terrified.

'What's happening here?' Richard said loudly.

The man spun around, levelling the automatic weapon at him.

'Slow down,' Richard said, raising his hand up in a stop position. 'You're obviously not a neighbour.' His mantra when flying was aviate, navigate, communicate. He'd start with 'communicate'.

Odell was befuddled, facing two people now. And one in a uniform. He yelled at Kiri, 'Don't move!' In the dining room, she had edged closer to the fireplace and within range of the tools.

'Who are you? The police? Are you a copper?' Odell's frontal lobe for complex thinking had shut down. Any abilities for making rational decisions and logical reasoning had left months before when he started popping the white pills.

'Get down here where I can see you!' Odell ordered, waving the gun. As Richard moved to the right, Odell moved backwards towards the lounge.

'I don't care if I shoot one or two of you,' Odell said in a low growl, pointing the gun at them but having a hard time planting his feet.

As he raised the automatic into a firing position, he edged further away. His heel caught on the step and he fell backwards. His weapon hand hit the floor and the automatic went off, firing a bullet through the glass slider.

Kiri screamed. Richard stomped on Odell's gun hand.

Odell released the automatic with a yelp. Richard followed through with a boot kick into Odell's arm, then swept the automatic across the wooden floor, clearing it out of Odell's reach.

Odell shook off the kick and jumped up. He was operating with strength beyond his normal capability, feeling no pain. He threw Richard into a wall, trying to choke him.

Kiri grabbed a poker next to the wood burner and hit Odell on the arm, but he barely noticed and kept hold of Richard. Odell's grip was almost superhuman as he tried to lift Richard off the floor.

Ric rushed into the dining room. For a second, a surge of electric fear exploded in him when he saw his mum in danger. He picked up the gun that Richard had kicked aside.

'Odell! Let him go!' He pointed the weapon at Odell.

Elaina grabbed Kiri and pulled her away from the dining table into the hall. Kiri had snatched her phone and starting dialling Triple One.

Ric exhaled in relief that Kiri was okay, while holding the 9mm automatic handgun squarely aimed at Odell.

Odell released Richard, turned and stared at Ric. He was dancing between confusion and euphoria. Anger winning out, he picked up a chair and threw it through the glass slider, which shattered into pieces. Odell rushed out through the opening onto the deck. He didn't see the crystal-clear glass railing in front of him. He hit it at full tilt.

And flipped over the armoured glass, disappearing from sight.

Kiri had finished explaining to the emergency person what was happening. The woman assured her police were already on the way. 'Stay on the line,' she ordered.

Elaina made a move towards Ric, but he held up his hand. 'Wait. Stay over there. There may be—'

Heavy footsteps came down through the house.

'Police, drop your weapons! Police … drop … your … weapons!' was repeated over and over again. The shouts from the stairs intensified.

Ric carefully placed the weapon on the dining table and stepped well away.

In seconds, four policemen in body armour rushed down the stairs. Elaina shouted and pointed to the balcony. 'Outside, he's outside. Over the edge.'

The police hustled outside to the lower yard. Odell had attempted flight, but landed on the dirt and been winded. He started getting up. First one, then two policemen tried to grab his arms. Finally, two of them sat on Odell, while the other two put him into restraints.

Meth pumped through Odell's body. He was definitely feeling no pain.

Chapter 47

A Promise Is a Promise

The Cliff House, Nelson, South Island
Elaina and Kiri went to the hospital to pick up John.

After phoning the airline to say he'd be unable to fly today, Richard helped Ric clear up the broken glass and tape a plastic sheet over the doorway. Then he brought the ferns down the stairs and set them on the dining table.

'Glad I was making a home delivery of these,' he said.

Ric realised that if Richard hadn't been there, things could have been very different.

'Your timing was impeccable like your flying,' he said to Richard and brewed him a coffee. A flat white.

Ric arranged the sofa so John could look at the sea. Elaina and Kiri helped him into the lounge, and Ric assisted him to the sofa. He waited until his father was settled before he told John the news.

'We found the cabin. It had everything Lenore needs for a DNA test. We got a few samples off this morning. Lenore will process them soon. They arrived while we were on our way here.' He rattled off in priority order what he thought his father wanted to hear.

A smile blossomed across John's face, and he nodded. 'Well done, Ric. Dear Elaina, thank you!' He reached out for their hands.

Richard stood up. 'Thanks for the coffee, Ric. It's been an entertaining morning. Hope you enjoy the native plants.'

Kiri filled John, Ric and Elaina in on the recent visit from Odell. 'Richard should get an Academy Award for his line "You're obviously not a neighbour",' Kiri said.

'Sounds like Odell has been strung out for a while,' Ric said.

'He kept telling the police that he had quite a story to tell,' Elaina mentioned.

Kiri took over being the senior nurse at The Cliff House recovery station. 'There's a man named Detective Inspector Hamish Parkhurst who needs to see you, Ric. I told him to come over and he's due here in about an hour. He only gets in the door if he brings some of that German bread your father likes from the bakery.'

'I like the way you organise things, Kiri,' Elaina said. 'Quid pro quo. That's my kind of deal.'

Franklin and George arrived with the campervan loaded with the boxes.

'Took us a while to get through the police blockade up that way,' George said, opening the camper door.

Ric and Elaina unloaded the boxes, stacking them in the sunroom in case DI Parkhurst wanted to inventory or review them. Ric put the rifle into his room at the top of stairs to give to Parkhurst when he arrived. He propped it next to his old bow and arrows from the garage.

George left to check out the Maitai River for fishing and Franklin tagged along.

Kiri set up a small portable table next to John, so he didn't have to move around.

John looked across the bay to Longboat Island. *After a year, Salvy. I'm so close. I promised you I'd work it through.*

Ric was finishing the in-house coffees when Parkhurst rang the ship's bell and Elaina went up to let him in.

'My first order of business,' she told him, 'is your coffee request.'

'Wow. A long black, please. I don't get this kind of treatment when I'm knocking on most doors,' Parkhurst said. 'DI Parkhurst is my official title, but Hamish works as well. And you are?'

'Elaina Williams, whom you read about in Ric's boating accident report. As long as that bag you're carrying is the famous German bread, you can proceed down the stairs,' Elaina said, laughing, and taking the bread to the kitchen.

Ten minutes of light discussion and then Hamish plunged into the deep end. He set his briefcase on the dining table and addressed them all.

'Ernest Bennett has been put under police arrest while he currently resides at Nelson Hospital. He was an accomplice in two murders that languished here in Nelson for almost a year.

'Ernest has seen the proverbial handwriting on the wall and decided he has plenty of knowledge stored in his memory that he'd like to divulge. He has access to a storage unit that contains most of the contents of Salvatore Marino's apartment. We've contacted the manager of the unit who had already put a lock on it and has given us access. For some reason, Ernest says a sheep farmer in Cable Bay has three boxes. We'll see how far Ernest's memory takes us.

'A rather angry Odell Rodman is under special custody in a detention holding cell. He's up for the murder of Tessa Bright because she was alive when he threw her into the sinkhole. We'll see if there's footage of her arrival at Reid Baxter's in Nelson where she was initially assaulted.

'Odell claims he has a digital copy of Baxter's killing of Salvatore at the former Parásita lab, on Longboat Island. He had no problem identifying his meth source hidden in the back roads well beyond Riwaka. We have a warrant in the works to go to the property.'

Kiri interjected. 'If you want an advanced copy of that Parásita digital camera feed, I have the full-length feature. It's the original security camera version and it's on a computer in the scullery.'

Hamish's mouth fell open. 'Ahhh. Great!' he said, taking this in. 'Then there's the multiple attempted murders with which you, of course, are familiar. Odell's not been able to find a barrister who wants to represent him, but once he does, I suspect we'll hear more.'

John was listening intently and sucked in a breath. Kiri came over to him to hold his hand.

'The mastermind of the murders, Reid Baxter, has more on his plate. You possibly recall the name Malcolm Sloan?' Hamish looked around.

Lights were clicking on in Ric's head like a flare path down a flight runway.

'About a year ago we suspected there was a money laundering, real estate and drug distribution scheme going on. There was a complex use of trusts to avoid identification of the actual owners.

'We contacted the State Crime Command in New South Wales Police. They have both the Criminal Groups Squad and Organised

Crime Squad and they gave us some advice. We also worked with a group within the State Intelligence Command. Our contact there was a Detective Inspector Jack McMasters. He's been working on a couple of covert operations there in Australia.

'We needed someone to run a covert op here in New Zealand. Someone who wasn't well known, but had a good enough backstory so that Reid Baxter would buy into it. Mr Baxter has been on our watchlist for a while. But he's a slick character. And he knows which political buttons to push.

'Jack and Malcolm created the escaped convict scenario which Reid Baxter snapped at like a hungry barracuda. He likes to feel like he has a hold over every one of his associates. Having someone in hiding was especially appealing to him.

'Except Malcolm wasn't there to hide out. He was there to gather information, which he did. Malcolm has put together so much evidence of the money-laundering schemes, as well as two actual murders, that Baxter will wish he'd gone down the hill with Ernest in this last Nelson mudslide.

'And we have you, Kiri and Elaina, to thank for your attempt to report an incident you thought important. We knew Nelson Police had a leak, but it's difficult to work that kind of case from the inside. We've been liaising with the Tasman District Commander for a year. Superintendent Andy Hastings was only too happy to set up surveillance on the suspect you both had identified. Constable Cox has recently had a change of uniform and a change of venue and he won't be leaving anytime soon.

'The meth manufacturing scheme has a special task force looking into it and I won't go into further details until certain other events occur.'

Hamish looked at his mobile phone. 'Perhaps relatively soon.'

'What about the cancer cluster?' Kiri asked. 'Surely the number of people who have died after having toxic material buried on their land should be investigated? If Baxter was burying toxic chemicals, he should be held accountable.'

'Absolutely,' said Hamish. 'There's an internal group working on that as well. We'll need any small bits of data that you've found.'

'We have an eye-witness account contained in fourteen boxes of material as well as twelve volumes of a detailed diary,' Ric said. 'That's probably enough to get them started.'

Hamish paused mid-swallow of his long black. '*What* do you have?' he asked incredulously. He'd thought he was providing the bulk of the information at this informal chat. He never expected there would be all this information coming back to him.

Ric took Hamish on a scenic tour of the sunroom with the boxes and lab books. He opened a few of the boxes, recounting some of the details they had found.

'This, and the computer in your scullery, will turn the tide on these investigations into a tsunami,' Hamish announced.

CHAPTER 48

GOOD AS ROBIN HOOD

Near The Cliff House, Nelson, South Island

Francis couldn't believe the rain was finally over. How many re-runs of *The Maltese Falcon* could he manage? Today the sun appeared and was toasting the morning. Time to knock this self-assignment off the list.

Francis parked down below the Peters' house on a side street called Sea Breeze. It was quiet and deserted. Several of the houses were under renovation and repair after the recent weather event and landslip.

He walked to the end of the street with his backpack and began the trudge up a steep hill with scattered vegetation.

The red-blooming pōhutukawa on the hillside, about twenty metres from The Cliff House, provided excellent cover. There were shrubs around the base that had been trampled down, probably by children playing.

Francis slid the black rod out of his backpack and assembled the barrel and firing mechanism. The weapon travelled well as an accumulation of camera and film shooting equipment, which ironically included the firing mechanism.

Ammunition was a little trickier. That had arrived via consignment from a specialist.

Francis had carefully considered his weapon for the job. He'd thought of the short-barrelled handgun he'd used for his work in Indonesia. It was nice and compact, easy to assemble and less obtrusive.

But then again, with its shorter barrel, it was not as accurate. And he didn't know how close he was going to be to the target. Not like at the restaurant.

The split rifle barrel was a good option this time out. The longer barrel would give him better accuracy, as this kill would be from a greater distance. Now he had a clear field of fire, and he had the cover for an easy retreat back.

Francis was already contemplating his drive through the hinterlands of the South Island, a quick drop-off of the rental car and his departure from Christchurch.

This was what he truly loved about his work. The symmetry of it all.

The killings could be technically difficult, usually because of location and circumstances. Each kill was 'bespoke'. He liked the sound of that word—made to order. He was most definitely not a bulk provider. He wasn't working on an assembly line or even 9 to 5.

The best part was the level of planning required. His kills were a premium product.

These two remaining targets, Peters and O'Neill, were the only blemishes on his long career. And soon he was going to erase the first one—Peters. His record would then be almost cleaned up and his reputation intact.

Francis looked around. He was concealed by the lower vegetation which ran up towards the house facing the sea. He noticed one of the glass doors on the lower level had plastic sheeting taped to it. Maybe the wind had broken it in that wretched storm. There were two vehicles on the drive. He had already seen some activity in the house on various levels.

It looked like two men were in a room up near the top of the driveway. One of them looked like Peters. There was a side door to that room that exited onto a patio.

All of a sudden he saw a young woman on a lower deck. She paused as if she was looking at the view.

He knew that woman. He had seen her before. At the Bay of Fires. When Peters had been holding her. He had debated then about taking her. He could easily fire and reload. Now, he sighted down his barrel …

Elaina had been on the lower deck looking at Tahunanui Beach. She glanced up at a man near a tree. He was parallel to the sunroom of The Cliff House. He was sighting down using something … she wasn't sure. Then he seemed to stare directly at her.

She knew that face. She had seen it when Ric showed her Hendrik's photo. The man had been in Tasmania. Trying to kill Ric then. *What exactly* was he holding now? She had to warn Ric. Or …

… and then the woman disappeared inside the house, seemingly oblivious to everything after looking at the beach. Francis focused back on the upper room, where one of the men was near the outside door, looking out.

Elaina bounded up the stairs. Kiri and John were taking a rest in their room and the door was closed. She could hear John snoring softly.

She raced past Ric's room, then took a step back. She grabbed Ric's bow. It was strung. Grabbed an arrow out of the quiver. Sped out the door and up the outside steps.

Behind Francis, the clouds scuttled across the sky and a ray of sunshine bounded out over the sea. Peters came onto a side deck of that upper room likely looking for the woman.

Francis moved forward, shifted some of the undergrowth that was in his line of sight. He wanted a straight shot. No mucking around this time with leaves, or boats, or water. He raised the barrel of his rifle …

At the corner of the garage, Elaina spotted the man below but was not in his field of vision. He was standing by the large red-blossoming tree and she could see his weapon in firing position. He was clearly focused on his target.

Ric was below her on the sunroom patio facing the sea. It was as if he had a target on his chest. He was probably looking for her!

Francis centred the scope on Peters. At this range, two quick taps. One to the head and one to the chest.

He put his finger next to the trigger guard.

Elaina's heart thumped and she felt suffocated as she tried to grab a breath and think at the same time.

She couldn't yell out or the man would fire. And Ric would be dead.

The man had moved some of the bushes aside. She could see his casual dress which faded into the greens and browns of his background.

What didn't fade was the long barrel, a rifle and scope pointed towards the side deck of the house.

Francis took a breath. It was always the breathing that created a perfect shot.

The barrel was in alignment with his target.

There was no time. Her future—their future—was seconds away from evaporating.

She grabbed the arrow. A field point for targets. Would have to do. She mounted it on the string. Stepped out to the side of the garage. She had a clear line of fire to the red blooming tree.

Elaina pulled the fletching on the arrow back to her cheek.

She took a yoga breath, simultaneously fixing the range.

She let loose the arrow with a twannnnggg.

Ahhhoooooouuuuuuccccchhhh.

Simultaneously, a shot rang out.

On the deck by the sunroom, Ric heard the short *swack* sound from the corner of the garage. At the same time a shot rang out from the bush and went high into the Colorbond steel siding at the peak of the roof.

'Hamish, get down!' he shouted.

Both hugged the ground like it was their final minute on earth. Ric and Hamish clung to a concrete retaining wall, trying to slow down their panic-breathing.

Empty-handed, Elaina hurried down the hill, reaching the deck by the sunroom. Ric was crouched by the short brick wall, listening to some unidentified sounds in the distance.

'Elaina, get down.' Still in a squatting position, he reached out with both hands to grab her, pulling her towards him.

'Ah, Ric, I think I just shot someone.'

Ric wasn't sure he'd heard right. 'Elaina, someone's firing a weapon. And something else from above … up there.'

'Yes, I know, Ric. A bow. I think we need to check on that man over by that red tree.'

'What's going here?' Hamish said, crawling towards them. He was still huddled down while looking around.

Elaina stood up. 'We need to go see if we can help that man.' She started moving briskly towards the pōhutukawa tree.

Ric and Hamish stood up, looking in the direction of the sound. Peering over the wall edge, in the distance by a tree they spied a man with his left hand up to his chest, screaming, and pulling at a long arrow shaft sticking out of his shoulder.

They both bounded over the wall, adrenaline and their reptilian brains kicking in—fight not flight.

Francis saw them coming and tried to run. He tripped on some vines in the undergrowth, landing on his back. He was hidden in the high grass with the exception of the arrow and its fletched end sticking up.

Francis's rifle lay alongside him in the dillweed.

For the third time in less than 48 hours, an ambulance was called to The Cliff House. The police emergency response that occurred at The Cliff House was hurried along with Hamish's swift directions.

Francis Holms was taken into custody and then transferred to Nelson General Hospital Emergency Room. On a gurney, he was shifted through the Emergency Department with the arrow still vertically protruding from his chest.

The Emergency Department staff hadn't had an arrow in the chest in years. Especially with the victim handcuffed to the gurney.

Ric slowly walked Elaina to the lower deck along the side of the house.

Elaina started hyperventilating, chest heaving, while trying to process the freight train of adrenaline coursing through her body. She held Ric's hand, asking repeatedly, 'Are you all right? Are you all right?' and examining him.

'You're okay, Elaina. Take a breath. Tell me what happened.' For the first time since she had known Ric, Elaina could hear a tremor in his voice.

'I saw the man. The man in the picture you showed me. From Hendrik. I didn't know what he was doing here. He was holding a rifle. I could see you down below. I couldn't yell. He'd have fired. I had no option. It was a field tip. Should only have wounded him.'

'You got him before he fired the rifle. His shot went wild, into the house. He missed me, because of you.'

Elaina reached up to touch Ric's face. Tears started streaming down her cheeks. 'I'm so glad he missed you. So glad. He ... he isn't dead, is he?'

Hamish had arrived to hear Elaina's question. 'No. But he won't be shooting anything for a while. I've had an earful from my command. Mr Holms is being held at Nelson General Hospital, restrained and under guard. He'll be charged with attempted murder and possession of a firearm. The possession pales in comparison to the murder part of his past background.'

Hamish recounted that Francis's entry into the country had unearthed his multiple identities. His background began to unravel as he became a chew toy between three Weimaraners.

The New Zealand Government and court system were processing him for attempted murder and illegal entry into the country as well as weapons charges.

The Australian Government wanted him for associated crimes in Australia, while the British Government was claiming him for possible connections to assassinations in the United Kingdom.

A fourth group coming to the party was the Indonesian State Intelligence Agency: Badan Intelligent Negara (BIN). BIN had detected Francis's arrival in Indonesia and associated it with the recent assassinations of two Australian diplomatic personnel. They'd had some help from ASIS.

Hamish broke into a song with a decent baritone.

'Extradition's in the air,' he sang.

'As I look all around.

'Extradition's in the air,

'With lots of sightings and heaps of sound.'

He concluded with, 'Of course, the New Zealand Government said it would all be sorted out once Francis recovers from his arrow wound.'

Kiri came out on the deck, holding John's hand. 'We've been hearing sirens for the last half hour. Have we missed anything?'

CHAPTER 49

THE D'URVILLE ISLAND STALKER

John walked back to his makeshift sofa, but his hand was clenched around his phone.

'Lenore called, said she was unable to get hold of Ric. The samples Ric sent her have tentatively confirmed that the skeletal remains found at the hazardous material site and at the Paxton farm were Salvatore Marino. He was my friend. A good friend,' John said in a low tone. 'I never try to make a promise I can't deliver on. Even though he wasn't around, I made a commitment to Salvy that I would find out who did this. I am grateful for all of you who helped me fulfil my promise.'

Ric went into the scullery to make Hamish another long black and Hamish followed with his briefcase. He set it down by the box of computer equipment.

'You'll be interested that The D'Urville Island Stalker has been short-circuited in more ways than one. I had wanted to give you something, Ric, before our brief intermission. After obtaining a search warrant on Baxter's top floor residence in Nelson this morning, we found a records room next to his computer set-up. He kept files on all of his activities. Very detailed files, some of which had their origins from police information. Amid the mountain of data we are collecting, there were four files I found that have absolutely no bearing on this case or the outcome of any of these investigations.'

Hamish handed Ric a bundle of files tied together.

Ric turned them over to read the labels.

John Peters
Kiri Peters
Ric Peters
Elaina Williams

Ric flipped through the loose pages of each file. Background checks, photographs, associations, articles. Baxter was an excessive-compulsive collector of antiques and used that same excessive-compulsive behaviour for any person he wanted control over.

'Thanks,' Ric said, tucking the files away to retrieve later.

'One intelligence person to another,' Hamish said, looking directly at Ric, who nodded.

Hamish switched gears and chatted a few more minutes while downing his long black. He arranged with Ric for the pick-up of all the boxes on the following day as Ric had told his father he would go through them that afternoon, in case there was anything to help Arabella or Cynthia Paxton.

While Kiri and Elaina cleaned up, and John was completing his second crossword, Ric dialled up Maximillian Oliver Williams, who had texted him twice that morning.

'Nice of you to check in, Ric,' Oliver said. 'I trust you've had a restful and pleasant holiday and are ready to get back to work?'

'Yes. Nothing but lying on the beach, Oliver. What's up?'

'We finally got the CCTV from the Indonesian Police from that restaurant Laurence Patterson so enjoyed—until a bullet went through his forehead.'

'Let me guess. They found a shooter that wasn't me.'

'Yes. We've helped identify the weapon. We analysed the film through a variety of AI Image scanners and found the clever way the shooting was accomplished.'

'A pea shooter?' Ric asked.

'Almost. A long pistol designed for concealment. AI found the barrel peeking out from the foliage. It was in the booth behind you. The Indonesian Police have decided you didn't do it.'

'Excited for their efforts. Guess I can now vacation in Bali … legally,' Ric said.

'And of course you heard about the Ambassador?' Oliver asked.

'Tick, heard it from Steven,' Ric said. For once he believed he was ahead of Oliver on the information stream which he quite enjoyed. With Oliver, that would probably last about thirty minutes.

'Thought you'd be glad you're off the hook for that one too. Gives you a clean slate when you're back with us next week. Give Elaina my love.'

Tahunanui Beach, Nelson

In the late afternoon, Ric and Elaina took a break and headed down to Tahunanui Beach. They swam and collected shells and made a sandcastle. Back on their towels, they watched three boys climb into a blow-up raft and paddle around.

'I've told Hendrik we have some time before we head back to Australia. Since possums are a pest in New Zealand, maybe Hendrik could provide a quick tracking tour while we're on the North Island.

'But, Ric, they're a protected species in Australia.' Then Elaina realised Ric was joking with her. 'There've been parts of this trip when it was fun to see you out of your element,' Elaina continued. 'You weren't always the competent tough-guy action hero, but a son, a lover, a friend, surrounded by his past and mending some long-downed fences. Sometimes like a kid again.'

'I want to go back to the tough-guy action hero image. Would you reveal which one?'

'Hmmm … I won't tell you. But this is our last day here before we fly up to Auckland tomorrow, and you said you wanted me to see the Nelson you knew, Ric. I at least want to get another Mr Whippy ice cream.'

'Now that is one request I'm only too happy to comply with.'

Chapter 50

Tracking Mandu: 17,508 Islands

Bali Airport, Denpasar, Indonesia

When Flynn and Hendrik checked in their SUV, a policeman strolled up. He tilted his head with his beret miraculously staying on his head.

'You haven't been in Bali long,' he said.

'Ahhh …' Flynn couldn't figure what the officer wanted.

Hendrik took over. 'Checking out locations for the BBC. We're making a wildlife documentary in the northern region.' With Hendrik's South African accent and his French army field jacket, he seemed to fit the exact attire that a film studio would require.

Besides the duty of protecting tourists in Bali, the police were very familiar with the need to accommodate any and all studio productions. They were free advertisements for Bali and had a direct impact on revenue.

The policeman smiled and touched his finger to his beret. '"May the force be with you."'

After their night flight took off, Hendrik ordered two whiskeys. 'I thought I was going to have to ask you to sing *Molly Malone* to get us out of there.'

Flynn smiled. 'I would have done it, even though I'm not in the mood.' Flynn looked out the window as the green island of Bali slipped away in the clouds.

At the Indonesian airport, Flynn had texted Ric that he would meet him in Auckland, like he'd promised he would. Just for a few hours. Then he'd head back to Tasmania. Get things squared away. And that would be it.

He took a sip of the whiskey. Then a large swallow. His first in weeks. It seemed to bathe his brain in pinpricks.

Hendrik looked at his friend. 'My brother, my *boet*, I've been thinking about what that Aussie monk said to us.'

'"May the force be with you?"'

'No, that was the police. The Aussie monk said something like, Mandu was going to take the last two people "to another island in the north, but I don't know which one".'

'Yes, I think he said something about "the 20,000 islands" in Indonesia.'

'No, he said 17,508 islands,' Hendrik said. 'And that's the thing. I know there's an island in Indonesia called North Pagai. It's off the coast of Sumatra. But I don't think there are many other islands in Indonesia called the "North" something island. So what if Mandu wasn't talking about Indonesia.'

Flynn had hit his call button to order another whiskey. 'But I know where there's a "North Island", Hendrik. I'm taking you to it.' Flynn fingered his glass looking for a refill.

'Yes, you are. And that's just it. It was something that Ric said to me that made me think. Auckland is on the North Island. And the Aussie monk said he almost missed seeing Mandu because he was staying at a monastery outside of Auckland. A monastery in the Forest Tradition. What if Mandu was taking the last two people to that monastery on the *North Island of New Zealand*?'

Flynn ran through what Hendrik, the tracker, had put together. He tilted his head trying to clear his thoughts.

The steward came by.

'No, thanks.' Flynn shook his head. 'Wouldn't the people who stayed in New Zealand have to be … New Zealanders?' he said slowly.

'Or Australians. If they were Australian citizens, they could go to New Zealand and stay indefinitely. It's reciprocity.'

The cloud in Flynn's brain cleared like cold water had been thrown on it.

The two people left could be at that monastery! 'Ahhh, it's worth a shot, Hendrik. It's worth a bloody shot to talk to that man and his son. If they are still there.'

Outskirts of Auckland, New Zealand

Flynn was driving the SUV while Hendrik navigated. Ric and Elaina sat in the backseat, buckled in for the entertainment provided by the driver and the tracker.

A small car cut in front of them on State Highway 1. 'Watch that bloody rhino, Flynn. He's hogging his lane and half of yours.'

A large truck whizzed by.

'Be careful of any wild game crossing this road,' Hendrik advised. 'The drivers here are worse than a sausage fly.'

'Hendrik, we're not on a dirt road in equatorial Africa. The most dangerous wild animal here is a possum.'

Elaina and Ric looked at each other and burst out laughing.

Ten minutes later they entered a small village deep in a forested area forty minutes from the airport.

'Where are we?' asked Elaina.

'One of the several Buddhist monasteries in New Zealand,' Hendrik said. 'We've been to three other monasteries and three other drop-off locations in Indonesia. This is what I'd call a long shot.'

Flynn explained, 'It's our last try at tracking what happened to the people that Mandu rescued from our village in Indonesia. Mandu rescued seven people. He promised to get them to friends or family. We also think Mandu talked to a monk in Bali about this place. If they are there, these are the last two that we know about.' Flynn took a breath. 'A man and his son.'

Still, disappointment broke out over Flynn's face like a bad rash. 'I've been hoping that maybe they know something of what happened to Gemi and Diah. Or maybe they saw them alive … before …'

This was the end of the line for Flynn's search. He and Hendrik were headed back to Tasmania via Sydney later that night. For Flynn it was the end of the line, full stop.

Flynn parked the SUV under a spreading shade tree. A stand with fruit and other food was set up alongside the road. The sign was clear. 'Free for anyone who needs it.'

Buddhist monastery, Forest Tradition, outside of Auckland, New Zealand

'I can't go in,' Flynn said, resting his head on the steering wheel. 'It's been too much.'

Ric came to the driver's window, putting his hand on Flynn's arm. 'I'll go for you, Flynn.' He and Hendrik headed towards the gates of the monastery.

Out of earshot, Hendrik muttered to Ric, 'Maybe I made a mistake. I thought if we could track down Mandu it would help ease Flynn towards resolution of their fate. You had mentioned that Flynn might only have a few meagre facts and that might be all he ever finds out. I wanted to ensure we'd scouted out every track line. It's what I do.'

Ric acknowledged Hendrik's efforts. 'You did fine, Hendrik. I have been in Flynn's shoes and the memories will always be there.'

Elaina got two water bottles and she and Flynn stood in the shadows of the shade tree.

'Have you ever come to a time in your life when you know what the answer is … but you don't want to know it?' Flynn asked.

'I think we all feel that at times,' Elaina said reflectively. 'Accepting reality has never been an easy one for me. My mother left when I was young. I never accepted that she wouldn't ever come back. It has been a stumbling block for me … until I met Ric.'

'I suppose this journey—first with Ric, then Hendrik, and now with you—is part of me saying goodbye,' Flynn said.

Elaina wasn't sure what and whom he was saying goodbye to. She reached out to hold his hand.

Ric and Hendrik reached the gates of the monastery. Tapping on the wooden door, they were admitted. After they disappeared behind the wood-and-iron door, it slapped shut with a thud.

Fifteen minutes later, the gate opened. Ric came out and headed towards the SUV. Elaina and Flynn trotted over to him.

'What happened?' Elaina asked.

Flynn couldn't speak and lowered his head.

'The last two people Mandu rescued are here.' Ric said. 'They're happy to talk to you, Flynn.'

They walked along the dusty road and passed back through the doors of the monastery, which opened into a garden of tranquillity, shaded by tall, cooling trees. Ric walked in front, leading them both off to the side of a large stone building, towards a short wall where Hendrik was standing talking to a man in a robe. On the other side of the wall was the monastery's fruit and vegetable gardens.

Various people were tending the gardens—trimming plants, pruning fruit trees and working patches of vegetables. Wearing a broad straw hat, a loose-fitting top and light cotton pants and sandals was a young person on a ladder, cutting back several branches of a fruit tree. Off to the side of the tree, a small child with short hair was playing with the sticks that fell down from the pruning. The child was crossing the sticks over each other, building little houses. Pausing for a moment on the ladder, the worker turned and stared at the four visitors from under the hat.

Flynn turned towards Elaina as if to speak; then put his hands to his mouth, trying to stifle a scream. He fell to his knees and started to sob uncontrollably, gulping in air. 'It can't be. It can't be,' he said.

The straw hat came off the worker. The haircut was short. Almost like one of the monks along the way. The tree-pruner didn't have long hair like Gemi had worn in their seven years of marriage. In her family, the women never cut their hair short. They only trimmed it occasionally.

But the face was that of a woman. She attempted to get off the ladder, almost falling. Then she ran towards Flynn. The child followed close behind.

Gemi fell to her knees and threw her arms around Flynn's neck, holding on to him. Young Diah did not remember the man. She had been taught by Gemi to stay clear of everyone. She stood back, watching her mother cry, and then she began to cry.

Elaina felt like her heart skipped a beat. It was the unbelievable reunion of a family that had been savagely torn apart. Through a circuitous journey, they had found each other again.

Elaina came close and put her arms around the little girl. When she was a child, her father and her uncle had often comforted her. She knew what to say. 'It's okay, sweet pea. You'll be fine, darling. Everything will be fine,' Elaina whispered to her. She took the little girl's hand and walked over to Ric.

Ric was tired and haggard, having spent three of the last four days trying to save others, as well as saving himself. The little girl held onto Ric's leg. It was something that she suddenly remembered from when she was with her Ayah in Indonesia.

Ric squatted down and looked at her face. 'I think I can take you to your Ayah, Diah.' He stood up, stiff in the knees, and walked the girl slowly over to Flynn.

Gemi and Flynn were kneeling on the ground, both crying and laughing. Diah grabbed onto her mother. Then she did something she had seen once. She patted the top of Flynn's head.

'That's a good start, Diah. That's a good start,' Flynn said.

Elaina took Ric's hand in hers. Ric lifted her hand and kissed the top of her fingers.

'I know you don't like the world that I work in,' he began, 'and I agree with you. You've asked me how I manage to bear working all the time in cloudy, murky environments where everything is in the shade, unclear, ill-defined. But these are the times that help me through. This is what allows me to bear it. And it makes being with you possible.' Ric took Elaina in his arms and kissed her.

Hendrik ambled over with Nāro, the senior monk at the monastery.

Nāro explained, 'A man named Mandu Olda brought them to us. They are Australian citizens so they can stay in this country as long as they like. They were afraid to return to Australia because there were some Australian men not happy with them. Mandu said to give things time … and it would work out. Mandu was very good at predicting this event.' The monk smiled.

'That sounds very Buddhist,' said Flynn, then realised what he had said.

Flynn's flight was rearranged to Nelson, along with Gemi and Diah. Ric's parents were delighted to have visitors after Ric and Elaina's departure. Ric thought a few weeks with Kiri and John would be helpful to both families.

On the plane back to Australia, Elaina held Ric's hand while Hendrik looked at an African travel magazine. Elaina watched him thumb through the photos, going back and forward on the ones that piqued his interest.

She was thinking of the small family that had waited almost two years to reunite. That seemed like such a long time.

'We don't need a big wedding, do we, Ric? How about a pop-up one? Sort of like an extended potluck dinner. Instead of spending months and months preparing for it, let's go to France. Then we can come back and have a quick pop-up wedding somewhere in Sydney.'

Ric looked at Elaina, then at Hendrik holding the African travel magazine. Hendrik was wondering how Ric was going to tackle that one.

Very rarely did Ric ever do anything spontaneously.

'*Oui, ma cherie*,' he said.

~~~

Three weeks later at Golden Bay, Tasman District, South Island

In the early morning on a Sunday, a small group of people came to a cemetery near a river. A massive boulder from Marble Mountain had been carefully carried down by truck and put over the top of a designated locale.

Arabella Marino and Julie Clark were seated in the front row. Thomas Murphy, the Site Manager, had spoken. Louise McKenny with her guitar and Bob Lambert had sung *Amazing Grace*. Tahi and the three other archaeological monitors stood next to Eric Roberts. Tyler, Arnie, Christie and Darrell were sitting behind John and Kiri.

John got up to speak about the importance of friendship.

Then he went back towards Kiri and sat on the other side of little Diah, who had been his constant companion during the past few weeks.

Flynn had his arm around Gemi, whose hair had grown out a few centimetres. He nodded as John spoke, realising the effort over the past two years that Ric, Elaina and Hendrik had made for him.

Ric and Elaina sat behind holding hands, having flown back to Nelson for this ceremony.

Salvatore Marino, his wife Tessa Bright-Marino and their child, Melissa, were laid to rest in Golden Bay. The headstone read:

Salvatore, Tessa and Melissa –

Together and at Peace

Taken from us but in Our Hearts Always.

Here lie brave warriors.

In the end, Tahi was right. The skull was that of a great warrior.
~~~

EPILOGUE

A full forensics examination of the remains of Tessa Bright and that of her child confirmed that Tessa was still alive when she was thrown into the sinkhole and died on impact with the ledge. RNA from beneath Tessa's fingernails (and DNA) were a match to Reid Baxter. The conclusion was that Tessa had tried to defend herself against Baxter when she was attacked.

The physical evidence was corroborated with a sworn statement from Odell Rodman. He came to Baxter's apartment and was told to remove the body and dump it. Further, it was discovered that Baxter had been treated for facial scratches he claimed to have received from a cat. CCTV footage from the Baxter apartment confirmed the arrival of Tessa Bright at the main entrance and the later removal of her body via the alley behind the building.

Odell Rodman had not realised that Tessa Bright was alive when he dumped her body; nevertheless it made him responsible for her death. Reid Baxter was an accessory to the murder, as he had first attacked Tessa Bright. Both men were charged in connection with her murder.

The skeletal remains of Salvatore Marino were examined, with the cause of death being a blow to the back of the head, resulting in a massive fracture of the skull. A digital copy of CCTV recordings obtained by Odell Rodman (as well as the original computer digital file) showed Salvatore being struck with a shovel by Reid Baxter at Parásita. Rodman had kept the copy as an insurance policy. He was the individual who buried Salvatore first at Parásita. When the cleanup was announced, Rodman was told to move the remains to the Paxton farm.

Ernest was implicated in the murder since he was the one who cleared out Salvatore's apartment in order to make it appear that the chemist had simply run off. Ernest was aware of Salvatore's death.

The hazardous clean-up site at Longboat Island would now undergo a full epidemiological investigation. The assessment would include evaluation of the plant's operations and the burial of hazardous substances in the local area. It would also investigate any potential cancer cluster affecting local inhabitants in the vicinity of Parásita. The government was seeking additional data from local health professionals and the public about other potential cases.

~~~

In Indonesia, at a residence of Ambassador Clarence Jenkins, a safe was found open and cash and valuables were gone. Jenkins was found dead on the floor. As private documents began to surface from unidentified sources, members of the Australian government called for an immediate Royal Commission of Inquiry. The commission would be investigating the destruction of several villages in Indonesia and the mass murder of many of their residents. Two of the main witnesses, Flynn and Gemi O'Neill, plus their daughter Diah, were in Nelson, New Zealand, staying with John and Kiri Peters. They were enjoying the protection of the New Zealand Police pending their return to Australia to give their testimony.

~~~

Hendrik Ackerman had headed to Sydney, then onto Tasmania to pick up Charlie, Flynn's dog. They would be staying in Flynn's house until the O'Neill family returned. Charlie enjoyed the tracking activities that Hendrik conducted around the property.

~~~

A four-way jurisdictional tug-of war erupted over the extradition of Francis Holms for crimes in the United Kingdom, Australia, Indonesia and New Zealand. For the first go-around, the United Kingdom drew the long straw, preparing to add Francis to their legal gristmill. While in custody, under heavy guard, Francis crafted a call of nature stop into an escape while transiting through Dubai. His ankle bracelet ended up in a piece of luggage on its way to the United States.

~~~

Salvatore's letter to John:
Dear John

This is a letter I have been dreading to write. I am very fearful for my life. I need to tell you a few things, and because of the lack of time I have it will be disjointed.

The good news in my life is that I married Tessa Bright. We were seeing each other privately. It was in part to protect her that we kept it quiet. Even better news is that we are expecting a child. We've already named our daughter Melissa.

Unfortunately, if you are reading this something has happened to me. As a precaution, I have moved all of my records up to the fishing cabin in Golden Bay to get it out of the hands of those at the plant. Things are not going well there, and I worry about retribution.

I put the cabin in your name. That was to disguise the ownership in case I wasn't around.

I would ask that you help Tessa and our daughter through this. I will surely miss seeing Melissa grow up and being with my family.

I can barely think about this last part, but if something should happen to Tessa, would you please keep a watch on Arabella, who I've moved to Golden Bay to keep her out of harm's way? I know you will figure out a way to find her.

My warmest regards to you, dear old friend. Thank you for being there for me.

Salvatore

AUTHOR'S NOTES

Insights Into Building the Yoga Mat Mysteries

The Series

Susan Rogers and John Roosen are the authors of the 'Yoga Mat Mysteries'. Two writers—one voice. The titles of the series refer to yoga poses that are an integral part of the story and reflect one or both of our protagonists. The series includes *Dead Man's Pose*, *Cobra Pose*, *Tree Pose* and *Warrior Pose*. Several manuscripts are in the editing phase, which include [working titles]: *Half Moon Pose* (the south of France), *Dragon Pose* (Melbourne, Australia), *Goddess Pose* (Greece) and *Boat Pose* (Amsterdam, the Netherlands). A further novel is in the works: *Camel Pose* involving the Middle East.

We often draw on our own backgrounds for the plotlines, events and details, as well as the backgrounds of friends, 'rellies' and experts we've run across. The following are a few examples from *Warrior Pose*.

Ground truthing

Susan Rogers and John Roosen conduct thorough ground truthing with every story created. Ground truthing is a direct observation process of visiting every area and location they write about to verify the accuracy of their descriptions. It ensures all the elements such as geography, transportation, foods, climatic conditions, travel times and history are verified. They follow a similar process for the characters they develop in their stories to ensure accuracy in each description and what they do, even as fictional characters.

'Wait, John, aren't they real?'

Boat decapitation

As maritime investigators, both John and Susan have investigated seagoing, port and boating accidents similar to the one described in the Marlborough Sounds. Worldwide, there are accidents that occur each year involving ships—from tankers to passenger liners to recreational vessels—as well as portside accidents involving land-based or maritime personnel.

One brutal accident they investigated included a decapitation when a large speedboat ran over a smaller vessel. A variety of recommendations came out of that investigation for improved maritime safety. Like many of their past experiences, Susan and John weave in factual occurrences within their stories.

Hazardous site clean-up

Part of this story involves the clean-up of a hazardous waste site. John and Susan have spent many years working around the world at a wide variety of sites. John, in particular, has conducted clean-ups at numerous sites around the globe. The Parásita waste site was modelled using some of the aspects of several of these sites.

The skull

During a hazardous material clean-up at one of these operational sites, a human skull was recovered by John Roosen and Susan Rogers. The skull was not found in a recognised burial area and the rest of the body was not located. The find was reported to police as a potential crime scene. The location of the skull in the area being excavated showed that it was not a historical or archaeological find. This was based on the depth of the find and objects around it. The skull was investigated by the police and never identified. After nearly a year, a burial and small ceremony were conducted. A memorial remains at the site.

CALL TO REVIEW

G'day, Reader:

We hope you enjoyed ***Warrior Pose*** as much as we took pleasure in writing it for you to read.

Your feedback helps us provide the best quality books and helps other readers like you discover great reads.

It would mean the world to us if you took two minutes to share your thoughts about this book as a review. You can leave a review online where you purchase the ebook or audiobook.

For example, find this book on Amazon and scroll down to 'Review This Product' – Write a customer review. Note that you may have to sign into Amazon along the way, depending on how your device is set up. All other sites (eBook, audiobook or print book) will have similar ways to review this series.

Thanks for reading ***Warrior Pose*** !! Book 1 in this series is ***Dead Man's Pose*** and can be found in your favourite online bookstore, as well as audiobook stores. Book 2 in this series is ***Cobra Pose***, and Book 3 is ***Tree Pose.*** Both are available as an eBook and an audiobook. Book 4 in this series, is ***Warrior Pose***, currently in eBook format and will soon be a print book and audiobook as well.

We wish you all the best,
John and Susan

ABOUT THE AUTHORS

What do a woman, who used to train military personnel how to shoot straight, and a man, skilled at eradicating all sorts of hazardous materials safely, have in common? Besides both being designated law enforcement officers, they are writing a 'knock 'em dead' mystery series of books … together!

John Roosen started his career as a biologist, served as a commissioned naval officer, a designated Federal Law Enforcement Officer, and an environmental emergency specialist in the United States. He has lived and worked in the Americas, Australasia, Antarctica and the Middle East. At a moment's notice, he would respond to chemical and refinery plant explosions, deal with rocket fuel plant meltdowns and dismantle illegal drug labs. As a change-up, John switched careers to chasing pirates and duelling with a con artist extraordinaire on a remote South Pacific island. In between, he organised jungle expeditions and deep-sea scuba diving. However, John's experience extends beyond responding to cataclysmic disasters and includes mastering the intricacies of making souffle omelettes without burning the edges.

Susan Rogers already knew she was a writer at age six, but as an adult she took a major detour to become a commissioned naval officer and a designated Federal Law Enforcement Officer. She has conducted sting operations, run extensive weapons training programmes and directed the restoration of a Presidential Yacht. In her spare time, she has written several books, run health and safety operations for multi-billion-dollar projects in Abu Dhabi and revamped a South Pacific maritime service. Susan continues to write – whether braced against the hull of a sailing vessel on a hard tack, during a crossing of the Middle East's empty quarter in a Mini, or bouncing around in a troop carrier in Australia's outback.

Hungry for more? ***Dead Man's Pose*** is first in the Yoga Mat Mysteries line-up, with ***Cobra Pose***, as number 2 and ***Tree Pose*** as number 3. ***Warrior Pose*** is number 4 while Book 5, (currently titled ***Half Moon Pose***) is coming soon!

ACKNOWLEDGEMENTS

When attempting this creative activity, there were always two of us to battle on … or battle with each other over the misplaced modifiers or the methods for murder. We were fortunate to a great team cheering us on. We had a focused team of advisers, editors, proofreaders, and technical personnel. They believed in our vision and helped us achieve it. This is the fourth book that Sherryl Clark has edited not once but twice for each manuscript. She helped us capture suspense, tension and a thrilling ending which is always good for a mystery. She knows (and believes in) our characters as much as we do! A talented and encouraging editor.

This book was supercharged by the special efforts of the incredible Tiffany Yates Martin (Fox Print Editorial). Once again, Tiffany read and provided in-depth commentary at a crucial moment in this story's creation. It was a marvellous experience with synergy and sparks flying both ways in the welding together of a more powerful story. We enjoy Tiffany's coaching, enthusiasm and extensive knowledge.

Many thanks as well to the hard-working Lesley Marshall who provided excellent proof reading and commentary. Lesley is exacting, has an eagle eye and very knowledgeable. Her New Zealand perspective was especially useful for this book with its New Zealand setting.

Technical expertise in an array of fields, including commercial piloting, was very important for this book. Senior pilot, Captain Richard Holmden, once again demonstrated his wide-ranging skillset in reviewing ***Warrior Pose*** multiple times to ensure we had the smallest detail correct. His in-depth knowledge, of flying and of New Zealand and Australia, gave this story a lift.

Glen Aspin, the extraordinary alpine expert, mountain climber and trainer provided his review and comments on the mountain and rescue sequences in ***Warrior Pose***. His reviews (and the major effort to get them to us) were crucial to these sequences.

You can definitely tell a book by its cover. We have a dream cover design team with: the wonderfully talented graphic artist Tess McCabe (with her fourth cover design); the film-writing team of Nicholas Roosen and Pooja Khatri; the artist-sculptor Colleen Dallimore; the critique-feedback section of Timothy Roosen and Melina Pappa. Individually and together, they created, critiqued, modelled and tweaked till the stunning cover of ***Warrior Pose*** came together.

Mark McCallum, technical writer and creative writer, provided comprehensive, as well as instantaneous feedback when we were stuck or needed help. We called on Mark throughout the book writing journey for help and encouragement.

Gerard Malan and Nick Roosen were our African and tracking guides as we crafted the important Hendrik and Flynn sections. They kept us on the trail of getting a great subplot throughout this book.

Numerous people served as book advisers during the development and marketing stages of this book. Our most sincere thanks to: Dave Chesson, Kindlepreneur; John Low, Ebook Launch; and Matthew J Holmes, guidance and encouragement, Geoff Affleck and Sandy Day.

We also thank those who kept the momentum going with their support, as well as critiquing covers, providing guidance and feedback, reading blurbs, listening to plotlines. Thanks to: Scott and Linda Cherry, Gary and Judy Siegel, Peter and Helen Klineberg, Jessica Aguilar, Carolyn Aguilar, Kaye and Robb Francis, Sharon Aguilar, Andreas Welte, and Fiona Welte, Russell Thompson, Kim O'Neil and John Mock.

WORKS BY AUTHORS

https://www.yogamatmysteries.com/

DEAD MAN'S POSE

From Sun Salutations to Shadowy Suspects

When a close friend dies mysteriously, spirited yoga teacher Elaina Williams and her enigmatic partner Ric Peters are thrust into a dangerous game of deception and murder.

Teaming up with a savvy outback detective, an eccentric academic, and a sharp-eyed yet sight-challenged witness, they follow a trail of secrets through Sydney's glittering facades and seedy underbelly.

Corrupt officials, ruthless criminals, and high-stakes chases stand between them and the truth. As Elaina and Ric close in on a killer, their own undeniable chemistry ignites, adding tension to an already deadly pursuit.

Blending the intricate puzzles of Agatha Christie with the pulse-pounding thrills of Michael Connelly, Dead Man's Pose launches the Yoga Mat Mysteries—a gripping whodunit with a twist of romance and a city full of secrets.

Will they solve the mystery before Sydney swallows them whole? Dive into the adventure today!

E-Book and Audiobook for ***DEAD MAN'S POSE*** available from Amazon / Audible, Spotify, Barnes & Noble and other eBook and audiobook retailers.

COBRA POSE

A Deadly Cyber Heist, A Missing Father, and a Race Against Time

When Elaina Williams' father, Edward, vanishes without a trace, the yoga instructor-turned-amateur sleuth is thrust into a deadly game of cat and mouse. A high-stakes cyber heist is about to rip through the global financial system, and her father may be caught in the crossfire.

With Ric Peters—a battle-hardened photojournalist with secrets of his own—by her side, Elaina follows a dangerous trail of digital deception from the sun-drenched streets of Brisbane to an isolated island off Queensland, Australia. The Cobra and The Wolf, a shadowy duo of international criminals, are ready to strike. Billions are at risk, and so are their lives.

As time runs out, Elaina and Ric must unravel the mystery before Edward disappears forever. But with ruthless hackers, corrupt officials, and an enemy who always seems one step ahead, can they outmanoeuvre the predators before it's too late?

Cobra Pose delivers a pulse-pounding mix of mystery, cyber intrigue, and slow-burn romance. Get ready for a heart-racing thriller where trust is a luxury—and survival is the ultimate challenge.

E-Book and Audiobook for ***COBRA POSE*** available from Amazon / Audible, Spotify, Barnes & Noble and other eBook and audiobook retailers.

TREE POSE

When the past refuses to stay buried, the roots of deception run deep…

Ric Peters and Elaina Williams sought peace in Tasmania, but their escape turns into a nightmare. The Devil's Island lives up to its name, stirring ghosts of its dark history—and unleashing Ric's own demons.

A vengeful enemy has tracked Ric down, seeking retribution for a past mistake that Ric has kept hidden from Elaina. Now, as his secrets threaten to unravel everything, Elaina becomes the next target. A ruthless hitman lurks in the shadows, waiting for the perfect moment to strike—collateral damage be damned.

As corrupt officials pull the strings and innocents are seduced into human trafficking, Detective Inspector Jack McMasters races to untangle the truth before time runs out. But with danger closing in from all sides, will Ric and Elaina survive the storm—or will the past destroy them both?

Murder, deception, and a past that won't stay buried—Tree Pose is a gripping mystery packed with suspense, secrets, ghosts, and an electrifying race against time.

E-Book and Audiobook for *TREE POSE* available from Amazon / Audible, Spotify, Barnes & Noble and other eBook and audiobook retailers.

WARRIOR POSE

Skulls, Hitmen, and Deadly Secrets—One Explosive Mystery

His life at a crossroads, Ric Peters is torn between his perilous job and dreams of a future with Elaina. But their trip to New Zealand throws them into chaos as they are swept up in a whirlwind of danger and dark family secrets.

As Ric grapples with accusations of murder back in Indonesia, the discovery of a mysterious skull at a toxic waste site near his family's home deepens the mystery. Bodies appear, old wounds reopen, and Ric's strained relationship with his father is tested by shadows of the past. An old friend's disappearance and deadly secrets unearthed at a chemical plant threaten to expose more than just the environmental sins of the region.

When a woman's body is found in the local hills, her face a mask of terror, the danger becomes deadly personal. With Ric's parents drawn into the fray and Elaina targeted by shadowy foes, the stakes soar. Meanwhile, Ric's friends back in Indonesia desperately need his help to evade police and a potential firing squad, relying on him from thousands of miles away.

From high-speed chases across mountainous terrain to close encounters with New Zealand's breathtaking landscapes and quirky characters, ***Warrior Pose*** is a relentless ride through betrayal, love, and survival. Join Ric and Elaina as they navigate a labyrinth of intrigue and danger in this explosive instalment of the Yoga Mat Mysteries.

Dive into another thrilling chapter of the Yoga Mat Mysteries, where secrets run as deep as the tides and trust is as fleeting as the shifting sands.

E-Book and Audiobook for DEAD MAN'S POSE available from Amazon / Audible, Spotify, Barnes & Noble and other eBook and audiobook retailers.

SUSAN ROGERS
JOHN ROOSEN
DEAD MAN'S
POSE
YOGA MAT MYSTERIES

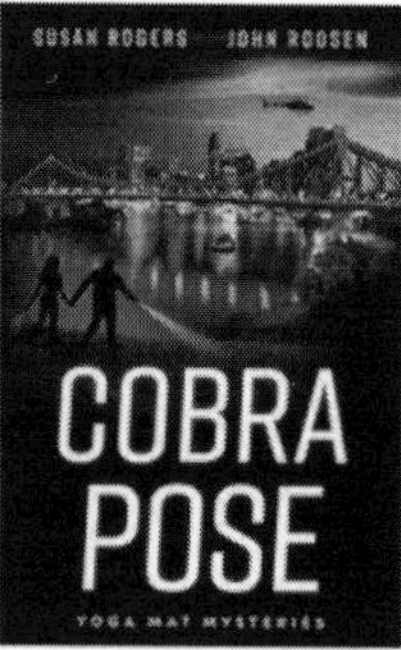
SUSAN ROGERS
JOHN ROOSEN
COBRA
POSE
YOGA MAT MYSTERIES

SUSAN ROGERS
JOHN ROOSEN
TREE
POSE
YOGA MAT MYSTERIES

SUSAN ROGERS
JOHN ROOSEN
WARRIOR
POSE
YOGA MAT MYSTERIES